The Return of Mayra

by Evelyn Green

Copyright Page

Content Warnings: This book includes strong sexual scenes, violence, and profanities.

Chapter 1

Michele Armstrong was ice skating on her Aunt Gloria's and Uncle Joe's pond, or at least trying —since she was sitting on the ice more than standing. She looked over at a bench and saw her grandma, Leewan Johnson, watching her. Michele skated, with her legs far apart and arms swinging, over to her grandma, then flopped down next to her. Looking at her grandma, she asked, "What are you doing here?"

"The paternity test results came back! Prince Macalla Williams is 99.9% your biological father."

"Oh! I bet his wife, Princess Lalirra, and her daughter, Amarina, don't like that!"

"No, they don't!" Leewan said with a laugh. "They keep arguing that the results have been rigged."

Michele laughed then said, "Wouldn't they be mad if I said I changed my mind and have decided to live in the castle's guest house with you!"

"Do you?"

"Sorry, grandma. You know I love it here in Michigan and want to finish my high school years here. Plus, I don't want to leave Paul!"

Leewan looked disappointed and said, "I know dear. We can just continue to talk in our dreams until you come to visit next summer. Is there anything you want me to tell the prince? I mean your dad!"

"Just let him know that I'm happy that I finally found my biological dad."

After a moment of silence, Michele asked, "Any word on what really happened to my mom?"

"No. Princess Lalirra's parents, Moki and Merrin Taylor, still deny having anything to do with her disappearance. Have you had any prophetic dreams about her?"

"No grandma. I wish I did."

"Well, if you ever need to talk, just say my name three times before you go to bed. Love you, Michele."

Michele woke up in bed. Her golden retriever, Mitch, was lying next to her, staring at her with her big, brown eyes. Michele looked at the clock; she still had a couple of hours to sleep before she had to get up for school.

*****

Michele's alarm went off at 6 a.m. She crawled out of bed and got dressed. When she walked downstairs, her Aunt Gloria and Uncle Joe were sitting at the kitchen table drinking their coffee and reading the morning newspaper. Joe looked up from his paper when she walked in. "Well good morning. Are you ready to go back to school after our visit to New Caledonia Island?"

"Not really." Michele went to the refrigerator, grabbed the orange juice, and then proceeded to pour herself a glass. After she sat down at the kitchen table with her glass, she poured herself some cereal and thought: *Wish I could tell my aunt and uncle about finding my biological father.* Michele couldn't tell her aunt and uncle about her biological father, who was a prince of the Hidden Islands of Honiawae, since their memories of meeting the prince, along with her boyfriend's (Paul's), were replaced by the mind-erasing witch. Gloria, Joe, and Paul now believed they went to New Caledonia Island to visit Michele's grandmother, Leewan. They had no memory of meeting her other grandparents, King Levi Williams, and his wife, Queen Chloe; and they had no memories of the Hidden Islands of Honiawae -- that consisted of seven islands located in the Pacific Ocean, somewhere between Australia and Hawaii. The islands were originally founded by two witches in the early 1700s, back when witches, and some innocent people, were capture, judged, and burned at the stake. One of the witches that founded the islands was Leewan's great, great, great grandmother, Martha Black. When Martha was young, her parents were captured by the men hunting witches. Running for her life, she called upon her whispers of the wind powers for guidance. The wind replied to her in the form of a storm cloud formation. It showed her the coordinates of the hidden islands and whispered: *take all.* She shared this information with her best friend Elizabeth since her husband, Abraham Williams, owned a large fishing company. Elizabeth had a hard time convincing her husband to use his ships to help Martha's plan of relocating most of the witches and their families, but he finally agreed when she told him she was one of the witches targeted for practicing witchcraft. After Abraham used his ships to transported three shiploads full of people and animals to the hidden islands, the residents claimed him as their king. The islands do show up on world maps; however, they are listed as uninhabited islands. These uninhabited islands are protected from passing boats by jagged, underwater mountains; there is only one safe entrance into the islands on the southside, and only narrative settlers know the whereabouts of the entrance. The islands are also protected from satellite detection by an old magical, boundary spell. Michele continued to stir her cereal with her spoon, she felt bad about keeping secrets from her aunt and uncle, but the whereabouts of the hidden islands could not be exposed.

Joe stood up and said, "Well, I better be getting to the police department. I'm sure they've missed me."

Gloria replied, "Of course they missed their number one detective."

"I wonder if they ever found anymore leads on that thug that broke into our house and killed my partner, Kevin."

Michele looked up and said, "I think he is long gone."

Joe looked at her and asked, "Why. Did you have any more dreams?"

Michele didn't know what to say at first, since she knew the thug was killed by the Moki Taylor, the Warden of Keelonie Island, and his wife Merrin. They had him executed for treason after he had confessed to Michele's grandmother -- that he had orders from the Taylors to take her daughter, Mayra, to a Russian agent in Australia. The thug also told Leewan, that the Taylors wanted Mayra out of the picture since their daughter, Lalirra, was betrothed to the prince, and Mayra and the prince were lovers. Of course, the Taylors denied these accusations to the king and queen and had the thug/spy executed for treason.

"Well Michele, did you have another dream?"

"No. That's just it. If I am not having any dreams, the thug must be gone."

"Humph! I wanted to get my hands on him. Teach him a lesson for breaking into the City Hall and killing my old partner." He bent down and kissed Gloria goodbye, then he looked at Michele and said, "Have a good day at school."

*****

When Michele got to school, her best friend Leah was standing by their shared locker. Leah looked at her and said, "About time you come back to school you slacker."

"I only missed two days. One before the Thanksgiving break and yesterday."

"So how was the trip?"

"It was nice visiting my grandmother. The island she lives on is tropical and beautiful."

"Any luck finding the whereabouts of your biological mother?"

"No. She disappeared when she was around my age. My grandmother lost all contact with her."

"Well, that's a bummer."

Paul walked up to Michele's locker and said, "Good morning beautiful. You ready to go to class?"

She grabbed his hand and smiled at Leah. "We'll talk more later."

*****

After school, the teenagers met in the school parking lot. Paul was leaning against Michele's car with Michele cradled in his arms. Leah was standing in front of them, hanging on to her boyfriend's, Jeff's, arm. "So, you going to tell us about your vacation?" Leah asked.

"What's to tell. We went to visit my grandmother on the Island of New Caledonia. The weather was perfect, in the mid-80s, and the island was gorgeous."

"What did you do for your 17th birthday?"

"Oh. We celebrated that at Paul's aunt and uncle's house in Australia. Look what Paul bought me!" Michele held out her hand. "My very own birthstone ring."

"Nice! Where did you get that crystal necklace?"

"Oh, this." Michele grabbed the multicolor crystal. "This was a gift from my grandmother. I guess her mother gave it to her."

"So, you told me there were no leads to your biological mother's whereabouts, but what about your dad. Did your grandmother know who your dad might be?"

"Yes and No."

"What?"

"There was a guy there, that my grandmother thought could be my biological dad."

"And…"

"I had the chance to meet him. He was really nice, and I did a paternity test before I left."

"So, when do you get to know the results?"

Michele looked down. She didn't want to tell her friend before she told her aunt and uncle. Moreover, she couldn't tell them her biological father was a prince of a magical kingdom. They'd treat her differently for sure... and think she was crazy.

Leah interrupted her thoughts and said, "Well."

"Oh sorry. I zoned out." Michele laughed and said, "Soon. I hope."

"How about your prophetic dreams. Have you had any more dreams about that guy that tried to jump you and Paul at the bonfire?"

Michele knew that she needed to update her friends but how much could she tell them? *Telling them right now, out in this freezing weather doesn't seem like a good option.* "No more dreams recently. Hopefully, that means the thug left town."

Leah nodded her head and said, "Good."

Paul looked at his watch and said, "I have to get going to work. My boss at the computer repair shop won't be too happy if I'm late again."

Leah said, "Yeah... Jeff and I have to get going too. But I wanted to ask both of you ... Do the two of you want to go to the city park with us this Saturday? There's supposed to be some sort of a winter festival with ice skating, sledding, food, and a Christmas tree-lighting ceremony. Thought it would be fun!"

"I think Paul and I are both free this Saturday?" She looked at Paul and he nodded his head. "So, I guess it's a date. We can talk more about it later."

Leah turned and waved goodbye. Jeff nodded his head at Paul and said, "See ya."

After Leah and Jeff left, Paul turned his attention to Michele. "Sorry, I have to go." Then he brushed her hair aside and gave her a big wet kiss. "Call me tonight, babe."

Chapter 2

When Michele got home, she helped her Aunt Gloria with the farm chores. After they were done feeding the barn cats, cows, and chickens, Gloria went back up to the house with the two golden retrieves, Ace and Mitch, while Michele fed and brushed her horse. "I missed you, Harley." The horse snorted. Michele laughed, then said, "What? Don't you believe me?"

Harley was officially Gloria's horse, but after Michele's adoptive parents died in a car accident, she moved in with her adoptive father's brother, Joe Armstrong, and sort of claimed the old, brown mare as hers. After Michele was done brushing the horse, she climbed on the horse's back and laid her head down on the horse's rump. Michele loved sitting/lying in the barn and talking to Harley – using Harley as a sounding board. "So, Harley. Guess my dad is a prince, who used to be in love with my mom when she was about my age. My dad broke her heart when he told her – he was betrothed to a woman named Lalirra Taylor. But that's not the worse part... My mother, Mayra, wanted to do the right thing, so she set up a date to meet him in the gardens to break up with him; however, the parents of the Lalirra found out about the love affair and ordered their guards to remove my mother from the picture by delivering her to a man from Russia. No one has heard or seen my mother since."

After a moment of silence, Michele told the horse, "Now don't tell anyone I told you that." The horse turned her head and nudged her leg. Michele laughed and dug a treat out of her coat pocket to give the horse. After a moment of silence, Michele jumped off the horse's back, untied her, then said, "I need to try to find my mom. Maybe if I repeat her name three times before I go to bed, I can find out something in my dreams. What do you think?" Harley nudged her with her nose, begging for another treat. Michele laughed, gave her a treat, then patted her on the neck before leaving.

Chapter 3

At the dinner table that night, Michele decided to tell her aunt and uncle that she found her biological father... *I just need to leave out the part about my dad being a prince.*

"Dinner is delicious Gloria."

"Thank you. It's an old family recipe. I'll have to teach you someday."

"How was your day at work Joe?"

"Same ole, same ole. You know...." Joe took another bite of his food then held up his fork. "But the department is working on one unsolved crime. Do you remember that lady they were talking about in the newspaper Gloria?"

"That older lady that was found dead by her family?"

"Yep. That's the one. They still haven't found the perpetrators who broke into her house to rob her."

"That's really sad," Gloria replied.

Michele interrupted, "My grandmother came to visit me in my dream last night."

"Oh!" Aunt Gloria said. "What did she have to say?"

"Do you remember that tall blonde man that my grandma thought was my dad?"

"Yes. The guy in the picture on your mother's old, bedroom dresser." Aunt Gloria said.

"Yes. That's the one." Michele waited to see if her aunt and uncle could remember anything else about the prince.

After a moment of silence, Aunt Gloria spoke up. "Well. Is he your father?"

"That's what my grandmother told me."

"Well... That's great news. Now when you go visit your grandmother next summer, you can also visit your biological dad."

"You don't look too happy about finding your biological father," Joe stated.

"It's just... I don't think his new wife, Lalirra, and their daughter, Amarina, like me."

"Oh... You met them?" Gloria asked.

Michele thought she messed up but quickly replied, "Yes. My grandmother took me over to meet him when we went to town."

"I didn't know that. Did you like him?"

"Yes. He was very nice."

"Well I'm glad you found your biological dad," Joe replied. "Too bad no one knows what happened to your mother all those years ago."

*****

Michele called Paul that evening while she was lying in bed with her furry companions: Mitch, and her cat, Pepper. "What are you doing?"

"Just relaxing in bed… thinking of you. Did your grandmother get ahold of you yet -- to let you know the results of the paternity test?"

"Yes. I guess Macalla Williams is 99.9% my biological dad!"

"Well, that's great. Now you can go to visit him next summer when you go back to New Caledonia Island to visit your grandmother." After a moment of silence, Paul asked, "Do you think that one thug that was searching for you is still out there somewhere?"

She thought: *No. That thug was killed for confessing the kidnapping of Mayra to my grandmother, but the Taylors covered up their involvement by saying the thug made up the story to protect his own life. What should I tell Paul?*

"My grandmother told me that he is no longer a threat. Guess he got himself killed – somehow."

"That's great! I mean… at least we know he's not still out there trying to kill you for some reason. Guess we will never know the reason."

She thought: *Cause I'm the prince's daughter,* but said, "Guess not."

After a moment of silence, Michele continued, "I need to let friends, Leah and Amy, know about me finding my biological dad and about the thug. Is it ok with you, if I invite Amy and her boyfriend, Mike, to the festival this weekend? And maybe Mike can spend the night

with you again, and Amy can stay over with me at
Leah's house? I would hate to make them drive all
the way home after the festival."

"I don't see why not. Mike stayed over
after the high school bonfire... He seems pretty
cool. I'll ask my mom. Shouldn't be a problem."

"Thanks! You're the greatest. Love you!"

"Love you too. See you tomorrow, at
school."

Chapter 4

Wednesday morning, while Michele was
sitting at the kitchen table with her uncle and aunt,
Joe started talking to his wife about work. "So,
another elderly lady was found, robbed, and left for
dead at her house. Luckily, the elderly lady's
daughter stops by every morning to check on her
mother on her way to work; if she didn't, I don't
think the lady would have survived.
Unfortunately, the elderly lady is unconscious and
in critical condition at the hospital. So far, the
police department doesn't have any leads on the
perpetrators."

"Oh, that just awful!" Aunt Gloria replied.
"I hope they find the criminals soon before
someone else gets hurt."

Uncle Joe looked at Michele expectedly
since Michele had prophet dreams before that had
helped the police department capture criminals.
"Any dreams lately?"

"Nope. Still quiet on the home front. Sorry
I can't help with this case."

*****

It seemed like time was moving in slow motion. Michele was bored out of her mind at school since every one of her teachers only wanted to discuss the finals that were coming up the next week. She sat in each of her classes watching the clock tick by slowly.

During Michele's last class (study hall), she couldn't stand looking at her review notes anymore so she started doodling on a piece of paper while daydreaming. Looking around the room her eyes roamed over to Paul. He was looking down at the table reviewing some of his notes. Michele thought: *He's such a nerd... but he's my handsome nerd! I bet he ends up being the Valedictorian.* Then she started reminiscing on how her friend, Leah, taught her how to break the ice and talk to him at the beginning of the school year -- she had to pretend she didn't understand how to do their homework assignment so he would volunteer to help her. Michele felt bad for having to tell the little white lie, but it had worked. They were a couple now and she was madly in love. Michele looked at his strong arms, broad shoulders, and soft-brown hair. She licked her lips and thought: *Boy did I get lucky... smart, good-looking, and sensitive.* Just looking at him made her blush -- remembering the first time they were alone in his parents' basement; when they did some heavy petting and exploring... Paul did look sad when Michele refused to go all the way, but he seemed to understand her fear of getting pregnant and he respected her wishes. What Michele failed to do, was to tell him that her friend, Leah, took her to a health clinic shortly after that encounter -- to help her get on some birth control. Michele knew Paul was the one for her and she wanted him to be her first. She also wanted to plan out her first time so it would be special. Michele continued to stare at Paul while daydreaming what she wanted to do to him.

Paul looked up and caught her staring. He smiled and sent an air kiss her way. She blushed, then quickly looked down at her paper, embarrassed by her wicked thoughts. When she looked at her paper, she was surprised by the image she drew of a man. She thought: *What the hell*! Then she added a little more shading and thought: *Wonder if this is the guy responsible for all the recent robberies?*

The bell rang, signaling the end of the day. Michele folded up the sheet of paper, threw it in her purse, then jumped up to catch up with Paul.

Chapter 5

After school, Michele had to go to work at her part-time job at the Country Crock. The restaurant was extremely busy that night which helped with the tip money, but by the time she made it home, she was totally exhausted. When she walked through the door, she looked at her aunt and uncle sitting in the living room and said, "I'm home."

Gloria looked up at her and asked, "How was your day?"

"Exhausting. I think I'll just go up to bed."

"Have a good night dear."

After Michele threw herself on the bed, she looked at her dog and said, "I need to call Amy first." Her friend, Amy Long, lived a couple of towns over. She was Michele's best friend from the previous school system that she attended for only one semester. Michele's adoptive father was a military man so Michele was constantly moving from town to town. After the freak car accident, where both of her adoptive parents drowned in an icy, cold pond, Michele moved to a new town to live with her Uncle Joe and Aunt Gloria. Even though Michele had to move again, she kept in contact with her friend Amy.

Amy answered her phone on the second ring.

"Hi, Amy. How's everything going?"

"Oh, you know… Getting ready for finals at school, hanging out at the house while my mom works all the time, and… Mike and I, sort of took our relationship to the next level."

"The next level?"

Amy laughed, "Yeah. You know what I mean. We're having sexual relations."

"What! Aren't you afraid of getting pregnant?"

"Nah. I'm smarter than that. I went to the health clinic to get on something before we took the next step."

"Leah took me took a health clinic too. But… I haven't told Paul yet."

"What you waiting for?"

"I don't know. Just haven't had time to make the first time special. You know."

"That reminds me. How was the trip to visit your grandmother in Australia?"

"That's what I want to talk to you about. What are you and Mike doing this Saturday?"

"Mike doesn't have to work at the gas station, but I'm supposed to work four hours at the fast-food drive-through… Maybe I can get someone to cover my shift?"

"Please try. I want you and Mike to meet Paul and me at a winter festival. Then maybe the two of you could spend the night again so we can all talk at Leah's house after the festival."

"Sounds like fun. Let me check into it. I can call you tomorrow."

"I have to work after school tomorrow. It might be easier for you to text me."

"Sounds good. I'll send you a text tomorrow."

After Michele hung up, she called Paul. He sounded half-asleep when he answered the phone, "Hello…."

"Sorry. Did I wake you?"

"No. No. I'm awake."

"Sure." Michele laughed. "I won't keep you… I just wanted to let you know – it looks like our plans are on for this weekend. Amy thinks Mike and her can make it."

"Sounds good. My mom said it's ok for Mike to stay the night."

"Great! Well… I won't keep you. Goodnight Paul. I love you."

"Love you too."

Chapter 6

The next morning, Michele gave her Uncle Joe the picture she drew during study hall.

"Hmmm. I don't recognize this guy, but guess I could have the guys down at the department run it through the criminal database – see if it gets any hits."

"Yeah. I'm not sure what it means. I sort of drew it subconsciously while I was doodling."

Aunt Gloria looked at Michele and asked, "Do you have to work again tonight after school?"

"Yeah. Even though I want to call-in since Paul has the night off and I have to work with Denise!"

"Who's Denise?"

"She's the head cheerleader from school, she thinks it's her job to socialize while I do all the work. So, if it's busy like it was last night, I'll really be exhausted tonight."

"Oh, honey. Take care of yourself."

"I will. Oh! By the way. Leah and Jeff want to do a double date this Saturday to the town's winter festival. Is it ok, if I spend the night at Leah's on Saturday?"

Uncle Joe looked up and asked, "No wild high school party tonight?"

She shook her head and said, "No parties. I swear!"

"Ok then. It's okay with me if ok with Gloria."

Gloria nodded her head.

"Thanks! I better be going to school." Michele ran around the table and gave Gloria and Joe a kiss goodbye on their foreheads.

*****

Michele ran into the restroom before starting her shift and saw Denise primping at the mirror. Denise glanced over at Michele, with her nose in the air, and said, "I hope you wore your roller skates. Looks like you're in for a busy night."

Michele went into a bathroom stall and sat down. She thought: *Is it too late to call-in?* Denise Johncock was a beautiful girl with long dark hair, big blue eyes, perfect complexion, and an hour-glass figure; however, she had the personality of being a presumptuous bitch. She came from money so she thought that working hard was beneath her. She only worked part-time since her parents insisted on it and for the social life. Most of the time at work, she would drag her feet while rubbing noses with the elite members of the city or flirting with the popular boys, forcing Michele to work double duty and pick up her slack. If customers sat in her section, that she felt was beneath her, she would make up some excuse so Michele would have to wait on them.

"Are you going to stay in there all night, Michele?" Denise asked while packing up her makeup.

Michele took a deep breath, then exhaled. "I'm coming."

*****

Michele was running her ass off. Every time she cleared off one of her tables, another group of people would sit down. She thought: *Where are all these people coming from?* She looked over at Denise's section and realized why she had so many customers… *Her tables are all dirty again!* Michele looked over to where Denise was standing. *Figures. She's too busy socializing with the town's mayor and his wife.*

The cook interrupted her thoughts and called out from the kitchen's window, "Michele, your order is up."

Michele threw the dirty dishcloth down on a table and rushed over to pick up the order. After she delivered the food, she looked over and saw Denise standing at one of her tables. From the distance, she could see Paul's friends, Tom and Mike. Michele walked over towards the table and watched as Denise flipped her long dark hair. She had one hand on Paul's shoulder and was saying, "Why are you dating someone like Michele when you could have me? I could show you a good time if you want to hook up sometime?"

Michele could only see red as she walked up to the table. When Paul notice her, he looked down at his hands on the table. Michele looked at Denise and said, "This table is in my section!"

Denise looked at her and said, "I noticed you were busy, so I thought I would help. I can get this table for you, besides... Paul and I were just talking about meeting up."

Michele's blood started to boil. The cook called her name for another order ready to be delivered. Michele turned to get her order and screamed, "Fine." When she turned, the mop bucket, that was sitting on the floor near Paul's table, started to vibrate and splash water all over the floor. By the time Michele got up to the kitchen window, she heard a loud crash. When she turned around, she saw Denise sitting on the floor -- holding her deformed wrist. Denise started screaming, "My wrist! My wrist! I think it's broken." The cook and Michele ran over to help Denise up. When Denise stood up, she was favoring one of her legs. "I think my ankle is sprained too. Who left that mop bucket there?" Denise glared at Michele.

"I was going to take care of it after I clean up the mess from the previous customers. I just never had the time. Sorry."

Michele and the cook helped Denise to one of her dirty tables. "Get your hands off me." Denise snapped at Michele. "And get me my phone so I can call my mom to come to get me."

The cook looked at Michele and said, "I'll go try to call another waitress into work if you'll go get her phone."

After Michele retrieved Denise's phone from the breakroom, she walked over to Paul's table with her pen and order slips in hand. While posing the pen on the paper, she asked in a firm voice, "You guys ready to order?"

Paul looked at Michele and said, "Don't be that way, babe. You know I came here to see you. I don't even like Denise."

Michele looked up with tears in her eyes and said, "Sure. That's your story!"

Paul stood up and hugged her. She let him hug her for a couple of seconds, then she pushed him away. She walked over to the next table, grabbed a napkin to wipe her tears, then returned to Paul's table and asked, "You guys want something to eat or not?"

Paul looked at Michele and said, "Just take Tom's and Mike's orders. I'm going to start busing some of the tables for you… until someone else shows up to help."

*****

Paul hung around the Country Crock until the end of Michele's shift, then he walked her to her car. When they reached her car's door, Michele turned to look up at him and said, "Thanks. I can take it from here."

Paul put one hand on the car and leaned over her while she rested against the car. He took his other hand and stroked the side of her face with his thumb. Michele jerked her head away from his touch. Paul shook his head, then brushed a strand of her long blonde hair away from her face while saying, "You should know I only have eyes for you."

Michele smiled slightly then turned to get into her car. Paul slid his hand down the car to blocked her exit with his arm. "What? No kiss goodnight!" Michele stretched up on her tippy toes to give him a quick peck, but Paul wrapped his arms around her, pulled her close, and started kissing her…. lightly at first, then he started teasing her with his tongue until she finally gave in and kissed him back full-heartily. When the young lovers finally came up for air, Paul looked into Michele's blue eyes and said, "I love you!"

"I love you too." She pulled away and started opening her car door.

"Let me get that for you." She stepped aside and let him open the door. He held the door while she got in, then said, "Are we good?"

"Yes. We're good. I'll see you tomorrow at school." She glanced at her watch then said, "I better get going before my aunt and uncle begin to worry… And thanks for the help!"

"Anytime." He closed her door and watched as she pulled away.

By the time Michele got home, her aunt and uncle had already retired to their bedroom. When she closed the front door, her aunt called out, "Michele! Is that you?"

"Yep. I'm finally home."

"How was work?"

"Exhausting."

"Get some rest sweetheart."

"I plan too."

Michele ran up to her room and got ready for bed. After she finally got into bed, she glanced at her cellphone. She had a message from Leah saying *everything is set for Saturday*, a message from Amy saying *I got someone to cover my shift*, and a message from Paul saying *sweet dreams, yours forever*. Michele smiled, plugged her phone into the charger, then snuggled up with her dog, Mitch. The cat jumped up on the bed, circled the foot of the bed, then plopped himself down. Michele looked down at the cat and said, "Good night Pepper."

Chapter 7

Michele woke up to Mitch licking her face. "Ok. Ok." Michele laughed and pushed the dog away. "Will these strange dreams ever stop?" Michele patted the dog on the head. Pepper mewed, mad at his bed companions for interrupting his sleep.

Michele got out of bed, turned on her desk lamped, and grabbed her notebook off her desk so she could write down the dream's imagery. After Michele wrote down the dream, she looked at her notes: *A one-story brick house with the front door broken in, the number 351, and the image of the guy she drew.* She thought: *Hmm. Not much better. Still missing the street name and the date this is supposed to happen. I need to contact my grandmother. See if she has any advice on how to make these crazy dreams give me more information.* She looked at the clock – 5:50 a.m. *Guess no time to contact her now!*

After Michele got dressed for school, she went downstairs to the kitchen to tell her uncle about the dream.

Joe listened attentively to the story, then replied, "A house address of 351, without a street name is like looking for a needle in a haystack. But at least we know it's a brick house. Did your grandmother give you any pointers for controlling these dreams while we were over there visiting?"

"Not really. But she did teach me how to contact her in my dreams if I needed to talk. I plan on trying to contact her tonight. See if she can help!"

"Good. You do that. But I do have some good news to tell you... The department got a hit on that picture you drew; guess that guy spent some time in jail on charges of assault and battery."

*****

Paul had to work Friday after school so Michele just drove home to help Gloria feed the farm animals. The weatherman had been right in predicting the snowstorm, Thursday night into Friday since a fresh powder of white snow covered the ground -- a good three to four inches. Michele laughed on the way out to the barnyard since the golden retrievers, Mitch and Ace, were having a hay-day running around, chasing each other, and rolling in the snow. After all the animals were fed, Gloria and Michele collected the eggs the chickens had laid then made their way back to the house. On their way back to the house, Gloria looked at Michele and said, "I think I'll order pizza tonight. I'm not in the mood to cook anything."

"Sounds good to me."

By the time the pizza was delivered, Joe, Gloria, and Michele were in the middle of watching a comedy movie on TV. Gloria went to the door, paid for the pizza, then dropped the pizza off on the coffee table for the group to share.

At the end of the movie, Michele looked at Joe and said, "Think I'm going to turn in now, I want to try to contact my grandmother tonight – see if she can help me figure out this last dream and the picture I drew."

Uncle Joe looked at her and replied, "Good luck! The police department does need your help in finding this crook before he kills again…. And tell your grandmother I said Hi!"

Michele gave her aunt and uncle a kiss goodnight then looked at Gloria and said, "Thanks for the pizza!"

"Anytime… And thank your grandmother when you see her -- for inviting us over to visit her!"

"Will do."

Chapter 8

While lying in bed, Michele called Paul to discuss their plans for Saturday. Paul sounded exhausted, so Michele kept the call short and sweet. After she hung up the phone, she closed her eyes and repeated her grandmother's name three times: *Leewan Johnson. Leewan Johnson. Leewan Johnson.*

Michele was sitting at a kitchen table with her grandmother. She looked around. They were at the castle's guest house; the house King Levi Williams offered to give Michele so she could stay with her grandmother while they ran the paternity test -- to see if she was his legitimate granddaughter. The guest house was located kitty-corner from the castle. It was a charming, three-story house with a glass cupola on top. Michele had agreed to a paternity test, but she didn't want to stay in the guest house since she wanted to finish her high-school years in America with Paul.

Michele looked at Leewan and said "Hi grandma!"

"Another visit so soon?"

"Yes. I'm here since you never had a chance to teach me how to control my powers."

"I know. I'm sorry. We were just so busy after that spy jumped you and Paul by the river. Did you have another dream?"

"Yes. I had a dream about a one-story brick house with the front door broken in, the number 351, and an image of a guy. The strange part is... I sort of drew a picture, subconsciously, of the guy before I had the dream -- while I was doodling."

"You drew a picture of the guy! Very interesting."

"What does it mean?"

"Well... Remember when I told you some powers don't pass down generation to generation and just, sort of, reappear whenever they feel like it."

"Yes."

"Well, I think you are developing more powers than your mom or I ever had. I just wish I gave your mom that crystal necklace I gave you. I think it could have protected her from the Taylors' spies sneaking up on her in the gardens -- where she went to meet your father. I feel her disappearance is all my fault. Like I told you, my mom died during childbirth, so she never told me the importance of the crystal necklace. My dad just told me my mother wanted me to have it and to pass the crystal down to any future descendants. I told you how that necklace protected me more than once. When I was about your age and started developing my powers, an evil sorceress came to me. She tried to get me to join her in her quest to overtake control of the islands. When I told her that I didn't want any part of her evil plans, she tried to take the necklace. I grabbed it, and like you with that evil spy at the river, the sorceress was thrown and knocked unconscious. I ran from the scene and the evil sorceress never challenged me again."

"Oh, grandmother. You didn't know anything about the necklace. It wasn't your fault Mayra was taken."

"I know. But I just can't help feeling guilty…. Do you remember what that spy said, at the river, when he confessed to me about the Taylors' plan to get Mayra out of the picture?"

"About delivering her to a man from Russia since their daughter, Lalirra, was betroth to the prince?"

"No. About the spies searching for you. After they found out about you -- they wanted to eliminate you so you could not help me find Mayra."

"Oh. Yeah. I remember."

"Well, I think that necklace might help you. Hold that crystal in your hand when you go to sleep at night and think of your mom. Concentrate on what you want to know about her: where she is, how she is, or try to meet her."

"I can do that?"

"Oh, I hope so. I just know she's alive out there -- somewhere."

"We will find her grandma. But you never told me how to control the dream I am having now! My Uncle Joe said there is a guy in my home town back in Michigan that is breaking into houses and killing the homeowners."

"Oh! Since your powers are not fully developed, that crystal could help. Just do what I told you to do to help you find your mother. Hold that crystal in your hand before you fall to sleep, then concentrate on what you want to know... the five W's -- who, what, where, when, and why."

Leewan started to fade. Michele screamed, "Grandma before you go! I think I might have injured a co-worker. Remember when you ask me if I could move things with my mind when I am upset. Well, now that I think about it, I might have had a hand in spilling water on the floor at the restaurant where I work, since I was mad at my co-worker for flirting with Paul."

"You need to be careful Michele. That's how the witch hunts started in the 1600s -- witches doing magic in public."

"I know. I didn't mean to break the girl's wrist. But she just made me so mad."

"You need to practice controlling your emotions with deep breathing and mind control; and you need to start practicing on how to control this new power. Start by staring at an object and pointing your finger to make it move. Remember what I did to the spy by the river?"

"Yes. You pointed your finger and lifted him up a good 20 feet up into the air; then threatened to drop him face-first on his head."

"Yes. So, start by practicing moving small objects. Only do this in private since most people are afraid of the things, they don't understand... And if you get mad, you need to try to control your anger and walk away. Give yourself time to think about the situation before you react."

Leewan started to fade again. "Sweet dreams Michele. I love you!"

"Love you too."

Chapter 9

Michele felt like a klutz trying to skate. Paul, being the true gentleman that he was, tried his best to keep Michele from falling on her butt again -- without success. Michele watched from her sitting position on the ice as Amy and Leah skated around the man-made skating rink with their dates -- like pros.

"Well everyone here can tell I wasn't born and raised on skates," Michele laughed as Paul helped her off the ice for the third time.

"Paul look at Michele and asked, "Do you want to retreat to the bench and have a hot cocoa with me?"

"I thought you'd never ask."

Paul held Michele why she half staggered, half skated to the bench. After getting her safely to the bench, he went to get their boots. After the couple changed their skates for their boots, Paul stood up and said, "You just wait here. I'll go return these and come back with some hot cocoa."

After he left, Amy came skating over to the bench. Sitting sideways on the bench, she asked Michele, "You ok?"

"Yes. Yes. I am great. You guys go have fun. I just didn't want to show off my skating skills and make you guys jealous."

"Yeah. I can tell. You missed your calling." Amy laughed, then took off to skate with Mike around the rink.

After Paul returned with their drinks, he sat down next to Michele and wrapped his arm around her. Michele sat in silence, enjoying the moment of hanging out with the love of her life, sipping her cocoa, and watching her friends' skate.

After the couples were done skating, they walked over to the community building. The inside of the building was decorated like a Christmas wonderland. One section of the building had carnival games for young children, and another area had a large, 360-degree, circular fireplace. The group walked over to the fireplace to find a place to sit and warm their toes. After the group sat down, Michele started looking around the place. She looked over at the children's area and noticed a line of kids waiting to see Santa. To the left of the children's area, there were some picnic tables and a couple of food stands. Her stomach began to rumble. She nudged Paul and said, "You hungry?"

He looked over in the direction she was looking and saw the food stands. He turned back and looked at the other couples, "You guys hungry?"

"I'm starving," Amy replied, then pulled Mike up, out of his chair. "Let's get something to eat."

"I'm game," Jeff responded, then looked at Leah.

Leah nodded her head, grabbed Jeff's hand, and then started following the group as they made their way over to the makeshift food court to get in line.

Looking up at the menu, Paul asked Michele, "What do you want, beautiful."

"I'll just take the cheeseburger meal deal."

"Sounds good. I can get our food if you want to go find us a table."

"Ok."

After the teenagers enjoyed their meals, they headed back outside to do some sledding. As Michele walked by the 25-foot Christmas tree, she read the sign: *Tree lighting ceremony at 6:30 p.m.* She looked at her watch: *4 p.m.* Then "Hey!" Michele screamed after getting hit dead center by a snowball. "That wasn't fair," she laughed, then grabbed a snowball and threw it back at Leah.

The group ran, dodging snowballs, all the way over to the park's sledding area. After waiting in line to rent their round saucers, the group walked over to the least crowded area of the hill and waited their turn. When the group made it to the front of the line, Jeff, said, "Let's have a race."

After everyone was situated on their saucers, Jeff shouted, "On your mark. Get set. Go!"

At first, the group was in a neck and neck race until Michele's sled hit a bump and sent her airborne. When the sled finally landed, it hit the ground sideways, causing her to spin around in circles. By the time she reached the bottom, in last place, she was facing backward. Paul walked over to her side to help her off the ground. Laughing, he said, "Show off."

Michele laughed as he helped her up. "That was fun... Let's do it again!" Then she looked over at Mike, who was proudly dancing around while holding his fingers up in the "L" shape, "I won! I won! Losers!"

Paul walked over to Mike, patted him on the back, and said, "You might have been the first one down the hill, but I think Michele beat you in the most sledding stunt driving department."

The couples slid down the hill a couple more times with the guys winning every race. After the final race, Paul looked at the girls and said, "You girls aren't much competition for us men."

Leah responded, "It's just because you boys weigh more --- makes you go faster!"

As the group climbed the hill for the third time, Michele claimed, "Sledding is fun, but it's also a lot of work. Think I'm ready to head back to the community building and check out the tree lighting ceremony."

The group returned their sleds then proceeded back to the community building. As they approached the large Christmas tree, Michele couldn't believe the number of people that were standing around the tree. She thought: *Looks like half of the town showed up.*

The group found an open space in the back of the crowd to stand. Michele snuggled next to Paul for warmth. After the mayor gave a short speech, he flipped a switch and turned on the Christmas tree.   Michele watched in awe as the crowd all started cheering and applauding. After a few minutes of admiring the lights, Amy asked the group, "Are you guys ready to head over to Leah's? My toes are frozen."

"I am!" Michele spoke up and looked at Leah.

"Sounds great to me. Jeff and I will meet you guys there."

Chapter 10

The couples met outside of Leah's house in the driveway. Michele looked at all the Christmas decorations around the house and said, "Your parents must really love Christmas."

"Yeah. My dad sort of goes overboard. You should see his hardware store!"

Leah worked, part-time, at her dad's, Mark Brown's, hardware store since the summer she turned 16. In truth, working at the hardware store was one of the best things that ever happened to Leah since it gave her the chance to meet Jeff. When Leah first moved into the area with her adoptive parents, she secretly had a crush on Jeff Backes, the star quarterback of their high school football team -- but never had an opportunity to meet him. Working at the hardware allowed Leah to talk to Jeff since, over that summer, he became a regular customer while helping his dad build a pole barn. Leah and Jeff became close acquaintances since Jeff frequently asked for Leah's help in finding supplies. After a month or so of meeting frequently at the store, Jeff finally asked her out... Michele thought: *fate has a strange way of bringing two people together. Those two are inseparable.*

When the teens walked into Leah's house, Michele noticed all the lights were off except the Christmas lights.

"Where are your parents?"

"They must still be at the winter festival. They took my younger brother there. I did see Theron once while we were sledding. I'm just surprised that I didn't run into my parents, but the place was packed."

After all the teens took their boots off in the foyer, Leah led the group to the basement.

Mike looked at the ping-pong table then asked Jeff, "You want to play?"

"Sure."

While the guys started playing their game, the rest of the group found a place to sit on the old couch and chairs that surrounded an old, console TV stand. Paul sat on one side of the couch with his arm draped around Michele, while Leah sat on the other side of the couch. Amy sat on the edge of one of the chairs and leaned forward to start the questioning, "So, tell us about your trip. Did your grandmother teach you how to control your dreams? Did you have fun?"

Leah spoke up, "And what about you getting a paternity test. Was that guy your biological father?"

"What!" Amy yelled. "You found your biological dad?"

Michele laughed, "One question at a time!"

"Ok." Leah laughed. Tell us about the paternity test first."

"My grandmother took me and Paul to meet this guy who lived on New Caledonia Island. The guy agreed he could be my biological father, so we both did a paternity test."

"And…" Amy encouraged more information.

"The test results came back 99.9% positive."

"That's great!" Amy shrieked.

Leah held her hand up to give Michele a high five.

"So, what does he look like? Was he nice?" asked Amy.

"He was blond like me. Tall and muscular."

"And was he nice? Did you like him? Are you leaving us to go live with him?"

"Wait a minute." Michele laughed. "No, I am not leaving you guys. I hardly know the guy. I'll probably go visit him next summer when I go to visit my grandmother."

Paul added, "And yes. I thought he was very nice. And he acted like he still cared about Michele's mom, Mayra, after all these years. He didn't seem to know what happened to her – she just, sort of disappeared." Paul squeezed Michele closer with his arm for a second then continued. "I don't think Michele's biological dad's new wife liked us much. What was her name?"

"Lalirra" Michele added.

"Yeah. Lalirra! She and her daughter, Amarina, were real bitches. They acted like Michele just showed up to get some money or some kind of handout from her dad."

Michele thought: *If Paul only remembered how much I had to gain, he would understand why Lalirra and Amarina acted like bitches.*

"So, the truth comes out…. Your step-mother is a real bitch! You would have left us to live with your dad if that bitch wasn't around," Leah chuckled.

"No. Really. I barely know the guy, besides… he did offer me a room to move into, but I told him I want to finish up my high school years here in Michigan with your guys and Paul."

"Aw," Amy said and jumped up to give Michele a hug. Leah and Paul also joined in, forming a big group hug.

Jeff looked over from the ping-pong table and said sarcastically, "Poor Paul, surrounded by all the estrogen."

Leah looked at Jeff and said playfully, "You're just jealous cause you weren't in the middle of that hug."

Jeff shrugged his shoulders, picked up the ball, and served it to Mike.

Amy sat back down and asked, "So, how about the vacation. Did you like the island?"

"Yes. It was beautiful. Like a tropical paradise. Paul said it reminded him of Hawaii."

Paul nodded his head.

"And did your grandmother get a chance to teach you how to control your crazy dreams so you can find out where that one thug is that was tracking you?"

"Yes, and No," Michele replied. "Yes, she told me how I could control my dreams with the help of this crystal necklace. She gave me this necklace for my 17th birthday. She told me to hold this crystal in one hand before I go to sleep, then think about what I needed to know." Michele lifted the crystal off her chest to show her friends, then continued, "And No. It will not help me find the one thug since my grandmother told me he, sort of, got himself killed – somehow."

"Well... I for one, am glad you don't have to worry about that thug anymore... But where did you get that beautiful ring?"

"Oh. Paul gave me this birthstone ring for my birthday." Michele held up her hand for Amy and Leah to admire.

Leah winked at Paul and said, "You did well."

*****

After the guys left, the girls said goodnight to Leah's parents, who were sitting in the living room watching TV, then made their way upstairs to Leah's room.

Michele looked at Amy and Leah and said, "I claim the floor."

Leah looked at Michele and said, "You don't need to sleep on the floor. We all squeezed into my queen-size bed last time."

"That's okay. I don't want to wake you guys up – in case I have another dream."

"Another dream?" Amy asked.

"Yeah," Michele told the girls about her latest dream. "I think this dream might be connected to some unsolved cases my uncle is working on. Some perpetrator is breaking into homes, beating the occupants half to death, then robbing them blind."

"Oh my!" Leah said.

"I want to try my grandmother's suggestion tonight, see if I can find out the five W's -- who, what, where, when, and why." Michele thought: *Sorry grams, I need to find out more about this dream before someone else gets killed. Mayra will have to wait. She's been missing for over 18 years; another day wouldn't hurt her.*

"Hope it works," Amy said. "Wake me if you need me!"

"I will. Thanks."

Michele made her makeshift bed on the floor. After the girls turned out the lights, she grabbed the crystal necklace and concentrated on the five W's.

*****

Michele woke up in a tangled mess on the floor. Disoriented, she started tugging, frantically, at the blankets that were restraining her body. When she finally untied herself, she sat up and tried to catch her breath. Her heart was pounding out of her chest and her body was soaking wet with perspiration. She grabbed one of her blankets and wiped her face. When she was finally able to focus her eyes, she looked around the room in the dim lighting that was shining through the bedroom window from the street lights down below. In the dim lighting, she could make out a bed with someone sleeping in it. It took a minute or two before she could comprehend where she was. She thought: *Oh, shit! It worked.*

Michele started crawling across the floor to find her purse and overnight bag. After she found them, she quietly unzipped her overnight bag and reached in it to get her paper notebook. She thought: *I'll just sneak out and write the dream's imagery down in the upstairs bathroom.*

She started crawling towards the door. Amy flipped on the bedside lamp. "What's going on?"

Michele looked up at Amy, caught in the act of leaving, "Go back to sleep. I just going down the hall --to write my dream imagery down."

"Oh, hell no! I came here to help you."

Leah woke up with a stretch and yawn. "What's going on?"

"Oh, hell," Michele said as she stood up. "I was trying to sneak out without waking the two of you up."

Amy scooted over in the bed towards Leah, then patted the spot right next to her. "Come on over here and let us help you decipher your dream."

Michele walked over to the bed, flopped down next to Amy, then opened her notebook. "I think the crystal worked. Let me write down everything I can remember first, then I'll let the two of you read the list."

After she wrote down her list, she handed it to friends to review: *The number 21. A mailbox with the number 351 on it. A street sign with Hawkins Lane written on it. The guy in the picture. A one-story, brick house. And an old lady lying on the floor.*

Amy looked at Michele and said, "Wow! I guess your grandmother's suggestion did work. According to your notes, it looks like the perpetrated you drew is planning on robbing an old lady's house located at 351 Hawkins Lane on December 21st."

Michele grabbed her cellphone and looked at her calendar. "So, December 21st is this coming Saturday. The beginning of Christmas break."

Leah looked at Michele and said, "We better call your Uncle Joe."

"Not right now. We have time.!" Michele threw her pillow at Leah and laughed. "I'm going back to sleep."

Chapter 11

Sunday afternoon, Michele went home and showed Joe her notes from her dream.

"Great! Now we have something to work with. I'll let the guys at the police department know tomorrow."

Michele smiled, then said, "I'm going upstairs to take a nap. Those girls didn't let me sleep last night."

After Michele woke up from her nap, she spent the rest of her day helping Gloria with the farm animals and then studying for her finals. Before she went to bed, she called Paul to update him on her newest dream. After she told him, she said, "I'm going to use my grandmother's advice and try to contact my mother tonight."

"I hope it works. Call me if you find out anything... good or bad!"

"Will do. Wish me luck."

"Sweet dreams, babe... Love you."

*****

Michele laid in bed with her faithful golden retriever by her side and Pepper, the cat, at her feet. She put one hand around the crystal necklace and repeated three times: *Mayra Johnson*. After she repeated her mother's name the third time, she thought: *I hope this works, grams*.

Michele was standing in a dark alley. Shivering, she hugged herself and looked around at all the old, tall buildings. When she looked down the alleyway, she thought: *Is that a dead body lying next to the garbage dumpster?* She walked closer, she noticed it wasn't a dead body after all. It was a woman, lying on her side in the fetal position, clutching her abdomen and softly moaning. Michele heard voices from behind her. She turned around and watched as three teenagers started walking down the alley towards her. They continued walking, right past her -- as if she wasn't there. They walked up to the woman lying on the ground. One of the teenagers kicked her. The woman let out a yelp. "Looks like she's alive," said the teenage boy with a thick accent. A girl spoke up, "We should call someone and get her some help! Looks like she's pregnant and withdrawing from drugs. Poor thing." The third teenager put his arm around the girl and said. "You're right. We can go and make an anonymous phone call. Come on. Let's get out of here and find someplace else to smoke this joint."

The dream started to fade. Michele woke up with a start. Her dog started licking her face.

Michele laughed and started petting the dog. "I'm okay Mitch."

Michele laid back down on her pillow, with her hands behind her head, as she remembered the story Anya Staevich had told her about her adoption: Anya worked at an orphanage in Moscow, Russia. A friend of hers that worked at a local hospital called and asked if the orphanage had room for another baby. Anya went to the hospital to pick up the baby and found out that baby's mom was found, withdrawing from drugs, on the streets of Moscow. After caring for Michele for over three months at the orphanage, Anya's boss told her that she had to find Michele a new home – so they could make room for new orphans. Anya wanted Michele to go to a special home so she thought of Michele's adoptive mom, Daria, since she used to work at the orphanage and was always sweet, loving, and caring with all the orphanage babies. Anya also knew Daria was about the right age to have a baby and that she was married to a military man from America. When Anya contacted Daria, Daria was more than eager to adopt the little girl since her husband and her been trying, without success, to have a child of their own. After the adoption, Daria sent Anya yearly pictures of Michele, until the car accident. During Michele's phone calls with Anya, Anya had told Michele that she didn't know what happened to her mother after she was discharged from the hospital and that the hospital closed down over ten years ago.

Shit! Michele thought. *That dream didn't tell me anything I didn't already know. But that reminds me… I promised Anya I would continue the tradition of sending her a picture of me yearly."* She looked at the dog and said, "Remind me tomorrow to send a picture to Anya."

The dog looked at Michele and barked.

Chapter 12

The last week of school, prior to Christmas break, flew by. Michele contacted her grandmother, in her dreams on Monday night to let her know the crystal didn't help her find Mayra's whereabouts... but she would keep trying. Uncle Joe had relayed Michele's dream to the police department and then told Michele that the department was planning on having 24-hour surveillance on the Hawkins Lane house all weekend.

Saturday morning, Michele and Leah went Christmas shopping since both of their boyfriends had to work. During their shopping trip, Michele told Leah how she planned to take -- her and Paul's relationship to the next level.

"Are you sure you're ready for that?"

"I love Paul. I want him to be my first."

"So, when are you planning this?"

"Paul said his parents both work Monday. I plan on sneaking over there after his parents leave for work."

*****

Early Sunday morning, Michele sat up in bed with a jolt. *Oh shit!* She looked at her clock – it displayed: *2 a.m.* She threw off her blankets and ran down the stairs. Pounding on Joe's bedroom door, Michele screamed, "He went to a different house!"

Michele heard footsteps, then the door flew open with Uncle Joe standing there -- tying up his bathrobe. Joe looked at Michele and said, "What?"

"The criminal! He drove up to the house on Hawkins Lane and parked down the road. While he was surveying the area, he spotted the stakeout car, so he drove right past the house. He took the first right, then went to a different house --

about six blocks away. It's a white, two-story house."

"Shit! Do you know how many white, two-story houses are in this town?"

"I know... but... he's driving an old, white SUV. Does that help?"

"It might. Let me call it in."

*****

A couple hours later, Michele woke up to the sound of a ringing phone. After listening to her uncle talk on the phone, she got up from the couch to find out what happened. Joe walked to the kitchen, turned on the light, and took a seat at the table. Gloria also got up and joined Michele and Joe in the kitchen.

"Good news Michele. They caught the perp in the act of robbing the house. Your car description paid off! Guess they spotted a white SUV parked outside of a two-story, white house. When they walked around the house, they found the backdoor kicked in -- so they snuck in the house and caught the perp loading up a bag of Christmas gifts. The police detective that called, told me that the homeowner was knocked unconscious -- but should survive."

Chapter 13

Early Monday morning, Michele climbed out of bed to get ready to go over to Paul's house. She took a quick shower then put on her lacy bra and throng -- that Leah had picked out for her at the mall. Looking at herself in the mirror, she smiled nervously and thought: *I hope I'm making the right decision. Maybe I should have talked to Gloria about my plans... but I know what she would say already.... I'm too young to be in love!* Michele felt bad for lying to Gloria, but she didn't want to hear the lecture; she had told Gloria that she and Paul were going out to breakfast, then sledding.

Michele almost turned the car around on the way to Paul's house; she was chickening out – thinking: *what if this step ruins our relationship? What if I'm no good in bed? What if Paul's parents come home and find us? What if Gloria realizes I lied?*

After Michele parked her car on the side of the street, just down the road from Paul's house, she dug through her purse to find the house key he gave her. She stared at the key for a minute or two, then thought: *If I really do love him. What am I so afraid of?*

When she crept into his bedroom, he was lying on his side with his back facing the door. From the doorway, she took a once over look at his room. It was well decorated, in a manly sort of way; the walls were painted maize and blue and it had Michigan Wolverines' football memorabilia hanging on the walls and on his desk. She also noticed his room was basically clean, which was a good thing since she was scared to death of cockroaches. When she looked over at his bedside stand, she noticed an 8 x 10 picture of her. Smiling, she proceeded to remove her clothes.

After removing her clothes, Michele slid under the covers in just her bra and underwear. She laid there staring at Paul's back until he began to stir. When he rolled over and noticed she was there, he reached his arm around her and pulled her up onto her side. With his forehead touching hers, he looked into her eyes and said, "Mmm... My dreams come true – waking up and finding you in my bed."

He reached a hand up to the side of her face and started running his fingers through her hair. "Are you sure this is what you want? If your nervous, we can wait. I'm happy with just snuggling up with you in my bed."

"Yes. I'm sure. I want you to be my first. I'm just not sure what to do."

Paul smiled, "You just need to lie there. I'll do the rest."

"Oh! And how do you know so much?"

"I've watched plenty of movies." Paul laughed. "Don't worry. No rush. If I do something you don't like, just say stop."

Paul started nibbling on her lip and teasing her with his tongue. Then he pushed Michele over onto her back and started showering her with kisses down her neck. When he reached the back of her neck, he whispered in her ear, "I love you."

Paul continued kissing her neck while his hand started stroking the side of her body – running shivers up her spine. When his hand started to roam up to her breast, he felt the lacy bra. "What's this? Let me see." Paul turned down the blanket to view Michele's matching bra and panties. "Nice."

"Leah helped me pick them out."

"Oh! Tell her she did well... But you didn't need to... since I just want you to take them off. All I'm wearing is my birthday suit."

Michele blushed. She didn't realize he was naked; she thought he had shorts or underwear on.

"Here. Let me help you," Paul said in a husky voice.

Paul pulled her bra's shoulder straps down, one at a time; then Michele turned away from him slightly so he could unhook the back. After Paul removed her bra and tossed it on the floor, he started messaging both of her breasts with his hands. Michele watched his facial expressions and his strong hands as he played with her breast and stimulated her nipples with his thumbs. She thought: *How did I get so lucky! He's so sexy with those strong arms, tousled-brown hair, dreamy-brown eyes, and long lashes.*

Michele gasped when Paul latched onto one of her nipples with his mouth; then she began to relax while he traced both of her nipples with his tongue. After a while, Paul scooted down, between her legs, and pulled her panties off. Kissing her thighs, he slowly started working his way up --- towards her hot spot. Michele's legs went tense when Paul's mouth settled on her clit. He continued to suck, lick, and tease her clitoris until she let a loud moan and shuttered with pleasure.

Looking up at Michele, Paul asked, "Can you get me wet?"

Paul rolled over and exposed his body. Michele turned on her side and traced her finger down his lean chest. When she looked at his penis, she was surprised to see how large it was. Michele reach down and began to stroke his long shaft. Then, leaning over him, she started licking it. While she was licking it, Paul reached down to touch the back of her head, then murmured, "Suck it, babe."

Michele took Paul's advice and started sucking and licking the head of his penis, like a lollipop. After a while, Paul let out a deep, throaty moan and said, "Stop. Lay back, I want it inside of you."

Michele laid back down on the bed while Paul positioned himself between her legs.

"I'll take it slow. Tell me if I hurt you."

Paul took his penis in his hand and started teasing Michele's opening -- then slowly, he thrust his hips downward. Michele started to tense. Paul pulled back slightly and said, "Just try to relax, babe. Spread your legs a little wider and let me slide inside."

Michele spread her legs a little more. Paul started making circular motions with his hips, driving his shaft in a little further with each circle -- until in one final thrust, he was buried deep inside of her. Paul learned down on his elbows and started biting and sucking on Michele's bottom lip while moving his hips, slowly up and down. Michele moaned, reached her arms around Paul, and dug her fingernails into his back. Paul responded by increasing his momentum, thrusting faster and deeper. Michele eagerly responded to each thrust by pushing her pelvis up to meet his. She closed her eyes and pushed her head back into the pillow -- truly enjoying the heavenly sensation. All at once, Michele's world exploded as Paul made one final thrust, burying his penis deep inside. Paul closed his eyes, threw his head back, and let out a small sigh of pleasure. After Paul's body shuddered, he collapsed on top of her.

Paul laid there, motionless for a while. Michele thought: *Did I kill him?* She turned her head and asked, "Are you okay?"

Paul laughed a deep, throaty laugh. He propped himself back up onto his elbows so he could look into her eyes. "Yes. I'm beyond okay. That was incredible!" He lowered his head and kissed Michele on the lips then murmured, "I love you."

*****

Laying on Paul's chest while he played with her hair, Michele asked, "So what now?"

Paul smiled, kissed the top of her head, then said, "I guess you'll have to marry me."

"We're only in eleventh grade, silly."

"Then someday?"

"Someday…" Michele looked at him and said, "Now seriously Paul. I meant what are we doing now? Today! You brat!" She hit him playfully.

Paul looked at her, pretending he was hurt. "Ouch!" Rubbing the spot where she hit him, he said playfully, "Anything you want to do, your majesty. Just don't beat me again… Please!"

Michele laughed but thought: *If he only knew how true that statement might be someday -- since I am first in line to inherit the throne of the seven islands of Honiawae. If he knew… that I am a princess… and a witch, I bet he would put his tail between his legs and run.*

"I won't beat you anymore if you will answer the question appropriately. Tell me what you want to do with the rest of the day. I told my aunt we were going to breakfast then out sledding."

"Well. I guess we need to go do that then. I don't want to make a liar out of you."

Chapter 14

Four months later, spring was in the air. Leah and Michele had joined the high school track team again and over the last several months: Paul and Michele had spent most of their spare time together and Michele had learned what the backseat of a car was for. Michele did try to contact her mother multiple times; however, her dreams were useless since they only showed the same dream over and over again -- of her mom lying in a dark alley. Michele had discussed the dream with her grandmother on multiple occasions, through her power of whispers in a dream, but they both were clueless on what else to try. Michele's criminal nightmares seemed to have stopped for the time being -- which gave her more time to practice her telekinesis (power of moving objects with her mind). To help her practice, Michele had bought a little basketball hoop to stick on her bedroom wall and practiced her telekinesis, almost daily, by making baskets with a wave of her finger. She also practiced her magic by waving her fingers and cleaning up her room. Over the months, Paul had frequently asked Michele if she was having any more nightmares. She would just shake her head and used the excuse: *It's probably too cold for criminals to be out.* Michele never told Paul about her power to move things since she was worried that kind of power would scare him away.

One night, while Michele was lying in bed trying to organizing her room with her powers, she tried picking up her carry-on bag that was sitting on the floor in her closet. When she picked it up, a rock fell out onto the floor. She dropped the bag and walked over to the closet to pick it up. She examined the half rock, half crystal, and thought: *I forgot all about this rock. And I was right, Leewan never noticed I borrowed it from Mayra's old bedroom.*

She carried the rock back over to her bed, climbed under the covers, then showed it to Mitch. "This rock came from my mother's rock collection. Isn't the crystal side beautiful?" Michele held onto the formed side of the rock and turned the cut-side of the rock around in the light; she loved all the sparkling diamonds that glittered within the pinkish hue colors of the rock. Looking at the dog, she said, "I can see why my mom liked this rock. At least I have something now, that used to belong to her."

Mitch barked once in agreement.

Michele patted the dog's head, then said, "It's getting late. We better be getting some sleep." She reached over, turned off the light, then held the rock close to her side while thinking: *I wish I knew where you were mom!*

*****

In the middle of the night, unbeknownst to Michele, the crystal rock began to glow. Mitch made a low, whimpering sound as she watched Michele kick her legs and shake her head from side to side. After a couple of minutes of tossing and turning, Michele started screaming, "What are you staring at? Why won't you talk to me? Where are we? What is this building? No. This can't be right!" The dog jumped up and started licking Michele's face.

Michele's bedroom door burst open, and Gloria came running through the door. Shaking Michele, she screamed, "Wake up Michele! Wake up. You're having another dream."

Michele bolted straight up in bed with tears in her eyes. Gasping for breath, she looked around the room, then looked at her aunt, "I saw my mom, or at least I think she was my mom. She was sitting in a wheelchair – outside, next to some big building, staring off into space. The building looked like one of those big institutions made for the criminally insane."

Gloria sat down on the side of the bed and hugged Michele. "Oh, Michele. I'm so sorry."

Michele looked up through tear-filled eyes. "Thanks. I better let my grandmother know."

After Gloria went back to bed. Michele grabbed her crystal necklace and repeated "Leewan Johnson" three times.

*****

Michele was sitting at her grandmother's kitchen table in her small cabin on Honiawae Island. Her grandmother, Leewan, was standing at the kitchen counter, pouring herself a cup of coffee. She turned, looked at Michele, then asked, "Do you want some coffee and a cinnamon roll?"

"Can I eat in my dreams?"

"Oh yes! On a visitation dream, you can. Here try one of my home-made cinnamon rolls."

Michele tore off a small piece of the fresh-backed cinnamon roll and popped it in her mouth. "Umm. This is really good, grams."

Leewan smiled. "I was going to contact you after I was done baking."

"I had a dream about my mom, Mayra."

Leewan slammed her coffee cup down on the kitchen table, splashing coffee all over. "What! Do you know where she is?"

"Not really. But I have some clues…. In my dream, it looked like she was sedated and was sitting in a wheelchair outside of some big mental institution."

"A mental institution. No wonder I couldn't contact her…. If she is sedated, my magic can't break through the mental fog. I'll let the prince know…. I mean your dad. Maybe he can find out more. Just wish we knew where this institution was. Must be near Moscow – somewhere."

Leewan started to fade. "Take your cinnamon roll with you."

"How do I do that?"

"Grab your necklace in the dream and grab the…"

Michele woke up in bed with the cinnamon roll. She thought: *I must have been holding the cinnamon roll when I grabbed my necklace. Wow. It really worked!* Looking at Mitch she asked, "Do you want a bite?" Michele tore off a piece of the cinnamon roll and gave it to the dog. Pepper, the cat, jumped up next to Michele and started meowing. "Ok. Ok. You can have a small piece too."

Chapter 15

Paul came to the track meet to watch Michele do her huddles and run the last leg of the 440-relay race. After Michele ran her races, she went up in the bleachers to sit by Paul, Gloria, and Joe.

Joe looked up as Michele approached. "There she is. The champion of the track team. You blew those girls away!"

Panting, Michele flopped down on the bench next to Paul. Looking over at Joe she said, "You're just saying that since you're my uncle... But I guess I did do a pretty good job. I didn't break any school records though."

"But your relay team won first place, Michele... Thanks to you," Gloria chimed in.

Paul patted Michele's leg and said, "You did great!"

"Thanks."

Leah came up to the bleachers to sit with Jeff and her parents, who were sitting one roll behind Michele's family. Michele looked up at Leah and asked, "How did you do at your high jump?"

"Third place overall."

"Nice."

Leah took a seat next to Jeff. Michele turned so she could address both, Paul and Leah, "I never got a chance to tell you guys at school, but I saw my mother last night in my dreams."

"You what? Where is she?" Leah asked.

"I'm not sure. She was unresponsive in a wheelchair outside some big building. I think it was a rehabilitation center or some kind of mental institution. All know is it was a large building with a fenced-in yard."

"Hmmm," Paul said. "The last time anyone knew her whereabouts was at the hospital in Moscow, Russia -- where she had you. I can do some research when I get home – check for mental institutions near Moscow. I would think the hospital would've discharged her to a local institution."

"Thanks. That would be helpful. My grandmother and my dad are also trying to look into it."

*****

Michele had to work at the Country Crock on Saturday. Denise just started back to work after taking an extended sick leave for breaking her wrist on the job. When Paul and his buddies came in, Denise just looked at them – then glared at Michele.

Paul looked at Michele and asked, "Which booths are in your section?"

"The clean ones, of course."

Paul and his buddies, Tom and Mike, took a seat in her section.

Michele followed them to the booth then asked, "You guys know what you want?"

After the boys ordered their drinks and burgers, Paul grabbed Michele's hand. "Are you still getting out of work at seven?"

"Yep."

"Want to go see that new movie with me tonight?"

"Sounds great to me."

"Movie starts at nine, so I'll pick you about around 8:30 p.m."

*****

When Paul arrived at Michele's house, Gloria invited him in to wait for Michele. Joe was sitting in his favorite recliner, watching TV. He looked up at Paul and said, "Have a seat, son."

Paul took a seat on the coach then looked over at Joe's gun sitting on the coffee table.

Joe looked at Paul and asked, "So, the two of you are not going to any parties tonight. Are you?"

"No sir. Just a movie."

"Good. I don't need any more drama. And remember, she has to be home by midnight."

"Yes sir. I remember."

Michele came down the stairs wearing a mini skirt and a low-cut shirt. Her Aunt Gloria looked up at her and asked, "Where did you get that outfit?"

"Leah helped me pick it out the other day. Do you like it?"

Paul sat on the couch with his mouth hanging open. Aunt Gloria said, "No. You'll catch your death of cold. You need something warmer than that!"

"I have a jacket." Michele grabbed her blue-jean jacket off the coat rack and opened the front door. "Are you ready Paul?"

Paul stood up and said, "I'll have her back by midnight."

The couple left out the front door. Gloria stood there with her mouth hanging open, staring at Joe.

Joe chuckled and said, "You used to wear outfits like that too Gloria."

Gloria turned to go back into the kitchen and said, "Well, I never!"

*****

On the way to the movie, Paul looked at Michele and said, "I really do like that outfit on you."

Michele blushed slightly and said, "You don't think it makes me look too trashy?"

"Hell no! But it might cause trouble when I have to fight all the other boys off you."

Michele laughed then looked out the car window thinking: *I bet my half-sister, Amarina, would think it was trashy.* The last time Michele saw her half-sister was at a dinner party in the castle's formal dining room. Amarina was wearing a gorgeous, sparkling, light-green gown that was adorned with rhinestones. Amarina had snickered when she heard the stories of Michele's upbringing and had made fun of Michele's cut-off shorts and t-shirt.

Paul interrupted Michele's thoughts and said, "I did a little research on your mother's whereabouts, but I'm afraid it's like looking for a needle in a haystack. There are just too many places that match the description of your dream."

"Thanks for trying. Hopefully, my grandmother and my dad have better luck."

*****

Michele enjoyed cuddling up with Paul at the movie theater. She loved the movie and Paul's company-- even though he complained about her putting way too much salt on their popcorn and acted grumpy when he had to get some refills on their pop.

After the movie, Paul asked Michele, "Do you want to go to the drive-through so we can get a late-night snack?"

"Sounds good… big spender," she laughed.

"Well, I have to have you home by midnight or your detective uncle will probably hunt me down."

Michele laughed. "Oh, Uncle Joe is harmless."

"That's what you think!"

Paul pulled into Michele's driveway at 11:50 p.m. Michele leaned over to kiss him goodnight, then whispered, "We still have time for a quickie." She jerked her head towards the back seat.

"Hell no! And take a chance of your uncle coming out here with his gun. You should have thought of that earlier!"

Michele laughed. "Then tomorrow?"

"Should I pick you up early for dinner at my parent's place, or should we just plan on leaving early?"

"Will just leave early."

The young lovers kissed one more time before Michele opened the door to get out.

"Michele. I really love that outfit on you!"

"Thanks." Michele closed the car door while someone simultaneously flipped on the front porch light.

Chapter 16

Michele barely fell to sleep when the visions started. Michele sat straight up in bed, threw back her covers, then ran down the stairs to wake up her uncle.

She pounded on Joe's and Gloria's bedroom door, then screamed, "It's happening now. It's happening now. You need to send someone over to the house."

Uncle Joe opened his bedroom door while tying up his bathroom robe. "What's happening now?"

Michele screamed hysterically, "Domestic violence or whatever you call? Broken glass, blood, a black eye, a gun, a little girl hiding under her bed. He's going to kill his wife and maybe the child. You need to stop it. Now!"

"Ok! Ok! Calm down, Michele. Come on to the kitchen so I can write down some more information." Joe walked to the kitchen and flipped on the light. Aunt Gloria came out of the bedroom and followed them to the kitchen table.

Michele sat on the edge of a chair and blurted out the address of the house. She watched as Joe wrote down the address then she leaped out of her seat and started pacing the floor. "We need to get someone over there now!"

Joe picked up the phone and dialed the number to the police department. After he reported the disturbance to one of his co-workers, he looked at Michele and said, "They're sending a car there now. Hopefully, they get there in time."

Gloria reached out her hand to stop Michele from pacing. "It's okay, baby. It's out of our hands now. All we can do now is pray."

Michele nodded her head in agreement. Joe looked at her and said, "You might as well go back to bed. I will let you know in the morning if they made it there on time."

Gloria walked Michele to the stairs. "You did a good thing. Hopefully, the cops will get there in time."

* * * * *

Michele woke up early and walked downstairs. Her Uncle Joe was sitting in the living room watching the 6 o'clock news. The news reporter was saying: *There was a standoff for a couple hours early this morning before the gunman finally surrendered. He was taken into police custody and is waiting at the county jail for arraignment. His wife is being treated at a local hospital. She is reported in fair condition. The child that was found at the scene has been released to the custody of local relatives.*

Joe turned around and saw Michele standing at the foot of the stairs.

"You did it, Michele! You saved that woman and her child."

"Thank God!" Michele sat down on the couch and put her head down into her hands.

*****

After breakfast, Michele went outside with Gloria to feed the farm animals and collect the eggs the chickens had laid. When they returned to the house, Michele set the eggs in the sink then looked at aunt and said, "Think I'm going to hang out in my bedroom until it's time to go to Paul's for dinner; I need to call Amy and Leah, get them caught up on my latest dreams."

After calling her friends, Michele searched through her closet for something to wear. Paul's parents were friendly enough but she still wanted to make a good impression since both of his parents were doctors. *I don't want them thinking I'm not good enough for their son.* After trying on numerous outfits, she finally settled on a conservative, knee-length, black skirt, and a short-sleeved shirt that matched the color of her blue eyes. Standing in front of the mirror, she noticed how her multicolored crystal, that her grandmother had given her for her 17th birthday, seem to change colors to match whatever outfit she wore. After she applied some light makeup, she made her way downstairs to say good-bye to Gloria and Joe.

Gloria looked up from the couch when Michele came down the stairs. "Well, don't you look nice!"

Joe turned in his chair to look at Michele. "What time do you plan to be home? You know it's a school night."

Michele smiled and said, "Yes I know. I should be home by 9 p.m. at the latest."

Joe returned his attention to the TV and Gloria continued to talk. "Make sure you thank Paul's parents again for helping us arrange our trip to Australia last fall. It made the trip so much more affordable to have a free place to stay at Mrs. Hudson's brother's house in Queensland, before meeting your grandmother at the ferry.... I wonder if they can help out again when you go to visit your grandmother this summer?"

"We still have a couple of months to plan. I'm sure Paul's parents will help out if needed."

"I hope so. Have you heard if your grandmother was going to help with the plane ticket? If I recall right, I don't think she has a lot of money."

"I think my dad is planning on paying for all of it."

"Oh. Well, that's nice of him. I'm just surprised since he only met you once... Well, have a good time at Paul's"

"Thanks." Michele gave Gloria a peck on the cheek then patted Joe on his shoulder. "I'll see you around 9."

Chapter 17

As Michele drove through the rich subdivision, she thought about where she would want to live when she grew up: *Would I want to settle down in a nice subdivision like this? Live in the country? Or live in the castle with my dad? The country for sure!* Michele knew she could not give up the country. She loved the privacy, the farm animals, and the gorgeous sunsets over the open fields. She still wasn't sure if she wanted to live in the countryside where her grandmother lived on Honiawae Island or settle down in America. *Guess I should discuss this with Paul; after all, he did propose to me.* Michele sighed as she pulled into Paul's driveway. *But Paul doesn't even remember Honiawae Island. Thank God I have another year of high school before I have to decide!*

When Michele started walking up the sidewalk towards the big two-story house with an attached four-car garage, the front door opened. Paul stood in the doorway and said, "You're five minutes late."

She laughed and walked up to him to give him a kiss. "Did you miss me?"

"Of course! Let me help you with your jacket." Paul helped her out of her jacket and hung it up in the foyer's closet while Michele admired the large crystal chandelier and spiral staircase… that led up to Paul's bedroom.

"My parents are sitting out in the living room; we should go hang out with them before dinner." Paul winked at Michele then led her by the hand to the living room.

When Michele entered the living room, Judy Hudson looked up and said, "Well, there she is. Jim and I were just talking about your Uncle Joe and Aunt Gloria; and how we should have invited them over for dinner too!"

"Maybe we should plan that some other time. I'm sure they would like that. Gloria wanted me to thank the two of you again, for helping them with the arrangements to go visit my grandmother. Without your help, I'm not sure if we would have been able to afford it without charging up their credit cards."

"Oh, anytime dear. Are you going to visit your grandmother again? I know my brother and his wife would love to see Paul again. Maybe next time you go, Jim and I can go with you guys and stay at my brother's."

"I'm planning on visiting my grandmother over the summer. I'm sure my aunt would be relieved if I traveled with someone they knew."

"Then it's a deal. Just let Paul know what day you want to leave. Jim, Paul, and I can book the same flight you take to Australia. Then I can rent a car and take you to the ferry to visit your grandmother, or you could stay a couple days at my brother's before you go. Do you need help buying your ticket? We should buy them at the same time so you and Paul can sit together."

"No. I'm pretty sure my grandmother and dad are making all the arrangements. I'll let Paul know when the arrangements have been made."

"Let me know as soon as you can so Jim and I can request work off and make arrangements with my brother, George."

"Ok. I'll call my grandmother sometime this week."

The maid walked out to the living room and announced, "Dinner is ready."

Michele looked at Paul and whispered, "I didn't know your parents had a maid."

Paul smiled and said, "We don't really have a maid. Wendy is our housekeeper. She comes over twice a week to clean; and on special occasions, she cooks for us for extra money."

"Oh! This is a special occasion?"

"You're here, so it must be special. Isn't it?" Paul laughed.

*****

Paul led Michele by the hand to the back of the house. "My mom wants us to eat dinner outside, on the back deck, since the weather is unseasonable warm."

Michele walked through the French doors and looked around the backyard. It was a beautiful, well-manicured, fenced-in yard with a stone walkway, water fountain, and flower garden. The stone walkway led the way to an inground pool with a built-in hot tub. Just beyond the pool, Michele could see a pool house and a work shed that matched the color of the house.

Paul pulled out a chair at the outdoor patio table for Michele to sit. After she sat down, Wendy dropped a plate in front of her with a Ribeye steak, baked potato, and grilled asparagus. Michele noticed an empty glass in front of her, a glass of water, and a house salad. She looked at Judy and Jim and said, "Wow. This dinner looks delicious."

Judy replied, "Figured it would be a good day to eat outside and enjoy the sunshine; after being cooped up inside all winter. Would you like lemonade or ice tea?"

"Lemonade please."

After dinner, Wendy bought out a pie for dessert.

Michele looked at the pie and said, "Banana cream! My favorite."

Judy chuckled and said, "That's what Paul told us. Guess he does know you pretty well."

After eating such a big meal, Michele could only choke down a small piece of the pie. When she was done with her pie, Michel stood up to clear her plate. Judy spoke up, "No Michele. You don't have to do that. That's what I'm paying Wendy for. Paul told me he rented a movie for the two of you to watch. The two of you should just go watch your movie."

Michele put her plate back on the table and looked at Wendy who was starting to pick up some of the plates off the table and said, "Thank you, Wendy. Everything was perfect."

Wendy smiled and said, "Your welcome."

Paul stood up and grabbed Michele's hand. Looking at his parents he said, "Thanks for the great dinner." Then he turned and led Michele back into the house to the downstairs den. "Have a seat while I get us some drinks." She took a sit on the oversized, stuffed couch while Paul walked over to the bar. Turning back towards Michele, he asked, "What do you want to drink?'

"Your parents let you drink?"

He laughed, "No. All the alcohol is locked up in those cabinets. I meant non-alcoholic drink, silly."

Michele blushed then said, "I'll just have some water, please."

"Do you want any popcorn, peanuts, or chips?"

"No. No. I can't even look at any more food right now."

Paul returned to the couch and set two drinks on the coffee table. Then he walked over to the gas fireplace and flipped a switch. After starting the fire, he dimmed the lights, sat on the couch, then grabbed the 75-inch TV remote to start the movie.

While a trailer about another movie started to play, Paul grabbed a couple of pillows and a blanket from a cabinet. He winked at Michele and said, "Thought we could cuddle up under this blanket to watch the movie."

Paul stood up so Michele could lay down sideways on the couch. After she was situated, he squeezed in behind her and threw the blanket over them.

During the movie, Paul's hand started to roam up her blouse to caress her breast. After a while of spooning and fondling her breast, his hand started roaming south. Michele turned slightly onto her back to give him access to her privates. While messaging her area between her legs, he whispered in a husky voice, "Take off your panties -- so I can play?"

She reached down, slipped off her panties, and pulled up her skirt to give him full access. When she laid back down, she turned her head towards the TV so she could finish watching the movie while he played; however, she found it hard to concentrate on the movie when Paul's hand started to explore the area between her legs. Moreover, she completely lost her ability to think when he took a moist finger and started stimulating her clit. After she shivered with delight and let out a low moan, Paul said, "Turn on your side so I can put it in you."

Michele looked at him in shock and said, "But your parents are right upstairs."

"So! They won't come down. Plus, if they do, we're just cuddling, innocently, on the couch watching the movie."

Michele turned on her side and let him have his way. After a while of slow, rhythmed movements, she heard the door at the top of the steps open. She stopped moving in fear of being caught and looked at Paul.

His mom called from the top of the steps, "Michele, you left your phone up here in the living room.

Michele heard footsteps coming down the stairs. Paul pulled her closer and whispered, "It's ok. Don't move!" Then he reached over her, grabbed the TV remote, and paused the movie.

When Judy appeared at the bottom of the steps, both Paul and Michele looked up at her.

"Sorry to interrupt. How's the movie?"

Paul pushed himself up onto his elbow to expose the top, clothed portion of his body, then said, "Great. Really good."

Judy continued, "I'll let the two of you get back to your movie, but I wanted to bring Michele her phone since it's been ringing off the hook. Looks like someone name Leah Brown is trying to get ahold of you.

Judy handed Michele her cellphone. Michele reached up from under the blanket, grabbed it, then said, "Thanks. Leah's my best friend from school. I'll give her a call."

"Ok then. Enjoy your movie." Judy turned to go back up the stairs.

Michele glanced at Paul and said, "I told you we would get busted."

Paul made a deep moan as he thrust his penis into her deeper, then said, "We weren't busted darling. We were just interrupted. Now back to what we started."

After the young lovers finished what they'd started, Michele's phone started ringing. Michele answered her phone and said, "Hi Leah. What's up?"

"My mom has been in a car accident! I've been trying to reach you. I'm here at the hospital now with my dad and Jeff. I need you! They took my mom to surgery. Please come!"

Michele sat up on the couch and said, "Oh my God! Yes. I'm on my way."

After Michele hung up her phone, Paul asked, "What?"

"Leah's mom was in a car accident. I need to go to the hospital. Now!"

Paul jumped up to turn off the TV and the fireplace. "I'm going with you. I'll drive while you call your aunt and uncle."

The teens ran up the stairs. Michele put on her jacket while Paul told his parents what happened and that they were going to the hospital to stay with Leah.

Judy looked at him and said, "I hope Leah's mom is ok! Call us when you know how the surgery went."

Chapter 18

When Paul and Michele arrived in the Critical Care Unit, Michele asked a nurse, "Can you tell me where Mary Brown is?"

"Are you related to the patient?"

"No. But her daughter is my best friend."

"Sorry, dear. Only the immediate family allowed in the room."

Paul looked around the unit and called out, "Leah."

Michele turned to walk away from the nursing station. Leah stepped out of a room crying. When she spotted Paul and Michele -- she ran to them sobbing. After hugging Michele, she started dragging her towards the room. The nurse spoke up, "Sorry dear. Only two visitors in the room at a time."

Leah glared at the nurse, then said, "Fine!" She looked back and Michele and said, "I can take the both of you to the waiting room where my brother, Theron, and Jeff are waiting. When my dad is ready to step out of the room for a couple of minutes, I'll come to get you."

*****

Leah led Paul and Michele to the waiting room. Theron jumped up when he saw his sister and asked, "Is she awake. Can I go see her now?"

"No. She's not awake. The doctor just left a few minutes ago. Guess she hit her head pretty hard when that other car T-boned her. The doctor said something about her having a ... subdural hematoma or some sort of bleeding in her head. He had to make a hole in her scalp to relieve the pressure. There is some sort of drain coming out of her head. He said they would watch her closely and repeat another CT or something in the morning to see if the bleeding has stopped. He also said there is a high chance that she might never wake up -- only time will tell. For now, all we can do is sit and wait. They are keeping her sedated and on a breathing machine so her body can rest... and hopefully heal."

"Can I go see her?" Theron asked.

"The nurse said only two people at a time. So, I can take you down there to stay with dad. But we're not supposed to touch anything. When the two of you are ready to leave the room, come back here so Michele and I can go see her."

Jeff looked up at Leah and asked, "Anything you want me to do?"

Leah looked at Jeff through tear-filled eyes and said, "Not right now. Thanks! Just wait here with Paul and Michele until I return."

Jeff looked at Paul and Michele and said, "Thanks for coming. I just feel so useless."

Paul forced a smile, then took the seat next to him. Michele sat in a chair on the other side of Paul. Paul looked at Jeff and said, "Nothing anyone of us can do now but to wait and be here to support the family."

When Leah returned, Jeff jumped up to hug her. She broke down crying and sobbed, "I hope she wakes up."

Michele stood up and hugged the backside of Leah. "We're here for you. I'm sure she'll wake up. I can feel it in my bones."

*****

After about ten minutes or so, Mark Brown and Theron came into the waiting room with bloodshot eyes. Mark looked at Leah and said, "If you and Michele want to go sit in your mother's room for a while, we'll stay out here with Jeff and Paul."

Leah jumped up and grabbed Michele's hand, "Come on Michele."

When Michele walked into the room, she noticed that all the lights were turned down low and that there were a lot of beeping noises coming from all the medical equipment. She looked at Leah's mom who was lying unconsciously in bed. She had a tube coming out of her mouth, a bunch of Intravenous (IV) tubes connected to a line in her neck, and some sort of drainage tube coming out of her shaved head -- draining bloody fluid.

Michele walked up to the bed and reached for her hand. When she squeezed Mary's hand, Michele felt her necklace start to heat up. Michele grabbed the crystal with one of her hands then noticed sun rays coming down, out of the ceiling, shining on Mary. Michele looked at Leah, standing on the other side of the bed, to see if she noticed anything strange. Leah just stood there, staring at her adoptive, foster-care mother. When Michele looked back at Mary, her eyes were fluttering. Michele turned her head and looked at the heart monitor -- the rate seemed to be increasing. When she looked back at Mary, Mary's other arm was reaching up towards the breathing tube. Michele looked at Leah and said, "Don't let her pull the tube out." Leah ran around to the other side of the bed and grabbed her arm. Mary opened her eyes wide and started thrashing around in the bed. Michele screamed, "Nurse. Nurse. We need some help in here!"

Some nurses came running into the room. A couple of nurses took over holding Mary down while another nurse at the door said, "I'll go get the doctor."

Within a couple of seconds, a doctor came through the door, "What's going on?"

He looked at the patient and said, "Looks like she's waking up." He glanced at one of the nurses and said, "I need a syringe so I can pull the tube."

Michele and Leah watched as the doctor pulled the tube out of Mary's mouth – the one that connected her to the breathing machine. After the tube was pulled, Mary started shouting, "Where am I? What happened?"

The doctor took Mary's hand and told her, "You're in the Intensive Care Unit. You were in a serious car accident."

Mary looked around the room and saw Leah. Leah ran to her mother's arms and started crying, "You woke up! You woke up!" Leah stood back up, wiped the tears from her face, and asked Michele, "Will you go get my dad."

Mary noticed Michele and said, "Hi Michele. Come closer so I can look at you." Mary put her hand out.

Michele walked up and took her hand and smiled. "Glad you're feeling better, Mrs. Brown."

"You can just call me Mary, or mom. You and Leah are so close I might as well be your mom."

Michele smiled and said, "Yes mom."

Mary started reaching for the top of her head where the drain was. "The doctor grabbed her head and said, "That's a ventricular drain that is draining the extra fluid from your head. If your pressure inside your head stays low, I can remove

that drain tomorrow. But you have to promise me
– you will not pull that drain out on your own."

"Yes, doctor. I promise."

Leah grabbed Michele's hand and said,
"Let's go tell the other's the good news."

Chapter 19

When Michele got home, it was closer to
10 p.m. Walking into the living she was greeted
by Joe and Gloria.

"So how is Mary Brown?" Gloria asked.

"She woke up! The doctor thinks it's a
miracle." Michele didn't tell them that she might
have had a hand in the miracle since they might
think she was losing her mind: They'd already
wanted to send her to get professional help when
she started having her prophetic dreams. Telling
them now, about her possibly having healing
power or about her advancing telekinesis skills --
might send them over the edge.

"Well praise the Lord!" Gloria proclaimed.

Michele smiled and thought about her
grandmother's, Leewan's, explanation of their
magical powers: *They are a gift from God.*
Looking at her aunt and uncle, she replied, "Well I
better be going to bed. See you in the morning."

*****

After Michele snuggled into bed with her
faithful golden retriever, she thought: *I need to
reach out to my grandmother to tell her about this
new power… and make plans for our summer visit.*

She closed her eyes, grabbed her crystal, and repeated Leewan's full name three times.

Michele was sitting at a long table by herself. She looked around the room and thought: *This is the council room where my grandmother first told the prince I was his child. What am I doing here in the castle on Honiawae Island?*

The council room door opened and her grandmother, Leewan, and her biological dad, Prince Macalla Williams, walked in.

Michele stood up in surprise. Leewan walked over to hug her, then stepped aside for the prince to address her.

"Hi, Michele. Do you have one of those hugs for your dad?"

Michele stood there awkwardly for a second; then dumbfoundedly said, "Of course."

After hugging her tall father awkwardly, Michele stood back, looked at Leewan, then said, "How can he be here in my dream? I didn't call him."

Leewan laughed and said, "Sit. Sit. We have a lot to talk about."

After everyone was seated, Leween leaned across the table and explained, "I linked your father to me – so when you called, he could attend the dream meeting. I have been staying at the castle's guest house for the last couple of days. When the prince returned from Russia, without any leads on your mom, he asked if he could talk to you. I told him I could link him to my dreams, so if you called, he could join in. I also told him if you didn't call me within the next couple of nights – I would reach out to you."

"Wow. That is so cool. You'll have to teach me sometime."

"Yes. I will. But we don't have much time in these dreams, so we better get down to business. We need to make plans for your visit this summer. You do still plan on coming... right?"

"Yes! Of course. That's why I wanted to contact you. Paul's parents are planning to help me again if needed. They said they wanted to go visit Paul's, mother's brother in Australia and they could book a flight with me so I wouldn't have to travel alone. They even..."

Leewan interrupted, "Fine. Fine. Do you have a date picked out yet?"

"I thought about flying out of Detroit on Monday, June 7th. Paul's mom, Judy, said she could pay for my ticket and she would rent a car. Then she asked if I wanted to stay awhile at her brother's before catching the ferry to the Island of New Caledonia."

Leween looked at the prince. "Do you want to tell her, or should I?"

Michele looked from her grandmother to her dad.

Macalla spoke up, "I planned on paying for it all: the flight, the rental car, the ferry... and give you some extra cash for food. I need to have some control of your whereabouts to make sure you're safe... I don't want you to come up missing like your mother, Mayra did. Will you let me?"

Michele's eyes got wide, then she said, "All I need is some help with my airline ticket and the ferry. I don't want your wife, Lalirra, or my half-sister, Amarina, thinking I am only out to claim my inheritance. I already told Paul's mom and dad you would probably help me pay for my ticket."

"Can I pay for yours and Paul's? You did want to bring Paul back for another visit, right?"

"Yes. That would be nice. If he wants to come."

Leewan nodded her head, "You should invite him."

Macalla continued, "If he does want to come. I want to pay for both of your plane tickets and the car rental so I can send some undercover agents to inspect everything before your arrival -- and to watch over you."

"You're sending people to spy on me? I'm old enough to take care of myself!"

Leewan patted the prince's hand in a motherly sort of way, then said, "Michele. He's just concerned for your wellbeing. He followed your leads to Russia and searched for Mayra -- without any luck. If what we believe is true, about Lalirra's parents having a hand in the disappearance of Mayra, we fear her family might try to make you disappear too."

Michele looked at her dad's concerned eyes and said, "Ok... I guess. Thank you!"

Prince Macalla smiled and said, "It's the least I can do since I haven't' been much of a father to you all of your life."

Michele shook her head and said, "Well, that's not your fault. You only found out about me last fall."

The prince smiled and said, "But I still want to make it up to you. I will have a package delivered to you first-class within a couple of weeks. If you need anything else, just let your grandmother know."

"Thank you, Prince Macalla."

"Please don't feel you need to address me formally. I'm your dad. If you don't want to call me dad yet... I understand. But you can just call me Macalla."

"Thanks, dad." Michele smiled as she thought: *I like that sound of saying that to my real, biological father.*

The room started to fade. Michele said, "One more thing Leewan. Can we talk freely?" She looked at her dad. "About our powers?"

"Yes. Of course. Your dad comes from a long generation of witches too; but like I said, sometimes the powers skip a generation or two. What up?"

"Is it possible for me to have healing powers?"

"What? Yes. I course. My grandmother had some healing powers. That's why I wanted to be a midwife. But for some reason, I never developed those powers. Oh, Michele, I'm so proud of you."

The dream faded away with her father smiling and Leewan blowing Michele a kiss goodbye.

Michele woke up in bed with her golden retriever lying next to her. She looked at the clock and said to the dog, "Looks like I might as well get up, my alarm is set to go off in ten minutes."

Chapter 20

When Michele got to school, she wasn't surprised to find no one standing by her shared locker since Leah was spending the next couple of days hanging out at the hospital with her mother. As she was hanging up her jacket, Paul approached and said, "Good morning beautiful. How was your night?"

Michele turned around and smiled. "Good. Now that I know Leah's mom is out of the woods. And I talked with my grandmother and my dad last night."

"Oh."

"Yep. My grandmother and dad invited you to the island for another visit this summer… if you want to go with me? And my dad insists on buying your plane ticket and paying for the rental car!"

"He doesn't have to do that. My parents can afford the added expense."

"Does that mean you want to go… with me?"

"I would love to. But I'll have to talk to my boss at work. I should be able to get some extra time off."

"Great!" Michele hugged him, then continued, "I told my dad he didn't have to pay for everything… But he insisted. And we picked a date to fly out: Monday, June 7th. My dad is going to order the tickets and have them delivered first class. I can let you know the flight number out of Detroit as soon as I get the package."

"Sounds good. I'll let my parents know." Paul grabbed Michele's hand and started walking towards their first class. "And we need to talk prom. I know it's three weeks out but my mom is bugging me on what color dress you're planning on wearing."

Michele laughed. "I almost forgot. My aunt plans on taking me shopping this Saturday – so, as soon as I know the color, I'll let you know."

*****

After school, Michele skipped track practice to go with Paul to the hospital to visit Leah. Leah had texted Michele during school, telling her that her mom was being moved to a step-down unit that allowed more visitors. When the couple walked into the room, Paul went over to a chair to visit with Leah's boyfriend, Jeff, while Michele joined Leah at the bedside.

"How are you feeling, Mrs. Brown... I mean mom."

"Much better. Thanks. I'm ready to fly this coop but the doctor states I have to stay another day for observation. Guess the CT scan this morning showed almost 100% resolution of the subdural hematoma so the doctor removed the awful drain. He said I am the first person he has ever seen to recover so fast from such a trauma."

Michele smiled and looked at Leah. "Did you get any sleep last night?"

"Not much. It's hard to sleep in a hospital – with all the noise and interruptions from the hospital staff. I might go home tonight since mom seems to so much better."

"Where's your dad and brother?"

"They just stepped out. Guess dad had to go check on something at the hardware store. Oh. Before I forget. When are you going shopping for your prom dress? The doctor told my mom if he does discharge her tomorrow, he wants her to stay home and take it easy for at least two weeks; so, I thought I could go dress shopping with you?"

"My aunt wants to take me this Saturday, but I'm sure she wouldn't mind if you wanted to come with us."

Chapter 21

By the time Saturday came, Michele wondered where the week went. Life was certainly busy with school, work, and track practice; she barely had time to breathe, yet spend quality-time with Paul.

"Michele!" Gloria called up from the bottom of the stairs. "Did you want to help me feed the animals before we go?"

"Sure. Be down in a sec." Michele looked at her Mitch and said, "I wonder why I can't contact my mom." Michele had been trying, almost nightly, to reach her mom. She was repeating her name three times and holding the crystal – but only came back to the same dream of her mom lying on the ground in a dark alley – where the teens found her. No more information about the building or institution where her mother was. Michele shook her head in disappointment then ran downstairs. Gloria was sitting in the kitchen with Joe, drinking coffee. "You want something to eat before we go?"

"No. I'm fine. Thanks."

Joe looked up and said, "Here Michele. This came in the mail for you yesterday. Looks like it's from your dad. Sorry. I didn't look at the mail yesterday. I just brought it in last night after work. I was too tired, so I just threw it on the shelf with the rest of the bills – figured I had to pay them all today."

Michele grabbed the envelop and tore the package open.

After a couple of seconds, Gloria asked Michele, "What is it?"

"It's my tickets from my dad for my trip to Australia."

"Oh!" Uncle Joe spoke up. "Your dad bought your tickets. That was nice of him. I figured he would chip in but I didn't think he would pay for all of them. I was planning on making a withdrawal from your trust -- from my brother's estate."

"Guess you won't have to. Looks like everything here." Michele started pulling out the contents while talking: "Two airline tickets for June 7th at 6 a.m., a rental car receipt with an open return date, two tickets for the ferry boat ride with cabin, a letter, and a check." Michele stared at the check and her eyes got big.

Aunt Gloria said, "What? What is it?"

"Oh. Nothing. Just a little extra spending money for the trip." Michele folded up the check, put it back in the envelope, then thought: *He didn't need to give me three thousand bucks. I'm giving most of that money back to him!*

Joe spoke up, "Two tickets? Who's the other ticket for?"

"Oh. Sorry. I didn't get a chance to tell you. My grandmother invited Paul over for a visit too. And Paul's parents want to book the same flight so they can go over and visit Paul's uncle."

"Well, that sure makes me feel better. I told Joe that I didn't want you traveling half-way around the world on your own." Gloria smiled at Joe then said to Michele, "Come on. The animals are waiting."

*****

Gloria rode shot-gun since Michele wanted to drive her car to the dress shop. After picking Leah up, Michele swung by the bank to deposit the check she got in the mail. At the dress shop, Michele and Leah grabbed a lot of the dresses off the bargain shelf to try on.   Most of the dresses were either too short or too large for Michele. After trying on numerous dresses, the girls decided they couldn't fit any of the dresses on clearance.

Rifling through the new dresses, Michele's eyes kept moving back to one particular dress. It was a limited edition. It reminded her of the blue, sparkling gown she saw on Queen Chloe the first time she met her--- Macalla's mom…her grandmother! Michele finally gave up and wandered over to the dress. Looking at the price tag, she almost fell over.

Leah walked up to the gown. "Wow! That's beautiful. It matches your eyes." Leah looked at the tag. "Looks like it was imported from Australia. Whew! Look at the price!"

Michele looked at the price tag; it read: *$799.99.*

A sales lady walked up and said, "You have great taste. That dress just arrived. It's a form-fitting dress with a nice slit up the side. The slit helps if you're planning on doing a lot of dancing."

Michele looked skeptically at the price tag. The sales lady went on, "It also comes with a tiara, matching necklace, and earrings. Wait here. I'll go get them."

Aunt Gloria walked up and said, "Nice looking gown." Then she looked at the price tag. "Hope you saved all your money from working; I only have about $100 to chip in."

Michele thought: *I do have some money in the bank, but I also have my dad's money… I could use some of my dad's money, then just save up all my tip money to pay him back.* "I'll try it on. It might just look good on the hanger."

Michele took the dress to the dressing room. Leah grabbed two dresses she was looking at then joined Michele in the dressing room. When Michele stepped out, wearing the dress, her aunt gasped and said, "Wow! That dress looks gorgeous… but it's like déjà vu. I swear I have seen that dress on you before; but your hair was put up in braids, woven together on top of your head." Gloria shook the image out of her head.

The sales lady walked up and said, "Oh my. Aren't you a site? You look like a true princess… Here. Try the tiara on."

Michele blushed and thought: *If she really only knew—that I am a true princess.*" She shook her head and laughed softly; then she put the crown on and looked in the mirror. "I…" She almost said: *I look like Queen Chloe,* but stopped herself. "I… guess I could use my savings."

Leah walked out of one of the changing booths wearing a black formal gown with silver rhinestones around the v-neckline and waist. "Wow! That dress looks great on you."

Michele looked at Leah and said, "That dress looks great on you! How much is that dress?"

Leah looked at the price tag and said, "$359." Then she looked at the saleslady. "Does this dress come with a tiara or matching necklace?

"Here. Let me look." The sales lady looked at some code on the sales tag then looked up, "Sorry. It doesn't. But we are having a sale right now on our tiaras and jewelry."

"Ok. I'll look at your tiaras. I already have some jewelry at home that should match."

Gloria looked at the sales lady and spoke up, "Can you grab a tiara for Leah to put on... I want to get a picture of them in their dresses."

"Sure."

When the sales lady reappeared, she placed a tiara with faux diamonds on Leah's head. "There. That looks, perfect."

Gloria stepped back and held up her cellphone, "Smile for the picture girls."

After numerous pictures, the girls returned to their changing rooms to take off the dresses. Michele hollered at Gloria from inside of the changing booth, "Make sure you send Leah and I copies of the pictures you took."

"I'm sending them now."

When the girls were done changing, they returned to the center of the dressing room where Gloria was waiting. Leah looked at Michele and said, "I think the sales lady purposely picked out the most expensive tiara in the place. Let me look at their other tiaras, then we can be on our way."

While Leah was paying for her gown and tiara, Michele looked down at the gown in her arms. She felt bad using her dad's money to buy the dress since she didn't know if she would be able to save enough money, in time, to pay him back. Maybe her uncle could get some of her money out of her trust… or she could borrow some money from her grandmother.

After Michele paid for her dress with her debit card, Gloria spoke up, "Where do you girls want to go to lunch? My treat!"

Chapter 22

Paul stopped over Saturday night after work to see Michele's dress. When Michele heard his car drive up, she went out onto the front porch to wait for him. When Paul reached the top of the pouch, Michele gave him a quick kiss and asked, "How was work?"

"Really busy. I think everyone's computer, that lives in this town, crashed."

"My laptop is running good!" Michele laughed. "Come on in. It's cold out here."

Michele grabbed Paul's hand and led him into the house. The golden retrievers, Ace and Mitch, met Paul at the door and started barking happily and jumping all over him.

"Down!" Michele laughed.

"I love your dogs." Paul reached down and started petting the dogs while they wagged their tails – happy to get attention.

Paul looked into the living room where Joe was sitting in his recliner, watching TV, and Gloria was in her favorite chair, doing needlepoint. Gloria looked at Paul and said, "Hi Paul. How was your day?"

"Good. Thank you."

Michele pointed to the couch. "Have a seat while I go get my dress."

Paul took a seat while Michele ran up the stairs to fetch her prom dress.

When Michele returned with the dress, Paul stood up to meet her by the bottom of the stairs. "Wow. I love the color. Aren't you going to put it on for me?"

"No. You have to wait. I just wanted you to see the color so you could take a picture of it to show your mom. I know she wanted to help you get a matching suit."

Paul looked disappointed but proceeded to take a picture of it as Michele held it up. After he took a couple of pictures, Michele ran the dress back up to her room. When she returned, she told Paul, "Come to the kitchen so I can show you the package I received from my dad."

Paul followed her into the kitchen and took a seat. Gloria also came out to the kitchen to stir her chili. While Michele emptied the contents of the package on the table, Gloria asked Paul, "Will you be staying for dinner."

"If you made enough? It sure does smell good."

"Oh, we have plenty. I usually make way too much and have leftovers for days."

Michele handed Paul his ticket for the flight and the car rental information.

Paul looked at the car rental information and said, "Your dad paid for the rental car, for my parents."

"Yep. As I said, he insisted."

"Wow. Not sure how my parents are going to feel about that. They're not used to having other people paying for their vacations. He even rented the biggest SUV." Paul looked down at his plane ticket then asked, "Where's the return flight ticket?"

"He told me in a note he sent, that he would buy your return flight ticket on which every day you decide to fly back home." She smiled, then handed him another ticket. "Here's your ticket for the ferry. Did you get a chance to talk to your boss yet?"

"Not yet. We've been busy. Plus, I need to talk with my parents about it first. Aren't you planning on spending the whole summer with your grandmother? Is your grandmother prepared to put me up for the whole summer?"

"Yes. My grandmother was the one that insisted that I invite you. Like I said, my dad, said he would get your return flight whenever you decide you had to go back."

"Well… I guess I need to stay all summer. I can't have you flying back to the states on your own -- you might get lost or something."

Michele hit Paul playfully. "I am old enough to take care of myself… But I would love for you to stay the whole summer."

"Let's play that by ear. See what your grandmother says, what my parents think, and see if my job will even let me take the whole summer off."

Michele started putting her tickets back into the envelope while Paul continued to talk, "You know it's my birthday, June 10th. My mom wants to celebrate my birthday at her brother's house in

Australia. Did you plan on taking the ferry to your grandmother's before my birthday?"

"No. I wanted to stay a couple of days with your family there if your Uncle George and Aunt Beth will have me."

"I'm sure that won't be a problem."

Michele looked at her Aunt Gloria, "How long before dinner? Do you want me and Paul to feed the animals?"

"The chili needs to simmer a while longer, so if the two of you want to go feed the animals first -- you have plenty of time."

*****

The dogs took off running and barking happily across the backyard while Michele and Paul made their way to the barn to feed the cats.

"Here kitty, kitty, kitty, kitty," Michele called while setting the food on the barn floor. Paul grabbed the water bowl to refill it with fresh water from the barn's hydrant. After setting it down, he smiled as he watched all the cat's dive into the food bowl. "How many cats do you guys have?"

"One house cat named Pepper and six barn cats. Come on. We have to feed the cows next." After feeding the four cows, then the six pigs, Michele fed her horse.

While the horse was eating her grain, Michele opened the stall door so she could pet her horse. Looking at Paul she said, "This is Harley. You should come over sometime so we can go riding together."

"I don't know about that! I never rode a horse before. Plus... you only have one."

Michele laughed. "We can ride double on Harley. My aunt has some trails back in the woods. It's quite peaceful back there. My uncle hunts the backwoods once in a while. Maybe if it's nice tomorrow afternoon, we could go for a short ride. I promise Harley will not throw you off."

"Hmm. Maybe."

Michele laughed and reached up to give Paul a quick peck on the check. He returned the gesture by grabbing her, pulling her close, and giving her a deep, passionate kiss. When he stepped back, Michele's head was spinning. She thought: *I'm in way over my head. How will I ever be able to make a good decision on where I want to live after high school ---right now I would live in a box -- as long as I could be with him.*

Michele shook her head, thankfully she had time to decide. "Come on. We have to go feed the chicken next."

Chapter 23

Sunday afternoon, the sun was shining and it was around 60 degrees. Paul stopped over at Michele's house to take her up on her offer to go horseback riding. After Michele saddled her horse up, she led Harley into the barnyard. "I'll let you ride in the saddle and I'll ride behind you on the horse's rump."

"Whoa. I told you I don't know how to ride."

"But you already know how to make a horse stop... by yelling whoa! See the horse looking at you." Michele laughed. "Don't worry. Harley here is a seasoned horse. Even a two-year-old could ride her. I'll be sitting right behind you. If things get out of control, I can easily reach around you and grab the reins."

"Just remember. You swore I wouldn't get thrown... Now how do I get on that contraption?" He pointed at the saddle.

"You just put one foot in the stirrup and hop up."

Paul looked at Michele dumbfounded. Michele pointed at the stirrup. Paul put his right foot in the stirrup.

Michele laughed and said, "No... Not that foot. Unless you want to swing your left foot over the saddle horn and sit backward. Here. Step aside. I'll show you first."

Michele put her left foot in the stirrup then hopped up on her right leg. She stood straight up with her left foot in the stirrup for a second -- then swung her right leg over the back of the saddle and took a seat. "You get down by doing the opposite... Just swing the right leg back over the saddle, then hop down." Michele demonstrated her dismount. "Now you try it."

Harley turned her head and nudge Paul closer. Paul hollowed, "Hey. Don't rush me."

Michele laughed. Paul put his left leg in the stirrup and started hopping up and down on his right leg. After four hops, he tried to swing his right leg over the horse but ended up kicking the horse in her rump. The horse made an abrupt, high-pitched squeal, moved forward two steps, and Paul fell to the ground.

Michele started laughing hysterically. Paul shot her an evil look from the ground. Michele started having a coughing fit, trying to cover up her laughter. Paul stood up, dusted off his pants, then said, "I don't think this is going to work. I can't even get on the horse."

"I know what to do. Let me help you." Michele bent forward and made a swing out of her two hands. "You step on my hands, grab the front of the saddle, and I'll boost you up high enough so you can swing your right leg over the back of the saddle."

Paul step on Michele's intertwined hands and tried to step up. Michele's hands fell apart and she screamed, "Ouch! That's not going to work."

Michele ran back towards the barn, grabbed a bucket, then said, "Here. Stand on this."

Paul stood on the bucket. Michele said, "Now put your left foot in the stirrup, push up with your left foot, then swing your right leg over."

Paul did as Michele instructed but only made his leg swing half-way over the saddle. Hanging on to the horn, with his left foot in the stirrup and right foot on top of the horse's rump, Paul's butt was being pulled down by gravity. Michele ran up to the horse's side and started shoving his butt up into the saddle. When Paul was finally sitting up in the saddle, holding onto the horn for dear life, he looked down at Michele. "There. Now I can tell everyone I rode a horse. Help me down now!"

Michele laughed. "Oh, come on. It'll be fun. I swear." She walked up to the side of the saddle and pulled his foot half-way out of the stirrup. "First lesson in safety. When you ride a horse, you should only have your toes in the stirrups, so if you fall, your foot doesn't get caught in it. I've heard stories of people getting dragged down the road by their horse because their feet got caught in the stirrup."

"Ok. That does it. Help me down."

"I swear Paul. Harley would never do that. Here. Take your foot out of the stirrup for a minute."

Michele pulled Paul's foot out of the stirrup, put her left foot in it, then hopped up onto the horse's rump. Reaching around Paul with her right hand, she grabbed the reins that were wrapped around the horn of the saddle. "Can you put your toes back in that stirrup?" Paul looked down and maneuvered the front of his tennis shoe into the stirrup.

"Now watch my hand. To go forward, I hold the reins loose and centered. If I want to turn, I just move my hand in whichever direction I want the horse to turn. Michele wrapped her right arm around Paul's waist and made a clucking sound with her tongue. The horse started to walk forward. "Now remember, if you say whoa, the horse will stop. Do you want to take the reins?"

"No!"

"Just hold the reins like I am holding them and I'll hold your hand to guide you."

He took the reins and she placed her hand around his. "Now we just have to stir Harley to the trailhead."

Once the horse was heading down the trail. Michele released Paul's hand so she could hug him with both of her arms. "See. Riding isn't that hard. Just keep the horse's reins loose and she will follow the trail."

Paul started to enjoy the ride through the woods with the sun shining through the leaves, the birds singing, and Michele holding him tight. After a while, the trail came to a little brook with a bridge over it. Harley walked right over the bridge like she knew where she was going. When the trail came to an opening, the horse stopped suddenly, snouted, then looked to the right. The underbrush started to shake, then outran a baby fawn. Michele pointed at the fawn as it ran across the grassy opening to his mother standing on the other side. The mother stared at Paul and Michele while it waited for the baby. When the baby was close, the doe turned and ran into the thicket. "Wasn't that beautiful," Michele proclaimed.

"It was," Paul said and glanced at Michele sitting behind him.

"The trail ends here and circles back to the barn. Just click your tongue… Harley knows the way back."

*****

When the teens made it back to the barn. Michele showed Paul the easy way to dismount by sliding down the horse's rump. It took Paul a second to get his butt over the back of the saddle, but when he finally did, he slid down the rump like a champ. Standing on the ground, right behind the horse, Paul said, "That was fun. Glad you talked me into it."

Michele smiled and led the horse into the barn. She didn't want to ruin their ride by telling

Paul he should never stand directly behind a horse, in their blind spot.

After putting the horse up for the night, Michele asked Paul, "Do you want to help me feed the rest of the animals?"

"Sure. I'll go feed the cows while you feed the pigs."

When all the animals were fed and the chicken eggs collected, Michele started climbing up the ladder that led to the haystack. "Come on. I want to show you something."

Paul followed Michele up the ladder then took a seat on a hay bale next to her. "What did you want to show me?"

"This." Michele swept her arm around then said, "A place for us to be alone." Michele smiled innocently, then leaned in for a kiss. Paul reciprocated the kiss eagerly and ended up pushing Michele backward into the hay. After five minutes of kissing and heavy petting, Michele heard her aunt calling, "Here kitty, kitty, kitty."

Michele sat up and looked at Paul. "My aunt is coming. We better get down."

Michele walked to the edge of the haystack and jumped. Paul looked over the edge and saw Michele laying in a big pile of hay. Michele jumped up on her feet, moved to the side, and said, "Hurry." He jumped out of the haystack and rolled in the hay pile below. When the barn door opened, Paul was standing up, brushing the hay off his pants.

Michele looked innocently at her aunt and said, "I'm glad you bought the cat food down. We just got done feeding all of the other animals.

Here. Let me help you." Michele grabbed the cats' water dish and handed it to Paul to fill.

"Thanks. So, all the other animals have been fed already?"

"Yep. Paul and I fed them."

"Great. Thanks. Are you staying for dinner Paul?"

"What are you having?"

"Spaghetti."

"Sounds good to me. This farming stuff can sure make a man hungry."

Michele giggled, grabbed the bowl of chicken eggs, and started walking with Paul towards the house.

Chapter 24

Michele said good-night to Paul and hung up the phone. She laid in bed, stared at the ceiling, and thought: *Boy am I exhausted.* It had been over two weeks since her shopping trip with Leah and Gloria to the dress shop. Time seemed to be flying by in a blink of an eye. Life was busy for Michele since her schedule was full, from dawn to dust, with school, track, work, and now... Leah, being the outgoing friend that she was, had volunteered them to be active members in the prom's planning committee. Michele felt her life was spinning out of control with all her obligations and responsibilities... and she was only 17! Michele looked at the dog, shook her head, and said, "I can't wait for my vacation to Australia, maybe I will finally get some rest!"

Mitch perked her ears up and looked at Michele with sad eyes.

"I know. I'll miss you too. But I'm sure your partner in crime, Ace, will love to keep you company."

Michele turned on her side and snuggled up with the dog; as soon as she closed her eyes, she was dead to the world.

*****

Michele was covered with scratches and blood. Paul was lying at her feet on the gym floor, unconscious. There were chunks of debris all around the room. The gym lights were blinking off and on, and some of them were hanging dangerously low to the floor, sparking with electricity. Michele looked around and saw fellow students screaming and running towards the exit signs. Some students were trapped on the floor from falling debris, screaming for help.

Michele woke up with Mitch licking her face. She pushed the dog aside then threw off her blanket. She was sweating to death and hyperventilating. She sat up, put her head down on her knees, and tried to take some deep breaths, in and out. While she tried to calm her breathing down, she raised one of her hands towards her chest since it felt like her heart was trying to pound a hole through it. She thought: *It was only a dream. Get yourself together.* After Michele touched her chest, her hand started to tingle – causing a cooling, relaxing calm.

Michele looked at her hand. It looked like a normal hand; but did it just do what she thought it did? Grabbing her notebook of dreams, she wrote down the imagery of the dream. *Oh shit! I need to cancel the prom.*

*****

Thursday morning, Michele met Leah at the locker. In a low, urgent voice she said, "We have to cancel the prom!"

"What! Are you crazy? Prom's this Saturday."

"I know. But I had a crazy dream. Somethings going to happen and a lot of people will be injured."

"Oh shit!"

"Exactly what I said."

"But we can't tell everyone that prom is canceled just because you had a dream."

"Right. Hmmm. Can we move the location?"

Leah laughed, "Yeah right. You're on the planning committee. Do you really think we can change the venue in less than three days?"

"But we have to do something! Maybe pretend there's a gas leak or something. Get my Uncle Joe involved."

"Michele. You can't ruin everyone's prom night. Look at all the work we put into this event. And our classmates have bought dresses, suits, corsages, you name it. There must be something else we can do to ward off whatever disaster you think is going to happen? Maybe you can go home tonight, have another dream… find out if there's any way we can prevent this dream from coming true?"

"Michele looked down and said, "Your right. I don't have all the details. Maybe it was just a loose light fixture or something."

"Hey, babe." Paul walked up to Michele's and Leah's locker. "You ready to go to class?"

"Sure." Michele grabbed her book and looked at Leah. I'll talk to you later."

Chapter 25

Paul had to work at the computer repair shop after school, so after track practice, Michele went home to help her aunt with the chores. During dinner, Michele bought up her dream.

"I had another crazy dream last night."

"Oh!" Aunt Gloria said.

"Yeah. This one had to do with our prom. I'm not sure what's going to happen; I just saw light fixtures hanging down and a bunch of debris scattered around the high school's gym. I know some of the students are going to be injured, but Leah told me it's too late to pick a different venue, and I can't tell my whole high school to cancer the prom just because I had a dream."

"Hmmm," Uncle Joe replied. Do you have any more details?"

"Not really. I just remember me having bloody scratches and Paul lying on the floor- unconscious."

"How scary!" Aunt Gloria emphasized.

"Can you cancel the prom Uncle Joe? Maybe call in a bomb threat or gas leak?"

Uncle Joe cleared his throat and said, "No. I can't believe you would even mention that.

Those are serious crimes, Michele. Do you want me to end up in jail?"

"Well… I just don't want anything bad to happen. I hate these stupid dreams!"

"Maybe I can help Michele. I can send a friend of mine, who is an electrician, to check the gym's lighting system. I can tell him you noticed a couple of light fixtures flashing on and off on different occasions and I just wanted to make sure everything was up to code. And maybe… I can get the chief of police to send some men over to monitor the school during the prom… since he knows how reliable your dreams can be."

"That might help. Thanks, Joe. That makes me feel a little better, but I'm still worried about Paul. Maybe I should tell him tonight -- on the phone… that I don't want to go to prom."

"Oh, Michele. I know how much you've been looking forward to this prom… And you look so beautiful in that dress. Maybe your dream won't come true this time. Maybe your just under a lot of stress and overworked? Your uncle could help monitor the situation… couldn't you Joe."

"Well yes. If Michele wants me there?"

"It would be nice to have you close in case I needed you. Maybe you could sit in your car in the school's parking lot?
"Will do."

*****

That night, Michele told Paul about her dream while they talked on the phone: "…Now I'm thinking about skipping prom."

"But your uncle said he would get the lights inspected and that he would have the school under surveillance."

"I know. I'm just worried something might happen to you! I already lost my parents after having one of these dreams."

"I know. I'm sorry…. Have you talked to your grandmother about this dream?"

"No. And I'm not sure if I should try to reach out to her tonight or try to get more details on this dream?"

"I think you should talk to your grandmother… And Michele. If you do decide you want to skip prom, that's ok with me. But I have to see you in that dress!! So, we need to, at least, go to dinner together as planned before the prom."

"I guess there's no harm in going to dinner."

"Great! Love you, babe."

"Love you too."

*****

Michele was twilling around her bedroom in front of her grandmother -- showing off her prom dress. Leewan was sitting on the edge of the bed, smiling. "Wow! That dress looks beautiful on you. Where did you get it?"

"I bought it from a local, formal-dress shop."

It looks like one of the dresses they make at the queen's shop; I mean your grandmother Chloe's shop."

"I thought this dress looked like the one Chloe was wearing the first time I met her; and the tag did say it was imported from Australia. I didn't realize my other grandmother owned a dress shop."

"Yes, Queen Chloe Williams owns a dress shop on Honiawae Island. The shop purchases silks and linens from Australia to make clothing for the residences that live on the Hidden Islands of Honiawae. A lot of the suits and dresses that are made there are for the king's army and the occupants of the castle; however, the shop also makes gowns and suits to sell to different shops on the mainland of Australia."

Michele plopped down on the bed next to Leewan. "So, I called you tonight since I wanted to show you my dress and because I had another strange dream…" After telling her grandmother all the details of the dream she said, "I want to cancel the prom."

Leewan patted Michele on her thigh. "Now you know you can't do that Michele. People don't understand our powers. They will call you crazy when you try to cancel the prom, then they will think your psycho – after your dream comes true. Plus, witches have to stick together. We can't have a repeat of the witch trials or let common people know about us."

"So what use are these dreams if I can't use them to protect people… And what about Paul?"

"You can use your power to protect Paul and yourself by changing your situation, location, or actions. Don't go inside the school! You can also help prevent a major disaster from happening by standing outside of the building, out of view of bystanders. If you notice anything strange, just use your power to divert the situation. Just make sure Michele... that no one sees your hand in diverting the situation."

Michele hugged her grandmother. "Thanks for the advice."

Her grandmother smiled and blew her a kiss while her image faded away.

Chapter 26

Late Friday afternoon, Michele walked into the Country Crock and saw Denise. She thought: *Oh great! I'm already exhausted from track practice, now I get to work by myself."*

Denise smiled when she saw Michele. She followed Michele to the timeclock and said, "I'm glad you're working tonight. We need to talk. I was going to call you during my break but now I can just talk to you in person." Michele stood there with her mouth hanging open – thinking: *What would Denise want to talk to me about?* Denise reached in front of Michele to punch in, then said, "You better punch in. Don't want to be late."

Michele punched in then walked over to the waitress she would be relieving. She glanced over at Denise and noticed a change in her: she seemed more friendly and sociable. After about an hour into her shift, Michele saw Paul's friend Tom come into the restaurant and stand by the door, looking for a place to sit. She walked over to him and said, "My section is over there." She pointed to some tables behind her then continued, "Aren't you here early? Paul doesn't get out of work for another ten minutes."

"I'm not meeting Paul."

Denise ran over from her section, put her arm through Tom's arm, and said, "This is what I wanted to talk to you about Michele. Tom and I are dating… and I was supposed to ask you if you don't mind, can Tom and I join you guys for the prom festivities?"

"You can't go…."

"Before you say anything, whatever your plans are for dinner before the prom is okay with me. I don't want to change anything. Tom just thought it would be nice if we all could hang out as friends."

"But…"

"Talk it over with Paul or at least think about it. It'll be fun." Denise started leading Tom to her section, looked over her shoulder, and mouthed, "Pleeease …...."

Michele went back to busing her tables. She thought: *It's nice that Denise wants to be friends, and Tom is one of Paul's best friends, but I don't want anyone to go to the prom.*

While Michele was taking an order from one of her tables, she heard the bell on the front door ring. When she looked up, she saw Paul walking into the diner. She waved at him then pointed to one of her booths. After she dropped the order off at the kitchen window, she grabbed Paul's favorite pop and walked over to his table. Before Michele made it to his table, Tom ran up to the booth, slid in next to Paul, and gave him a side bearhug with one arm while ruffling up his hair with the other hand. "Surprise!"

Paul looked at him and said, "What are you doing here?"

Tom jerked his head to the side, "I'm here with Denise."

Paul glanced at Denise then said, "So the two of you really hit it off then."

"Yep. Thanks to you."

"I didn't really do anything. I just told you I didn't think she was dating anyone exclusively— so if you like her, ask her out."

"Yeah. Well. If you didn't encourage me, I won't have asked her out."

Tom looked at Michele, then said, "Well. I better let the two of you talk." He jumped up, winked at her, then walked back to his table.

Michele sat down next to Paul. She looked at him, then put her elbows on the table and dropped her head into the palms of her hands.

Paul looked at her shaking her head from side to side, then said, "That bad, huh?"

Michele looked sideways at him and said, "Yeah. Denise and Tom want to go to prom with us."

"They do? That's great!"

She glared at him and said, "I thought you would understand."

"Oh, come on Michele. Hanging out with Denise for one night won't kill you. Besides, you'll have Leah and me to protect you. You don't even have to talk to her if you don't want to. You know… you would be doing Tom a big favor since he probably just wants to hang out with me and Jeff."

"I don't care about that. Denise isn't that bad. It's my dream that is bugging me... Or don't you remember?"

"Yes, I remember. But you told me at school today that you'd talked with your grandmother last night and she said it would be okay to go to prom. And you also said the police and your uncle would be there, so what could go wrong?"

"I don't know. I'm just worried. I saw you lying on the floor, unconscious, in my dream."

Paul grabbed her hands, "I know. I know. I love you too! Just don't worry so much. I want to dance with you in that beautiful dress you bought… Let's just play it by ear. Let me know if you have another dream tonight."

Michele nodded her head, then said, "You can tell Tom we decide they could join us."

"Great!   And I'll call the restaurant to let them know we are bringing two more people." He tugged playfully on her ponytail, then continued, "If you have any more dreams about the prom, we'll just stand outside of the school and dance under the stars."

The cook called from the kitchen counter, "Michele. Your order is up."

Michele started to get up, Paul grabbed her hand and said, "Will you get me a cheeseburger and fries when you get the chance."

She smiled and said, "Sure."

Chapter 27

Paul called Michele Saturday morning. "Good morning sunshine. Any rotten dreams last night?"

"No. Believe it or not. I slept pretty well."

"Great. That means everything is set for a great evening tonight. Can't wait to see you in that dress! I'll pick you up around 3:30 p.m."

"I'll be waiting with bells on," she chuckled.

After she hung up the phone, she walked downstairs to the living room. Her Uncle Joe was sitting in his favorite recliner, watching the weather report on TV: "...*With the unstable air mass, we might see popup storms tonight, and some might be severe.*"

"That's just great! It's going to rain on my parade. I guess no dancing under the stars for me."

Uncle Joe looked up at her and replied, "At least it's warm. In Michigan, you never know what the weather might be, especially in May... And don't worry. It's only a 30% chance of rain."

"The way my luck is, it's more like a 99.9% chance of rain."

Uncle Joe laughed, then asked, "Any more dreams?"

"No. Thank God! Maybe the disaster has been diverted."

"I sure hope so. But if you need me, I'll just be one ring away. I plan on sitting in my car in the back parking lot so I can have a good view of the whole school."

"Thanks. I really appreciate it."

*****

Michele stood in front of the mirror staring at her prom dress; the glittering, baby-blue, form-fitting dress had transformed her from the girl next door to a lady. She'd given Leah the faux-diamond necklace and matching earrings that had come with the dress since she refused to take off the crystal necklace that her grandmother had given her and she preferred to wear a pair of crystal earrings that she had found in her adoptive mom's jewelry box -- after she'd died. Looking in the mirror, she noticed how the dress's low-cut, square neckline showed off her cleavage and how her crystal necklace had turned a shade of blue to match the dress. When she turned sideways, she couldn't help but admire the lacy, short-cut sleeves, and the sexy, high-cut, slit. She stuck her leg through the slit in the dress to check out the shoes her Aunt Gloria had bought her. The rhinestone-studded sandals were classy with the added crisscross straps around her ankles, but they were also practical since the heels were flat and only one-inch tall. Michele thought: *I couldn't have picked better shoes for myself. Now I won't have to worry about tripping in high heels and making a fool out of myself... and I might be able to dance without looking like a klutz.*

Michele heard the doorbell ring. She glanced at her clock: *3:20 p.m. He's early.* She glanced in the mirror one more time to make sure her hair looked alright, then thought: *Chloe was right. I do resemble her with my hair swept up in this twisted, crown-braid with a tiara on top.* She pulled on the two wisps of hair that fell on both sides of her face, grabbed the rhinestone handbag off the bed that her aunt had bought her, then thought: *Gloria does have good taste.*

When Michele started to walk down the stairs, she noticed that Paul and Gloria were waiting at the bottom for her. Paul looked up at her and put a hand to his heart. "Be still my heart. You're in the presents of a queen." He took a short bow, then said, "Are you ready to go beautiful? Your chariot awaits you."

She paused for a moment, confused. *Does he remember the castle and who my real father is?* She shook her head. *No. I don't think the mind-erasing spell wears off?*

Paul looked at her, "Are you alright?"

Michele nodded her head, laughed softly, then continued down the last few steps. "Yes, I'm alright. I was just thinking how handsome you look in your white suit with your light blue cummerbund – but where's the tie?"

"No tie for me. That's where I draw the line." He laughed then started to put his arm up to escort her but stopped short when he saw the corsage. "Here I almost forgot." Paul handed her the corsage to wear around her wrist. "Gloria helped me pin on my boutonniere." He winked at Gloria.

Michele slipped on the corsage and admired the delicate, blue-colored rose buds with white baby's breath.

Paul put his arm back up and said, "Should we go?"

Gloria screeched, "No wait. I have to take pictures. Let's go out to the front porch and get some pictures on the swing and then a couple by the flowering tree in the front yard."

After Gloria took multiple pictures, the couple started walking towards the limousine that Paul's parents had rented for the occasion. Michele stopped short and looked at her aunt. "Do you want to meet us at the restaurant since we are planning on taking some group pictures in the park that is located across the street?"

"I would love to. I'll meet you there."

"Meet us there around 4:45 p.m. We still have to swing by Leah's house to pick up the rest of the group."

Chapter 28

The restaurant Paul picked out was a good 25 minutes away since it was a fancy restaurant located in a larger city. Michele could tell that Denise was falling in love with Tom since her personality had made a 180-degree turn; Instead of acting superior and flirting with all the guys, Denise clung to Tom and seemed more sociable. During the limousine ride, she snuggled up next to Tom and shared an exaggerated story on how she met him: "It was fate that brought us together. Without Tom being in the right place at the right time, I might have died. I was watching one of the boys' softball games and a hard hit, foul ball almost hit me right in the face. Tom here, ran over from third base and saved the day. After he saved me from near inches of my life, I just had to thank him; so, after the game, I caught up with him -- and he asked me out! The rest is history." Everyone laughed as Denise gave Tom a quick peck on the check.

Gloria was standing outside of the restaurant's door when the limousine pulled up. After she took some pictures of the group exiting the limousine, the group walked across the street to take some pictures in the city park. After taking multiple pictures by the river and on the walk-bridge, the group said their goodbyes to Gloria then walked back to the restaurant to order their dinners.

Looking at the menu, Michele said, "Wow. Look at these prices."

Paul smiled and said, "Get whatever you want. The sky's the limit."

She settled for a chief salad; the cheapest thing on the menu for only $25.

After dinner, the group piled back into the limousine to make their way to the high school. While getting in the limo, Michele noticed some dark clouds coming over the horizon. Looking at Paul, she said, "Great. Looks like we might get rain."

By the time the teens arrived at the high school, the sun had been displaced by clouds and the wind was whipping around, spitting light rain around - sideways. Grabbing her evening handbag, Michele made a mad dash for the high school's front entrance. Once inside the building, Michele got the feeling of déjà vu. The closer she walked to the gymnasium's front door, the harder it was for her to breathe. She started sweating and shaking profusely. When Michele was just steps from the main entrance, she slid to a stop. Frozen in fear, she grabbed Leah. "Don't go in."

Leah looked at Michele and said, "It will be alright Michele. As you said, you didn't have any more dreams so the disaster must be diverted. Come on in. We did a lot of planning for this. Let's reap our just rewards."

Leah grabbed Jeff's hand and proceeded to the check-in table that was located just inside the door. Tom put his hand on Paul's shoulder and said, "Are you guys coming in?"

"Go ahead and get a table. I'm going to wait here in the hall with Michele for a while."

"Ok then." Tom smiled, took Denise by the hand, then walked up to the check-in table.

Michele started walking back and forth down the hall in front of the entrance – disrupting the flow of traffic entering the school. Paul grabbed Michele's hand and said, "Come with me." Paul led Michele down the hall to a bench that was sitting outside of the administrative offices.

After the couple took a seat on the bench, Paul wiped a strand of hair out of Michele's face. "It's ok Michele. If you don't want to go in, we can just stay here. I can hear the music from here and we can have our own private dance here in the hallway."

Michele looked at Paul and smiled. "You'd do that for me. You don't think I'm crazy?"

"Yes, I would do that for you, and no, I don't think you're crazy. I love you, Michele. Like I told you before… I want to marry you someday. Just because you are nervous about one of your dreams does not change the way I feel about you. Plus, your dreams have proven to be reliable before. I won't make you do anything you don't feel comfortable doing. If one of our friends happen to come back to check on us, I'll just tell them we want to spend some time alone… and then I'll ask them to bring us some punch and a plate of hors d'oeuvres."

Michele's eyes started to water. "I'm sorry that I'm ruining your prom. You should be in with your friends – having fun. I just have a bad feeling and can't bring myself to walk in there."

"It's ok. Like I told you. I rather spend my time with you. But we'll have to go and stand by the open doors so I can show off my date… the most beautiful girl in the school."

Michele smiled, wiped her tears from her eyes, then said, "It's a deal."

*****

After most of the guests had found their seats, the DJ made an announcement to kick off the high school's prom. Michele noticed, as the music started to play, someone had dimmed the gym's lights. From the doorway, Michele looked around the gym at all the decorations she had a hand in designing. The gym looked like a fairytale princess land: it had water fountains, green foliage, and a photo booth adorned with flowers and tiny, flying fairies. There were dangling white Christmas lights sporadically hung around the gymnasium, and a long, decorative table filled with snacks. While Michele was admiring the decorations, Leah and Jeff showed up at the gym's door.

Placing a hand on Michele's shoulder, Leah said, "Oh honey. I wish you didn't worry so much. But I do understand why. Let me bring you and Paul a couple of chairs so both of you can sit out here."

Leah turned to fetch some chairs. Paul reach out and grabbed Jeff's arm. "Can you bring Michele and me a couple of drinks and a plate of snacks?"

Jeff smiled and said, "Sure."

*****

Michele and Paul sat on folding chairs, munching on their snacks while watching their fellow students' dance. After Paul finished most of his snacks, he set his plate on the floor and moved his chair closer to Michele so he could hold her hand. At the end of one of the upbeat songs, the DJ announced, "We're going to slow it down now and play one of my favorite songs from Eric Clapton. This song is dedicated to Michele, with love, from Paul." Most of the people on the dance floor started looking around for Michele but only a few knew where to look. After Leah and Denise waved at her, they grabbed their partners and started dancing to the song, "Wonderful Tonight."

Paul stood up from his chair, held out his hand, and said, "May I have this dance?"

Michele blushed, stood up, then fell into step with Paul. Resting her head on his broad shoulder, Michele could have sworn she saw stars shining in the hallway.

When the song was over, Michele almost jumped out of her skin to the sound and a flash of a large lightning bolt that hit close to the school. Michele looked down the hall, towards the school's glass doors. The rain was coming down in sheets and hitting the glass sideways. Within seconds, the rain turned into golf-ball-sized hail -- pounding on the glass. Michele watched in horror as one of the doors started to crack from the impact of the hail. Turning her attention to the gym, Michele saw the gym's roof start to crack, and all of the small windows that aligned the roof's top start to crash inward. Within seconds, the whole roof was starting to cave inward. People started pointing and screaming while the roof started to fall down upon them. Michele instinctively grabbed her crystal necklace with one hand while raising her other hand up towards the sky. With a swipe of her hand, the direction of the roof changed directions and was lifted up into the sky with a single gust of wind.

After the roof was thrown away from the building, the rain started coming down into the gym. The students that were in the gym started running for the exits. Paul pulled Michele to the side of the door so they wouldn't be trampled by people. When they were a safe distance from the door, away from the traffic, he questioned, "What in the hell was that?"

Before Michele had time to answer, Leah came running out of the gym's door. When she spotted Michele, she ran up to her and hugged her. "Oh my God. You were right! But I think everyone is alright. Luckily the storm took the roof off the building."

"Michele! Michele!"

"Over here, Joe."

Joe ran over to Michele and hugged her. "Glad you're alright! That was a freak tornado. The weather channel didn't even put out a warning. Come on. Let's get you guys out of here."

When the group walked out to the parking lot, it looked like a disaster zone; half of the cars were flipped on their sides or thrown against the building. The back-parking lot, where her Uncle

Joe was parked, was untouched. In the distance, Michele could hear sirens coming.

Joe looked at the group and said, "Luckily, the limo was parked in the back parking lot next to me. You kids can get a ride home in the limo. I'm taking Michele with me."

Joe took Michele's hand and started leading her back to his car. Michele looked at Paul and said, "I'll call you later."

*****

When Michele and Joe walked into the house, Gloria was watching the breaking news on the TV. She turned when she heard them enter and ran to Michele to hug her. "Thank God you're alright! I just heard on the TV what happened. How awful!" Then she turned her attention to Joe and hugged him. "I was so worried. I just heard a lot of the cars were tossed around like they were toys. I was just getting ready to try to call you guys."

Joe said, 'We're okay. Let's all go have a seat in the living room and I'll tell you all about it." He gently stirred Gloria to her favorite chair in the living room, then took a seat on one end of the couch, near her.

Michele stood by and listened as Joe's recapped the awful events. When Joe finished, he looked at Michele and asked, "Did I miss anything?"

"No. That's basically what happened." She looked at Gloria and asked, "Did the news say if anyone was hurt?"

"No. The news reporter said, at that time, there were no reported injuries...but authorities were still investigating the incident."

"Good." Michele reached down and hugged Gloria, then said, "If you don't mind, think I'll go up to bed now. I want to call Paul. Make sure he made it home alright."

"Sure, honey. Have a goodnight."

Chapter 29

Michele looked in the mirror, one last time, at her prom dress. She could picture herself wearing the dress the next time she goes to the castle to see her younger, half-sister Amarina: *Amarina and her mother, Lalirra, won't make fun of me in this dress like they did when I first came to meet the king and queen in my shorts and t-shirt.* Leewan had taken Michele and her guest to meet the king and queen during her first visit to Honiawae Island -- after one of Lalirra's parents' spies tried to jump Michele and Paul in a park. Leewan took them to the castle so she could report the incident to Prince Macalla, the head of the king's army. That's also when Michele first found out that Leewan suspected that the prince was her biological father – since he and Leewan's daughter, Mayra, were lovers prior to Mayra's disappearance.

Michele shook her head and proceeded to get ready for bed. When she returned from the bathroom, she noticed the dog sleeping across the bed. Laughing, she said, "Mitch. You don't need to hog the whole bed. Move over so I can call Paul."

Paul answered the phone on the second ring, "Hi."

"Hi, Paul. Did everyone make it home alright?"

"Yes. Hold on one second so I can take my phone up to my room -- I just finished telling my parents about the tornado tearing the gym's roof off."

After a couple of minutes, that seemed like hours, Paul said, "Ok. I'm in my room now. Can you tell me what happened? I think I'm going crazy! I swear I saw that roof caving inward... Then I saw you lift your arm and toss the roof away with a flick of your wrist. You didn't change the direction of the wind, did you?"

Michele chuckled, "How could I do that? I just instinctively put my hand up to protect myself from any falling debris. I guess it might have looked silly since the cave-in wasn't even close to the hall -- where we were standing."

Paul gave out a half-laugh, "I guess you're right. But I could have sworn you had a look of determination in your eyes... instead of fear."

"Oh, Paul. It happened so fast. Maybe you mistook the look of shock on my face as determination."

"Yeah. You're probably right. You might have prophetic dreams, but you don't have magical powers to control the wind... or control the minds of people."

Michele chuckled nervously, "Of course not. Must have been an act of God."

"Yeah. A real miracle. I was just feeling unsure. I thought if you could control the weather, maybe you could control the way I feel about you?"

Michele gasped and thought: *How could he even think that?* "No Paul. Even if I did have some sort of magical power to control the wind, in which I don't... I would never use my power to manipulate the way someone feels about me. I can't even imagine you thinking that I would."

"I know. I'm sorry. I just never felt this way about anyone. And it scares me sometimes. Some of my friends tell me I'm way too young to settle for my first love."

"Oh! Is that how you feel? That we're too young to know what true love is. Well, I say bullshit to whomever your friends are that told you that. They're just jealous. You know Paul... I truly love you?"

"I know. And I love you too... Sorry for even thinking you had some kind of mind-controlling magic."

Michele was quiet for a minute. She thought: *Could I have mind-controlling power.... And this whole relationship with Paul is just a fantasy I concocted?"*

"It's been a long day Paul. Can I come over tomorrow? So, we can talk?"

"Sounds good to me."

"I love you, Paul."

"Love you too."

After Michele hung up the phone, she thought: *I need to talk to my grandmother... tonight!* She reached for her crystal necklace, held it tight, then repeated her grandmother's name three times.

*****

She was sitting at the kitchen table at her grandmother's house on Honiawae Island. Her grandmother was sipping tea. "Would you like some tea, dear?"

"No thank you."

"I was hoping you would contact me. How was the prom?"

"I did what you told me to do. I stood outside of the gym and watched. I was able to divert the disaster, but I fear Paul might have witnessed my hand in diverting the situation."

"Oh! I was afraid someone might see you. Should I send a mind-erasing witch over to help you clear up the situation? I might be able to send her over in one of Paul's dreams... I've never tried it before, but I read in one of my great, great, great grandmother's books that it is possible to access a human in their dreams. If it doesn't work. She would have to take a plane... which could take a couple of days for her to get there."

"No. I think I have the situation under control. I don't want someone manipulating Paul's memories again. But I do need to tell Paul about my powers -- if I ever want to have an open, honest relationship with him.... I was thinking of telling him when we come to visit you this summer. If he still wants to come? I thought I could tell him at your house. If he takes it badly and doesn't want anything to do with me, can you invite the mind-erasing witch over... so she can erase the memory?"

"Sure honey. Anything you want."

"Hopefully he excepts me as I am, or I guess, I will have to end our relationship."

"Well, I hope he does, for your sake. I can tell how much you care for him... And he seemed like a very nice, young man when I meet him on your last visit."

"I do love him! And grams... Can you tell me why I didn't have a dream about the tornado Friday night? I think I should've had another dream -- showing me more details?"

"The whispers of a dream are strange. Like before, when the Taylors' spy jumped you and Paul in the park, here on the island; your dream didn't warn you since it knew you had the matter under control."

"I guess that makes sense."

Michele was quiet for a minute then asked, "Grams... is there any way I could be manipulating Paul's feelings for me?"

"Hmm... I guess it is possible.... But highly unlikely."

"What?"

"Why do you think your manipulation Paul's feelings?"

"Paul bought it up. He said he was worried after he thought he saw me raise my arm and toss the roof away... that maybe, I had some sort of magical powers that could control the wind... and control how people feel."

"Oh, honey. Even though it is possible to control how someone feels... it's highly unlikely to do it subconsciously. It takes a lot of concentration and practice. It's almost like hypnosis. Besides, you and Paul were together before the development of all your powers. You might even develop more powers over time, but I doubt you have the power to control people's thoughts and feelings now. Only time will tell if you will develop this rare power."

Michele thought about what her grandmother said before she replied, "Thank you for the reassurance. I didn't want to believe what Paul and I have could of all been manipulated by my powers. And he did mention, that some of his friends think we are too young to know what real love is."

Leewan laughed, "Ha! I know that's not true. Like I told you before, I ran away with your grandfather when I was about your age. He was the love of my life... and I know I would've still been with him today, if not for the farming accident that took his life."

"I remember. Wish I could have met my grandfather... So, you never met anyone else... after your husband passed?"

"Oh," Leewan chuckled. "There's been plenty of other suitors. I just never felt the same way about any of them -- as I did for your grandfather." Leewan started to fade. "Looks like our time is up. Sweet dreams Michele. Contact me if you do need any help with Paul. We can't have him exposing you to the world... scaring people into thinking they need to reenact the witch trials again."

"I will. Love you!"

Michele woke up in her bed, daylight had just started to creep in through her bedroom window.

Chapter 30

Sunday afternoon, Michele drove over to Paul's parents' house. Paul met her at the front door as he usually does, but this time Michele saw an emptiness in his eyes. While she was taking off her shoes, Paul's mom came out of the kitchen. "Hi, Michele. I'm glad you're here. Paul's been in one of his moods all morning. Maybe seeing you will snap him out of it?"

Michele smiled at her, then looked at Paul and thought: *I sure hope so.*

Paul looked at his mom and said, "We're going down to the basement to watch a movie."

"Sounds good. Should I make lunch for both of you and bring it down? You haven't eaten anything all morning."

Michele looked at Paul. Paul replied, "I'm good. Are you hungry Michele?"

"No. I'm good too. Thanks for asking, Judy."

"You're welcome. If you change your mind, just holler."

Michele and Paul turned to leave the foyer. Judy spoke up, "After the two of you are done watching your movie, Jim and I want to discuss the upcoming trip…. You are planning on staying for dinner Michele. Right?

"I wouldn't miss it for the world."

Paul opened the door that led downstairs, then started descending the steps. Michele followed closely behind Paul to the downstairs react room. Once there, Paul plopped down on the couch. Michele approached him slowly, then folded one leg up on the couch so she could sit on it sideways, facing Paul. "What's wrong Paul? Did I do or say something to make you upset?"

"No. I'm just mad at myself for saying things that might have made you upset or ruined our relationship. I shouldn't have told you what some of my friends were saying about our relationship. It's none of their business anyways...they just don't understand how you make me feel."

"And how is that?"

"Happy."

Michele smiled and said, "You make me very happy too."

Paul reached up and pushed a strand of hair away from her face. "So, you're not mad at me or think I'm crazy for accusing you of being a witch. I know there's no such thing as magic or mind control."

"Of course not. I'm not mad and I don't think you're crazy. It was a stressful night for both of us. If anything, you should be mad at me for ruining your prom and refusing to go into the gymnasium to sit with our friends."

"I kind of enjoyed our time alone."

She smiled and said, "Me too. We didn't get a chance to dance under the stars, but the hallway did seem to provide some sort of serenity."

Paul smiled, then reached up to gently caress the side of her face with his fingers before leaning in for a kiss. The kiss started slow, with Paul nipping at her lips while looking into her eyes until Michele hungrily pulled him close. After a long, eager kiss, she pulled away and asked, "So was this our first fight?"

Paul chuckled, then said, "I wouldn't call it a fight. Maybe just a misunderstanding. I could never fight with you. I might get mad from time to time, but I'm willing to talk things out to make things work. You can be a real mystery at times, but a mystery I would like to solve."

She smiled and mumbled under her breath, "Maybe sooner than you expect."

Paul looked at her confused and asked, "What did you say?"

"Oh, nothing. I was just wondering if you really had a good movie for us to watch?"

Paul smiled and grabbed the TV remote. "There must be something good on one of these premium channels."

After finally finding a good movie -- that they both agreed upon, the young lovers snuggled up on the couch to watch it.

*****

After the movie, Michele and Paul went upstairs to discuss their trip to Australia with Paul's parents. "So, the date is set for June 7th at 6 a.m., flying out of Detroit. Right?" Judy asked Michele.

"Yes."

"Paul told us that your dad already sent you your tickets for the flight and the ferry boat. He also told us your dad bought him a flight ticket and a ticket for the ferry so he can go with you to the Island of New Caledonia. Did you decide what day you wanted to leave on the ferry? I wanted to celebrate Paul's birthday at my brother's house, so I need to know if you planning on staying at my brother's house for Paul's birthday on June 10th or should I celebrate his birthday earlier?"

"I would like to stay at Paul's aunt and uncle's house until the 11th... If they will have me?"

"I'm sure that wouldn't be a problem," Judy smiled. "And make sure you thank your dad for reserving the rental car for us and for buying Paul his tickets. He didn't have to do that!"

"I know. I told him not to. But he insisted."

"It was very generous of him. But I'm worried about Paul's return flight. Should I give Paul money to buy his return flight?"

"No. You don't have to. My dad told me he would buy Paul's return ticket when he knew what date Paul wanted to leave. I'm sure my dad will even have him personally escorted back to the airport by some of his... umm... staff."

"Escorted? Your dad must have a good-paying job on the Island of New Caledonia. What does your dad do for a living?"

"Umm. I'm not really sure. I know he's in charge of a lot of people and I think he has something to do with real estate or something like that." She thought: *I can't tell them that he's a prince and leads an army. Oh, how I hate lying to them!*

"I'm sure real estate is quite expensive over there. What do you think Jim? Do you think Paul's old enough to spend a summer abroad?"

"I would leave that choice to Paul; however, Michele's dad was right in leaving the decision to Paul... for when he might want to return since Paul has his job to think about." He looked at Paul and asked, "Did you talk to your boss yet?"

"Yes. I don't think he was too thrilled about me asking for the whole summer off, but he did say he would think about it. I told him I enjoyed my job but I really wanted to go on this vacation."

"Well, hopefully, he will at least give you two weeks off." Judy smiled then looked down at her watch. "I think dinner should be about ready."

*****

Amy called Michele during her ride home from Paul's. Michele answered the call with her car's hands-free system. "Hi, Amy."

"Oh my God Michele! Why didn't you call me? I just heard on the news about your school getting hit by a tornado during your prom. I'm glad everyone made it out of the gymnasium alright. Didn't you have any dreams to warn you?"

At first, Michele didn't know what to say. She just sat there and continued to drive, in silence.

"Are you there? Michele!"

"Yes. Sorry. Just on my way home from Paul's. I'm sorry I didn't call you. Figured no big deal since no one was hurt; however, it did put a damper on our prom night... But on a good note, we did get some good pictures at the restaurant before going to the prom."

"A damper... I call it a disaster! Our prom is this coming weekend. I hope ours goes off without a hitch.... And make sure you send me some of those pictures. I would love to see what type of dress you picked out."

"I can send them to you as soon as I get home… And you better send me some of your prom pictures too."

"Will do… So, what else is new? I take it you and Paul are doing good?"

"Yep. How about you and Mike?"

"We had a rough patch for a while, but things are good now."

"And you're yelling at me for not calling you! What happened?"

"Mike told me we're too young for a long-term relationship and that he thought we should try dating other people for a while… But I think, he had his eye on this other girl – and his friends encouraged him to shop around."

"Oh, Amy. I'm so sorry. I don't know about these men and their peer pressure. Paul told me some of his friends think we are too young to have a serious relationship too."

"What did you do? Did the two of you break up too?"

"No. Luckily Paul realizes what we have is special and that he shouldn't always listen to his friends."

"You're lucky. Sounds like Paul has a good head on his shoulders. I won't wish the pain of heartbreak on anyone."

"So sorry I wasn't there for you… You should have called me!"

"I know. I should have, but I was just so devastated -- for over a month. I didn't want to talk to anyone who had a good relationship or who might tell me I was better off without him…"

"You know I am here for you. If you need to talk… I'm a good listener."

"I know. I don't know why I didn't call you. I just sort of claimed up. I did try to date a couple of guys... but... you know. It just wasn't there. I never found anyone that sparked my interest like Mike did."

"So how did the two of you end up back together?" Michele pulled into her driveway and put the car in park so she could finish her phone call with Amy.

"I think Mike finally realized the grass wasn't greener on the other side. He showed up at my door one day with flowers. He cried and asked for forgiveness. I should have made him suffer for a couple more days, but instead, I asked if he had a date for the prom."

"Well, I'm glad the two of you made up. I think the two of you make a great couple."

"Thanks, Michele. I appreciated that."

Michele watched as someone flipped on the front porch light, then replied, "I better get going since I just got home. But I promise to call more or at least text."

"Sounds good. I will too." Amy chuckled. "Don't forget to text me some of your pictures."

"Will do. Bye."

When Michele hung up the phone, she was happy Amy didn't bring up her dreams again since she didn't know how much she could tell Amy without making up lies. Amy knew about her prophetic dreams, but she didn't know about Michele's telekinesis powers or her new healing power. Michele wondered: *How much longer can I keep up with these charades? Maybe I'll have to make a decision, sooner rather than later, to finish high school in America or move in with my*

*grandmother on the Island of Honiawae – it's hard
keeping all these secrets from my friends and
family.*

Chapter 31

The school was closed on Monday and
Tuesday due to the damage done by the tornado.
During the time off, Michele took the opportunity
to earn extra cash by signing up to work extra
shifts since she wanted to replace the money she
had borrowed from her dad -- to pay for her prom
dress.

Tuesday night, Michele's grandmother
Leewan came to visit her in her dream... Leewan
was sitting on the edge of Michele's bed, petting
Mitch. Michele looked up at her and asked, "What
are you doing here?"

"I have some bad news."

Michele sat up and asked, "What. Are you
ok?"

"Yes. Yes, honey. Nothing about me. It's
about your mom, Mayra."

"What? Is she dead?"

"No. No. I can still feel her in my bones.
It's just... The prince has called off the search.
They have searched every known mental
institution near Moscow, without any leads. Have
you had any more dreams about her?"

"No. Sorry. Every time I try to reach out
to her. I just keep returning to the alley where
those teenagers found her. I can't even get the
same dream back that showed her at the
institution."

"Well keep trying... Did you happen to do something different the night you saw her at the institution?"

"Not that I remember. I just grabbed the crystal, as you taught me, and repeated her name three times before going to bed."

"Hmmm. Well, don't give up. Please!"

"Never."

"Well, I better get going. You have to get up for school. See you soon."

Leewan faded away and Michele's alarm went off.

Chapter 32

The school year was over before Michele knew it. While she was packing up her luggage for the trip to Australia, she looked over at her cat playing on her dresser.

"What are you doing over there?"

Michele walked over to her dresser and noticed Pepper pawing at the rock she brought home from her mother's old bedroom.

"What made you so enthused about that rock all of the sudden?" Michele watched in wonder as the cat pawed at the sparkling crystals.

"That's it. Oh, Pepper, you're a genius. The night I had the dream of my mom at a mental institution, I had that crystal rock in bed with me."

Michele grabbed the rock and put it in her suitcase.

*****

Paul's parents, Jim and Judy Hudson picked Michele up the day before the flight to Australia. Their flight was scheduled to leave early the next morning, so Jim and Judy figured they would stay at an airport hotel the night before – that way they could leave their car at the hotel and catch a shuttle to the airport.

Michele's uncle and aunt helped Michele carry her bags out to the SUV. While Joe was helping Jim load her bags into the car carrier, Gloria hugged Michele and said, "We're going to miss you. Make sure you call me when you get to Paul's uncle's house so I know you made it there safely." Gloria looked at Michele with tears in her eyes and asked, "You do plan on coming back. Right?"

Michele looked at Gloria, trying to decide if she should lie or not; she wasn't sure if she was going to stay with her grandmother or come back to live with Gloria and Joe to finish her senior year – it all depended on how Paul took the news. Michele swallowed a lump in her throat, fighting back the tears that this might be her final goodbye, and said, "I'm planning on it."

Uncle Joe walked up to Michele, put a hand on her shoulder, and said, "Guess that's it. Have a safe trip."

Michele hugged Joe and said, "Thanks Joe, for everything!" When she stepped back, she told her aunt and uncle, "I'm going to miss you guys. I love you both."

Gloria hugged Michele one more time and whisper, "I love you too."

Michele walked over to the car where Paul was standing, holding the backseat door open for her. She looked around at the farmhouse, pond, and barnyard one last time, then looked at Joe and Gloria standing side by side with their arms around each other. "Bye!" She waved, then hopped into the car. Paul closed her door then walked around to the other side of the car to get in while waving at Joe and Gloria, "See you later."

Jim honked the horn as the car pulled away while Judy waved out the passenger side window.

During the long drive to the airport, Michele was both excited and nervous. She was excited to spend time with her grandmother and her biological dad, but she was also nervous since she was making a life-changing decision – telling Paul about her hidden secrets of being a witch and the first-born daughter of a prince. Michele glanced over at Paul who was staring out the backseat window, watching the scenery: *I'd give a penny for his thoughts.* Then she wondered how he might react when he hears the news: *Will he think I'm crazy and not want anything to do with me or will he accept me as I am?* She looked down at their joined hands. She wanted to believe their relationship was fate and that it could weather any storm, but….

Paul looked over at Michele and squeezed her hand. "Are you excited?"

Michele smiled and nodded her head.

"I am too. But I'm not looking forward to this long flight."

Judy looked back at the two of them and said, "We reserved two rooms with two queen-size beds. The rooms are supposed to have an adjourning door. I figured the girls could sleep in one room and the boys in the other."

Michele smiled and said, "Sounds good. Thank you!"

Chapter 33

The flight from Detroit, Michigan to Brisbane, the capital of Queensland, Australia, was a long 18-hour flight. By the time the plane touched down in Brisbane, with the time change, it was around 3 p.m. When Michele exited the crowded, airport's ramp, a muscular, young man in his early twenties, with a bulky hearing aid -- bumped into her. He reached down to pick something off the ground then handed Michele a card. In a low voice, he whispered, "Welcome Michele. Your dad wants you to call the number on this card if you see anything suspicious."

She looked down at the card and read it when she looked back up, the guy was gone. Paul walked up behind her and asked, "Is everything ok?"

She shoved the small card into her short's pocket, smiled at Paul, and said, "Just peachy."

When Paul's parents exited the ramp, Judy said, "Don't know about you guys, but I need to find a restroom before we pick up our luggage and get the rental car. It's going to be a long six-hour drive to my brother's house."

The group walked down the hall of the busy airport looking for a restroom. As Michele walked with Paul, she looked around searching for the man that bumped into her, but he disappeared. After using the restroom, Michele noticed a tall man standing by the restroom's exit door. The man had the same hearing aid or was it a blue-tooth phone in one of his ears. He smiled at Michele as she walked by, then continued to stand by the door -- like he was waiting for someone else.

After the group collected their bags from the baggage claim area, they walked to the car rental desk. After Jim showed the clerk his reservations. The clerk told him, "Wait here! I'll have someone show you to your car."

When the clerk returned, the tall, muscular man that appeared with him was the same young man that had bumped into Michele when she first got off the plane. The man smiled at Michele, then said to the group, "Follow me."

Michele started dragging her luggage behind her. The man looked over his shoulder and saw Michele struggling. He turned slightly, reached for her bag, and said, "Here. Let me help you." The man easily lifted the suitcase and continued leading the group to a loaded, black, armored SUV. When the man unlocked the sport utility vehicle, Jim stopped in his tracks and stared at it. After a moment of standing with his mouth open, he asked the younger man, "Are you sure this car is for us. I would think this type of car would be reserved for high-profile visitors or even the President of the United States."

The man smiled, glanced at Michele and raised his eyebrows, then said, "Yes Sir. This is the car that was reserved for you. The reservation also has unlimited drivers, so anyone in your party can drive it." The man handed the keys to Jim, then proceeded to help everyone load their suitcases into the back of the extra-long SUV. When the young man went to grab Michele's carry-on bag, he let his hand linger on hers longer than necessary while giving her a special look. When the moment was over, he winked at her then loaded her bag. Paul noticed the exchanged and marched to the back seat of the SUV. Michele followed him and hopped in the seat next to him, but when she turned to close her door, the handsome, young man was standing at her door. He looked at her and said, "Safe travels."

After the man closed her door, the group was on their way. Paul sat in silence, staring out his window, while Michele looked out her window, admiring the scenery. After Jim found the ramp leading to the interstate, Michele watched a black sedan cut across two lanes of traffic to follow them. She thought: *My dad sure went overboard sending people to watch me, but how am I supposed to know who is following me...? Are the people that are following me now -- sent over from my dad to protect me or are they people sent over by the Taylors to make sure I don't make it back to the hidden islands?* After a while of watching the black sedan following in the distance, she reached for Paul's hand but he jerked it away and said, "Don't."

Michele looked at him and said, "What's wrong?"

He looked at her and spoke in a low voice so his parents wouldn't hear him over the radio. "That man was flirting with you... And you let him! I bet that piece of paper he handed you at the airport had his phone number on it. Didn't it?"

Michele thought: *Shit! It is a business card with a phone number on it. What was she going to say to cover this situation up?*

Paul looked at her with angry, watery eyes and said, "Well! Are you going to show me the card he gave you or deny it?"

She reached into her pocket, pulled out the card, and said, "It's not what you think. My dad's just overprotective. He sent that guy over to make sure I made it in one piece. I swear... I'm not looking for anyone else. I only want you!" She handed him the card.

Paul looked at the card; all it had was the name Jayden Hoekstra and phone number on it. He picked up the card and acted like he was going to tear it up. Michele said, "Don't.... Please!"

Paul urgently whispered back, "You swear that man was sent to protect you... by your dad."

"Yes. I never met him before."

"So, you don't mind if I hold onto the card then?"

"Be my guest."

Paul took out his wallet and acted like he was going to put the card into it. Then he looked at Michele and handed her the card back. "Sorry! I believe you. I guess I was just jealous. I should know better; You've never lied to me before."

Michele took the card back and thought: *I just haven't told you the whole truth. I guess only time will tell if you can handle the truth.*

*****

Halfway through the drive, Jim stopped the car for a pitstop. After filling the tank up with gas, he drove up to the travel plaza. "Who's hungry?"

Judy looked at teens in the backseat and said, "I know I am. Are you guys ready to get something to eat?"

Michele nodded her head and Paul mumbled, "Yeah. I could eat."

Before getting out of the car, Michele looked around the parking lot for the black sedan. When she couldn't find it, she quickly opened her door and made a fast dash towards the travel center.

Paul walked fast to catch up with her and asked, "Where's the fire?"

Michele looked at him over her shoulder while walking. "I just realized how bad I need to go to the bathroom."

Paul laughed and followed her into the center.

While in the restroom. Michele got out her cellphone and called the number on the card.

After the first ring, Jayden answered and said, "Hello. What's wrong?"

"Nothing. I hope... But there's a black sedan following us and I just wanted to make sure it's one of my father's cars and not the Taylor's."

Jayden laughed, then said, "That obvious, huh? Guess I need to talk to those agents. They are supposed to be trained to tail a car and not be conspicuous."

"I didn't mean to get anyone in trouble. No one else in the car noticed. Guess I'm just more observant."

"Well, I guess it's good for you to be able to tell our guys from anyone else's that might be following you. So, if someone gets too close to you, look for a gold pin on their left shirt collar. It should be a round pin with a black capital "W" on it-- which stands for King Williams's Army."

"Ok. Thanks! I better get going."

When Michele exited the restroom, Paul was standing outside the door waiting for her. "About time," he laughed. My parents went to the restaurant to find a seat."

Paul took Michele's hand and started leading her towards the restaurant. While walking, she looked over her right shoulder at the exit door and saw two men standing there. One of the men pointed at her, then they both started walking fast -- towards her. When the men were within 20-feet of intercepting her, some other men walked up behind them and stopped the followers instantly by jabbing something into their backs. Michele turned her head to watch as the first, two men were ushered out of the building.

"Watch it," Paul said. Michele stopped just in the nick of time and let out a screech; she almost had a head-on collision with a ten-year-old boy who was running towards the restrooms. After watching the boy run by, Paul asked Michele, "What were you daydreaming about."

"Oh, nothing. Guess I'm just jet-lagged and not paying attention."

*****

After the group had something to eat, they were on the road again. By the time the group got to Paul's Uncle George's and Aunt Beth's house, it was close to midnight. Michele hadn't seen the black sedan again after the rest stop. She wondered if the driver got in trouble or if he was waylaid by the incident at the rest stop; either way, Michele still felt someone's presence, watching her, as she got out of the SUV.

Paul's uncle's house was lit up like a Christmas tree. George must have turned on every light in the place so his sister Judy could find the right house. As soon as Jim put the SUV in park, George and Beth came out of the house to give their guests hugs and to help them unload.

While getting the luggage out of the back of the SUV, George looked at Jim and said, "Wow. You must be doing good in America. You rented a high dollar Lincoln Navigator!"

"No. I mean Yes. Your sister and I do make a decent living in America – since we're both doctors. But I would have settled for a full-size car. I have Michele's dad to thank for the Lincoln Navigator."

George looked at Michele and said, "I might have to meet your dad one of these days. Does he need a yacht?" George laughed lightly.

Michele grabbed one of her bags and said, "I don't know. I can ask him."

George laughed again and said, "You do that. If he ever needs a private yacht, I can hook him up."

After all the luggage was carried into the house, Beth told her guest, "I've made sleeping arrangements for everyone. Hope you don't mind Paul, but I gave you the couch in the living room so your parents can have one of the guest rooms upstairs and Michele can have our second spare room?"

"No problem. The couch is good for me. Thanks."

After all the guests were shown their assigned quarters, Michele closed her bedroom door and started unpacking. While she was unpacking, someone knocked on her door. When she opened the door, Paul walked in and said, "I just wanted to say goodnight."

"You shouldn't be in here; your parents are right next door!"

Paul laughed. "So. The door is wide open… And I just wanted to give you a kiss goodnight." He put one arm around her back to pull her close. He gently pushed a lock of hair away from her face and said, "You're so beautiful. Sorry I was jealous."

"It's al…" Michele wasn't able to finish her sentence since Paul claimed her lips with his.

"Ah hum," Jim said from the hallway. "Think that's long enough. We all should be getting to bed. George has big plans for us tomorrow."

Paul looked at Michele and said, "Sweet dreams," then left. After he closed the door, she thought: *That's right. I need to see if my mother's rock really helps with my dreams, but first, I need to text my aunt… let her know I made it here in one piece."*

Chapter 34

After Michele settled into bed, she grabbed her crystal necklace and pulled the crystal rock to her side. She looked up at the ceiling and repeated her mother's name three times: *Mayra Johnson, Mayra Johnson, Mayra Johnson.*

Michele was standing on a sidewalk, outside a large brick building with multiple windows. The breeze was chilly against her bare legs. She looked down and noticed she was still wearing her long, light blue, bedtime t-shirt. Directly in front of her was a lady sitting in a wheelchair with her head bent down. Michele looked around the gated area and noticed green trees, green grass, and other patients.   Some of the other patients were in wheelchairs, like the lady sitting in front of her, and other patients seemed to be walking around aimlessly, talking to themselves. In the distance, she could see two people in white uniforms sitting on a bench. Michele turned her attention back to the lady sitting in front of her -- she had greasy, dishwater-blonde hair pulled back in a bun. *Could this be my biological mom?* Michele knelt on one knee and looked up into the lady's face. "Mom! Mayra! Can you hear me?" The lady just sat there, staring down at the dirt. Her eyes were light blue, like Michele's -- but lifeless.

"Come on Jane. It's time to take you inside and feed you some lunch."

Michele looked up and noticed a middle-aged woman wearing a white uniform had just grabbed the handles on the back of the wheelchair so she stood up and stepped to the side. The women pushed the wheelchair right past Michele without even acknowledging that anyone was there. Michele thought: *She must not be able to see me or this is a vision from the past.* She started following the woman and the wheelchair down the sidewalk and called out, "Stop! I want to talk to Jane."

The image started to fade and Michele woke up in a bed, confused. She looked around the room and thought: *Where in the hell am I now?* She started to get out of bed and felt the crystal rock lying in the bed next to her. Looking at it in the dim light from the window, she realized: *Oh. I'm at Paul's uncle's house.* She glanced at the clock sitting on the bedside stand: *9 a.m. Guess I might as well get up.*

*****

When Michele walked down the stairs, she saw the group sitting around the dining room table.

"Well good morning sleepyhead," Paul said with a smile.

Paul's Aunt Beth said, "Have a seat, Michele. There's plenty of food on the table."

She took a seat at the table and looked around at the spread. There was an assortment of breakfast foods such as biscuits and gravy, scrambled eggs, pancakes, bacon, and ham to choose from.

"Please pass the orange juice and pancakes."

While she was eating, Paul's mom Judy asked, "You and Paul are still planning on taking the ferry to visit your grandmother on Friday, right?"

"Yes, if it's no bother for George and Beth."

Beth spoke up, "No problem at all. Plus, we want you here to help celebrate Paul's birthday on the 10th."

Judy asked, "Have you called your grandmother yet? I hope she's not upset that you're spending some of your time with us."

"I was planning on calling my grandmother tonight after I knew for sure what day I would be taking the ferry over. I'd already told her before we left off my plans to stay here and celebrate Paul's birthday. She didn't seem upset."

"Great. Then it's settled. After breakfast, my brother has plans to take us to the Yacht Club, where he works. He states he has big plans for us." Judy smiled at her brother.

George smiled back, then looked at Michele and said, "I hope you like fishing and boat rides."

"I have never gone fishing and I don't have much experience with boat rides since I've only ridden on a ferry boat once, last fall when I went to visit my grandmother."

Beth smiled, "Don't worry. Us women can just sit on the top deck and enjoy the sun while the men go fishing."

Michele smiled and said, "That sounds nice. And if you don't mind, can we stop somewhere, either today or tomorrow, so I can buy something for Paul's birthday?"

Beth looked questioning at her husband. He spoke up and said, "There is a gift shop down at the yacht club or you could always wait until tomorrow to shopping in town."

"Thanks."

Paul's dad added, "You know Michele, your dad paid for the rental car... so, if you and Paul want to take it to tomorrow to explore the area -- the rental contract does cover any driver."

Michele looked at Paul and smiled, "Sounds like fun to me."

Paul reached under the table and gave Michele's hand a quick squeeze.

Chapter 35

The ride to the yacht club in Yeppoon took about 25 minutes. The group didn't need to drive separately since the rented SUV was large enough to transport all six of the occupants, with room to spare. During the ride, Michele felt her phone vibrate. Looking at the screen, she noticed that the call was from Jayden. She looked around, to make sure no-one was watching, then opened the message. "Good morning princess. Where are you going? I want to send some men there before your arrival to scope out the place." Michele deleted the message right away, looked around the car to ensure no-one was watching, then sent her reply.

When the group arrived at the yacht club, Paul's Uncle George introduced them to some of his co-workers, then led them to his private fishing yacht. "Here she is, the Queen of the Coral Sea. George helped his wife and all the guests board the main fishing deck. After everyone was on board, George explained how he designed yachts for a living and how he designed this boat. "The first floor here..." George waved his arm around, "has this outdoor fishing deck and a glassed-in sunroom. The glassed-in sunroom has a cleaning station, a live well, and a chest freezer. There is even a half-bath located towards the front on this floor since my wife didn't want the smell of dead fish lingering on the other floors." George looked at his wife and winked. "There are two sets of stairs by the bathroom. The stairs that go down will take you to sleeping quarters, the engine room, and a full bath. The stairs that go up will lead you to the living quarters. I designed the living quarters as an open floor plan, dividing the kitchen from the living room with an island. The upstairs also has a half-bath. From living quarters, you can climb up a ladder that will take you to the captain's chair and sundeck. A dingy is stored on the front of the boat for safety purposes or for cruising around a marina. Feel free to give yourselves a self-guided tour while I prepare the boat for the voyage."

Michele grabbed Paul's hand and smiled. "Lead the way, my prince." Paul started leading her to the back of the boat through the sliding doors. Michele thought: *Why did I call him my prince?*

*****

While the men were fishing for tuna, Beth manned the captain's chair and Michele and Judy lounged around on the top sundeck -- sipping strawberry margaritas. Michele was more than a little surprised when Paul's Aunt Beth offered her an alcoholic beverage, but she accepted it immediately. Sitting back in her lounge chair, Michele marveled at the beauty of the Pacific Ocean through her sunglasses. The water sparkled like diamonds under the direct sunlight. In the distance, she could see other fishing boats, yachts, and sailboats. She could also see the shoreline of Australia and the outline of distant islands. She grabbed a pair of binoculars that were sitting on a tray next to her so she could observe the boats around them. The first boat she spotted was a fishing boat; she watched the crew members on that boat struggle to haul in a large fish. The next boat she spotted was a sailboat; she watched a man while he adjusted the sails. When she searched the open seas for another boat, she found another fishing yacht -- like the one they were on. She searched the decks for any occupants and spotted a lady staring right back at her through another pair of binoculars. Michele gasped and dropped the binoculars. Judy looked at Michele and asked, "Everything alright?"

Michele picked up the binoculars off the deck floor and said, "Yep. Guess the alcohol and the sun is making me see things." She picked up the binoculars again and looked over at the fishing yacht. The lady that was staring at her only moments ago appeared to be making small circles with the palms of her hands above the water while saying something. Michele thought: *It looks like she's trying to enchant the water.* The lady had dark skin and was wearing a red sundress. Her long, black hair was blowing in the wind, and two taller men in white, short outfits were standing on both sides of her. Michele surveyed the boat and notice a large, red emblem on the side of the bow, that had a large, black "T" inside of it.

Michele dropped the binoculars into her lap and thought: *Shit. Could the Taylors' guards have followed me out here…? And brought a witch.* I wonder what that witch is doing to the water? She stood up and walked to the port side of the sundeck. Looking over the rail into the water, she noticed a bunch of fins coming towards the boat. Michele pointed to the fins and yelled at Beth who was at the helm of the boat, "What are those?"

Beth stood up and looked where Michele was pointing. "Looks like a school of great white sharks."

While Michele watched as the sharks swam closer to their boat, she heard a loud splash on the starboard side. When she turned her head to look, she saw a spot of water coming towards the boat. Michele pointed and Beth screamed, "A whale."

The boat started to capsize to the left as the whale began to surface. Michele grabbed onto the side rail as the boat started to tip, towards the waiting sharks. She looked and the sharks and screamed, "Stop!" Everything froze. Michele looked around -- stunned at what she did. She saw Judy's lounge chair pushed up against the guardrail and Beth, standing sideways -- holding onto the steering wheel of the boat. Michele held onto the side rail and made her way to the back of the sundeck so she could check on the men. She looked over the side rail and saw George and Jim lying on the deck floor and Paul in mid-flight, flipping over the portside railing -- with the sharks paused in a circle just feet below him. She used her finger and her power of telekinesis to flip Paul back onto the boat -- next to Jim and George. Then she turned her attention to the whale. With all her might and concentration, she pushed her hands out and away from her body so she could magically push the whale a good fifty feet from the boat. *Ok. That should do it.* "Go!" she shouted.

Time returned. The whale drove back down into the ocean and started swimming parallel to the boat. The wave created by the whale started to recede causing the boat to rock back and forth until it settled in an upright position. Beth climbed back up into the captain's chair and said, "Wow! That was close."

Judy stood up and pulled her chair back to the center of the sunning deck. She looked at Michele and asked, "Are you alright?"

Michele nodded her head and said, "Yes. I better go check on the guys." She walked to the back of the sundeck and looked over the railing at the back-fishing deck. Paul's Uncle George was pointing at the school of sharks in the water. She watched as George ran into the glassed-in room below and came out holding a flare gun. George pointed the gun into the water and shot at the sharks, causing them to disperse and leave the area. After shooting the flare gun, he looked up at Michele and shouted, "You girls alright?"

Michele screamed back, "Yes. We're fine."

Paul looked up at her and waved. She smiled then turned around to find the binoculars. After she found the binoculars, thrown up against the front corner of the guardrail, she looked through them at the Taylors' boat. The witch with the long black hair was staring back at her through a pair of binoculars. Michele squinted her eyes and pushed one hand, palm out towards the witch. The witch was thrown backward against the boat's cabin wall. On impact, the witched bounced forward and landed on the boat's deck. Michele watched as the two men on the boat rushed to the witch's aide. When she noticed the witch wasn't getting up. She smiled and thought: *Servers her right. I must have knocked her unconscious.*

George came up the ladder and said to his wife, "I'll take over from here. We better start heading back to shore if there's a whale out here." He glanced at his watch and continued, "It's about time for us to get something to eat at the yacht club anyway."

Beth stood up so George could sit at the helm. "Did you guys get a chance to catch any tuna?"

"Paul and Jim pulled one in each and put them in the live well."

Michele climbed down the ladder and met Paul in the living quarters. He smiled when he saw her and said, "I was just coming up to find you. Boy was that some excitement or what?"

"Yeah. Too much for my likings. Did you enjoy fishing?"

"Yes. You should come to see the big tuna I caught." He took her by the hand and led her down to the lower deck.

Chapter 36

Sitting outside, at a round table under a large umbrella, Michele told the waiter what she wanted to order off the yacht club's menu. After she ordered her food, she started looking around at the people. George was standing by an outside bar, busy telling his friends and co-workers the story of the whale, Paul was talking to the waiter about the menu, and Jim and Judy were still studying their menus. Michele continued looking around the patio and spotted Jayden looking at her. When their eyes met, he smiled and motioned her to come over to the side of the building.

Michele waited until Paul was done ordering, then excused herself to go find the restroom.

"We just went when we got here," Paul said.

She blushed and said, "Well, nature calls me again."

Michele got up from the table and walked inside of the building. After a couple of seconds, she peeked back out the door to make sure no one was watching, then snuck around the side of the building to meet Jayden.

When Jayden saw her, he said, "Come with me." He turned, walked down the side of the building, then opened a service door for her. "Go on in." He waited until she was inside, then closed the door behind them. Once inside the building, Michele noticed they were in the club's storage room. Jayden grabbed her hands, looked at her with concern in his eyes, then said, "I heard what happened out on the water! I think it's too risky for you to stay here. Your father would kill me if anything ever happened to you. I think it's best if you leave now! The security team has a private yacht on standby so we can take you to the castle immediately."

She jerked her hands away and replied, "And leave Paul and his family here! I can't do that!"

"You can tell them there's a family emergency. Make up some story about your grandmother being ill or something like that. It's just too dangerous for you to stay here – out in the open. One of my men just returned from the islands. He told me that the Taylors are spreading false rumors to all of the islands about you being a threat to their way of living and that you're planning to expose the islands to the world."

"That's not true... and I can take care of myself! Besides... it's Paul's birthday in two days. I will go with you on Friday as planned. And hopefully, bring Paul."

Jayden shook his head and said, "Paul's the problem. He's an outsider. That's how the Taylors convinced some of the witches to work for them. They told them that you and Paul have plans to expose the islands – which could lead to another world panic and the witch trials starting all over again."

"That's all nonsense!"

"I agree. But you have to understand. These people have been living under the radar all their lives. They have only heard stories of the witch trials in the late 1600s and they don't want to repeat history. The Taylors have them convinced if the world does find out about the Hidden Islands of Honiawae, and all the witches living there, they will send in military troops and take over the islands."

"Is my half-sister, Amarina, and her mother, Lalirra, still living at the castle?"

"Yes. Your grandparents, King Levi Williams and Queen Chloe, cannot find any proof that the Lalirra parents, Moki and Merrin Taylor, are the ones that started these vicious rumors; nor can they find any proof that they are behind the disappearance of your mother, Mayra.

"This is ridiculous. I have no intention of exposing the island. My grandmother, Leewan, is making arrangements to have a mind-erasing witch available, to erase Paul's memories if he doesn't take the truth well. I love Paul and want to spend the rest of my life with him. If I have to... I choose Paul over the kingdom. You can tell my father that!"

Jayden stared at her in disbelief. "You would choose a boy over the right to inherit the kingdom – with all the money in the world to buy anything you ever dreamed of and all the power to rule over the Hidden Islands of Honiawae?"

"Yes." She looked down at her watch. "I better get back to my table. Is there a way to go through the building so it looks like I am returning from the restroom?"

Jayden shook his head in disbelief, bowed slightly, and said, "If that's your wish.... Follow me, princess."

*****

That night, after everyone retired for the evening, Michele looked out the window and saw a car parked down the road. She texted Jayden to ensure the car was one of them. After receiving a quick reply: "Yes." Michele went to bed and repeated her grandmother's name, Leewan Johnson, three times.

Michele was sitting at the Leewan's kitchen table on Honiawae Island. Leewan was sipping some tea. "About time you came to visit me!" Leewan said with a smile. "I heard you refused

Jayden's request to leave the mainland, immediately."

"How did you hear about that when no phone signal can reach the islands?"

"Jayden sent a guard back to relay the incident to your father."

"Figures."

"I also heard you scared a witch from Keelonie Island. A friend of mine, from that island, told me when one of their witches returned from the Taylors' castle, she wouldn't tell a soul where she had been, but she did say she wouldn't be taking any more assignments from the Taylors to find you.... and putting her life at risk -- ever again! What did you do to the poor girl?"

"I just tossed her up in the air as you did to that spy that worked for the Taylors... But... I might have slammed her against the boat's cabin wall a little too hard... knocking her unconscious."

"Oh! Nice. I suppose."

"You suppose? She deserved it. She tried to feed me and my guest to the sharks."

"Why do you think she had anything to do with it? All I heard was you were being followed and the boat you were on almost capsizing from a whale swimming too close to it. Do you have proof she did it? If you do, I can bring it up at the witch's council."

"Witch's council. You guys have such a thing?"

"Yes. I can tell you more about it if you ever decide you want to join... But for now, we need to get back to the task at hand.... Do you have any proof?"

No. It's just my word against hers. But I did see her staring at our boat through binoculars and I did see her making motions over the water prior to the incident, so.... I just took put two and two together."

"Your instincts are probably dead on but not enough for me to press charges... I can't wait until I get to see you in person this Friday."

"Are you mad that I am bringing Paul? Do you think I am comprising the security of the islands by bringing him?"

"Of course not. I was young and in love once too. Just like you, I wouldn't let the opinion of others stand in our way."

"Thank you."

"I did make the arrangements with the mind-erasing witch to be at my house on Friday... Just in case we need her."

"I appreciate it. I love you, grams."

"I love you too. Stay safe and if you have to use your powers -- make sure no one notices."

"Will do."

The dream faded and Michele woke up in bed. The sun was peeking in through the window so she decided she might as well get up.

Chapter 37

After Michele put her shorts and t-shirt on, she snuck down the stairs so she wouldn't wake anybody up. She walked into the living room and saw Paul sleeping on the couch. She stood there for a while, watching him sleep in the early dawn's light. He looked so peaceful... and handsome; the vision initiated a burning desire inside her -- to reach out and touch him. Michele crept slowly towards the sofa, then reached down to push a stray hair from his face. Just as her finger was about to touch his hair, Paul's hand shot up and grabbed her wrist. She stifled a screamed and jerked back. He continued to hold her wrist, smiled up at her, and whispered, "Is anyone else up?"

She shook her head.

Paul moved back against the couch, lifted the blanket, then whispered, "Then slide in here. I was just dreaming about you. Come lay beside me."

Michele looked at his bare chest. A red blush overcame her cheeks. She looked over her shoulder then back, and whispered, "What if someone gets up and finds us? Do you have any clothes on?"

Paul made a husky laugh. "Yes. I have my undershorts on. See." He lifted the blanket so she could see his black underwear.

"I better not. I'm sure your aunt or uncle wouldn't appreciate finding us in a comprising position."

"If I put my jeans and shirt on... will you?"

Michele looked at Paul's clothes on the coffee table, then nodded."

He sat up on the side of the couch to get dressed. Michele turned her head to look the other way. Paul chuckled and said, "Oh come on Michele. It's not like you haven't seen me naked before."

She turned her head back and looked at him. Her eyes traced down his chest to his underwear. Her eyes got big when she noticed the bulge in his shorts.

Paul grabbed his shorts and said, "Don't worry darling. I promise to be good." After he slipped on his T-shirt and shorts, he laid back down on the couch and held the blanket up for her to climb in. Michele complied and laid on the couch beside him. He wrapped the blanket around her and pulled her in close. Then he propped his head up, stroked the side of her face, and said, "You're so beautiful." She looked at him and smiled. He took the opportunity to give her a good morning kiss -- that turned into a needed, hungry kiss – leaving Michele breathless. When the kiss was through, Paul laid his head on the pillow and started stroking her hair. "So, what are you doing up so early?"

She didn't want to tell him about her visiting her grandmother in her dreams so she told him, "I just couldn't sleep… and I wanted to see you."

Paul grinned and snuggled her closer.

After a while, Michele spoke up. "So, do you think your parents will really let us use the car to go shopping today? I need to pick you up something for your 18th birthday."

"Umm. I don't know. But I sure hope so. Guess we can double-check at breakfast."

"You never told me what you wanted."

"I want to take you someplace where we can be alone. Maybe at a private beach or a secluded park somewhere, so we can try out the rental car's back seat together."

Michele laughed and punched him lightly in the arm. "You men and your one-track minds."

"Well, you asked me what I wanted."

"I meant… What do you want for your birthday… silly?"

"I just want you."

She smiled and asked, "And how are you going to unwrap me, in front of your parents, on your birthday?"

"That might be a problem."

Michele laughed and said, "Seriously. You better tell me what you want or you're getting a big, fat nothing!"

Paul laughed, then said, "Time alone with you is all I want. But I guess if we do go shopping, maybe I can find something I like… If that'll make you happy?"

"Yes. And do you know what else would make me happy?"

"Name it."

"Will you turn on the TV… so, it will look like we are just in here watching TV – in case anyone else wakes up early."

"If I have to." Paul reached up, over his head and grabbed the TV remote off the end table.

*****

Michele sat up faster than a wink of an eye when she heard someone coming down the stairs. She tossed the blanket to one side of the couch with one hand and nudged Paul up with the other hand. "Sit up," Michele whispered, urgently. By the time Paul's mom walked into the room the couple was sitting side by side, with Paul's arm resting on the back of the couch and Michele's hand resting on his thigh, pretending they were watching the TV.

Judy looked at the couple, then looked at the TV. "Anything exciting on the news?"

"Oh, same ole, same ole," Paul replied.

"Well, I'm glad your both up. I wanted to talk to you about our plans today."

"What's up?"

"I know Michele wants to do a little shopping, so I thought we could all make a day of it. Maybe go out someplace to eat breakfast first, then do a little shopping at the outlet stores down by the pier."

Paul moaned since it wasn't what he had planned for the day.

"Sounds great to me," Michele replied, then looked at Paul innocently. Paul stared back at her, speechless. She hit his leg and rolled her eyes. Paul took the subtle hint, looked at his mom, and said, "Sounds like fun."

Chapter 38

After everyone was dressed, the group headed into town in the SUV. While the adults chit-chatted up in the front of the car, Michele and Paul sat in the back -- half- haphazardly playing pea-knuckle with their thumbs while watching the scenery roll by. When Michele glanced out the back window of the SUV, she spotted the black sedan and wondered: *What would the people do if Paul and I did go parking? We'll never get any time to be alone with those guards following us. I'll just have to figure out a way to lose them.*

After the group arrived at the restaurant, Michele and Paul sat at one booth so the adults could sit together in another one. After the couple ordered their food, she took his hand and started tracing hearts in his palm. When she looked up into his deep, brown eyes, she saw a glint of amusement.

"I love you too," he whispered with a smile.

She blushed, then said, "I wanted to talk to you about going to see my grandmother... If you still want to go with me?"

"Why wouldn't I?"

"I don't know. Just wondering if you were having second thoughts?"

He laughed, then said, "I wouldn't miss spending time with you for the world. My boss might have only approved two weeks off from work, but I plan on staying as long as you want me to. The whole summer – if you want."

"But what about your job?"

"I thought about that. I'm just going to call my boss, once we get to the island, and tell him I need the whole summer off. If he has to hire someone else, I'll understand. But hopefully, he will at least have a part-time job for me when I come back in the fall."

"You're going to quit your job for me?"

Paul squeezed her hand and said, "You're worth it, babe."

She smiled while thinking: *If you only knew what I was prepared to give up for you.*

*****

After breakfast, the group huddled together just outside the restaurant's front door. Judy looked at her husband and said, "I know you don't want to browse the same shops I do. If you want to look around the pier with George, I'll hang out with Beth. We can all meet here, say, about four o'clock sharp."

"Sounds good to me. Come on George, show me that fishing shop you were talking about the other day." Jim gave Judy a peck on the cheek then took off with George.

Judy looked at Michele and Paul. "Do the two of you want to hang out with us or split up and meet us back here around three?"

Paul spoke up, "Will meet you here at four. See ya!" He grabbed Michele's hand and started dragging her off in the opposite direction. She smiled and waved at Beth and Judy before stumbling into step with Paul.

"Why are you walking so fast?" Michele laughed at Paul.

"I want to get this shopping thing done so we can have some time to find someplace to be alone."

"I think the pier is way too busy to find someplace to be alone."

Paul dangled the keys in front of her face.

"How did you get them?"

He smiled and said, "My dad gave them to me. I told him I wasn't in the mood for shopping all day and that there is a park, with a beach, just a couple miles down the road I wanted to check out."

"You bad boy."

"I know. But you love me anyway."

The young lovers walked down the pier hand and hand. Michele enjoyed the warm, sunny weather and the seagulls flying all over the place. She looked at all the shops and restaurants as they passed by -- there was an ice cream shop, fresh fish, a Crab Leg House, a coffee house... then two men staring at her. *Oh shit!* she thought. *Those men look like the same two men that were on that boat with that witch. I'm being followed.* She looked straight ahead and tried to act casual. *Those men might not know that I recognized them.* When she looked ahead to the next shop, Paul jerked her hand and made a beeline for it; it was a t-shirt shop. "Come on Michele. The sooner I pick out a t-shirt, the sooner we can be on our way."

As Paul dragged Michele closer to the shop's entrance, she noticed two large men standing near the door -- trying to act casual: talking to each other and looking in every direction except towards her. The sunshine reflected off a pin on the men's collars. When Michele got closer, she glanced at one of the gold pins and notice a large "W". She smiled and let Paul lead her into the shop. Once inside, Paul released her hand so he could look at some t-shirts. Michele waited a couple of minutes then backtracked towards the door so she could speak to her dad's guards. "Hi boys, you're doing a great job watching me, but I think you should also be looking out for those two guys that work for the Taylors." The men looked at her in shock, then looked in the direction she was pointing. When the men spotted the Taylors' spies, the spies took off walking fast in the other direction. Michele smiled when the two guards took off after the Taylors' spies and thought: *That was too easy... now Paul and I can slip off to have some alone time. But I need to do something about my cellphone.* She took her phone out of her pocket, held it tight, and whispered: *Don't let anyone track me.*

Paul came back out of the shop's entrance holding a T-shirt that advocated Queensland, Australia. "What are you doing out here?"

"Oh. Nothing," Michele said shaking her head. "I just thought I saw my dad."

"Well, I think I found what I want for my birthday. But the prices here are ridiculous. If you want to wait, you can just buy me something from the island where your grandmother lives."

"Let me see." Michele grabbed the price tag and her eyes got big. She shook her head and replied, "That's not too bad. Plus, you're well worth it. Just let me pay for it and we can be on our way."

Chapter 39

Michele walked into the shop and looked around for a sales clerk. When she spotted a young lady behind a counter, she grabbed the shirt from Paul and started walking up to the counter. When the lady behind the counter looked up and saw her coming, she turned all red, stood at attention, then started curtseying over and over again. "I. I. I'm sorry. I didn't know you were coming here, your highness. Let me go get the manager." The girl turned around and ran into the backroom.

Paul looked at Michele and said, "What was that all about?"

"I'm not sure. She must have mistaken me for someone else."

Within a minute, an older lady came out smiling. She looked at Michele, then Paul. "How can I be of service?"

Michele held up the t-shirt. "I just want to pay for this t-shirt."

"Oh. Let me see." The lady grabbed the t-shirt then started shaking her head. "Did you know this t-shirt is on sale --buy one, get one free?" She looked at Paul, "Don't you want to pick out your free t-shirt?"

Paul looked at Michele, then back to the lady. "Ok. Just give me a second." He walked back over to t-shirts. The lady whispered over the counter, "Welcome Michele. Your dad's guards told me you might be coming by. This shop here belongs to your grandmother, Queen Chloe. Anything you want from here is free. We even have a dress-shop attached to this shop. Right through those doors --if you want to look?"

"That's okay. I think I better pay for the t-shirts."

"Does that mean you haven't told Paul… about the islands?"

Michele blushed, then whispered back. "No. I haven't told him about the hidden islands. I am waiting to tell him about who I really am when we get to my grandmothers—so my grandmother can help me erase his memories if it doesn't turn out well."

The lady patted Michele's hand. "I knew those rumors were just lies spread by the Taylors"

Paul walked back up to the counter with another t-shirt. Michele reached into her handbag to pay for the shirts. The lady looked at the tags again and said, "Today's your lucky day. This shirt is also on clearance, so you will only be half-price for one of the shirts."

Michele paid the lady and the lady winked at her, "Don't forget to check out the dress shop. If there is anything you want me to put on layaway, just let me know. We can always ship the dresses to you -- if you don't have time to come back and pick them up."

Michele grabbed Paul's hand and said, "Can we just walk through the dress shop so I can dream."

Paul looked at his watch and said, "Sure. But we need to hurry if we want to have time to go to the park."

$$*****$$

Michele was impressed with the assortment of dresses on display. There were dresses for every occasion. Some of the dresses were modern, everyday wear, some were business attire, and some of them were formal wear for proms, weddings, or princesses. She looked over to one corner of the room and also noticed a display of jewelry and tiaras. "I might have to see if my grandmother will let me come back here to do a little shopping."

Paul looked at one of the price tags on a dress and whistled, "Well, I hope your grandmother has money; don't think you can afford any of these dresses on a waitress salary."

She smiled, then replied, "I guess you're right. But I can dream."

"If you really want one of these dresses, I probably could chip in on one before we return to Michigan."

Michele looked at him and said, "You'd really do that?"

"Sure, why not? How often does someone get the chance to buy something special from another country?"

"We better get heading to the car if you want to go to the park." She grabbed his hand and started walking out the door. At the door, she stopped and looked right then left. Paul looked at her and asked, "What are you looking for?"

"Oh. Like I said. I swore I saw my dad out here. Let's take the back alley to the car. I think it will be faster since it is less congested with shoppers."

Chapter 40

The couple made their way, swiftly, to the Lincoln Navigator. When they got close to the car, Paul looked at Michele and asked, "Do you want to drive?"

"No. You can drive since you know where you are going."

Michele enjoyed the scenery while Paul drove the SUV north along the scenic, ocean drive to the park's entrance. While Paul paid for a daily pass at the front gate, she admired the park's landscaping: the freshly manicured lawns, eucalyptus trees swaying in the breeze, and all flowering floras. After Paul paid for the daily pass, he drove down the main drive while Michele read all the directional signs: One sign pointed towards the pavilions, one pointed towards the natural trails, one pointed towards a lighthouse, one pointed towards a fishing pier, and one pointed towards a public beach. "Let's check out the public beach first."

"I wanted to see the secluded natural trails," Paul laughed. "But I guess we have time to cruise by the beach first."

The beach area was beautiful with the sparkling, turquoise-blue water and white sand. Michele watched as children played in the water, teens played volleyball, and someone was flying a kite. As Paul drove around the loop, the scenery began to change. Michele watched out the window as they passed some dunes. At the end of the beach drive, Paul turned left -- back towards the hiking trails. As Michele watch out the window, admiring the green flora, flowering bushes, and sparing, arranged eucalyptus trees, she noticed some movement out of the corner of her eyes. "Wait. I thought I saw something!" Paul slowed the car down and looked out the passenger's window. When the car reached a clearing, Paul stopped the car and looked out into the open field. From the window, the couple could see two red kangaroos eating in an open area. When the kangaroos noticed the car, they took off hopping in the opposite direction.

"That was cool. I've never seen a wild kangaroo."

Paul smiled, "Did you see the baby in the kangaroo's pouch?"

"No. I didn't notice."

"Well keep your eyes open. Maybe we'll see them again."

Paul followed the park's signs to a staging area. After he parked the car, the couple got out and walked up to a large sign with a map of the trails. "Let's take that trail," he said as he pointed to a three-mile loop that went up to a lookout point. "It's not that long and looks like it has some benches along the way."

Michele smiled, took his hand, and said, "Come on then. Times a wasting."

The couple took the trail, hand in hand, through the eucalyptus forest and green foliage. They stopped once on a wooded bridge that provided passage over a river. Michele looked down into the clear water and saw some sort of strange fish swimming around. "What type of fish is that?"

"I think that's what they call a lungfish. They are native to Australia."

Paul looked up the trail, then said, "Let's go. I think the lookout point is just beyond that hill."

Michele was breathless by the time she reached the top of the hill. Throwing herself down onto a bench, she looked at Paul and said, "Boy am I out of shape."

"You look great to me," he said with a wink. He took a seat next to her, wrapped one arm around her shoulders, and then looked out over the trees at the view. In the distance he could see the dunes they drove past and then the sparkling, turquoise water, that seemed to go on forever.

Michele stared in wonder and said, "Wow. How breathtaking. It's all so beautiful."

Paul took her chin and turned her face to look at him. "Not as beautiful as my view."

She started to laugh but was cut short by Paul's lips.

In between kisses and caresses, Paul whispered, "I've been waiting to get my hands on you for far too long." He started reaching one of his hands up her blouse.

Michele giggled and swatted his hand away. "Not here. Someone could walk up that trail any minute."

Paul sat back with disappointment in his eyes. Michele glanced at her watch. "We better be getting back if we want to meet the others on time." She stood up, started to walk away, then looked back at him when he didn't move. "Oh, come on. We have all summer." Michele held out her hand. Paul reluctantly took it and stood up, but before she could start walking away, he pulled her in for one more kiss.

By the time the kiss was through, Michele's head was spinning and her whole body was numb and tingling. She would've collapsed to the ground if Paul didn't hold her steady. "Are you okay?"

She blushed slightly at her body's reaction to his touch. "Yeah. I think I just need something to drink."

"Sorry. I left our water in the car. At least the trail is all downhill from here."

As the couple walked down the trail, Michele said to Paul, "I'm so glad you decided to take this trip with me. You know how much I love you, right?"

He glanced at her, squeezed her hand, then said, "And I love you too."

*****

Paul wasted a good fifteen minutes trying to find someplace to park. After he parked the car, he jumped out and ran around the car to open Michele's door; however, Michele beat him to the punch and was already halfway out the passenger door. Paul grabbed her hand and said, "We'll have to run to make it to the meeting place on time."

Paul jogged and maneuvered his way through the busy streets -- pulling a laughing Michele behind him. "Excuse us. Excuse us. Coming through," was all Paul said all the way to the restaurant's door. Paul's mom, Judy, was staring at her watch when the couple pulled up, laughing and out of breath.

Judy looked up and said, "About time. I was beginning to worry."

Paul looked at his watch and said, "Oh mom. It's only five minutes after four."

Michele glanced around the busy streets and saw one of her father's guards staring at her. She thought: *He doesn't look too happy... I wonder where the other guard is?*

As Paul led the group back to the SUV, Michele reached down in her handbag to take her cellphone off vibrate. Looking down at her phone, she noticed she had over 10 missed calls and multiple text messages from Jayden. Skimming through some of the messages, she read: *Where in the hell are you? Why can't we track your phone? Text me right away. If I have to tell your dad we lost you, I could lose my job! Are you okay?* Michele smiled when she realized her incantation had worked on hiding the location of the phone;

however, she was worried about Jayden. Did she get him in trouble with her dad? She thought: *If Jayden does get in trouble, I'll just tell my dad it all my fault. I was the one that used magic so I could sneak away.*

Chapter 41

That night, before Michele went to bed, she looked out the window and saw the black sedan parked down the road. She smiled and thought: *I better text Jayden to see if he's alright.* She hopped on her bed and took out her cellphone. She typed a message to Jayden: *Sorry I ditched the guards. I just wanted to spend some time with Paul... alone! If my dad gives you any trouble, just let me know. I'll have my grandmother, Leewan, talk to him.*

Michele laid in bed and waited for a response, but before one ever came, she drifted off into a blissful sleep.

*****

During breakfast, Beth was going over the plans for Paul's 18th birthday. "Jim and George can grill the tuna and some baked potatoes; Judy and I will make Paul's birthday cake and maybe some broccoli casserole to go with the fish."

"What do you need me to do?" Michele asked.

"Your job is to keep the birthday-boy busy. Maybe go for a walk or watch some movies... Or there is the heated pool in the backyard. I know it's considered winter time here in Yeppoon,

Queensland, but our average temperature is over 70 degrees in the winter, and it's supposed to reach a record high of 84 degrees today."

Michele felt a little guilty for not helping out, but she did thoroughly enjoy the day lazing around the pool with Paul; and whenever Paul wasn't watching, she would check her phone and wonder: *Where are you Jayden? Why haven't you texted me back!*

"Why are you looking at your phone again?" Paul asked from the side of the pool.

Michele glanced up from the lounge chair, embarrassed she was caught. "I. I guess I'm just a little bit homesick. I was thinking about calling my aunt and uncle."

"You probably should call them. I'm sure they would love to hear from you."

She put her phone back down and said, "I probably will later." Then she got up from the chair and jumped into the pool, cannonballing Paul in the process.

*****

Michele never tried grilled tuna steak before, but she had to admit, it was delicious. "Thank you, George and Jim, for grilling the fish. I think you made a fish lover out of me."

Beth looked up and said, "Well, I guess I should go get the birthday cake now." She walked into the kitchen then reappeared carrying a large sheet cake. Michele look at the cake and said, "Nice job! Who did all the fancy decorations?"

Beth smile, then said, "Judy did most of the artwork and borders. She really is quite talented."

Michele looked at Judy and said, "I didn't know you were a doctor and a cake decorator."

Judy smiled and said, "I took a couple of cake decorating classes before getting into med school."

Beth sat the cake down in front of Paul. He took his finger and tried a bit of the frosting. Judy looked at him and said, "You can have a piece of cake after we sing to you."

Paul sat on his hand, as to hide the evidence, then said with a laugh, "Then hurry up!"

After blowing out the candles, Beth took the cake to cut it up while Judy handed Paul his birthday cards. Both of the cards, from his mom and dad and his aunt and uncle, had cash inside of them for him to spend on his vacation with Michele. After Paul opened, read, and thanked everyone for his cards, Michele handed him the present she bought. Paul acted like he was surprised as he pulled the t-shirts out of the gift bag.

"Wow!" Judy exclaimed. "Let me see those shirts."

Paul passed the shirts down to his mom. After examining the tags, Judy proclaimed, "Island Dreams. I think we went into that same store. Didn't they have an attached dress shop?"

"As a matter of fact, they did," Michele replied.

"That store was quite expensive and you bought Paul two t-shirts from there!"

Paul spoke up. "They were having a two for one sale; and the first shirt she bought was marked down, half-off."

"We didn't see any signs announcing any sales. Dang. We missed it. And I really liked their merchandise. We might need to go back there before Jim and I leave." Judy looked at Beth for confirmation; Beth nodded her head.

"We didn't see any signs either," Paul declared. "But the lady at the counter checked the tags and told us about the sale." He looked at Michele for validation.

Michele nodded her head, then asked, "Will you have time to go back there.... before you leave?" She thought: *I better contact the store and tell them to give Paul's mom and aunt a discount. They can just bill me the difference.*

"Oh, we'll have plenty of time. We'll just stop there after we drop the both of you off at the ferry tomorrow," Beth professed.

Michele smiled while her brain ran 50 miles a minute debating how she was going to notify the store. *Maybe I can text someone a picture of them together. I just have to figure out how I can get a picture.... I know....* "Can the two of you stand together? I forgot to get a picture of Paul's birthday cake with the two professional cake decorators."

Judy looked at the cake with the missing pieces arranged on dishes – ready to be passed out.

Michele noticed the missing pieces and spoke up. "That's ok. I can take a wide shot to include the pieces you cut out and the two professional bakers. It will be better that way since it shows the type of cake – marble."

Judy and Beth poised for a picture, then started handing out the cake -- saving the biggest piece for the birthday boy. After everyone finished eating their cake, Michele excused herself to go to the bathroom so she could call her Grandma Chloe's dress shop. Sitting on the bathroom's commode, she googled the name of the dress shop. A lady answered the phone on the third ring, "Island Dreams. How can I help you?"

"Hi. My name is Michele. I was in your store yesterday and bought two t-shirts for my boyfriend's birthday. I was wondering…"

The lady cut her off and declared, "Michele! Michele Williams?"

"Well, it's Michele Armstrong, but my father is Macalla Williams."

"Oh, thank heavens you're okay. I was worried about you. I've heard that some of the prince's guards have gone missing."

"Gone missing?" She thought: *Must be why Jayden hasn't returned any of my messages. I hope he's ok.* "Do they have any leads where they might be?"

"The guard that told me said he had a couple of men searching for them and that he also sent the yacht's crew back to the islands to get some backup. Oh, Michele. There is so much uprising on the islands. I don't think it's safe for you and your boyfriend to go."

"Uprising! Why?"

"Because of that rumor, I told you about. People are going crazy. There's been a lot of protesting and some riots. They don't want you or that outsider coming to the islands and exposing them to the world. They fear the two of you will bring war and civil unrest. They fear history will be repeated with the outside world taking over their islands and reenacting the witch trials. The royal family, I mean your grandparents and father, gave a speech yesterday; they tried to assure the people that there was no truth to these vicious rumors, but you know how fear can cloud some people's judgment."

"I'm so sorry that my very existence has led to all this unrest. I will talk with my grandmother, Leewan, tonight. Let her decide what I should do. Maybe I will just go back to America... or meet my grandmother someplace else." Michele thought: *Or maybe I should meet my grandmother on the Island of New Caledonia since that's where Paul thinks she really lives.*

"That might be for the best, my dear. I'm afraid if any harm did come to you, the islands would end up in full-blown civil war."

Michele wiped a tear from her eye. She had finally found her real family, but finding them had turned into a nightmare for everyone involved. *I can't be responsible for the death of innocent people who are acting out of fear.*

"Are you still there Michele."

"Yes. I'm sorry I caused so much trouble. I never wanted any of this. I just wanted to find my true roots – since I was adopted as a baby."

"I know. Maybe someday you can come back to the islands to visit your family without people being afraid of you."

"I hope so…. And before I forget. The reason I called you was to ask if you have a cellphone?"

"Yes. Why?"

"I wanted to ask you a favor. My boyfriend's mom and his aunt are planning on shopping at my grandmother's store tomorrow. I was wondering if you could give them a discount or something. I promise to pay the difference."

The woman laughed, then said, "Any friend of yours is a friend of mine. Just send me their pictures by text, I'll give them a really good deal. And no need to worry about paying the difference. I am sure your grandmother, Queen Chloe, would kill me if I tried to charge you the difference. Besides, this store is part of your inheritance. Your grandmother had me witness the changing of the real estate title."

"She did what? She didn't have to do that!"

"She told me you would probably say that. She also told me she wanted the store in your name since she didn't want her money-hungry daughter-in-law, Princess Lalirra, getting her hands on it."

Michele chuckled softly, then asked, "I never got your name."

"Oh, just call me Elanora."

After getting Elanora's phone number, Michele sent her the picture of Judy and Beth -- then checked her phone for any missed calls from Jayden. *Still no reply.* Maybe I should try to call him? She called his number but it just rang and rang. *Shit! I have no way of contacting anyone on Honiawae Island since the hidden islands are protected by that stupid boundary spell. I'll just have to wait to contact my grandma tonight in my dreams.*

*****

That evening after packing, Michele was sitting next to Paul at the patio table that overlooked the pool -- enjoying the full moon and the soothing song the crickets were singing. After a while of admiring the stars, she turned towards Paul, took his hand, and said, "Last chance to change your mind if you don't want to waste your summer visiting my grandmother. You might get bored!"

"Bored. Never! Not when I'm with you. Why do you keep asking me if I want to go? Are you having second thoughts about taking me?"

"No. No. It' just ... I'm worried about you losing your job..." She blushed slightly and thought: *And your safety.*

Paul squeezed her hand and said, "Life is not about a job. It's about spending time with the people you love... Unless you are having second thoughts. Does it have anything to do with that guy we saw at the airport?"

She took her hand out of his hand and said, "Shit! No. Why would you even think that?"

"Well, you have been acting a little preoccupied lately. You always seem to be looking over your shoulders or checking your cellphone. Have you been calling that guy? Jayden. Wasn't that his name? The guy you said your dad sent to protect you. Protect you from what? Something doesn't seem right."

Paul looked at Michele with suspicious eyes. She grabbed her phone and threw it on the table. "No, I haven't called him. Do you want to check my phone?"

He stared at her phone. After a minute or so, that seemed like an hour, he said, "No. I don't want to check your phone. I trust you. Sorry." He reached for her hand, pulled it to his lips, and gently kissed it. When he looked up at her with sad puppy dog eyes, he asked, "Do you forgive me?"

Michele was starting to sweat but smiled in relief when he said he didn't need to look at her cellphone. Her mind had been racing over a mile a minute, trying to remember if she deleted the history of the last outgoing call to Jayden.

Michele grabbed her cellphone off the table and slipped it back into the pocket of her shorts. "Of course, I forgive. And I guess I might have been preoccupied, wondering why my dad feels he has to have someone follow me. Guess he must be... sort of... overprotective."

"You can say that again. Whose dad sends a security guard to watch over their daughter while their daughter is on vacation?"

"I know. Crazy."

Paul reached for her hand again and asked, "You want to go snuggle on the couch and watch a movie?"

Michele smiled and said, "Sounds good to me."

Chapter 42

After the movie, Michele looked at Paul and said, "We better be getting to bed; we have to get up early to catch the ferry."

"Wish you could sleep here with me on the couch," he said in a husky voice.

"That would be nice." Michele said sarcastically, "I'm sure your mom or dad wouldn't mind. I could go ask them. They have been sitting out there in the dining room, keeping one eye on us all night... And you make fun of my dad for sending a security guard." She laughed and started to get up. Paul pulled her back down, gave her a quick kiss goodnight, then asked, "Did you ever get a chance to call your aunt and uncle?"

"No. I completely forgot. I'll send them a quick test before I go to bed." She started getting up again but Paul pulled her close, looked her in the eyes, and said, "I love you."

"I love you too. Now you better let me go. I think your mom and dad are getting tired." she laughed softly, then got up off the couch.

Paul reached up and smacked her on the butt. "Party pooper."

"Ouch! I'll see you in the morning, you brat."

Michele said her goodnights to Paul's parents and relatives, then made her way to the guest room. After she closed the door, she looked at her cellphone history. *Shit! I didn't delete the last outgoing call to Jayden. Thank God Paul didn't really look at my phone.* She shook her head, deleted the history, then sent a quick text to her aunt and uncle.

After getting ready for bed, Michele walked over to the bedroom window and looked down the street for the black sedan. *Wonder if anyone is going to be watching the house tonight? I don't see any car, but someone is sitting in that van.* Maybe I should try to check with Jayden again. She grabbed her phone and texted his number: *Are some of your guards watching the house in the white van?*

Several minutes after she sent the text, a response finally came back, "Yes. Can you come out here? We need to talk."

Michele got an eerie feeling in the pit of her stomach and thought: *Something isn't right.* After debating what to do, she decided to text back: *Can't come out right now. My grandmother, Leewan, is here. I'm safe for now; however, if it's important, I can ask her if she wants to come outside with me.*

After sending the message, a response returned almost immediately: *No. That's ok. If you are safe there with Leewan, no need for us to talk.*

Michele smiled as she watched the van make a U-turn -- then drove out of sight.
****

Michele closed the bedroom curtains and thought: *Maybe I should sleep with the bedroom lamp on – in case they come back.* She crawled under the covers, looked up at the ceiling, and repeated her grandmother's name three times.

Leewan and Prince Macalla were sitting at the table in the castle's council room. They both stood up when they saw Michele. Michele walked over to her grandmother and gave her a big hug. Then she looked up at her dad and asked, "What happened to Jayden?"

The prince glanced at Leewan then looked back at Michele, "I'm not sure. Your grandmother and I just recently found out about the missing guards. I sent more guards over to search for them and to watch over you."

"You lost Jayden?" Michele looked at her grandmother. "Have you tried to find him in your dreams?"

"I was going too dear, but you contacted us first."

Michele looked back at her dad, "These new guards. Are they driving a white van?"

The prince looked surprised, "A white van. I don't own any white van on the mainland."

The prince looked at Leewan, she looked at Michele and asked, "Is there a white van watching the house right now... while you are sleeping?"

"There was, but I chased them off by saying you were there visiting."

"Good girl." Leewan smiled and began walking around the room. "But they might relay that message back to whoever sent them and find out the truth... that I am still here at the castle. We better send you back with a protection spell -- so you can use it to protect all the occupants in the house."

Michele nodded her head, then continued. "So, I heard the islanders are in an uproar. They think Paul and I plan to expose the hidden islands to the world. Do you think it's a good idea for us to come? Maybe we should just catch a shuttle to the Island of New Caledonia and meet you there? We could stay at a hotel or something. Say your house is getting remodeled.... or something like that."

"Oh, nonsense! No one scares me or my granddaughter away. The prince, I mean your father and I did make some changes to the plan. We're sending a private yacht to bring the two of you to the island -- and your dad and I plan on being on it. Just walk up to the ferry's boarding dock as planned. Some of your dad's guards, wearing gold pins with a capital "W" on their shirt collars, will meet you on the docks so they can escort both of you to the yacht."

Michele nodded her head in understanding.

"Follow me, Michele. We need to find a rock to put under your pillow."

Michele and the prince, followed Leewan out into the streets, then over to the guest house. As the group approached the house, the wrought iron gates magically unlocked and opened inward, welcoming the group in. As the group passed through the gates, Michele looked up at the palm trees that were illuminated by the street lights; they were blowing gently in the wind and she thought she heard them echoing: *Welcome home, Michele.* As the group walked towards the house, Michele glanced up at the three-story house sitting silently in the dark. From the distance, she could make out the front porch swing swaying back and forth, as if a person was sitting on it -- waiting for them. Michele looked up at the glass cupola that sat on top of the house. She remembered her time alone with Paul there, enjoying the view of the surrounding village. While skimming the windows with her eyes, she stopped, startled. "There's someone up there watching us."

Leewan stopped dead in her tracks. She looked up to the glass cupola, where Michele was pointing. "I don't see anyone."

"I swear I saw someone."

Leewan laughed softly. "I believe you. Rumor has it, my great, great, great, grandmother, Martha, still roams the halls of this house along with her daughter, Sasha." Leewan walked up to the large front porch with pillars. Once there, she knelt and started digging in the flower garden.

"What are you looking for?" Michele asked.

The prince put his arm around her shoulders and said, "She's looking for a rock so she can put a protection spell on it."

"Here!" Leewan held up a sparkling, white-washed stone. "This will work."

Michele saw the glitter of the rock and remembered her last dream about her mom. "That reminds me, grams. I sort of took one of my mom's rocks from her collection home with me. And I think I found a way to find her."

Leewan jumped up. "You did?"

Michele hung her head and said, "I know. I shouldn't have taken it from her bedroom. But it was only one rock. I didn't think you would miss it."

"I'm not worried about that. Maybe it was for the best that you took something that belonged to your mother; now we might be able to find her... But first things first. I need to put a spell on this stone so you can put it under your pillow. It will protect all the occupants in the house. No one will be able to enter or touch the house within a 20-foot perimeter."

Leewan held the stone up to the full-moon and chanted a spell in a foreign language. The stone began to glow for a minute or two, then faded away. She handed the stone to Michele and said, "You better get going, before those thugs show up again. Your dad and I will see you in the morning at the yacht."

"What about Jayden?"

"I will try to contact him after you leave. Those gold pins are linked to me. It shouldn't be a problem -- as long as he still has his pin on." Leewan and the prince began to fade. Prince Macalla said, "Can't wait to see you in person tomorrow."

*****

Unbeknownst to Michele, the rock under her pillow started to glow when a witch and a warlock from the hidden islands tried to sneak up to the house around 2 a.m. The witch and the warlock had told the occupants in the van that they were sick and tired of sitting around, waiting for a chance to capture Michele and Paul. They had already captured and tortured Jayden and his guards, then left them tied up at an abandoned house after all their harrowing came up empty-handed; the guards just denied knowing anything about Michele's and Paul's plans to expose or take over the islands.

When the witch and warlock were within twenty feet of the house, an invisible forcefield threw them back a good 25 to 30 feet. Both the witch and warlock stared at each other in disbelief. The witch stood back up and approach the house slowly -- with her hand out. When she reached the perimeter of the house, her fingertips felt a slight jolt of electricity. She jerked her hand back, kissed her fingertips, then looked at the warlock and said, "Shit! We don't know what we are dealing with. I not going to give my life trying to figure out if the rumors are true. I guess we will just have to deal with the truth if it comes to that point. Besides, I've been thinking, why would Leewan's granddaughter want to expose the islands when she is a witch herself. Maybe these rumors are just that -- rumors to get support to prevent Michele from inheriting the kingdom."

"I never thought about it that way. But you could be right. The Taylors from Keelonie Island have a lot to lose if Michele claims her rights to the throne. Guess I'm out of here too."

Chapter 43

Michele woke up to the sunlight shining through the bedroom window. She stretched her arms above her head, feeling refreshed. Glancing at the clock, she thought: *I better get dress so we can make it to the docks on time. Hope grams found Jayden and his men.*

After dressing, Michele walked down to the kitchen dragging all her luggage behind her. When she walked into the kitchen, she found everyone sitting around the table – eating breakfast. Paul stood up and kissed her on her cheek. "Good morning, beautiful." He glanced at his watch. "I was just getting ready to come pound on your door. We have to leave soon."

She blushed then said, "Sorry. I slept in. But I'm ready to go now."

Beth looked at her, "Don't you want something to eat?"

"No. Thank you. I'll just take a water bottle from the refrigerator and a couple of pieces of that bacon."

Judy stood up, kissed Jim on the cheek, then said, "I'm ready. Let's get going, Beth. After we see these two off, we can do some shopping."

Paul hugged his dad goodbye then turned to grab Michele's suitcases. "Thanks for having us, Uncle George."

"No problem. Anytime. Hope the two of you have a nice trip; and… if you guys need anything, give Beth or me a call."

"We will. Thank you," Michele replied.

*****

While Michele helped Paul load the car, she looked around the neighborhood and thought: *Good. It doesn't look like the white van ever returned.* After everything was loaded, Beth pulled out of the drive and started down the road. Michele watched as a dark color car started following them in the distance and thought: *That must be the new guards my dad sent over.* She continued watching out the window on their drive to the boat docks admiring all the rivers, marshlands, and the mountain tops that she could see in the distance.

As the car approached the city limits, Michele looked down at Paul's hand, holding hers, and started worrying about his safety. *Would the mob from the island try to hurt him?* She released his hand and dug through her purse. After she found a hair tie, she knotted her hair up in a messy bun then dug through her purse to find her sunglasses. Looking at Paul, she asked, "Do you have an extra ballcap?"

He grabbed his shoulder bag and said, "Yes. Why do you want a ballcap?"

"Oh, no reason. I just remembered the last time we rode the ferry. A lot of people stared at us since we're outsiders. Maybe if I wear a ballcap they will not notice that we are Americans."

Paul nodded his head and handed her the ballcap. She thought: *Hopefully my dad's security guards will recognize me.* Then she turned in her seat and saw the dark-colored car following in the distance. *If they watch me exit this car, they should know my disguise.*

*****

The boat docks were busy at eight in the morning. Judy and Beth walked with Michele and Paul up to the ticket booth. Judy hugged Michele and said, "Have a good trip."

"We will. Thank you."

Then Judy turned towards Paul and hugged him. "Text me when you get to Michele's grandmother's house. I want to make sure the two of you get there in one piece."

Michele's mind started racing. She knew cellphones didn't work on the hidden islands. *What should I tell Paul's mom so she won't worry?* She looked at her and told another white lie, "It might be a few days before Paul can text you. The cellphone service is awful in the secluded part of the island where my grandmother lives."

"Oh," Judy replied then looked at Paul. "Then just text me whenever you get the chance."

Beth pointed at the Island of New Caledonia Ferry Boat, "Is that the boat the two of you are taking?"

"No. My grandmother called me late last night. My dad and grandmother had a change of plans. Instead of us taking the public ferry-boat over to the island, my dad and grandmother are picking us up on a private yacht."

Paul looked at Michele in surprise and asked, "And when were you planning on telling me about this change?"

She blushed, then replied, "I wanted you to be surprised. Surprise! We're riding in style to my grandmother's island."

He looked around and said, "Well... Where's the yacht?"

Michele looked around and said, "I truthfully don't know. I was just told to come here, to the docks, and some of my dad's crew members would come and find us."

"How exciting," Beth proclaimed.

"Can we board your dad's yacht? I would love to see it," Judy professed.

Michele started nervously biting her fingernails and looking around – silently kicking herself in the butt. *What did I just do? I just told Judy and Beth about the yacht ride since I didn't want to lie to them again!* Michele knew the original plan was to pretend/lie that they were riding the ferry boat to the Island of New Caledonia when actually, they were riding on a large boat that was disguised as an industrial-size fishing boat. The fishing boat was built by the kingdom to serve a dual purpose: It exported and imported goods for the people of the hidden islands and it served as a form of public transportation for the residents. Now that the cat was out of the bag, Beth and Judy wanted to see the yacht, potentially putting themselves in danger.

"What's wrong?" Paul asked.

"Nothing!" she half-shouted. "I mean. I just don't see any of the crew members."

Paul grabbed her hand and said, "It's ok. We'll find them. Let's start walking down the street and look at all the boats. Maybe you'll recognize someone?"

Judy patted her on the shoulder, in a motherly sort-of-way. "Yes, Michele. We'll find them. Maybe they're just running late. Can you call them?"

Michele started shaking her head, then said, "Let's just walk down the street and look first."

The group started walking down the street, away from the fishing boat that provided passage to the hidden islands. As they walked, Michele noticed a lot of people standing in different locations, looking around. She thought: *I wonder if any of those people are searching for me? They might be from the uprising group and want to stop us from returning to the hidden islands. Glad I wore my hair up under this hat.*

As the group approached a private yacht club's entrance, Michele noticed a hint of gold reflecting off a man's collar in the bright sunlight. The man seemed to be in deep conversation with a couple of other men. All the men were wearing white uniforms with blue stripes on their shoulders. The man whose gold pin was shining in the sunlight had a captain's hat on. Michele pulled Paul to a stop. "Wait here with your mom and aunt. I think I recognize that man's outfit." Paul started to object, but Michele made a beeline through the crowded street to the man standing near the entrance. As she approached the man, he quit talking and looked at her. She stood in front of him, staring at his gold pin to see if it had a "W" on it.

One of the men looked at her outfit (an old, worn-out t-shirt, long, baggy, boy-shorts, and a ballcap) and mistakenly thought she was a scrounger. "Move along son. We're not offering any handouts here." The man reached to escort her away just as she spotted the "W" on the pin. "Wait! I just want to know if you guys know where Leewan Johnson's boat is?

The man with the captain's hat on said, "No. Never heard of her."

"Where did you get that pin?"

The captain glanced at his pin then back at her. "From my job. What's it to you?"

"My father gives all his employees a pin like that. The "W" stands for his last name."

The men looked at each other in confusion, then back to her. The captain asked, "What's your name son?"

"Michele."

The men stared at her in disbelief for a couple of seconds until the captain finally spoke up and said, "Well. What are you waiting for men? Help the young lady board."

The other two men bowed their heads slightly to Michele and asked, "Do you have any luggage?"

She pointed at Paul standing by all their luggage. "Over there with my boyfriend. I also want to bring his mom and aunt on the yacht so they can see the boat."

"I'll have to check with the prin...my boss." The captain grabbed his two-way radio that was hanging from his belt.

"Tell my dad... I insist!"

The captain glanced at her -- then nodded while making contact with the yacht.

The other two men came back up to the club's entrance carrying Michele's luggage while Paul, along with his mom and Aunt Beth, following close behind. Judy stopped by Michele and said, "Those crew members said we are not allowed on the yacht."

Michele looked at the captain who was just clipping his two-way radio back on his belt. The captain took off his hat and bowed slightly to the women. "I'm sorry for their mistake. They didn't realize who you were." The captain looked at the other two men and said with a wink, "Take our guest to the yacht. Leewan and Michele's dad is waiting for them."

One of the crewmembers nodded, then said, "Follow us, please."

Chapter 44

Leewan and Prince Macalla were waiting on the main floor of the yacht as the group climbed the entrance ramp. Leewan waved the crewmembers aside and whispered, "Take the luggage inside and remember, the prince is not a prince in front of these guests." After the crewmember left, she turned her attention to

Michele and gave her a big hug. "You made it. Love the outfit! Now, introduce me to your guest."

"This is my grandmother, Leewan Johnson. Grams meet Paul's mom, Judy, and his Aunt Beth."

"Welcome aboard!" Leewan reached out to shake their hands then turned towards the prince. "This is Macalla Williams, Michele's dad."

Macalla bowed slightly and said, "Welcome aboard, ladies."

Both Judy and Beth blushed at the sight of him since Michele's dad was a looker – tall, blonde, with blue eyes, and a tanned, muscular body that stretched the limits of his white uniform. After a moment of awkward silence, Judy stammered, "Thank... Thank... you. For inviting Paul over for a visit. And you didn't have to pay for his ticket."

"It was my pleasure." Macalla bowed again, then asked Leewan "Would you like to show the ladies around."

Leewan smiled and said, "This way, please."

Paul started to follow Michele and the group, but Macalla pulled him back, put his arm around his shoulders, and said, "Welcome aboard son." He squeezed Paul's shoulder a couple of times then whispered in a low voice, "If you are going to date my daughter, we need to set down some ground rules... We'll talk – later." Macalla smiled, condescendingly down at him, then left to follow the ladies.

When Michele noticed Paul wasn't with the group, she stopped and turned around. She watched as her dad passed by with a wink, then looked at Paul's sunken face and asked, "What did my dad say to you?"

"He said if I was going to date you, we needed to talk about some ground rules."

Michele's jaw dropped, then she said, "I'm so sorry. My dad can be a little overprotective."

"That's alright. If you were my daughter. I think I would be a little overprotective too."

Michele smiled, grabbed his hand, then pulled him in the direction of the tour.

Beth was in awe at the size of the yacht. "Wow. My husband designs yachts for a living; I wonder if he had a hand in designing this one? With all the emendates this yacht has to offer, this yacht is fit for a king."

Macalla chuckled and winked at Michele.

After the short, mini-tour, the group returned to the main deck. Beth looked around at all the men positioned around the boat. "You sure do have a lot of crewmembers, Mr. Williams. You must use this boat a lot."

Macalla cleared his throat, then said, "The boat belongs to my dad. And he does do a lot of traveling, from island to island."

"Well, we better get going!" Leewan interjected. "Sorry ladies, I'm going to have to ask you to leave. We have a lot of things planned for this evening. And Judy, don't worry about your son. I will personally take great care of him -- as if he was one of my own. And when he is ready to go home, either Macalla or I will personally escort him back to the airport."

Judy smiled and said, "Thank you. That's very reassuring. It was very nice meeting the both of you."

A couple of the crewmembers assisted the ladies off the boat. The captain of the yacht, tooted the horn -- signally the crewmembers to prepare for departure. As the boat backed away from the docks, Judy and Beth waved goodbye.

When the boat started heading out to sea, Leewan put her arms around Paul and Michele and said, "Come on inside now. We've planned a surprise for the two of you." She winked at Michele. Michele nodded her head in understanding – Leewan wanted the two of them out of view of any suspicious onlookers.

*****

Leewan led Michele and Paul into the main dining room. Once inside, Michele removed her glasses, ballcap, and messy buns. Running her fingers through her long blonde hair she said, "That feels better. Those ballcaps are hot." She looked around the room. She noticed that the room was surrounded by large, tinted windows. Looking at her grandmother, she asked, "Is it safe for me to remove my disguise?"

"Yes, the windows are bulletproof and are like a two-way mirror -- the occupants in this room can see out, but anyone from the outside cannot see in."

Paul looked confused and asked, "I don't understand. Why do you need a disguise?"

'Umm. Umm." She looked a Leewan for help.

"Oh, nothing really. Michele's dad is just over-cautious. What Michele probably hasn't told you, is that her dad comes from money. I think he watches too many movies. He's worried about Michele being kidnapped and held for ransom or something worse." She winked at the prince; the prince cleared his throat, then replied, "Well, better safe than sorry."

Paul nodded his head and gave Michele a meaningful look.

Leewan clapped her hands and said, "Have a seat while I go get the surprise." After Michele, Macalla, and Paul were seated, Leewan disappeared through a servant's door. When she reappeared, she was followed by servants carrying an assortment of fruits, finger foods, and desserts. Another servant walked around the table and offered the guest a choice of coffee or fresh pineapple juice. Michele grabbed a fresh banana off a tray, but before she had a chance to start peeling it, her grandmother walked up behind her and whispered in her ear, "Come with me."

Michele looked at Paul and said, "I'll be right back." He started to object, feeling nervous about being left alone with her dad, but Michele was up and halfway out of the room before he had a chance. Paul turned his head and looked at Michele's dad. Macalla smiled….

Michele followed Leewan down the stairs to a room that said "private office". When Leewan opened the door, Michele saw Jayden lying on a couch and the other two guards, that had been following her, were sitting at a table, eating breakfast. Jayden looked like a train wreck. From what she could see in the dim light from the portholes, he had a bandage wrapped around his head, multiple cuts on his face, and two black eyes. She started walking towards the couch but Leewan grabbed her hand and said, "Let him sleep for now. I need your help."

The guards that were eating at the table nodded at the two women -- in acknowledgment. Michele noticed scratches and bruises on both of the guards' faces similar to Jayden's. *They must have been tortured... because of me!*

Leewan led Michele to another unoccupied table near the back of the room. After Michele took a seat, Leewan walked over to a wall safe. Michele looked around the room and saw multiple monitors mounted on the walls. Some of the monitors showed live feeds from various security cameras located around the yacht; other monitors showed the depth of the water and shadows of fish swimming under the boat. A desk with large computer screens was located adjacent to her chair. Leewan returned to the table with a large, black handbag that contained six candles and an old book. Michele looked at the old book's purple velvet cover. The front of the book had gold and red swills on it, but the sides had two spines. "How do we open the book if it has two spines?"

Leewan smiled, then said, "Give me your hand." She placed Michele's hand on the front of the book; Michele could feel a tingling in her hand. "Now just tell the book to open to a spell on making an object invisible." Michele did what her grandmother told her to do and the book plopped open to an invisibility spell.

"We're going to use this spell to make the yacht invisible – that way, if anyone is following us, it will seem like the boat just disappeared." Leewan looked up at all the monitors on the screens to ensure no other boats were around then told Michele. "First, we make sure we have all the ingredients."

Michele read the list of ingredients out loud: "Six candles and a personal item from the subject or object." She looked questioning at Leewan and asked, "What are we going to use for a personal item?"

"We need something from the boat itself, so... maybe a piece of the flooring or a chip of old paint from a wall." Leewan reached into her black bag and pulled out a knife.

"What are you going to do with that?"

Leewan looked at the knife and chuckled, "What do you think?"

Michele's eyes got big as she thought: *I'm not cutting my palm open like they do in the movies.*

"I'm just going to use it to cut a small piece of the carpet. Maybe we should cut a piece out in a corner -- so it's not noticeable." Leewan walked to the corner of the room. When she returned, she had a small piece of carpet in her hand. "This should do. Now you light the candles."

Michele looked at her grandmother puzzled, "I don't have any matches."

Leewan shook her head, "We have some work to do this summer. Haven't you ever tried to light a candle?"

"No. Can I do that?"

"Not sure if you have developed all your powers yet, but if you have the power of telekinesis, you should have the power to light fires."

"Oh. How do I do that?"

"Just concentrate on lighting the candles while holding your hands out towards them."

Michele tried to light the candles without success.

Leewan said, "I'll start them, we don't have time to practice today." She flipped her wrist and all six of the candles burst to life. "Now, scoot your chair over here next to me and hold onto one end of this carpet while I hold the other."

Michele moved her seat closer to Leewan and held onto the carpet as instructed. Leewan looked at her and said, "Now we'll read the spell together." After they read the incantation, the candle flames flickered twice then rose a good three-inches high before smoldering out.

"Is it done?" Michele asked.

"Yes."

Michele looked over at Jayden. "Is he going to be alright?"

"Yes. He just needs to rest."

"So, I don't need to try my new healing powers on him?"

Leewan thought about it for a minute, then said, "Why not. It wouldn't hurt him to recuperate faster."

"Where did you find him?"

"I was able to track the two guards that were with him to an abandoned house. Your dad sent a team of men over there, along with a warlock, to rescue them; but for some reason, the abductors had fled the scene -- leaving Jayden and his men tied up."

"I'm glad you found them."

"What about the group of people you saw in the white van -- that were watching Paul's aunt's and uncle's house? Did they give you any trouble?"

"No. Just like the abandoned house, the people in the van fled the scene."

"Hmm. Hopefully, that means the people in the uprising group are starting to question that stupid rumor about you and Paul exposing the islands."

Michele dragged one of the chairs over to the couch where Jayden was lying. While the two guards at the other table watched, Michele laid both of her hands-on Jayden's swollen wrists. *These cutmarks must be from the zip-ties they used to tie him up.* As she covered the wounds with her hands, she felt her hands start to tingle and warm up. Within seconds, Jayden began to open his eyes. When Michele removed her hands, she noticed the cutmarks and bruises on his wrists and face had healed. Jayden sat up with a jolt. He looked around the room hysterically and said, "Where am I?"

"It's okay Jayden. Your safe here with us. On King Levi's yacht," Leewan replied.

The two men that were sitting at the table, jumped out of their chairs, and rushed over to the couch. "Thank God you're okay," said one of the men. "Michele just healed you! We witnessed it."

Jayden stared at Michele, then said, "Thank you! Guess I forgive you for ditching us the other day."

She blushed, then said, "I wouldn't let you take the rap for me ditching you. I was going to admit to my part of that deception to my father if he said anything to you."

"I appreciate that. Is there anything I can do for you?"

"Stay out of sight for a while. I think Paul is jealous of you. He thinks you like me or something like that," she laughed.

"Well, I'm not going to say Paul's instincts are wrong." He reached for her forearm and started caressing it.

Michele looked down at her arm and noticed the tingling his touch made on her skin. Looking up into his eyes she realized, she was instinctively drawn to Jayden -- with his tan, masculine body, strong jawline, tussled light-brown hair, and caring composure. She jerked her arm away from him, with a flash of guilt -- like she cheated on Paul with her mind. "Just do me a favor…. and stay out of sight for a while."

"Anything for you, princess," he said in a husky voice while staring at her with his baby-blue eyes.

Michele stood up and started walking towards the door, she glanced once on her way out of the room at the sexy male sitting on the edge of the couch. *Shit! I better stay away from him. Something about him makes me want to run to him and have him wrap me up in those big strong arms.*

Chapter 45

After Leewan and Michele walked out into the hall, Leewan closed the door quietly and said, "We need to tell Paul the truth about you before we get to the island of Honiawae -- in case we run into trouble with any of the protestors."

"What if he doesn't take it well?"

"I brought the mind-erasing witch with me and your father wants to be present during the conversation -- so he'll know if Paul knows the truth or not."

She nodded her head in understanding, then thought: *The final moment has arrived. Will Paul accept me for who I am or will I have to continue to live a lie to be with him. Did I make a mistake by bringing him to the islands, believing love could conquer all?*

When they returned to the main dining room, Paul looked at them with relief. Michele looked around the room and noticed Paul was alone in the room with her father and the dark-haired, mind-erasing witch that she met on their last trip to the islands. *I hope they didn't interrogate him too badly.* She took a seat next to Paul; he immediately reached for her hand under the table. When he squeezed her hand tight, she knew things had been bad since his hand was perspiring. She looked at him, gave him a little smile, and thought: *I'm so sorry Paul. Things are only going to get worse.*

Prince Macalla looked a Leewan as she took a seat across from Michele, next to the mind-erasing witch. Leewan nodded at the prince and said, "It is done. We are all set."

The prince smiled then turned his attention to Michele. "So glad you are back. Paul was just telling us his true intentions for dating you."

Her jaw dropped. She glared at her father and asked, "So, what did he tell you?"

"All good I assure you... I guess he passes my scrutiny... for the time being." Macalla nodded his head at Leewan. Michele shook her head and squeezed Paul's hand.

Leewan cleared her voice, then asked Michele, "So, do you want to tell Paul the truth or should I?"

Paul looked at Michele in surprise. Michele said, "I'll start... Paul. You know I love you. But I have to come clean-- about my family." Paul took a deep breath, relieved the secret was about her family, but he wondered: *How bad could her family be? Maybe they're part of the mafia!* Michele continued, "My family comes from a long line of witches." She paused to gauge his reaction. When the news didn't seem to faze him, she continued, "You know about my prophetic dreams, but I also have the power to communicate with others in my sleep, I have the power of telekinesis, and I have the power to heal."

Paul stared at her trying to comprehend what she just told him. When he finally spoke up, he said, "So, you can also move things with your mind and have psionic healing powers- like Pokémon?"

Michele nodded, "Yes. Watch." She pointed her finger at a bowl of fruit, then with a flick of her finger, she moved the bowl down the table."

Paul flinched, then said, "Wow. Pretty neat." Then Paul looked around the table and asked, "So does everyone around this table possess the same powers?"

Leewan spoke up, "No Paul. Sometimes the gift of magic skips a generation. Michele's dad, for instance, does not possess any magic, and some witches possess different powers. Like

Diane here, she possesses the ability to erase memories."

Paul felt relieved when he heard the news about Michele's dad. Then he looked at Michele, "Is that all. I thought you were going to tell me your family was part of the mafia or something like that."

She laughed then said, "No. Nothing like that. But my dad and his parents are the rulers of seven islands, which puts me in line to inherit a kingdom."

Paul's mouth hung open, then he laughed, "Yeah right. Now you're making up stories. There is no kingdom on New Caledonia Island."

"No Paul. I am telling you the truth. We are not going to New Caledonia Island. We are going to the Hidden Islands of Honiawae. The Hidden Islands of Honiawae consists of seven islands located in the middle of the Pacific Ocean. The islands were founded by our distant relatives back in the times of the witch trials when multiple families had to flee for their lives."

Paul shook his head, trying to comprehend all the information. After a moment of silence, he looked at her and asked, "If there are hidden islands with a kingdom, why don't I remember any of this from our last trip to your grandmother?"

Michele pointed at Diane. "She replaced your memories."

Paul looked upset. "What else don't I remember?"

Leewan reached for Paul's hands across the table. With a motherly voice she said, "If you want, Diane can return all your memories of your last visit. But I need to warn you, if... the memories are too much to handle, we might have to take them all back. The location of the islands cannot be exposed. Michele wants you to have your memories back since she believes you are capable of keeping our secret and she wants an open, truthful relationship with you."

Paul glanced at Michele then back at Leewan, "Do it!"

Diane looked at the prince, the prince nodded. She put her hands out on the table, looked at Paul, and said, "Give me your hands." After reciting an incantation in Latin, she released his hands. Paul sat silently staring off into space for a couple of minutes, then he dropped his head down into his hands.

Michele looked at Leewan. Leewan shrugged her shoulders.

After a couple of minutes, that seemed like a lifetime, Paul finally lifted his head and looked at Diane, "Are these memories the truth?" She nodded. He turned his head and looked at Michele's dad. "So, you are Prince Macalla Williams. Your parents are King Levi Williams and the queen, Chloe Williams. You live in a castle and are married to a woman named Lalirra Taylor. You and Lalirra have a daughter named Amarina – that is two years younger than Michele." The prince nodded. Paul turned his attention to Leewan. "Your daughter is Mayra, who is Michele's birth mom. Mayra disappeared before Michele was ever born, but you believe she's still alive, somewhere. You work with Prince Macalla, leading the king's army. I also remember you using magic to get information on your daughter's disappearance from one of Lalirra's parents' spies."

Leewan nodded, then asked, "And how do you feel about all the information?"

Paul looked around the table -- thinking more about his last trip to the island of Honiawae. When his eyes landed on Diane, he shouted, "I'm outraged!" Paul slammed his fist down on the table. Michele jumped back into her seat, surprised by his act of aggression. Paul started shaking his finger at Diane in rage as he went on a rampage, "How dare you take my memories away. You had no right to mess with my head! Why did you take my memories of the time I spent with Michele... or the time I spent with her family? Why did you do that?"

Paul started to stand up and knocked his chair over backward. The chair landed with a loud crash. He marched around the table, his face red with anger directed at Diane. Diane held her hand up, ready to use her magic to subdue Paul. She glanced at Leewan for reassurance while Paul homed in on her. Leewan shook her head while Michele started screaming, "Don't hurt him."

Paul stopped inches from Diane's upheld hand, "Do it! Do it! I don't care what you do to me. All I know is.... no-one has the right to meddle with Michele's and my relationship!" He shoved her upheld hand aside. She squinted her eyes and had that look (if looks could kill). Paul bent down closer to her face and shouted, "So, tell me. Why did..."

Michele jumped out of her seat and screamed, "Stop it! Now!" Paul stood frozen in time, pointing his finger in Diane's face, mouth wide open. Diane sat frozen in time with hatred in her eyes and her pointer finger curled in an awkward position.

Macalla stood up and started clapping his hands, "Well played. Well played. Paul has my blessings to marry you!"

Michele looked at her dad in disbelief with her mouth hanging open. Leewan smiled and walked around the table to Michele. Putting one arm around her, she pointed at the now frozen Paul and Diane. "Well done my dear. I was just getting ready to throw both of them to the floor. But I like this better. I didn't know you could freeze matter. You must be the chosen one."

"Chosen for what?"

Leewan patted Michele's back and said, "I'll tell you about that story at a later date. For now, let's try to find a solution to this problem."

Michele looked at Paul and Diane, "I'm sorry I froze them. I just couldn't stand to hear them fighting. One of them was going to get hurt, and more than likely, it would have been Paul."

"Yes, dear. You did the right thing. But did you hear what Paul said? He wasn't upset about you being a witch or the daughter of a prince; he was upset at Diane -- for erasing his memories of the time he had spent with you."

"So, what do we do now?" Michele pointed her outstretched arm at Paul and Diane.

"We reposition them both -- out of harm's way, then you can bring them back to real-time."

"Where should we put them?"

"Let's put Diane over in that chair facing the window. Macalla, can you carry Diane over there than open the window?"

"Sure thing," he replied as he walked over to pick Diane up.

Michele looked at Paul and asked Leewan, "What do we do with Paul?"

"Help me slide one of those cushioned chairs in front of him, in case he falls over, face first."

After rearranging the scenario, Michele looked at Leewan, "Are we ready."

"I think so. Go ahead and unfreeze them."

"Go!"

Paul jerked forward and fell headfirst into the chair. Standing up instantly, he said, "What the hell." He looked around the room in confusion. "What happened?"

Leewan smiled, "Michele froze both of you to prevent either of you from getting hurt."

Paul looked over to Diane, still frozen in time. "Good. Leave her that way. I don't trust her."

Michele looked at Paul, "I can't do that to her." Then she asked Leewan, "Why didn't Diane come back?"

"Did you really want her too?"

Michele hung her head down and said, "No."

Paul interjected, "I know. Maybe I'll just go downstairs to the main deck and wait for you. You can wake Diane up after I leave."

Michele smiled and looked at Leewan and Macalla. "Is there anywhere Paul and I can go to be alone so we can talk things out -- after I bring Diane back?"

Macalla looked down and grumbled, "Alone."

Leewan laughed and said to him, "I left you and Mayra alone at their age."

He looked up and said, "And your point?"

"They are young and in love. We need to trust them at some point to make the right decisions."

"But you know what happened to Mayra."

"I know. And I wouldn't trade having a granddaughter for the world."

Macalla shuffled his feet, looked at Michele, then said, "If you go down to the bottom deck, the two of you can TALK in the first guest room on the right."

Michele smiled and said, "Thanks, dad!" Then she looked at Paul and told him, "I'll meet you down there after I figure out how to wake Diane up."

Paul left the room, Michele looked at Leewan and asked, "Any suggestions?"

"You woke Paul when you truly wanted something and said it with emotion. You have to really want to wake Diane and say it with emotion."

Michele looked at Diane, sitting in an awkward position in the chair. "She does look uncomfortable and she only did what the king and queen wanted her to do, for the protection of the islands... Maybe... Diane, you can wake up now."

Diane's finger went straight and a bolt of light shot out of her finger. Michele watched as the bolt of light shot straight out the window, into the sky, then disappeared. Diane looked around the room and asked, "What happened?"

Leewan put her arm around Michele and bragged, "My granddaughter diffused the situation. Everything going to be alright."

Diane looked at Michele and nodded her head in appreciation. Michele blushed slightly, then said, "I better go talk to Paul. See where we stand!"

Chapter 46

Michele walked into the guest room. Paul was sitting at a desk, writing something down on a sheet of paper. When Paul heard her coming, he wrinkled up the sheet of paper.

"What are you writing?" Michele asked.

"Oh, nothing. Just a list of the advantages and disadvantages of dating a witch."

"And."

"The advantages surely outweigh the disadvantages, but I'm not sure how I would ever tell my parents."

Michele laughed softly then said, "I don't think we can ever tell them the truth." She grabbed a chair and pulled it up to the desk. "I have to tell you why Diane erased your memories. It has to do with the protection of the Hidden Islands of Honiawae." After she explained how the king, her grandfather, had instructed Diane to erase all the visitor's memories, why the brainwashing didn't work on her, and the current uprising of the islands, she waited for him to respond. When he didn't respond, she asked, "Do you want to update your list?"

He looked at the wrinkled-up sheet of paper and shook his head no.

Michele reached for his hand, then said with a tear in her voice, "I know this is a lot to ask of you… So, if you want. I can tell my grandmother to turn the yacht around. We can take you back to Yeppoon so you can call your parents. You could tell them we got in a big fight and broke up – if that's what you want?"

"Is that what you want?"

"No!" After a moment of silence, Michele continued, "If you don't want to go to the Honiawae with me, because of the uprising, maybe I can get my grandmother and dad to take us to the Island of New Caledonia for a week. After a week, we can take you back to the plane, tell your parents you had a change of heart, and wanted to go back to work?"

"No. I want to stay all summer with you." He reached up and softly stroked the side of her face with his thumb. "Those island people don't scare me. Plus, after what I saw. I know you can protect me…" He chuckled softly.

*****

After a while of sitting in silence, holding each other's hands, the couple moved to the bed to relax in each other's arms. Michele must have drifted off to sleep at some point since the next thing she knew someone was knocking on their door. "Come in." Michele sat up on the side of the bed while Leewan walked into the room.

"We'll be docking on the island soon. I need you to help me take the invisibility spell off the yacht."

Michele stood up and looked at Paul. "I'll see you in a few. You want to meet me upstairs in the dining room?"

"Why can't I come with you? I would love to see you and your grandmother in action."

Michele looked at Leewan and remembered Jayden. Seeing the look on Michele's face, Leewan realized Michele didn't want Paul to see the guards. Looking at Paul, Leewan interjected, "We need to be alone for this spell to work. Maybe next time."

Paul looked at Michele and said, "I'll just wait here if you don't mind. Not sure if I'm ready to face your dad and Diane on my own."

Michele smiled and said, "Okay. I'll be back shortly."

*****

When Michele walked into the room, Jayden and the two guards were playing cards at one of the round tables. Jayden jumped up when he saw her and Leewan walk into the room. "Is everything okay?"

"Yes. Yes," Leewan replied. "Just continue what you were doing. Michele and I just need to remove the invisibility spell."

Jayden walked up to Michele and grabbed her hand. Michele looked down at their joined hands as she felt a spark, then a tingle -- crawl up her arm.

"I never got a chance to properly thank you for healing my wounds. I'm forever in your debt." He lifted her hand to his lips and kissed it softly.

Michele blushed and stared at her hand.

Leewan looked at their joined hands and wondered: *Maybe Paul isn't the one that is fated for Michele?*

Jayden grabbed Michele's other hand and began to laugh… "I have to tell you what one of the crew members told us. We," Jayden looked at the other guards, "laughed our heads off for hours."

Michele looked at the other guards, laughing at the mention of the incident.

"What's so funny," Michele asked, half laughing with their contagious laughter.

"Well, the crewmember felt so bad. He said he was looking for a beautiful princess with long blonde hair. But…" Jayden laughed and hit his thigh with his hand, "…. he said when you walked up, he mistook you for a boy vagabond and told you to be on your way." The guards all started rolling in laughter.

Michele laughed too remembering the incident at the docks. In between laughs, she blurted out, "I need to find that guy and talk with him. That poor guy. He had no idea I had disguised myself to look like a boy."

After a minute of two of more laughter, Leewan interjected, "Michele, I need your help now."

"Yes. I'm ready." She reluctantly walked away from Jayden, smiling at him over her shoulder as she walked.

After the spell was removed from the yacht, Michele followed Leewan from the room. Jayden called to her as she left the room, "Until we meet again my fair princess… So glad you'll be staying at the castle."

When Leewan closed the door, Michele asked, "We're not staying at your house on the island?"

"No. I thought I told you. I have been staying at the guest house next to the castle. There is just too much turmoil going on right now. It's safer inside the castle's walls."

Chapter 47

Michele, Paul, and Leewan watched out the captain's window as the yacht approached the Hidden Islands of Honiawae. Leewan readied herself for war if anyone tried to hurt her granddaughter. Macalla paced around the captain's room, getting an update from his mother, Queen Chloe, on his island cellphone.

As Paul stared at the islands, he mumbled, "I know I said it last November when we came here, but the islands sure do remind me of the pictures that I've seen of Hawaiian Islands."

The captain chuckled, "You tourist. You think every tropical island with mountains and palm trees look like Hawaii. The Hidden Islands of Honiawae are in the Pacific Ocean, but they are more than 3,000 miles away from Hawaii. Sort of the halfway point between Queensland and Hawaii, if you drew a V line."

Paul just stared out the window and said, "The islands sure do look beautiful from here."

Michele smiled, squeezed his hand, then thought: *Maybe one day-- we might considerate this our home.*

After Macalla got off the phone, he approached the group with his arms wide open, like an eagle spreading its wings, to engulf the entire group in a large, friendly, bear hug. "My mother had good news to share! She told me, for some reason, the uprising has died down. Most of the witches and warlocks have returned to their homes and refuse to support the peaceful protesters. She also told me that we shouldn't have any problems exiting the yacht or in making our way to the castle in the waiting, horse-drawn carriages."

Leewan felt relieved and replied, "Excellent news! Will the queen be meeting us at the docks?"

"Unfortunately, my mother said she will not be meeting us at the docks since my father doesn't think it's safe for her to roam outside of the castle walls. She did send her love and told me to tell Michele, and Paul—welcome home."

Michele smiled, looked down at her outfit, and thought: *Oh shit! I should have changed into something more appropriate. I don't want to go to the castle in these baggy boy-shorts and t-shirt. Amarina and her mother will certainly have a hay-day making fun of me in this outfit.* She looked a Leewan in panic, then nervously asked her dad, "Are the carriages taking us directly to the castle?"

"No. Your carriage is taking you, Paul, and Leewan to the guest house. My mother thought you guys would want to relax and freshen up before joining them for dinner. My carriage is taking me directly to the castle, along with the injured spies we have bought back with us."

Michele was relieved when she heard her father's response. "Yes. I do need some time to freshen up."

Paul looked at Macalla and questioned, "Injured spies?"

Macalla glanced at Michele. She nodded her head and replied, "Yes. Tell Paul about the injured spies. I don't want any more secrets."

"I had spies following you and Michele back on the mainland. I just didn't want anything to happen to the two of you – due to this uprising."

"How did the spies get injured?"

"A group from the uprising captured them and tried to make them confess yours and Michele's plans for exposing the islands to the world. When the spies denied any such plans, the captures tortured them."

"I'm so sorry."

Macalla smacked his hand down on Paul's back and said, "No problem. It wasn't your fault son."

Michele smiled up at her dad, happy to know that he was starting to accept hers and Paul's relationship.

The captain grabbed the microphone and announced to the crewmembers, "Prepare for docking."

*****

Michele rode in silence in the back of the enclosed carriage as she watched the peaceful protesters out her window. Leewan had insisted that Paul sit in-between her and Michele so the witches could protect the carriage -- in case any bystanders started throwing things at them. Michele heard mean and nasty things as they made their way to the castle walls: "Go back where you came from, leave us alone, you're not welcomed here, traitors, imposters, liars, you should hang, etc."

At the main drawbridge that provided passage, over a raging river, to the main gates of the castle walls, the protesters were pushed back by the king's guards, allowing the carriages to continue, unharmed. After traveling through the village that was located within the castle walls, the carriage rolled to a stop. Some guards, dressed in blue, opened the carriage's doors and assisted the occupants out while other guards climbed up on top of the carriage, to retrieve the occupants' suitcases.

Michele walked up to the wrought iron gates that provided entrance to the guest house. Before a guard could unlock the gate, the gates opened inward on their own accord. Michele looked at the guard and shrugged her shoulders. "Just have your guards leave out suitcases on the front porch. I think we can manage everything else on our own. Thank you!"

The guard bowed to her then set off to help with the suitcases. Paul grinned over at Michele and said, "I guess I have to start getting used to a lot of new things."

"Not that much will change," she replied. I just won't have to hide my magic from you anymore."

"That and all the people bowing to you." Paul bowed and said, "Anything I can do for you, your majesty?"

She hit him in the arm and laughed, "You don't have to bow to me, you brat."

He lifted his eyebrows twice, then stuck out his arm and asked, "Shall I escort you, my dear?"

She laughed and grabbed his arm. "Please do."

*****

Paul escorted Michele down the stone walkway to the front porch, passing the flowing bushes and swaying palm trees. As they approached the front door, with the fanlight window and gargoyle door knocker, the door opened inward. Michele smiled at Paul and said, "Guess the house was expecting us."

"Looks spooky to me."

When Michele walked into the front foyer of the house, with the high-vaulted ceiling, she stopped dead in her tracks. Everything looked the same as the last time she visited. The library was located on her right, the kitchen to her left, and the split staircase was directly in front of her. Remembering the last time that they were both here, she looked a Paul with a mischievous grin and said, "Want to race?"

Paul leaped in front of her and took off racing up the steps, when the couple reached the split landing, Michele took the stairs to the right while Paul took the stairs to the left. Paul reached the middle of the second floor's balcony first; he grabbed the hand railing and announced, "I won!".

Michele crashed into him at the center of the balcony. Laughing and out of breath, she declared, "You cheated!"

"How did I cheat?"

"You took off before I said, Go."

"You're just a sore loser." He laughed, grabbed her face, and gave her a big kiss.

"What'd you do that for?"

"For returning all my memories of you in this house. Swear to me you will never let someone do that to me again, without my consent."

"I swear." She looked over the balcony as the guards brought in their suitcases. After placing all the suitcases on the floor, Leewan thanked the guards then sent them on their way. When Leewan looked up at Paul and Michele, she asked, "Do you guys want me to make something for us to eat? We won't be going to the castle until later tonight."

Michele looked at Paul, he shook his head, then she replied, "I think we're good. I just want to get settled in. Are the rooms we had before unoccupied?"

"Yes. You can have the first room to the right and Paul the first room to the left."

"Thanks."

Michele and Paul walked back down the stairs so they could retrieve their luggage.

*****

After Michele unpacked her bags in the room with the four-poster bed. She flopped herself on the bed and admired all the antique furnishings. Paul walked into her room and asked, "What are the plans?"

"I want to take a shower and then get dressed in my prom dress for dinner at the castle."

"I could join you in the shower," Paul said with a wicked smile.

She laughed, "I don't think my grandmother would approve."

"Maybe we could send her to the store or something."

Michele laughed, then looked at the jeans and t-shirt Paul was wearing. "Did you bring anything nice to wear to the castle?"

He looked at his outfit and replied, "No. When we planned this trip, I didn't remember anything about your family. Remember?"

"I know. I'm sorry... I wonder if my dad has anything you could wear? I don't want my dad's estranged wife, Lalirra, and my half-sister, Amarina, making fun of our outfits or upbringing again."

"For one, I'm not as tall or muscular as your dad; and two, Lalirra is not your dad's estranged wife, she still lives in the castle."

"I know. Maybe my grandmother, Leewan, can figure something out for you to wear. And, I do consider Lalirra my dad's estranged wife since they live in separate bedchambers. The only reason they are still together is because of some stupid tradition of arranged marriages -- and their daughter, Amarina."

Paul looked down at his outfit again. "I think I look dam good in my jeans and the t-shirt you bought me for my birthday. I don't know whether to take that as an insult or what?"

Michele jumped off the bed, "I love you just the way you are. I don't expect you dress up like a prince, like my dad, but I don't want Princess Lalirra, and my half-sister looking down their noses at us; like we're some sort of peasants. Please dress up for me!"

"If it will make you feel better… Let's go ask your grandmother if she can find me something to wear."

Michele and Paul found Leewan outside in the fenced-in flower garden that was located behind the house. She was sitting on a bench watching birds eat from a feeder and bath in a birdbath.

"Grams. I wanted to wear my prom dress for dinner, but Paul only has jeans or shorts to wear. Can you help?"

Leewan stood up, looked at her watch, then said, "We should have time to do a little shopping. There's a clothing store located just down the street."

Paul looked at Leewan while digging into his pants pocket to see how much cash he had. "What type of currency do they use on this island?"

Leewan patted Paul on the shoulder, "Don't worry about that. Anything you want will be charged to the castle."

Paul looked at Michele, Michele replied, "We don't want any handouts. I still have to pay my dad back for the money he lent me for this trip."

"Oh, nonsense. The two of you are guests here at the castle. And I know your grandmother Chloe. She doesn't let her guest pay for anything; and your dad gave you that money Michele. I'm sure he would never let you pay him back." Leewan looked at Paul and asked, "Can you be ready in five? I'll just inform the guards of our plans. I doubt they'll let us walk down to the store ourselves, but we could take a carriage. Did you want to go, Michele?"

"No. The two of you go and have fun. I need to shower and do something with my hair."

"You shower and get dressed. I'll help you with your hair when I get back."

Chapter 48

"Here. Try this shirt on. I think this silver silk shirt will look great with those black, dress pants. And here's a blue and gray tie."

"No ties," Paul insisted.

Leewan chuckled.

When Paul came out of the changing booth, Leewan's jaw dropped. "Wow! I can see what Michele sees in you. Boy, do you clean up nice! How does the outfit feel?"

Paul looked at himself in the mirror and replied, "Quite comfortable, surprisingly."

"Great. That didn't take long at all. Now change back to your clothes so we can find you some shoes."

*****

On the carriage ride back to the guest house, Leewan asked Paul. "So, Paul, tell me your plans for the future."

"At this point, I am not sure. I know I want to spend the rest of my life with Michele but she's only 17 and I'm only 18. I was planning on going to college to obtain a degree in either computers or finance. I wanted to propose to Michele before going off to college, so we could live together. But now, with my memories restored, I'm not sure what Michele will want to do? She just found you, so I'm not sure if she is going to want to go off to college with me or return here to live with you?

Leewan patted him on the leg, "Don't throw your dreams away yet. Only time will tell what Michele wants to do with her life. I for one, am not going to force Michele to decide between family or love. I know I chose love when I was her age."

*****

When Leewan and Paul entered the guest house, Michele came running to the upstairs balcony, looked down at them, and hysterically cried, "Great. Your finally back. I need help with this zipper. It's stuck and I'm afraid I might break it."

Paul looked up at her with her long, wet hair and sparkling, baby-blue gown hanging off her shoulders. She was a picture of youth and beauty. Paul took the steps, two at a time, until he met her on the balcony. As he zipped up the back of her dress, he whispered in her ear, "Don't be nervous about tonight, you look beautiful in any outfit you decide to wear."

After he zipped her dress, she ran back to her room to blow dry her hair. She called over her shoulder as she left, "Did you find anything to wear?"

"Yep. I'm all set."

****

After Leewan threw on one of her casual dresses, she went up to help Michele with her hair.

Brushing out Michele's long, blonde hair, she said, "You know Michele, you could just wear your hair down—if that makes you more comfortable."

"Thanks, grams, but I think I would prefer it up tonight."

"Your choice."

Leewan began braiding some of Michele's hair, then took the braids from both sides of her head and looped them up in a stylish fashion. The braids came together in the back of Michele's head, then Leewan added more hair to the braid and made one long continuous braid the full length of her hair. "There. Put your earrings on then look in the mirror. See if you like it that way."

Michele did what Leewan told her to do, then said. "Wow. It's great! Thanks!"

"You're welcome. You do look gorgeous… and I'm not just saying that since I am your grandmother."

Michele blushed, then curtsied to Leewan.

"Much better than the last time you were here."

"I've been practicing."

Michele walked across the hall and knocked on Paul's bedroom door, "How are you doing in there?"

"Just putting my shoes on. You can come in if you like."

She opened the door just as he was starting to stand up from a chair. When Paul turned and looked at her, he asked, "Well. How do I look?"

At first, Michele couldn't breathe. Boy did he look sexy! His brown hair was styled to frame his dark, tanned face and strong jawline. His dreamy, dark-brown, bedroom eyes looked inviting and complimented his outfit since he left the first couple of buttons undone on his new shirt. The form-fitting shirt showed off his muscular physique, while the black dress pants slimmed his hips. When he turned around to show off his outfit, he shook his butt at her. Looking over his shoulder, he playfully asked, "Do these pants make my butt look big?"

Michele started fanning herself, unable to handle the sudden increase in the room's temperature. It took all her strength not to run over and grab his behind.

When Paul turned back around, he asked, "Well. How do I look?"

Michele shook herself out of the daze and said, "Great! How do I look?" She twirled around to show off her dress.

"Well. It's not like I haven't seen that dress on you before…your hair looks nice."

She walked over and punched him in the arm.

"Ouch! What'd you do that for?"

"That's not the reaction I wanted."

"I told you before, your gorgeous in anything you wear. Besides, I don't want you getting a big head and start thinking you're too good for me."

"I would never think that!"

Leewan walked into the room. "Are the two of you ready?"

Michele looked at Paul and said, "Yes."

Paul put out his arm to escort her. She hesitated at first, since she was still mad at him, but finally conceded.

Chapter 49

After the guard announced their presence, Michele and Paul followed Leewan into the castle's formal dining room. Looking at the royal party sitting around the rectangular table, Michele noticed they had the same seating arrangement as they did last November -- with the king and queen sitting on opposite ends of the table. Princess Lalirra and her daughter, Amarina, were sitting at the far side of the table, to the right of the king, while her dad, Prince Macalla, was sitting closer to the main entrance, to the left of his mother, the queen. Michele and Leewan curtsied to the royal party while Paul made a quick bow.

Queen Chloe jumped from her seat to greet Michele with a big hug. After she hugged her, she led her to the table. As they were walking, she said, "You don't have to curtsy to us. You're one of us. And I love your dress."

Michele took a seat next to her dad and waved Paul over. Leewan took the seat on the right side of the queen. After everyone was seated, the queen rang the dinner bell. Servants started appearing from the kitchen door, that was situated beyond the king's chair.

While the party feasted on an assortment of every kind of food imaginable, the queen asked Michele, "Where did you buy the dress?"

"At a dress shop in the states. I bought it for prom."

"Prom?"

"Yes. Prom is a formal dance for high school students."

"Oh. How nice. Sort of like a ball?"

"Sort of. But our prom was located in our high school gym. Is the dress from one of your shops?"

"I think it is. In a matter of fact, I think I have the same dress. Must be we have the same taste in dresses." The queen smiled.

During dinner, Leewan listed with one ear to Michele's, Paul's, Prince Macalla's, and Queen Chloe's conversations, and used her other ear to try to decipher what the king was discussing with Princess Lalirra. To Leewan's eye, the king and Lalirra seemed quite cozy with their whispering and the princess's giggling every once in a while. Leewan also noticed Michele's half-sister making googly eyes at Paul, whenever he happened to look her way. Leewan thought: *This can't be good.*

After dinner, while the party was eating their desserts and sipping on some of the island's apricot wine, Chloe brought up the uprising: "Michele, you and Paul are free to roam the inside of the castle walls. There is a horse stable down the road from the guest house -- in case the two of you want to go riding. I know you probably miss your horseback at your aunt's and uncle's house. Explore the village all you want…. but you must stay inside the castle walls! Even though the uprising has died down some, there are still people protesting your and Paul's arrival. They think the two of you mean to bring change to their way of living—and expose the islands to the world."

"Why would they ever think that?" Michele asked. "Do you think the Taylors had any part in starting these rumors?"

The room went silent. Princess Lalirra stared at Michele with a look of contempt -- then grabbed the king's arm and began sulking, "How could she say such a mean thing about my parents."

Michele turned red and realized her mistake: *Open mouth, enter foot.*

The king patted the princess's hand. "It's ok, Lalirra. Michele's new to the islands." The king cleared his throat and looked at Michele. "I know you are my son's illegitimate daughter, but we will have no more conversations, inside of these castle walls, about these false accusations of Lalirra's parents having anything to do with the uprising or the disappearance of your mother. Is that clear?"

Leewan started to speak up. Queen Chloe grabbed her hand, squeezed it, then looked at her with pleading eyes. Leewan looked at the prince, he had sadness in his eyes. She looked down at her carrot cake and started moving the cake around with her fork.

The queen leaned over to Michele and whispered. "It's ok Michele. You didn't do anything wrong voicing your opinion. I think the princess has my husband brainwashed." She patted Michele's hand, then continued, "We'll talk later." The queen lifted her head, look straight at the king, and said in a firm voice, "Michele is my granddaughter! She has the right to her opinion; however, to make you and the princess happy, she will not voice her suspicions around either of you."

The king stared at his wife, then threw his napkin on the table. He knew his wife didn't get mad at him often, but when she did, he knew it was better for him to take his leave. "I must excuse myself; I'm not feeling well." Then he looked at

Michele and Paul and said, "Welcome to the castle, anything the two of you need or want is at your disposal." Then he looked back at his wife and nodded, "We can talk later -- my dear."

Princess Lalirra stood up shortly after the king left. Looking at her daughter, Amarina, she said, "We should be leaving too. Let your father spend time with his illegitimate daughter!" Lalirra nodded at Macalla and started walking away. Amarina stood up and smiled wickedly at Michele, "I'll see you around." Then she looked at Paul and said with a wink, "Hope to see you too, Paul. I could show you around the castle if you like?"

"Sounds good. Have a good night, Amarina."

Michele waited until she left the room, then she punched Paul in the arm. "What was that all about?"

"What? She is your half-sister. Thought we might as well make a friend out of her."

"Sure!" Michele said without conviction.

Leewan looked at Michele and said, "I agree with Paul. You should try to bond with your half-sister. If her grandparents did have anything to do with all this turmoil, it's not any fault of hers."

Michele sat silently, sulking. Queen Chloe reached over and hugged her. "I can tell you are my granddaughter. We are both alike – speak our minds. We're going to get along just great." The queen looked at Leewan. "It's getting late. And I do need to have a heart to heart discussion with my husband—if you know what I mean? We can catch up sometime tomorrow."

Leewan stood to leave and Michele and Paul followed suit. The queen walked over to Michele to admire the gown. Looking at her hair, she said, "No matter what my butthole of a husband said -- You are a princess! You can do as you want. You don't have to dress up to please others or to play a part. Just be yourself.... And, I think I like your hair down better, with the shorts and t-shirt you wore on your last visit. Show the world who you really are; a lovely, strong-minded woman – that will not be pushed around to conform to other people's ways of thinking."

Chapter 50

The sun was setting while Michele, Paul, and Leewan made their way back to the guest house. Michele glanced over her shoulder as they walked by the white, sparkling, stone-washed castle and thought: *It sure does look pretty, the way it glitters in the setting sun.* While admiring the castle, she looked up at the blue and white flags on top of the towers and noticed her half-sister in one of the tower's balconies, watching the sunset. Looking at Amarina, she had to admit, her 15-year-old, half-sister was a beauty -- with her long brown, wavy hair blowing in the wind. Michele worried: *Would Paul grow to like Amarina, more than he likes me?* She shook her head, and squeezed Paul's hand while thinking: *Never! We have too much history – even though I lied to him for more than half of our relationship.*

When the group returned to the guest house, she looked at Leewan. "I need to change my dress; I'll meet you down in the back-sitting room after I've changed."

Paul looked down at his clothes and said, "I need to change too."

*****

While Michele was changing, she heard a knock at her door. "I'm still changing. I'll only be a minute."

Paul called from the other side of the door, "Do you know what I'm supposed to do with my dirty laundry?"

"Just leave it in a pile outside of my door. I saw a laundry hamper in my closet. I'll put yours in there with mine... I'll meet you downstairs in five."

"Sounds good. I'll wait for you downstairs."

After Michele finished slipping on her jeans and a t-shirt, she opened the door to pick up Paul's laundry. While checking the pockets of his jeans before throwing his clothes in the basket, she felt a piece of paper; she pulled it out and noticed it was his crinkled-up list he made on the yacht. She thought: *I shouldn't read it.... But what harm could it do? No, I shouldn't. I should just give it back to him. Tell him I found it in his jeans. Hmm.*

Curiosity got the best of her so she straightened out the piece of paper and skimmed over his list of advantages and disadvantages of dating a witch. One of the disadvantages was underlined, it read: *Will I ever really know if I am truly in love with Michele or if it's all a lie, manipulated by some kind of spell she put on me?*

Michele let the list fall to the ground. Tears started falling down her face. She grabbed her head with both hands while shaking it, then thought: *I can't take this anymore! I need to get out of this place. Find someplace I can be alone – so I can think things over.*

She rushed to the doorway with tear-blurred vision, then looked in both directions before she tiptoed down the stairs to the front foyer. When she reached the front door, she could hear voices from the back of the house, so she opened it quietly and snuck out. She ran into one of the guards at the front gate. After she apologized, she said, "If anyone asks, I just went for a walk." The guard bowed slightly then stepped aside.

Michele started walking along the front of the castle walls. When she finally got to the far side of the castle, she turned right to walk around the castle. The side of the castle was bathed in shadows. Feeling nervous, she took off running towards the back of the castle where she saw more lights. When she finally reached the back of the castle, she turned right and ran straight into another guard.

"Whoa. Slow down," the guard said.

Michele looked up into Jayden's caring eyes.

"Everything okay, little one?" he asked in a low voice.

Michele collapsed into Jayden's strong arms. While sobbing, she said, "No. Everyone here hates me: the island people, the king, my step-mother, my half-sister; and Paul doesn't even trust me. I just want to go back home, to my safe house with my aunt and uncle. I never asked for any of this!"

Jayden started stroking her hair while talking in a soothing voice, "Oh, come on Michele. It can't be that bad. Lots of people here love you."

She stepped back, wiped her face with her hand, and said, "Sorry, I slobbered all over your outfit."

"Oh. This old thing. No matter.... Come with me. I can help you find someplace safe to relax." He put his arm around her and led her into the back of the castle -- through a staff entrance door. From there, he led her down a hall then steered her into a breakroom designed for employees. The room had a kitchenette, some tables with chairs, and a living room set with a couple of overstuffed couches. He pointed at one of the couches and said, "Have a seat." Michele sat down on the couch while Jayden went over to the kitchen area. When he returned, he handed her a box of tissue then set a glass of water on the coffee table in front of her. "Do you want to talk about it? Or, should I just stand guard outside of the room --- if you want time to be alone?"

Michele blew her nose then looked up at him while thinking: *Not good. This just complicates things more.* She didn't trust herself to be alone with Jayden. Something about him pulled on her heartstrings.

"Wow. That's cool. Your necklace is glowing!" Jayden declared.

She looked down at the crystal necklace she got from Leewan. She picked up the crystal and said, "That's strange. My grandmother gave me this necklace for protection and to help me…"

She stopped herself from saying anything more. She didn't know how much she should tell Jayden – about her prophetic dreams. She thought: *Maybe the necklace is glowing because Jayden is dangerous?"*

Jayden, sensing Michele's reluctance to talk about the necklace, changed the subject. "So, tell me why you think everyone here hates you."

Michele told Jayden about what the peaceful protestors screamed at her on her way to the castle and how she felt out of place – since she was only Prince Macalla's illegitimate daughter.

"That's crazy. Those people are probably all from the island of Keeloni. You know Lalirra's dad is the Warden of Keeloni, and most of those protesters are wearing red -- the color of Keeloni's flag. Lalirra's parents are probably the crazy people that started that rumor about you and Paul. They probably feel threaten. I bet they're afraid that Prince Macalla and the queen might declare you the legitimate heir to the throne; after all, you are a descendent of the true founder of the islands, Martha Black. I learned through my history lessons, that Martha used her power of the wind to help her escape the witch trials – and found these islands. She told her friend Elizabeth Williams about the vision and had her convenience her husband, Abraham, to use his shipping company to help transport their fellow witches to these islands. The early settlers only chose Elizabeth's husband to be their king since Martha didn't want anything to do with leading the people. After Abraham Williams step up as their leader, he had the guest house built for Martha, so she could live close to her friend, Elizabeth."

Michele thought: *How can Jayden be bad when he knows so much about the history of the islands? I need to ask Leewan more about this necklace...* She looked up into his handsome face and realized she needed to return to the guest house... Now! She couldn't fight the urge any longer -- to snuggle up in his safe, strong arms and forget about the world. Plus, Paul and Leewan might have noticed by now that she'd snuck out and they'd be worried.

"Thank you, Jayden. I think I'm feeling better now. Can you point me in the direction of the guest house?"

"I'll do more than that. It would be my pleasure to escort you there. And, if you ever need a sounding board again, I'm here for you!"

*****

Paul and Leewan were talking with the guards outside of the guest house gates when Michele returned with Jayden. Paul looked at Michele, then Jayden. Michele saw the flash of red in his eyes. *Oh shit!* she thought. *I screwed up again!*

Leewan ran over to her. "Where have you been?"

Paul just turned around and marched back into the house.

"I just went for a walk -- to clear my head. I ran into Jayden while I was out. He helped me find my way back."

Leewan smiled suspiciously at Jayden, then said, "Thank you Jayden. Come on inside, Michele. We need to talk."

Chapter 51

Leewan walked with Michele to the TV/sitting room in the back of the house. Paul was sitting on the couch, mindlessly watching some DVD he found in the blue ray player. Michele sat next to him while Leewan took a seat in the chair next to the couch. Leaning forward, Leewan asked, "Why did you leave the house without us, Michele? If you wanted to explore the kingdom, we would've gone with you."

"She wanted to be alone with Jayden," Paul hissed. "That's why she left without us!"

Michele glared at Paul and screamed, "No. I had no plans on running into Jayden. If you really must know, I left without you because I can't take any more drama! All those mean things those protestors said on my way here, my grandfather scolding me for asking a question, and then to top it off... I found your list! The list on the disadvantages of dating a witch; with the underlined disadvantage of how you really feel – that you don't trust me. You think I put a spell on you to make you like me."

Paul's jaw dropped and Michele could see the anger building up in his eyes. After a few minutes of glaring at her, he retorted in a low, harsh voice, "That was private. How dare you dig through my belongings."

She argued back, "I didn't dig through your belongings. I was just making sure your pants pockets were empty before I threw them in the laundry basket. Ugh... I can't take this anymore!"

She jumped up and turned to leave, "I'm going to bed!"

Leewan grabbed her hand and said, "Sit. Please."

Michele looked at Leewan with tears in her eyes. After a moment, she sat back down on the far end of the couch, the farthest she could get away from Paul. Leewan reached for her hand and started, "I know this is a very stressful time, but it shall all pass. We are here to support one another, not tear each other apart. Michele glanced at Paul, then looked back at Leewan. Leewan continued, "I for one, feel you have every right to be upset."

Paul tried to interrupt, "But…"

Leewan held up her hand, "Let me finish… Michele. Don't you think Paul also has every right to be upset? He came to the island to be with you. He found out that you have been keeping secrets from him and that all his memories of these islands were erased by a witch. Then, to top it off, you run off without telling anyone and come back with a striking, good-looking, young man."

Michele started to protest, "I. I."

Leewan held up her hand. I think you both need time to think about what you really want. Maybe you both should sleep on it. Tomorrow is a new day. After a good night's rest, the two of you should spend the day together so you can discuss things… But for now. I need your help.

Michele looked at Paul. She knew Leewan was right. They were all exhausted and fighting with each other while exhausted was bound to lead to disaster – with people saying or doing things they truly didn't mean and could never take back.

She looked back at Leewan and asked, "What do you need?"

"Remember that night, in your dream, when we were at the guest house searching for a rock to put that protection spell on Paul's aunt and uncle's house? You told me that night that your mother's stone, the one you took from her room, might be able to help us find her."

Michele nodded her head.

"Can you tell me why you think the stone can help us? I really want to find my daughter."

"I wanted to tell you sooner but really never had the chance. I think the stone is linked to Mayra. At Paul's aunt's and uncle's house, I fell asleep with the rock next to me. The dream I had of Mayra had more details. I now know that staff, at whatever mental institution she is at, call her Jane. So, we've been searching mental institutions near Mosco for a Mayra Johnson; but of course, none of the staff members know her as Mayra Johnson."

"Well, that is helpful. Now if we could just find out more details of the mental institution."

"I can try sleeping with the stone tonight. Maybe I can find out more?"

Leewan smiled and patted her on the leg. "I hope so. Well, I think we should all be getting to bed. It's been a long day." Leewan turned off the lights then led the group up the stairs. Michele stopped at the threshold of the room and looked over at Paul standing by his doorway. "Good night Paul. We can talk tomorrow."

He smiled briefly, then said, "Goodnight."

*****

As Michele lied in bed, she gripped her crystal necklace with one hand and put her other hand on her mother's rock that was lying next to her. After repeating her mother's name three times, she closed her eyes, and sleep overtook her body instantly.

"Are you okay, Michele?"

Michele looked around the dimly lit room. "Where am I?"

Jayden looked around the room, "You're in my bedroom. Sorry. I must have been thinking about you before I went to sleep." He pulled his covers back and said, "Excuse me while I put some clothes on."

Michele tried to look away as Jayden walked over to his dresser, but she couldn't stop herself from staring at his formed backline. After Jayden pulled on some sweat pants, he turned around and caught her staring. She immediately looked down at her hands. Jayden chuckled as he walked over to her. "Guess I would stare too -- if there was a naked woman in front of me. Should we go downstairs, to the kitchen, to talk? I'm sure you might feel uncomfortable being in here in my bedroom."

Michele followed Jayden down the stairs and wondered: *How in the hell did I end up here? I said my mother's name before I went to sleep!*

Jayden pulled a chair out for Michele. After she sat down, he took a seat right next to her. Michele looked down at the table and started shaking her head. Jayden gently pushed her hair back from her face, then said, "I'm sorry Michele. I have the power to dream walk too; I wanted to check on you while you were sleeping but I must have called you to me. I just wanted to make sure that you were alright."

Michele looked at him with his muscular chest and tussled hair; she didn't trust herself to be alone with him – even if it was just a dream. "I shouldn't be here. I'm in a relationship with Paul."

Jayden smiled and put his hands up. "No harm is done. I just wanted you to know if you ever need anyone…. to talk too. I'm here for you."

Michele smiled shyly; Jayden began to fade and was replaced by the image of a cafeteria. Michele was sitting at a table with two other ladies. She looked around the room and noticed multiple tables with people/patients sitting around them. Staff members, with white uniforms on, were walking around the room delivering food trays. One of the ladies at the table had a baby doll. The other lady grabbed the doll and said, "My baby." A struggle ensued, with both of the ladies screaming and tugging on the doll's arms. A woman in a blue uniform ran over. "Jane! Jane! Stop it now. You know that doll doesn't belong to you?"

"I want my baby."

"Orderlies!" The staff member called out. "I need some help restraining Jane while I go get some more Haldol. She's having one of her moments. That doctor needs to increase her medications again."

Jane started tugging on the baby doll and screaming, "I want to go home -- where the witches live! I want my mother! Give me back my baby!"

As the orderlies started coming over from across the room, the staff member in blue said, "Not this story again Jane. As I told you before, there is no such thing as witches and you don't have a baby. Now let go of Judy's baby doll."

When the orderlies reached Jane, they tried to make her release the doll. Jane finally let go of the doll but started swinging her fist at the orderlies. The staff member in blue turned and started walking fast towards the medication cart. When she was halfway to the cart, a telephone started ringing. The staff member changed direction and walked over to the phone. "Hello. Brightside Long-term Care. How can I help you?"

The image began to fade. Michele woke up in bed. The sun was shining through the window. She grabbed her cellphone off the nightstand – it read 10 a.m. She jumped out of bed. She had to find Leewan and tell her the good news -- she found Mayra.

*****

Michele ran down the stairs and found Paul sitting at the kitchen table listening to Leewan talk about the islands while she was cooking blueberry pancakes for breakfast. Leewan looked up from the griddle when Michele walked into the room. "Well good morning sunshine. Did you sleep well?"

Michele smiled cautiously at Paul then took a seat at the table. "Yes, I did. And I have some good news to tell you."

"Oh," Leewan said as she slid a plateful of pancakes on the table. After Leewan took a seat, she said, "Shoot. I'm all ears."

"I think I know where Mayra is."

"You do!"

"Someplace in Russia called Brightside Long-term Care."

"Brightside… Hmm. That name sounds familiar. I think your dad already checked there."

"Yeah. He might have. But he was looking for Mayra Johnson. Not a patient named Jane. And I'm wondering if they call Jane the common name that they name people in America – when they don't know who they are, Jane Doe."

"Jane Doe you say."

"Could be. But we need to check this place out again."

"Then we shall. We can call your dad after we eat. See what he can do to help us."

Chapter 52

Leewan tried to call the prince's cellphone after breakfast but it went straight to voicemail -- so she left a message: *Good morning Prince Macalla. When you get a chance, please call me. I think we know where Mayra is.* After leaving the message, she looked at Michele and said, "I bet your dad is busy holding court in the throne room, along with his mom and dad. I need to go to work for a couple of hours today at the guards' house. I'll let you know as soon as I hear back from your dad. The two of you just make yourself at home. You can explore the house or get some needed rest while I'm gone."

"Speaking of exploring the house," Michele spoke up. "Last time we were here. Paul and I found a locked room on the third floor. Do you know what's in that room?"

"Supposedly, that room was my great, great, great grandmother's, Martha Black's, old bedroom. I have never been able to open that door."

"Interesting," Michele replied.

Leewan grabbed her purse and looked at the two, "Call me if you need me."

After Leewan left, Michele looked at Paul. He had been watching her, but when she turned his way, he quickly looked down at the kitchen table. Michele could tell, by the way, he been acting, that he was still upset with her. Putting her hand on top of his, she asked, "Do you want to go up to the glass cupola with me?" He shrugged his shoulders. Michele got up from the kitchen table and looked at him. "Come on Paul. Please! We need to talk." He stood up and jerked his head to the left, towards the foyer. Michele took the hint and lead the way.

On the third floor, before going up to the rooftop, Michele walked over to the locked room and put her hand on the door. She stood silently for a minute and thought: *Martha, if you and your daughter are still here in spirit, I could use a little guidance. Please help me make the right decisions.* As in reply, a sudden warmth enveloped her hand for a brief second. After the heat subsided, she tried the doorknob, without any luck. Smiling at Paul, she said, "Shall we go up?"

When the couple walked into the glass cupola, they started wandering around the room aimlessly looking out the windows at the castle and the surrounding village. After a while, Michele took a seat in the loveseat, leaving room for Paul; however, instead of sitting next to her, he sat in the flowered, upholstery chair that was situated on the other side of the end table.

Michele looked across the end table and said, "I'm truly sorry. I didn't have any plans to run out last night and meet up with Jayden. I was just upset by everything that happened yesterday, and then, after reading your list, I just couldn't take anymore."

"You weren't supposed to ever read that list."

"I know. I'm sorry. I shouldn't have read it without your permission, but I'm glad I did. We shouldn't be keeping secrets from each other anymore. I need to know how you really feel so we can discuss things."

When Paul didn't reply, she continued, "You do have the right to your private thoughts— but I still can't believe you could think so low of me. Do you really think I'm that ugly, that I would need to put a spell on someone – to make them love me?"

"No. I think you're the most beautiful woman I have ever set eyes on. And that just my point… I've never felt this way about any other woman. Can't you understand why I might feel that way, after all those secrets you kept from me? You should know it will take some time for me to truly trust you again."

"I know. I'm truly sorry. But if it will make you feel better, I did ask my grandmother the last time you brought it up – if I could unknowingly put a spell on you to make you want me."

"And?"

"She said a spell-like that usually takes a lot of concentration and time – like hypnosis; and that it was highly unlikely for someone to do it subconsciously."

"Highly unlikely… but possible?"

"I don't know. I guess." Michele sat in silence for a minute or two-- just staring at her fingernails and thinking about what Paul said. She started having doubts and wondered: *Could I've done it? Maybe I did put a spell on him, unknowingly. In the very beginning, I truly did want him to like me!*

She looked back at Paul and said, "I don't think I placed a spell on you, but I guess it's a question we both need to find out the answer to. I don't want a false relationship any more than you do. I... I guess I could ask my grandmother if you want me to-- see if it's possible to do it unknowingly."

"No. Don't get her involved."

"Then how will we know for sure? Maybe I should try a spell on you to make you confess you're true feelings."

"No. I don't like knowing someone is messing with my head. That's the only part of you being a witch that really scares me."

Michele nodded her head and said, "I understand how you feel. I'm just not sure what you would like me to do about it?"

"I guess your understanding and declaration of not knowing is good enough for me-- if it's good enough for you?"

Michele's eyes filled with tears as she nodded. Paul stood up, walked over to the love seat, and took the seat next to her. Putting his arm around her, he said, "Sorry about the list. Now... will you tell me truthfully. Is there any reason I should be concerned about you hanging out with Jayden?"

Michele looked at him, with his solemn, brown eyes and thought: *I really don't know. For some reason, I feel this attraction or pull towards Jayden. Do I dare tell Paul the truth?*

After a moment of silence, Paul jumped up to look out the window and muttered, "Oh never mind. Your silence says it all!" Michele followed him to the window to console him, but when she reached out to touch him, he jerked away. "Don't! Just don't."

She looked out the window. Standing shoulder to shoulder, she replied. "I know I love you, Paul. You are my first and always will be. If you want me to be truthful, I have to admit that there is some attraction there. I can't explain it. But I do know, I don't want to lose you."

He looked at her and asked, "Have the two of you ... Did you?"

"No!"

"Do I still have a chance?"

"Yes! Yes," Michele shouted and fell into his arms crying.

Paul put his arms around her then turned his head to look out the window. Through his tear, blurred eyes, he saw Jayden walking down the cobbled street in front of the castle, side by side, with Leewan. Turning his head back to smell Michele's hair, he thought: *I'm going to kill him.*

*****

"I'm back!" Leewan screamed up from the bottom of the third-floor stairs.

Michele broke off the kiss, wiped her tear-streaked face with her hand, then asked Paul, "Do I look okay?"

He looked at her with her mascara running down both cheeks and hollered back to Leewan, "We'll be down in a second." Then he took off his shirt and handed it to Michele. "Here. Use this."

She wiped her face, then blew her nose on the back of his shirt. "Thanks."

"Shall we?" Paul motioned towards the stairs.

"What about your shirt?" Michele held the dirt shirt out to Paul.

"You keep it. I can grab another one from the room on the way down."

*****

On the way down to the kitchen, Michele stopped at her room to throw Paul's dirty shirt in the laundry hamper while Paul stopped at his room to grab another shirt. When Paul walked out into the hall, shirtless, Michele stared at his muscular six-pack – and started feeling a warm, fuzzy feeling in her loins. Thinking to herself, Michele wondered: *What's wrong with you. Your hormones have gone crazy - like a dam broke or something.*

Paul stood there smiling, perceiving Michele's look of desire. "Do you like the view?"

he chuckled. "I can show you more if you like."
He reached down for his zipper.

Michele turned away and blushed with embarrassment.

"No need to be embarrassed. I look at you with the same longing all the time. It's been a while, Michele." He took a couple of steps closer and started reaching for her. She stepped back and said, "Not now. My grandmother is downstairs waiting for us."

Paul grasped her shoulders, then whispered in her ear, "Soon then. Promise me."

She nodded her head slightly.

He smiled and repeated, "Soon."

*****

When Michele and Paul walked into the kitchen, hand in hand, Leewan was cleaning up the breakfast dishes.

"Sorry grams. I should have cleaned that up."

"Oh, nonsense. I never asked you to. I knew you and Paul needed time alone." Leewan glanced at their joined hands then winked at Paul. Turning her attention back to Michele, she said, "I hope the both of you have a better understanding now… about your true feelings, and we will not have another repeat of yesterday."

"We talked."

Leewan nodded. "Did the two of you have lunch yet?"

"No," they said in unison.

"Good, cause your father finally texted me; the court is taking a lunch break soon and he wants us to join them at the castle."

Michele looked down at her outfit. "Should I change?"

Leewan shook her head. "No. You heard the queen. You're family. No need to dress up for the family."

"But… will they be dressed up?"

"Of course, darling. But they just finished hearing complaints from the island people in the throne room. They are expected to make an appearance."

Chapter 53

When Michele walked into the castle's formal dining room, the royal family was seated around the table. As Michele suspected, King Levi Williams and her dad had their royal uniforms on while Queen Chloe, Princess Lalirra, and Amarina all had gorgeous dresses with tiaras on their heads. Michele watched as Lalirra and Amarina surveyed her attire, snickered with the king, then shoved their noses up in the air. Her grandmother, Chloe, jumped from her seat as usual to meet her guest. "So glad you could join us." Chloe hugged Michele and whispered in her ear, "Don't mind the two snarling bitches at the end of the table. Their bark is worse than their bite." Chloe smiled, looked at Michele's outfit, and said. "I'm glad you wore your shorts, no need to dress up for your family. I want you to be yourself. The clothes one wears does not make a person -- no matter what your money-hungry step-mother thinks."

Michele thought about what she said then replied, "Yes…. She is my step-mother. Wonder what she would think if I ran over there to give her a big hug." Michele laughed out loud. Leewan gave her a strange looked, then laughed softly.

After everyone was seated, Macalla asked Michele, "Leewan said you had something important to tell us – about Mayra?"

"Yes. I think I know where she is."

Amarina spoke up, "She's probably six-foot under, where she belongs. Why are you wasting the court's precious time and money searching for a peasant?"

Lalirra grinned and patted her daughter's thigh in agreement.

Michele's eyes boiled with anger. She screamed at Amarina, "Go… Go…." Glancing around, she saw Leewan cringe and Chloe cover her mouth. "Go take a shower!" At Michele's command, the chair Amarina was sitting in, instantly pulled her a good six feet away from the table. A storm cloud suddenly appeared and hovered above Amarina's head; with a loud crack of thunder, lightning stuck the floor, and then a gush of water poured out of the cloud."

Michele threw her hand up in the air and said, "Oh no! Go away!"

The storm cloud disappeared, leaving Amarina drenched in her chair. Lalirra started jumping up and down next to her chair, swiping at the water that had splattered her dress. Glaring at Michele, she screamed, "You ruined my dress!" The king was sitting straight up in his chair -- with a look of shock on his face, and Macalla -- started laughing.

When Macalla could finally control his laughter, he looked at Michele and said, "You're truly are mine and Mayra's daughter. Your mother had the power of the wind, and my ancestors had the power to move things. It skipped my generation; but my dad has it -- not that strong. He has been known to move things when he is truly upset." Macalla looked at his dad, and said, "Like that time you threw that guy off his horse -- since he threatened you."

Michele looked at the king, the king nodded.

Macalla continued, "Did Leewan ever tell you the story about how my great, great, great, great grandmother, Elizabeth Williams, foundered the islands along with Leewan's great, great, great grandmother, Martha?"

Michele nodded.

"I'll have to show you their tombs sometime. They are located under the city streets, in the catacomb. Maybe one day, Amarina might start developing the power of telekinesis – and she'll need an older sister's advice." Macalla winked at Amarina.

"Never," screamed Amarina. "I will never need any help from her." She jumped out of her chair and started marching out of the room. Her mother, Princess Lalirra, looked at her husband and said, "Now look what you have done. I'll take my lunch in my bedchamber." She ran after Amarina. "Wait up darling."

King Levi looked at Michele and asked, "Why did you do that?"

Michele glared at the king, "You know how Lalirra and Amarina treat me and you heard what

Amarina said about my mother. Why didn't you tell her to stop?"

Queen Chloe smiled – she was proud of Michele for standing up for herself. She turned her head, looked intensely at the king, and asked, "Yes dear. Why haven't you asked them to stop?"

The king squirmed nervously in his seat. He cleared his throat and said, "I will talk with them. Sorry, Michele. You are part of this family and they should treat you as such."

"Thank you," she replied.

She nodded her head at her husband then looked at Michele, "Now what were you saying about your mother – I'm sure the king will agree with anything you need to help find her." The queen looked at her husband; he nodded in agreement.

Michele told Levi, Chloe, and her dad about her dream. After she finished, Macalla spoke up. "I have to speak at scheduled appearances on all the surrounding islands. I need to reassure the people that the rumors are all false; however, I do believe my dad will approve of sending some of our best guards with you for protection and agree to foot the bill."

Michele looked at her grandfather, the king smiled and nodded his head. "I'll make all the arrangements personally. Can you give me a day or two?"

Michele smiled and said, "Yes. Thank you!"

Queen Chloe clapped her hands together once and said, "I don't know about any of you, but I'm starved." She picked up her bell and rung it.

Chapter 54

That night, Leewan walked with Michele and Paul to a local tavern for dinner. She introduced Paul and Michele to most of the locals they met on the streets and boasted how she found her granddaughter living in America. Leewan even told some of the locals how Michele might have located the whereabouts of her daughter, Mayra. The locals welcome Michele and Paul to the kingdom and a lot of them even started bowing and/or curtsying when they saw her walking next to Leewan.

During dinner at the tavern, one of the locals stood up and proclaimed, "I propose a toast to Michele, the chosen one. Welcome home!" Everyone in the tavern raised their glasses and someone hollered, "Cheers to the newly found princess." Michele blushed and Paul squeezed her hand under the table. Leewan whispered across the table, "Don't worry Michele. It's still your decision whether you want to live on the islands or go back to the states. No rush in making that decision. You're only 17."

On the walk home from the tavern, Leewan told them, "I need to work tomorrow since I need to help the king's guards plan their trip to the other islands with your dad. I also need to call on a lot of my allies, witch friends, to find out where most of the unrest is located. I want the local witches from those islands to support your dad's movement for peace."

"Will my dad be safe? Maybe we should hold off on finding my mother and go with my dad?"

"Your dad will be safe. I am putting a protection spell on him and having my allied, witch friends watch out for his wellbeing. Besides, the protestors are scared of you and Paul. If you arrived at their islands, they might take that as a threat. It's for the best that the two of you stay tucked away until the islanders are ready to meet you." Michele nodded her head in agreement.

As the group continued down the street, towards the guest house, Michele walked hand in hand with Paul. She smiled at all the locals as they pointed, waved, and bowed in her direction. Leewan watched the street corners. She recognized a lot of the king's guards and spies standing guard, watching their progression. Leewan smiled to herself, it was nice to know that Michele's grandmother, Queen Chloe, and her dad, Prince Macalla, were doing their part in ensuring the protection of Michele. As Leewan looked further up the cobbled streets, she noticed Jayden, standing in the shadows – watching. Not wanting Paul to see Jayden, Leewan pointed to the castle towers. "That far tower to the left contains Lalirra and Amarina bedchambers, the center tower's balcony is where the king and queen address the people, and the far tower, is where your father's bedchamber is." After Leewan was sure that they'd passed Jayden, she made a beeline towards the guest house. "I don't know about the two of you, but I'm ready for bed."

"It has been a long day," Michele replied. Then looking a Leewan she asked, "Would it be ok if Paul and I rode horses around the village tomorrow?"

"Yes. Yes. Enjoy yourself. The two of you are safe within the castle walls. You can even ride my horse if you want. Windfire is stabled at the local livery."

When the group entered the guest house's foyer, and Michele started walking up the stairs, Leewan grabbed her hand and said, "I need to talk to you, alone please."

Michele looked at Paul. He nodded and said, "I'll just go on up and start getting ready for bed."

Michele followed Leewan to the back sitting-room. Leewan turned on a lamp then took a seat next to Michele on the couch. Looking at Michele she asked, "What's going on between you and Jayden?"

Michele's jaw dropped open, then she said, "Nothing!"

"You can be honest with me. I see how he looks at you, and I've seen how you look at him. He stopped me on the streets today -- and asked how you were."

"He did?" Michele asked then shook her head. "I swear, nothing is going on…. But there is some sort of pull or attraction to him. And I've been meaning to ask you when I ran into him the other night -- my crystal necklace started to glow."

"Interesting."

"What does it mean?"

"I don't know."

"And did you know he has the whispers of a dream power?"

"He does?"

"Yes. He talked to me in my dream the other night."

"Hmm. That power is rare. I know it runs in our family but I never knew of any of the other witches on these islands possessing that kind of power. Let me do some research on where Jayden grew up."

"Do you think he's dangerous?"

"No. No. He's worked for the king's army for more than five years now. I think he volunteered when he was only 19. He moved up the ranks fast and has proven to be irreplaceable. Just do me a favor."

"Anything."

"Use caution when around him, until I can figure out where he came from."

"Ok. And grams."

"Yes."

"How come my grandfather, King Levi, acts so nervous when Chloe gets mad at him? Does Chloe possess some sort of magic?"

Leewan chuckled. "Queen Chloe does possess some magic, but not the type of magic you and I have. Her magic comes from her personality. Everyone on the seven islands, respects and trusts her. She is the main decision-maker for the kingdom. She is always fair and is very intelligent. Chloe is from Black Sands Island. Her family was the first settlers that made trade possible with the mainland. At that time, the king's family was poor; the taxes they collected from the citizens could barely pay all the bills the running the castle incurred. The king's family didn't want to raise the taxes so they arranged the marriage between Levi and Chloe. Your grandfather, King Levi, has grown to love and respect his wife over the years.

The decisions she has made has brought peace and prosperity to the kingdom."

"Wow. Very interesting story. I know I love Chloe's personality too. She's so down to earth."

Leewan looked at her watch and started getting up off the couch. "Oh dear, look at the time. I better be getting to bed. I have to get up early."

Michele followed her up the stairs. At Michele's bedroom door, Michele learned over and kissed Leewan on the cheek, "Good night grams."

"Good night sweetheart." Leewan smiled then walked further down the hall to her room. Michele stood in the hallway and watched as Leewan walked into her room and closed her door. Once the door was closed, she walked across the hall and knocked softly on Paul's bedroom door. He opened the door a crack to see who it was. When he didn't see Leewan, he opened his door. Michele saw him standing in his underwear. He reached up, grabbed her arm, then pulled her into his room. After shutting his door quietly, he said in a husky voice, "I finally get you alone." He took her into his arms and started kissing her. While Paul was eagerly kissing her, she could feel his arousal against her body. Breathing heavily, she pushed him away, and said, "We can't. Not now."

Paul looked at her with sad, puppy-dog eyes.

"My grandmother has to work early tomorrow. Can you wait until tomorrow morning?"

Paul glanced down at his shorts, then replied, "Not really. Guess I can go take a cold shower."

Michele glanced down and said, "I'm sorry. I just don't feel right with my grandmother sleeping one door down." She kissed him goodnight, then said, "I love you Paul... until tomorrow."

He smiled and said, "Until tomorrow."

Chapter 55

Paul snuck into Michele's room bright and early after he heard the front door close. He crawled under the covers and wrapped himself around Michele's sleeping body. Lying on his side, spooning her, he started kissing the back of her neck. When he reached the back of her ear, he nibbled on her ear and whispered, "Are you awake?"

Michele rolled over onto her back. She smiled and said, "Yes. I'm awake."

With an evil grin and a twinkle in his eye, Paul replied, "Mmmmm... Good morning sugar. Your grandmother has left the house!" He leaned over her and eagerly took her lips in his while his hand started exploring her body. In between kisses, he said in a husky voice, "Take off your clothes – I want to see all of you."

She removed her t-shirt and underpants then laid back down in bed so Paul could enjoy the full view. He whispered while caressing her body, "You're so beautiful." She closed her eyes and gave him free rein as he took his time kissing and exploring every inch of her body. After she climaxed a couple of times, she sat up, shoved him down on the bed, and said, "My turn to explore." He grinned and threw his hands up in total surrender.

During Michele's turn to explore, Paul reached down to touch her head and said, "Stop. I'm close." She smiled up at him, then laid back down on the bed. Paul climbed on top and slowly entered her. She let out a gasp of delight as he took his time thrusting, in and out, at a slow even rhythm, while kissing her neck, face, and lips. As the need and desire increased, so did the intensity of the thrusting until they both flew over the edge in total ecstasy.

After the explosion of fireworks, Paul's world went black. He laid on top of her for a couple of minutes, unable to move – like he'd been drugged. When he finally came to his senses, he whispered in her ear, "Oh Baby…. Marry me!"

Michele starting kissing his face and said, "Yes. I'll marry you… Someday. But I think we should wait… at least until we finish high school."

Paul laughed softly and propped himself up onto his elbows. Looking into her eyes he said, "Very true. We probably should wait until we graduate, but I want the world to know you belong to me. Waiting another year is too dam long."

Michele smiled, "Then you should buy me an engagement ring."

Paul thought about what she said for a minute or two, then said, "Will you take a zirconium diamond? I don't think I can afford much more, especially since I might not have a job once we return to the states."

Michele laughed and kissed him on the cheek. "I would take a ring from a bubblegum machine from you!"

*****

After the young lovers dressed, they went down to the kitchen to find something to eat. When Michele walked into the kitchen, she saw a note lying on the table. Reading the note out loud, it read:

If you guys want something to eat… you can either call the castle for room service or go to any local café. The local cafes can charge the bill to the castle's account.

Love, Leewan

Putting the letter back on the kitchen table, Michele asked Paul, "What do you want to do?"

"I would like to explore the island, but since we can't go outside of the castle's walls, I guess exploring the village will do."

"Let's go then."

The couple walked out the door and down the path to the main gate. At the gate, Michele stopped to talk to one of the guards. "Can you point us in the best direction to find a café that serves breakfast?" The guard bowed then pointed down the street to the right.

Michele and Paul walked hand and hand down the street. Michele felt like a celebrity while exploring the village since she noticed a lot of people stopping and staring at her or pointing her way. The people that did pass her on the sidewalk would either smile and step to the side or bow their heads in acknowledgment. Michele smiled back at all the strangers and greeted them by saying: good morning, nice day, no need to bow, etc...

While walking, Michele asked Paul, "How does everyone seem to know who I am?" He pointed up at a streetlight and said, "Looks like your dad had someone hang posters of you all around the village."

Michele looked up at the streetlight's pole and saw a poster of her blowing in the wind. The sign read: *Please welcome Prince Macalla's daughter, Michele, to the village.* Michele blushed and said, "Leave it to my dad. No trying to blend in."

When Paul opened the café's door for Michele to enter, a little bell attached to the door rang. As Michele entered the café, the staff all turned then stood at attention. At the site of Michele, the hostess ran from her desk and curtsied. Michele smiled at the hostess and nodded her head. The hostess looked around the café in a panic and stammered, "The best table is taken, but I will chase the occupants out immediately."

"No. No. Don't do that. We'll just take any table you have available or we can wait until one comes available."

The hostess blushed and said, "But all we have available is that small table in the middle of the dining room."

"That will do just fine." Michele smiled.

The hostess rushed to grab some menus, tripped, then led the couple to the table. After the hostess made it to the table, she looked at them and asked, "Is there anything I can get you to drink?"

"Just water for me," Michele replied. Paul nodded his head in agreement and said, "I'll just have water for now too, please."

The hostess scattered away while Paul pulled out a chair for Michele to sit in. As soon as Michele sat down, a well-dressed man showed up at the table. After taking a short bow, he introduced himself, "My name is Jarius Niang. I'm the manager on duty. I'm at your service. And thank you, Princess Michele, for allowing us the privilege to serve you. Our breakfast specials for today are Eggs Benedict or strawberry waffles."

"Thank you very much," Michele said with a smile. "I think we would like some time to look over the menu."

"Yes. Of course." The manager back away from the table, bowing all the way.

After Michele and Paul reviewed their menus, Michele glanced up. Instantly, the manager returned to the table. Bowing, the manager asked, "Have you decided what you would like to order."

"Yes. We have. And... um... can you do me a favor?"

"Anything. Anything at all."

"Please don't bow to me. Just act like I'm one of your normal customers, please."

"Yes. Yes. As you like." The manager said as he was bowing continuously. Then he caught himself and said, "Sorry, princess."

Michele laughed softly and said, "No worries." Then she looked at Paul and asked, "Do you want to order first?"

*****

Michele found it hard to eat her breakfast with everyone in the café staring and burning a hole into the back of her head. She thought: *Why is everyone staring at me? Am I eating my food with the right fork? Hope I'm setting a good example of how a princess should behave.*

As she slowly finished her Eggs Benedict, she noticed a little, brown-hair girl pointing at her. "Momma. Is that the other princess?"

"Yes, dear. But it's not polite to point."

"How come she isn't wearing a gown as Princess Amarina does?"

"Shh. It's not nice to talk about other people."

Michele turned towards the little girl. The mother pulled her daughter back, afraid Michele would do something to her impolite daughter.

Michele got up from the table and bent down next to the little girl. "Hi. My name is Michele. What is your name?"

"Mandy."

"That's a pretty name…. And to answer your questions, yes, my dad is Prince Macalla, so that makes me a princess just like my half-sister, Princess Amarina. I don't have to dress up in a gown to be a princess. I like wearing shorts and a tank top just like you. Dresses are nice for formal occasions. But don't you agree, shorts and a tank top give you more room to run and play."

The little girl nodded her head. "I do like your tank top. It glitters like mine."

Michele nodded, "You do look beautiful in your tank top." Mandy looked down at her shirt and smiled.

Mandy's mom spoke up, "What do we say, Mandy, when someone gives you a compliment?"

The little girl looked up and said, "Thank you. You're beautiful too."

Michele put out her hand and said, "It was very nice meeting you, Miss Mandy."

The little girl shook her hand and said, "It was very nice meeting you too, Princess Michele."

The manager saw Michele on the floor and ran over to assist her. "Is everything ok?"

"Yes. Yes. Thank you! Can we get our bill now?"

"No. There is no bill."

"Is my father covering my bill?"

"No. King Levi is paying for anything you need. I received a message from the castle a couple of days ago."

Oh really! Michele thought as she stood up. Looking at the manager she said with a smile, "If my grandfather is paying for anything I need, then I need to buy everyone's breakfast." She waved her arm out to encompass all the customers.

"Everyone's?"

"Yes. Is that a problem?"

"No. No. Not at all. I'll take care of it right away."

The manager started walking away but Michele called him back. "Can you do me one more favor?"

The manager bowed and said, "As you wish."

"Please give yourself and all your staff a 40% tip. Everyone here did a great job and I appreciate you making me and Paul feel welcomed."

"Yes. Yes. Thank you!" The manager said while bowing – then caught himself. "Oops. I did it again! Sorry, princess!" The manager stood up straight, laughed nervously, then announced, "Everyone's food bill will be paid for by Princess Michele."

All the customers in the café started clapping their hands and chanting, "Princess Michele, Princess Michele."

Michele walked over to Paul and took his hand. When he stood up, she lifted his arm and publicized, "I want everyone to meet my boyfriend, Paul."

Some of the people in the crowd started yelling: *Hi Paul, nice to meet you Paul, welcome Paul, etc.*

Michele and Paul waved goodbye as they made their way to the door. At the café's door, Michele announced, "If you see me on the streets, please just wave or say hi. No need to bow or curtsy; I'm just like any of you, a citizen of Honiawae Island."

As the café's door closed, Michele could hear cheering and clapping coming from the café. Paul put his arm around her as they walked away, down the cobbled street.

Chapter 56

After the young lovers walked a good five blocks away from the castle, they happened upon a livery stable. Michele looked at Paul and said, "Bet we could see more of the village if we rode."

Paul looked nervously at Michele since he really didn't trust horses; but if she wanted to ride, he would give it a try -- so he forced a smile and nodded.

"Great." She pulled on his arm and led him into the livery stable. The man working at the front desk saw Michele and immediately bowed. "How can I help you, princess?"

She blushed and said, "You can just call me Michele. And you don't need to bow – I'm just a teenager here visiting my grandparents." She glanced around the stables and saw a bunch of horses looking at her from their stalls. "Do you have a couple of horses that we can rent – to ride around the village?"

"No. But I have a couple of horses you can borrow. Leewan's horse, Windfire, is here, and we do have several extra horses you can pick from." The man looked at Paul, "Are you an experienced rider?"

"No. I only rode once -- with Michele on back of me."

The man nodded. "Then I suggest you take one of the older horses that are less spirited."

"Less spirited sounds good to me."

Michele spoke up, "I'll take Windfire."

"As you wish, princess... I mean Michele. Wait there on that bench while I have someone saddle the horses for you."

Michele and Paul sat on a bench near the front entrance. After about five minutes or so, a young boy bought both of the horses out. Windfire snorted and nodded her head when she saw Michele. The boy leading the horses bowed then handed Michele the reins to Windfire and Paul the reins to a white, dappled mare. The boy looked at Paul and said, "Your horse's name is White Lightning. But don't worry. She's retired from the king's army and doesn't like to run anymore." The boy turned and ran to the wall. He returned to Michele's side with a set of steps. "For you princess, to help you mount."

"Thank you." She climbed up the steps and mounted Windfire.

Paul watched Michele mount, then stared at his saddle. "This saddle doesn't have a horn. How am I supposed to get on?"

Michele chuckled softly and said, "The same way you got on Harley at my house. Just grab the front edge of the saddle in place of the horn."

Paul put his left foot in the iron stirrup, grabbed the front and back of the saddle, and tried to mount three times -- but failed. When he looked over at Michele, she tried to hide her laughter. "Ug hum." She looked at the stable boy. "Can you give Paul the steps?"

The boy bowed and ran the steps over to Paul. Paul climbed up the three steps, put his left foot in the stirrup, and swung his right leg over the horse's rump. Once mounted, he looked at Michele with apprehension and said, "We are only going to walk the horses around the village. Right?"

She smiled, nodded her head, then started riding away from the stables. Paul started kicking his horse and clucking his tongue, but the horse refused to move. The stable boy swatted the horse on the rump – which caused the horse to leap forward. Paul almost fell off the horse but was able to pull himself up by having a death grip on the pommel. After the death-defying leap, the horse continued down the street following Windfire for a couple of blocks, then decided to stop again. Paul squeezed his legs and made a clucking noise, but the horse refused to go. He called out Michele. "Wait up. My horse will not move."

Michele turned Windfire around. She rode up to the other horse and grabbed the side of one of the reins. She tried to pull the horse forward, but the horse wouldn't budge. "Let me have the reins." She tugged hard on both of the reins, but the horse fought back by rearing. Michele screamed as she watched Paul being thrown from the saddle. After he landed on the ground, she asked, "Are you alright?"

He stood up, dusted himself off, and glared at her. "I'm not getting back on that old nag."

Michele looked at White Lightening with an evil look. "I wouldn't blame you. I'll switch horses with you." She dismounted and held onto both horses.

Paul looked at her and asked, "How am I supposed to get on Windfire without the steps?"

"Just put your left foot in the stirrup; when you try to jump up, I'll help push you up."

He walked over to the side of the horse. Windfire turned her head and sniffed him. Sensing Paul's fear, the horse bowed.

Paul looked at Michele. She laughed. "The horse is lowing herself so you can get on."

After Paul mounted Windfire, the horse stood back up. Michele pulled down on White Lightning's reins so she could look the horse in the eye. "Listen here. I'm the boss. So, you either cooperate or I'll make you wish you had."

The horse sniffed Michele, snorted, then nodded her head.

The horses rode side by side after the incident without any further disturbances. As the couple rode around the village, they saw a lot of people going about their business: doing yard work, watching their children play, etc. Most of the people stopped what they were doing and waved when they saw Michele and Paul riding down the street. The couple would wave back and/or greet them with a friendly hello.

While riding one of the back streets of the village, Michele heard a young girl squeal with delight at the sight of the horses. The little girl ran up to a lady that was raking a flower bed. Michele listened to what the little girl said as she pulled on the lady's arm. "Momma. Momma. Horses are coming. Can we go pet them?" The lady dropped her rake on the ground while the child started dragging her to the roadside. "Hurry, momma! Hurry!"

As the horses approached the front yard, the girl shouted, "Can I pet your horses? My mother said I could have a horse... someday."

Michele and Paul stopped their horse. Michele smiled down at the little girl and said, "Sure."

The little girl's face lit up but her mother pulled her back and gave Michele an evil look. "No honey. That's Princess Michele there. I'm sure she is way too busy to stop for the likes of us."

Michele smiled at the little girl. "I'm not busy at all. If you want. I can even let you sit on my horse while I lead you around the yard."

"See momma. She's not too busy. Pleeease…"

The mother looked at her daughter's pleading eyes and gave in. "Just once then."

The little girl screamed with delight while Michele dismounted her horse. Michele looked at the mother before putting the child on the horse. "May I put her on the horse or would you like to?"

The mother nodded and said, "You may."

Michele lifted the squealing child onto the saddle. "Hold on to the front of the saddle while I lead you around." While Michele was leading the little girl around the yard, she asked, "What's your name?"

"Zoe."

"That's a beautiful name."

"Thank you. I love horses." After riding around the front yard once, the little girl screamed at her mom, "Can I go again?"

"That's up to the princess."

Michele smiled at the mother and started taking the little girl around again.

When they were halfway around the circle, the little girl said, "My grandmother and grandfather say you are mean."

Michele looked at the little girl and asked, "Why would they say that? Have they ever met me?"

"I don't think so. They live on Keelonie Island. We live here since my daddy works for the king. He does the landscaping."

"I don't think I'm mean. Do you?"

"No. I think you're nice. And a lot prettier than that poster my grandpa gave my parents."

"Your parents have a poster of me?"

"Yep. It's an ugly drawing of you, with evil eyes."

Michele just smiled, then looked ahead at the little girl's mom."

"Again. Again!" the little girl said.

Her mom just shook her head. "I think that's enough for today; but I want you to smile, really big, for a picture." The little girl said, "Cheeeessse," while her mom took a picture of her on the horse with Michele holding the reins. Then her mom walked over to the saddle to help the daughter down.

"Momma. Can we show Princess Michele the poster of her -- that granddaddy brought over?"

The mother's jaw dropped down. She lifted her daughter from the saddle, put her on the ground, then said, "Now thank the princess for the ride."

"Thank you!"

"You're welcome." Michele smiled at the little girl then looked at her mother.

The mother just said, "Thank you," then scooped up her daughter and walked away.

Michele mounted her horse, waved goodbye to the little girl, then proceeded down the road with Paul. When the couple was out of earshot, Michele looked at Paul, "What did you and mother talk about while I was leading the girl around?"

"Oh, nothing much. She just wanted to know how I liked the kingdom and if we would be staying long."

"What did you tell her?"

"I told her that I like the kingdom fair enough but I had heard there were crazy rumors, out on the other islands, saying you and I were planning on exposing the islands. I told her those rumors are just plain stupid and that you and I had planned no such thing. I also told her that we were only visiting your family for the summer... That's the truth. Right?"

Michele looked ahead for a second or two and thought: *Do I want to go back to America at the end of summer?* Then she looked at Paul and nodded her head, "Yep. That's the truth."

*****

After Michele and Paul returned their horses, the couple walked back towards the guest house. Paul grabbed Michele's hand as they walked so, he could show off their relationship to the village people. After walking a couple of blocks, Paul said, "I'm starving."

"Leewan should be home by now. We can get something to snack on when we get back."

As the couple continued to walk down the busy street, a lot of the locals acknowledged them with either a tip of the head, a smile, and/or a wave. Michele and Paul returned the gestures with either a pleasant smile or verbal reception. As the couple made their way down the street, Michele heard some horses coming up from behind.

"Move! Get out of the way!" someone howled.

Michele and Paul jumped to the side and watched as three guards rode by followed by one of the king's carriages. As the carriage rolled by, Michele saw her half-sister, Amarina, and her step-mother, Lalirra. Amarina, dressed to the hilt, gave Michele a dirty look. Michele thought: *Now I've done it! Walking down the streets in filthy clothes from a day of riding. I am never going to live this one down!*

Paul looked at the back of the ensemble and said, "No wonder they need three guards in the front and two in the back, looks like they bought the stores out."

Michele looked at him and said sarcastically, "I'm sure they only bought the things they truly needed."

They both laughed at the joke and continued walking down the crowded streets.

Chapter 57

When the couple walked into the house, Leewan said, "There's the two of you. We're late for a meeting at the castle."

"Can we change and grab a bite to eat first?" Michele asked.

Leewan looked at their dirty outfits and said, "I guess you better change. I'll make you a quick snack to eat on the way."

*****

Michele and Paul gobbled down their ham sandwiches on the short walk to the castle.

"Thanks, Leewan, that hit the spot," Paul said.

The guards at the castle's entrance bowed to Michele; then one of them said, "Follow me to the council room."

When the trio walked into the room, Michele noticed Jayden sitting at the table along with the other two guards that were assigned to watch her in Queensland; they were deep in conversation with King Levi. Queen Chloe turned when the trio walked into the room. She ran up to greet Michele, then said, "Come in. Have a seat." Michele walked over to the table and took a seat between her dad and one of the guards.

Leewan stood next to Paul momentary. She watched as Paul stared at Jayden's backside with hatred and anger brewing in his eyes. She touched his shoulder lightly and pulled him from the daze. She smiled sympathetically and said, "Go ask that guard sitting next to Michele to move so you can sit there."

Paul walked over to where Michele was sitting, shooting evil looks at Jayden all the way. He touched the guard on the shoulder and asked, "Do you mind moving so I can sit by Michele." The guard looked at him, then Michele.

Michele nodded her head and said, "Will you please sit on the other side of the table, by Leewan."

"As you wish, princess." The guard stood up and moved.

After everyone was seated, the king looked at his watch then cleared his throat. "Now that we're all finally here, I thought we all could discuss the plans for your trip to Russia. Jayden here made all the plane and hotel reservations. He and these two guards will escort you to Queensland on my yacht. From there, you will be driven to the airport in Brisbane. Jayden made reservations at a hotel near the Brightside Long-term Care Institution for two nights. That should give you plenty of time to find out whether or not your mother is at this institution. If she is there, Jayden has my full blessings to make any decision he needs -- to bring your mother home safely."

Michele smiled and said, "Thank you, grandpa."

The king turned red and squirmed in his chair when he heard her call him grandpa. "Um-hum." He cleared his throat and said, "You're welcome."

Macalla looked at his daughter and said, "I know you've met Jayden and his men before since I had them follow you in Queensland. Jayden is one of our top security guards. I'm sending him since I can't go with you and I know he will protect you with his life."

Paul's face turned red as he dug his fingers into Michele's thigh.

"Ouch," she gave him a dirty look.

He released his grip and whispered, "Sorry."

Macalla looked at Paul briefly, then continued, "And Dwayne and Charles are top-notched guards too. They have proven their worth over and over again. I believe these men will do everything in their power to keep you, Paul, and Leewan safe."

Looking at Jayden, Michele asked, "When do we leave?"

"First thing in the morning; if that okay with everyone."

Leewan and Michele nodded their heads while Paul just stared.

Chloe spoke up, "Before you leave tomorrow, a language-barrier witch will put a spell on everyone who is traveling to Moscow – so you'll be able to speak and understand their language…. Macalla, are your plans all set for traveling to the islands?"

"Yes, we leave first thing in the morning too. I am taking a shipload of guards with me. Our first stop is the Island of Keelonie. I'll be staying at the castle there with Lalirra's parents, Moki and Merrin Taylor."

"Good. Now that everything is all settled, can we all adjourn to the formal dining room?"

The king stood up, rubbed his belly, and said, "Sounds like a splendid idea to me, my dear." He walked over to the queen and stuck out his arm. The queen took her husband's arm and winked at Leewan.

*****

After dinner, Michele, Paul, and Leewan went back to the guest house to pack. Paul avoided Michele while packing and gave her the cold shoulder while they carried their luggage down the stairs.

At the bottom of the stairs, Michele asked, "What's wrong with you?"

Paul blew up, "You know what's wrong. Why does Jayden, of all people, have to escort us to Russia?"

"You heard my dad; he's one of their top guards."

"One of them. So, there should be someone else, anyone else, that can escort us to Russia."

Paul slammed his carry-on bag on the foyer's floor. Leewan walked out of the kitchen. "What's all the commotion about?"

Paul just stared at Michele. His face red.

Michele looked at Leewan, "Paul doesn't want Jayden to go."

Leewan nodded her head and mumbled, "Understandably."

"What? You're taking his side?"

Leewan looked at Paul and said, "If it will make you feel better, against my better judgment, you can share one of the hotel rooms with Michele and I'll take the other room."

"What?" Michele couldn't believe her ears.

Leewan looked at her, "I ran away with your grandfather when I was only 16. I'm not naive. I know the two of you have been sleeping together."

Michele looked down at the floor, embarrassed.

Leewan looked at Paul. "Will that make you feel better?"

Paul nodded his head and indecisively said, "Yeah. That would make me feel better. If Michele agrees?"

Michele looked up at him and said, "Yes. I agree. But you better not tell anyone in America."

He replied with a smile, "Just our little secret."

Chapter 58

Michele looked around a dark room and wondered: *Where am I?* She looked out a window and saw a village down below and some boat docks. *I must be up in a tower... And that ship tied to the boat dock looks like one of King Levi's ships.* When she turned around, she thought she saw someone lying on a bed in the dim moonlight. She walked closer to the bed and noticed that the person was her father, Prince Macalla. He was lying on his side, clutching his gut and groaning. His breathing was ragged. She took a seat on the edge of the bed and placed her hands on him. "Dad. Are you ok? What did they do to you?" When he didn't respond, she started shaking him. "Dad. Wake up! Dad!" She looked around the room for help. She noticed a poster sitting on the bedside table. She held the picture up so she could see it in the moonlight. It was a picture of her with Zoe on White Lightning; the caption read: *Does this look like a criminal to you?*

"Wake up Michele." Paul was shaking her. "Are you ok? You were squirming in your seat. You're all sweaty."

"Oh no! Why did you wake me up?" Michele looked around in the dark cabin of the plane. Just then, the cabin lights flicked on. The captain announced on the intercom, "We will be making landfall within 30 minutes. Flight attendants, please prepare the cabin for our final descent."

"Oh no! Where's Leewan?"

"She's sitting near the back of the plane," Paul replied.

"I have to talk to her." Michele looked over the back of her seat and called her name. When she couldn't see her, she unclamped her seat belt and started to get up. A flight attendant looked at her and said, "Ma'am, you need to sit back down. The seat belt light is on. We'll be landing soon."

Michele sat back in her seat with a huff.

Paul looked at her watery eyes and asked, "What's wrong?"

"My dad. I saw him in my dream. I think the Taylors poisoned him. I need to talk to my grandmother."

Paul tried to comfort her, but she just pushed his hand away and stared out the window.

*****

When the plane landed, Michele walked into the airport lobby. She looked at Paul through tear-filled eyes and said, "When my grandmother gets off the plane, send her over to me. I'm going to go find a couple of seats over there." She pointed to some vacant chairs.

When Jayden walked out of the tunnel, he saw Michele talking to Paul -- with tears in her eyes. He watched as she walked away. Out of concern for Michele, he took off after her, passing by Paul in the progress. Paul noticed Jayden following Michele so he walked up behind him and shoved him off track with his shoulder. Jayden looked at him with surprise and said, "What the hell."

Paul glared at Jayden and said, "Don't worry about Michele. I'll comfort her. Just do your job and watch for anyone that might be following us."

Jayden put his hands up in surrender. "No harm done. I just wanted to make sure she was ok."

"She needs to talk to her grandmother. Not you."

Leewan walked up at that moment, "What's going on boys?"

Paul pointed to Michele, "She needs to talk to you. It's about her dad."

*****

"What's wrong dear?"

After Michele told Leewan about the dream, Leewan just sat there, speechless.

Michele argued, "What good is my magic if I can't go back and help him. We can't even call someone to go help him since that stupid boundary spell. I need to get to the hotel – so I can try to get back to sleep."

"So, we shall."

During the car ride to the hotel, Michele stared out the window while Leewan filled Paul in on the dream.

"Oh shit. I'm so sorry Michele -- for waking you."

"It's not your fault," she mumbled.

After checking into their rooms, Michele and Paul stopped at the first room the group came to. Paul handed Leewan his key, then went into the room with Michele. Standing in the hallway, Jayden looked at Leewan and said, "They're sharing a room?"

Leewan smiled, "Yes. I thought it was best."

Jayden stood there in surprise as Leewan walked down the hall to the next room.

*****

Some hours later, Michele called Leewan's room. "It didn't work. I took a nap but didn't have any dreams."

"Hopefully that means he's ok. Maybe you healed him?"

"Do you think so?"

"Like I told you before. The whispers of a dream are like that. They only show you things you might be able to change. All we can do now is to pray."

Michele was quiet for a couple of seconds, then said, "Could he have died."

Leewan didn't respond.

Michele broke down crying.

Leewan said, "Nothing we can do about it now. We just need to hope for the best, pull ourselves together, and try to find your mother. Then we can all go back to the islands to try to find your dad."

Michele nodded silently then replied, "Ok."

Paul and Michele ordered room service and spent the rest of the day lying around in bed watching TV. Paul tried to comfort Michele the best he could but felt guilty for waking her up.

Chapter 59

The next morning, the group met in the hotel's restaurant for breakfast. Leewan looked at the group to discuss the final plans for the day: "So, Michele and I will go into Brightside and check on Jane, while you guys wait outside. I have this burner-phone so I can call you guys if we need any assistance. Hopefully, she's there, and we can just sign her out and take her home."

The group nodded in agreement.

After the food bill was paid, the assembly made their way to their cars.

*****

When Michele and Leewan walked through the double doors into Brightside's front entrance, Michele noticed two large security doors with some chairs situated to the left of them and a security office on the right. She walked up to the glass window at the security office and told the guard, "We're here to see Jane."

"Jane who?" the security guard asked.

"Jane Doe." Michele took a guess.

The guard looked at some list on the computer screen. "There's no patient here named Jane Doe."

Michele started arguing, "I know Jane is here! She has dishwater-blonde hair, light-blue eyes, about 5'6", and around 155 pounds. She usually sits around in a wheelchair asking for her baby."

A nurse that was standing near a file cabinet in the security office, looking over at Michele and said, "We do have a patient that meets that description. Who did you say you were?"

"I'm Michele, her daughter. And this is her mother, Leewan. We've been searching for her."

"Leewan you say. Hmmm. Jane Five does call out the name Leewan every so often when she's upset. We have so many Jane Does here, that we had to start changing their last names to numbers." The nurse looked at the security guard, "I'll take these ladies to see Jane Five. See if she's the one they're looking for?"

"Your call." The security guard buzzed the security doors. The nurse walked out of the office, opened one of the doors, then said, "Follow me."

*****

The nurse led the two of them down a couple of halls then turned into a patient's room. When Michele walked in, she saw the woman from her dreams sitting in a wheelchair -- staring aimlessly out the window. Leewan recognized her daughter immediately. She rushed over to the wheelchair, grabbed her hand, and said, "Mayra! Baby cakes! It's me.... Your mother.... Leewan."

The woman turned her eyes in the direction of Leewan and crooked, "Leewan?"

"Yes! Yes! It's me, baby cakes."

The woman smiled briefly then returned her attention to the window. Michele tried talking to her, "Mom it's me. Your baby." But the woman just stared off into space.

The nurse spoke up, "Are you sure this is really who you are looking for?"

"Yes. Yes. This is my daughter. I want to take her home!"

"I'm not sure about that. She needs 24/7 care and has violent outbreaks."

"I don't care. She's my daughter. And to prove it, I bet she has a birthmark in the shape of a crescent moon on the inside of her left thigh."

The nurse walked over to the wheelchair and pulled up the patient's dress to expose the thigh. "I guess you're right. This must be your daughter."

"Can I take her home today?"

"Hold on. There's a lot of paperwork and red tape we have to go through first. And I would have to get ahold of the physician so he could write your scripts for all her medications and all the medical equipment you may need at home. Then you'll need some way to transport her since she is wheelchair-bound. Do you have a wheelchair or hospital bed at home? And are you prepared to handle such a load of caring for an in-valent daughter?"

"Yes. Can we start the paperwork today?"

The nurse looked at the visitors pleading eyes, then said, "I'll go get the release forms."

After the nurse left, Michele and Leewan tried multiple times to get Mayra to respond but she acted like she was in a different world. Leewan looked at Michele and said, "They most have her on a lot of drugs. That's probably why I was never able to contact her."

When the nurse came back with all the paperwork, Leewan took the papers and said, "Is there someplace we can go to fill these out... and get the ball rolling?"

The nurse smiled and said, "Sure. You can follow me to my office."

*****

While Leewan was filling out the paperwork, she asked the nurse, "How long before I'll be able to take her home?"

The nurse looked up from her desk thoughtfully, then replied, "I don't know... a month or two."

"A month or two! I can't wait that long. I wanted to take her home today. Tomorrow at the latest. We live in Queensland!"

"I'm so sorry. That's nearly impossible. You see, Jane Five is an award of the state -- meaning she has a power of attorney making all the decisions for her healthcare needs. They might need to investigate where Jane Five is being discharged to; and possibly do a home inspection -- to ensure that you have all the adequate supplies for caring for someone -- such as Jane. In addition, the doctor has to write the discharge papers, order all the prescriptions, and you might need to take a couple of classes on how to care for her. Like I said before, a lot of red-tape."

"That will not do!" Leewan started to get up from the table. Michele grabbed her arm and shook her head. Leewan took a couple deep breaths, then looked at the nurse. "I'll take these forms with me and drop them off tomorrow."

The nurse nodded. "I'm sorry about the inconvenience."

*****

Back at the hotel, the group discussed their options for breaking Mayra out of Brightside. They all came to a final conclusion… the only way they were going to get Mayra out of the institution was with magic; and for the plan to work, they needed the help of the mind-erasing witch.

Michele looked at Jayden and said, "We'll just have to extend our stay here and wait for Diane to get here. I can try to call her tonight in my dreams."

Jayden nodded his head, "I'll take care of the hotel and the plane reservations. Dwayne and Charles can go and pick up all the supplies we'll need."

Dwayne and Charles nodded in agreement.

Michele looked at Leewan and asked, "And what about my dad? I wanted to try to reach him tonight, but I can't do both."

"I can try to reach your dad tonight. You just concentrate on reaching Diane… after you do get a hold of her, maybe she'll know where your dad is?"

Michele nodded her head. Leewan continued talking to the group, "And remember, no phone calls, room to room, tonight or in the morning – unless it's an emergency. We don't need a ringing phone waking Michele or me up from a dream. We can meet for breakfast tomorrow morning in the hotel's restaurant, around 9:30 or 10."

Jayden looked at Michele and said, "If it will make you feel any better, I can send one of my men back to the hidden islands first thing in the morning – if you or Leewan cannot find Prince Macalla tonight."

"But don't you need your men here?"

"Doesn't look like anyone followed us, plus, I have you and Leewan... I don't think anyone, in their right mind, would want to piss off the two of you."

Michele smiled, "Thank you. That would make me feel better. There must be some way of opening up the communication lines to the islands without exposing all the witches."

Chapter 60

Michele was discussing her plans in bed while Paul massaged her back. "I just hope I can reach Diane tonight in my dreams. Otherwise, we might just have to turn in the forms to Brightside and return to Honiawae without my mother... And, I kind just kind of want to return to the islands so I can check on my dad.... I feel so useless right now."

"It'll be alright. I have faith in you. You'll be able to contact Diane tonight and find out your dad is alright; then Diane will be on the first flight over here."

"I hope your right. Now if I can just relax... so I can get to sleep. I'm just too wired."

Paul looks at her with a grin and said, "I think I can help you with that!" He walked over to his suitcase and pulled out a bottle of wine and a wine opener.

"Where did you get that?"

"I picked it up at the hotel's gift shop – just in case we needed it."

After a couple glasses of wine, Michele lied down on the bed feeling light-headed. Paul crawled over to her and started kissing her tenderly. After making slow, compassionate love, Michele repeated Diane's name three times and fell into a blissful sleep while holding her crystal necklace.

*****

Diane looked up from the book she was reading and asked, "What are you doing here?"

"I need your help."

Diane closed her book and said, "I'm all ears."

"I had a dream; my dad was sick. I think he was in the Taylors' castle."

"Your dad is fine. Guess he had a stomach bug or something – from something he ate at the Taylors' feast. He gave his speech on Keelonie Island today and is on his way to Mysteria Island as we speak. He reported back to his mom that the speech was well received and that he found posters of you nailed to trees. I guess the posters show you leading a little girl around on a horse. You did a good deed, Michele. The people are starting to trust you."

"You don't know how good that makes me feel."

"Well, you deserve to. That was nice of you to take the time and offer that little girl a horseback ride."

Michele laughed softly, "I didn't mean that. I meant about my dad. I was worried about him."

Diane smiled, "It's a father's job to worry about his daughter, not the other way around. By the way, he is worried about you. How are things going over there?"

"We found my mom."

"You what! That's great!"

"No. We hit a stone wall – head-on. The institution she's at said it will take a month or two to go through all the red tape of releasing her and that they may need to do a home visit – to make sure we have adequate space and supplies for caring for her."

"What?"

"Yeah. It's crazy. My mom is sort of out of it. Not sure what is wrong with her. So that's where you come in."

"What do you need me to do?"

Michele explained the situation and the plan to Diane. As the image began to fade, Diane nodded her head and shouted, "I'll catch the first flight I can find."

*****

Michele opened her sleepy eyes and looked at the ceiling. After her eyes began to focus, and she began to realize where she was, she turned her head and noticed Paul, propped up on one of his elbows, staring at her.

"You okay, babe?" he whispered while reaching out his hand to pull her body closer.

Michele turned slightly towards him and said, "Yes. I'm great! I was able to reach Diane, just like you said I would. She reassured me that my father was ok and she plans on flying here on the first flight she can catch."

"I'm glad your dad's ok, but I'm not sure how I feel about seeing Diane. I'm still mad at her for erasing most of my memories."

Michele reached up and started tracing small circles on his arm. "I know, babe. But the king made her do it…. for the protection of the islands."

"I know. But I'm still mad."

"Do you want me to try to make it all better?" she said with an evil grin.

Paul raise one eyebrow and asked, "Do you think you can?"

"Just lie there and let me try."

Paul rolled onto his back while Michele pulled down the covers. "Looks like you already had plans to make me feel better."

"No plans, but I was hopeful."

Michele climbed on top of him, grabbed his large dick, then slowly lowered herself down.

*****

"Come and take a shower with me before we go downstairs for breakfast."

"If I have to," Paul complained while he eagerly following Michele into the bathroom. After the couple took turns washing each other's bodies, Paul looked at her, swept his fingers through her hair, and asked, "Do we have time to go back to bed?"

Michele looked down at Paul's large growth between his legs and said, "I guess we have to."

*****

At the doorway, Paul put out his arm and asked Michele, "Shall I escort you to breakfast Madame."

She smiled, took his arm, and thought: *I could get used to this.*

Paul strutted into the hotel's restaurant with Michele on his arm. He glanced at Jayden and gave him a superior look. At the sight of Michele, Leewan jumped up from the table and said, "Good news... I got ahold of your dad last night. He's fine. He's just worried about you."

"And I got a hold of Diane, she's on her way."

Leewan hugged Michele then said, "Come. Come. We can share all the details over breakfast. I selected this back table so we can be out of earshot from any prying ears."

After everyone was seated, Paul slid his arm around the back of Michele's chair and continued to eye Jayden – daring him to try to make a move on his girl.

The waiter came over to the table to take everyone's orders. "We'll just have coffee and water for now," Leewan declared. "And I think we all want the buffet?" She looked around the table while everyone nodded their heads in agreement. After the waiter left, Leewan grabbed Michele's hands and said, "You first."

Michele told the group about her dream. Jayden spoke up. "Great! Diane should be here by tomorrow - at the latest. Guess me and my men have our work cut out for us today – getting everything ready for tomorrow. Charles purchased a wheelchair for Mayra yesterday."

Leewan nodded her head in approval, then said, "I met the prince on the ship last night. He thinks someone put poison in his ale during the Taylors' feast, but somehow he miraculously recovered."

"What? Did he have them arrested?" Michele exclaimed.

Leewan patted her hand. "No. He said there wasn't any way he could prove it and he's ok now. Your dad did laugh and say Merrin Taylor almost fainted when she saw him the next morning. I think you cured him Michele -- when you went to see him in your dream."

Michele put a hand over her mouth in relief, then said, "Oh thank God!"

"Your father also said that he found a lot of posters of you -- posted all over the island. I guess the poster had a picture of you leading a little girl around on a horse?"

"Yes. I saw that poster in my dream."

Leewan smiled, "Well you did good Michele. The people are seeing you for who you are. A lot of the people are turning away from the uprising. They no longer feel you are a threat to their way of living, but we still have a long road in front of us to convince the rest of the population."

Chapter 61

Diane called Leewan from Australia, "My flight is due to arrive in Moscow around 8 a.m."

"Great. I'll send one of the guards to pick you up."

"So, are we breaking Mayra out tomorrow then?"

"I'll leave that up to you; if you want one day to rest or if you think we should proceed."

"I'll be fine. The sooner we get this done the better."

"Great. I'll let Jayden know so he can make all the arrangements."

*****

Diane arrived at the hotel around 10 a.m. The group met in one of the hotel's conference room to make the final plans. After the plans were finalized, the group decided the best time to go would be around 2 p.m. when the residence would be either laying down in their rooms or watching TV in the recreation room -- and the staff members wouldn't be busy with morning meds or meals.

After the group had lunch, they drove over to Brightside. Jayden followed them in a rented, handicapped van. He had already made the arrangements for a private jet that was waiting, on standby, at a local, privately-owned airport for the rich and elite. When the group arrived, Diane and Dwayne pinned name tags on and grabbed an official-looking folder declaring information needed for a surprise government inspection.

Diane walked up to the security officer at the main entrance. She smiled and showed her badge. "Hi. Can I talk to the person in charge? We were sent here for a surprise inspection."

"Yes. Right away ma'am." The guard nervously shuffled some papers he was reading then called the nurse in charge.

The charge nurse appeared almost instantly. Shaking hands with Diane, she said, "My name is Gretchen Yoder, how can I help you?"

Diane introduced her partner then looked down at her clipboard and said, "We've had some complaints. Can you set up a meeting for me to discuss the complaints with your staff so we can all brainstorm some options for improvement?"

"Yes. Of course."

"While you're doing that, my associate and I will take a quick walkthrough to see if these complaints are warranted."

"Of course. I can take you on a tour and have my lead nurse notify all the staff of a mandatory meeting, say about three?"

"Diane smiled, "That should do fine."

The manager picked up her cellphone to fill the lead nurse in on the surprise inspection, "Have all the available staff meet in the residence's cafeteria at three."

*****

During the inspector's walkthrough, Michele and Leewan walked into the facility to visit Jane Five. Diane nodded her head at the pair while passing in the hall – secretly communicating the meeting time and place with Leewan telepathically.

When Michele and Leewan walked into Mayra's room, she was sleeping peacefully. As Michele walked around the side of the bed, she looked at her grandmother and said, "I bet they have her sedated again."

Leewan nodded, then took her phone out of her purse to call Jayden. "It's going down at three in the resident's cafeteria. Have Paul ready with the getaway car for Michele, Diane, and me. You and Charles come on in the building at three, tie the security guard up, then break into the manager's office to get any files they have on Jane Five. After we secured most of the staff at the meeting, we'll search for any staff members left out on the floors and bring them to the front entrance -- so Diane can work her magic."

"Paul is insisting that he wants to help. He said he could start rounding up staff members, requesting their assistance, while we take care of the security guard."

"Then let him. Michele and I are packing up Mayra's belongings now."

At 3 p.m. sharp, Michele and Leewan made their way to the resident's cafeteria. Most of the staff members there were just finding their seats. The manager looked over at Michele and Leewan when they walked in and thought: *What are they doing here?* She started walking towards them to request their leave when Michele screamed, "Stop." Everyone in the room froze except for the three witches. Leewan closed the doors and Diane proceeded by lifting her hands up, palms down and chanting in a foreign language. Michele listened in amazement as Diane erased all the staff's memories of ever having a patient named Jane Five and changed the agenda of the mandatory meeting into a discussion on decreasing the patient/staff ratios. After Diane's work was done, Leewan said, "Come. We have to find the outliers."

Michele looked at the staff members frozen in time. "What about them?"

"Leave them. We'll unfreeze them after we get Mayra in the van."

****

Leewan, Michele, and Diane found Jayden in the front entrance, by the security office. He had his gun pointed at the security guard and some of the staff members that were sitting on the floor. When the group walked in, he glanced at them and said, "Oh good, you're here. That one there will not quit crying. She's giving me a headache."

Michele looked at the young woman that Jayden pointed his gun at. "Don't worry. It will all be over soon. No one will get hurt if they just listen to what they are told to do."

The woman looked at Michele with her teared-soaked face and said, "Please don't let him hurt me. I have young children at home!"

"Just sit there and you will be able to see your children tonight."

Paul walked into the room, shoving a man in a white uniform. "I think he's the last one."

"Sit." Jayden pointed his gun at the orderly.

Charles walked in. "Think we have everyone. I couldn't find anyone else. We need to get this done. The patients are getting restless out there."

Leewan said, "Ok. Paul and Charles get Mayra into the van. Don't forget to strip her bed and grab the bag with her belongings. It's in the closet. Text us when it's done on the group message so we know when it's safe to proceed. Jayden, you stay here with Diane. You can untie the security guard after Diane does her magic. Michele and I will return to the cafeteria. We'll unfreeze the staff as soon as we get the text."

Chapter 62

During the flight back to Queensland, Mayra just sat quietly, staring off into space. She smelled like urine and her hair was dull and greasy. Michele looked at Leewan and asked, "What did they do to her?"

"I'm not sure dear. But I fear the worst is yet to come when she starts withdrawing from whatever drugs they have her hooked on."

"You don't think they used shock therapy on her or she had some sort of head injury to make her this way?"

"I don't think so. I didn't see any scars on her head. But who knows what happened to her before she got caught up in the system?"

*****

When the jet landed in Queensland early the next morning, some of the yacht's crew members were already there waiting in cars. Before moving Mayra from the plane, Jayden stood up from his seat, looked at Michele with concern in his eyes, then said, "Sorry I have to ask." He looked at Leewan, sitting next to Michele, and asked, "Do you think we should restrain Mayra with my handcuffs before putting her in the car? Just in case she becomes violent. We don't want to have to use any physical force on her."

Michele looked at Leewan in horror, "No! They can't treat her that way."

Leewan patted her leg and replied, "I know dear. It sounds cruel, but it's for her own safety." Then she looked at Jayden and said, "I don't think we need to restrain her in the car since I think we still have time – before the drugs wear off. But I do think Michele should ride with you and the guards on the way to the yacht...just in case she does gets violent and can tap into her powers."

Leewan noticed a flash of red in Paul's eyes. She looked back at Jayden and saw him smirk at Paul. *Oh great! Jayden sure isn't helping to make this situation any better.* "Paul. I need your help loading all our luggage into the cars."

Paul glared at Jayden one last time, then uttered, "Sure. I'll go start loading up the cars." He jumped up from his seat then bumped into Jayden, hard while exiting the plane. Jayden stumbled backward but caught himself from falling. Paul shot Jayden a look over his shoulder and said, "Sorry about that."

*****

Michele looked at Paul before she got into the car. She waved slightly and shouted, "See you at the docks." The driver held the door open while she crawled into the SUV's third roll of seats -- with Jayden. Jayden smiled at her while she thought: *Oh shit! Paul's mad. Guess I can't blame him. What did I get myself into?*

Dwayne and Charles put Mayra in the second roll of seats, situated between them. As the driver pulled away, Jayden rested his hand on Michele's leg. She instantly felt a warm tingling feeling in her leg. As she looked down at his hand, she noticed out of the corner of her eye that her crystal necklace was glowing. *What the fuck?* She looked up into Jayden's baby-blue eyes. He gave her a sexy smile and said, "Just remember Michele, if you ever need anything. I'm here for you."

"I appreciate that." She turned her head to look out the window, unable to ignore the sensation from his hand on her thigh.

****

Mayra never made a peep during the car ride to the boat docks, she mostly just slept or stared aimlessly at the car's ceiling with her head cocked to the side. Charles had to use his handkerchief frequently to dab at the drool coming from her mouth. The cars did stop, one time on the way to the docks, at a local drive-through so everyone could grab a bite to eat. After ordering their food, Michele swapped places with Charles so she could try to feed Mayra.

When they finally made it to the boat docks, the guards transferred Mayra to a wheelchair. Michele and Jayden followed close behind the wheelchair as Charles pushed her to the yacht, surveying the surroundings for anything unusual. Once onboard, Leewan grabbed Michele's hand and pulled her to the side. "Everything okay?"

Michele nodded her head.

"You know they have to tie Mayra up in bed since she might wake up... and go batshit crazy. We do have one injection of Ativan to give her – if need be. If you want to go upstairs and keep watch with Diane and Paul, I'll stay in Mayra's room with the guards... or vice versa."

Michele shrugged her shoulders and said, "Whatever you think is best."

"It's not my decision. You have to decide what is best for you. And I'm not just talking about Mayra."

Michele jerked her head up. "What are you saying?"

"You know what I mean. The decisions you make now will affect the rest of your life... not mine."

Michele nodded while she glanced at Paul, then Jayden. "I'll go upstairs with Paul."

*****

The guards, disguised as crewmembers, walked the top decks while Michele, Diane, and Paul watched out the bulletproof windows from the inside yacht. After a couple of hours of watching out the windows in silence, Diane got up from her seat and poured herself some lemonade. She looked at the couple staring out the windows and said, "I'm going up to visit the captain so you guys can have some time alone."

After Diane left, Michele sat in silence thinking about what Leewan said. She looked at Paul and asked, "Are you mad at me?"

"No. Should I be? I'm just giving you time to think about who you really want. I don't want to force you to choose me!"

Michele didn't know how to respond so just continued to watch out the windows. After a while of sipping lemonade and watching, Michele looked at Paul and said, "I can't wait until we get back to the guest house. I'm exhausted." When he didn't respond, she asked, "Paul. Did you hear me?"

He dropped his binoculars down into his lap and replied, "Yes. I'm just wondering if I'm seeing things or if those two spots, I see in the distance, are two boats waiting to intercept us at the opening to the hidden islands' waterway.

Michele grabbed her binoculars off the coffee table and looked where Paul was pointing. "I think your right. We better go alert the guards and my grandmother."

*****

Leewan joined Michele, Paul, and Diane up in the captain's room to watch the approaching boats. After looking through a pair of binoculars, Leewan said, "They look like a couple of the Taylors' boats. I think I can make out there red and white flags."

As the yacht approached the opening to the hidden islands, the two boats they were watching disappeared; however, the ocean's waves began to kick up -- making it hard for the captain to navigate the boat through the narrow passage. Watching the underwater sonar cameras, Leewan pointed out the underwater mountains reaching up towards the yacht. "Those six-foot waves are pushing us dangerously close to those jagged peaks. If our boat hits one of them, those rocks are bound to rip a hole into the side of this yacht. The Taylors must have some witch or warlock working for them."

"Look," The captain let out a hollow and pointed at a large twelve-foot wave heading towards the port side of the boat. "Take cover."

Most of the people on the boat started screaming and running for cover. Michele stepped out onto the top deck and held both of her hands up into the wind. She squinted her eyes so she could see through the water splatter; then with all her might she pushed out her hands and screamed, "Stop!" The wave froze instantly while the boat continued forward out of harm's way. Once the boat was out of danger, she dropped her hands and the wave came crashing down behind them.

Leewan ran up to her, hugged her, and said, "You did it! You saved us all."

Michele looked around the open sea and said, "I just wish I knew where those boats were hiding."

*****

The yacht made it into port without any further incident. When the group disembarked, they found the queen waiting for them at the dock's entrance. When the queen saw Michele, she ran up to her to give her a hug. "I'm so glad you guys made it back." Then she turned and saw Mayra sitting in a wheelchair and said, "Oh my heavens!" She grabbed the arm of a passing guard and said, "Take her to the medical center at once."

Leewan spoke up, "No. No disrespect Queen Chloe. But I prefer to nurse her back on my own at the guest house."

The queen nodded and replied, "As you wish. But if you change your mind, there's always a room available for her at the medical center – free of charge. I can send a physician over to the guest house tonight so the two of you can discuss what supplies you might need."

"Thank you! You've been more than kind."

Michele interrupted their conversation and asked Chloe, "Is my dad back yet?"

"No dear. He's still out visiting all of the islands. You can call him from the guest house once you get settled…. But I would wait until this evening when he should have more free time on his hands."

Chapter 63

While Leewan was trying to feed Mayra in the kitchen, there was a knock on the door. Michele opened the door and was greeted by her dad's mother, Chloe. "How's everything going?"

"Okay. I guess."

"I brought Dr. Niec and his nurse with me. I also took the liberty of having my staff bring over a hospital bed, bedside commode, and some much need medical supplies."

"Thank you! Come on in."

Michele looked into the kitchen where Leewan was sitting and asked, "Where should the staff put the hospital bed?"

"See if they can rearrange the furniture in the back sitting-room so the hospital bed can face the sliding-glass door that leads to the sunroom and flower garden."

After the bed was set up and Chloe's staff members left, Leewan rolled Mayra's wheelchair to the sitting-room then, with the help of the nurse, put Mayra into the bed. The doctor reviewed Mayra's hospital records then performed a thorough examination. When he was done, he announced, "She looks perfectly healthy -- except for her mental status. Not sure about her mental compacity—since I'm not a psychiatrist. But in my opinion, she should wake up more after she goes through withdrawals. Only time will tell if she'll ever have the mental compacity to care for herself."

Leewan shook her head and looked down at her once vivant daughter lying motionlessly in bed. The doctor continued, "I'm sorry to have to tell you such a poor prognosis... I just don't want to give you any false hope. Like I said... Only time will tell. I will leave you with some medications to help with the withdrawals -- along with the instructions on what doses to give and how often." He reached into his pocket and held out a card. "Here's my private number. You can call me anytime, day or night, if you need anything else."

Leewan smiled slightly, then said, "Thank you for all your help. I will be calling you if we run into any trouble."

Chloe looked at her diamond watch. "Look at the time. Guess we should be going. I'm sure you guys need your rest after such a journey."

Michele looked up from the couch at the queen. "Can I talk to you before you leave? Privately."

"Of course, dear."

Michele and her grandmother walked to the library. Michele pulled the doors shut and told Chloe about the incident out at sea. "I can't be sure, but Leewan thought she saw some red and white flags on the boats."

"Very interesting. I'm not convenience the Taylors didn't have anything to do with the disappearance of your mother, unlike your grandfather. I'll ask around."

"Thanks, grandma."

Chloe started walking towards the door then stopped. "Michele. You know you can come to visit me anytime you like at the castle. My home is yours. And, feel free to explore it, if you want to."

"I might just do that! I do want to explore the catacombs."

"Anytime. They're part of your history too."

After Chloe and the guest left, Michele and Paul helped Leewan bring down her beddings and some of her belongings to the sitting-room so Leewan could make her bed on the couch. While sitting down on the couch, Leewan looked at the pair and said, "Thanks for the help. I'll be sleeping down here with Mayra until she gets better. The two of you can retire to your own rooms... I'll call you if I need any help."

Michele and Paul made their way up the stairs. At the threshold of her room, Michele turned, looked at Paul, and said, "Good night."

Paul asked, "Can't I come in?"

She shook her head and said, "You heard my grandmother. She wanted us to go to our own rooms, plus I'm exhausted. Paul looked at her, clearly upset. She gave him a quick peck on the cheek and said, "I'll see you in the morning." She closed her bedroom door, leaned her back up against it, and thought about what her grandmother had said: *The decisions I make today will affect the rest of my life.*

*****

The next morning, when Paul got up, he noticed Michele was already gone from her room. When he walked downstairs, he found her and Leewan sitting in the back sitting-room staring at Mayra. They both looked exhausted. "How was her night?" he asked.

"Awful," Leewan replied. "She started going through withdrawal. We just finally got her to sleep."

"Why didn't you wake me?"

Michele looked up and said, "Because she was seizing. Leewan couldn't give her a shot with her thrashing about so she needed me to freeze her while she gave her a shot. When Mayra finally quit shacking, we had to pad her bed railings to prevent her from hurting herself."

"Anything you want me to do?"

"Michele and I have it handled. But thank you. You can just make yourself at home. There's plenty of food and coffee in the kitchen. Just help yourself."

Michele stayed with Leewan the rest of the day, caring for Mayra. Mayra woke up several times, all hot and sweaty. And when she did, she would thrash around the bed and scream incoherent things; however, a couple of times she did scream comprehensible words such as, "No. No. Stop. Please stop." Michele and Leewan worked tirelessly bathing her with washcloths, medicating her, and trying to console her. Michele even tried to use her healing powers a couple of times on Mayra -- to no avail.

Paul made Leewan and Michele turkey sandwiches for a late lunch. He handed a sandwich to Michele and said, "Here. You need to eat." She took one bite of the sandwich, forced a smile, then set it back down on the plate. After Paul finished his sandwich, he looked at Michele and asked, "Can we talk?"

She just shook her head and said, "What's there to talk about. My mother needs me."

Paul shook his head and said, "Then I'm going for a walk." He jumped up out of the chair and stormed out the front door. Michele glanced at Leewan, Leewan shrugged her shoulders. Michele hopped out of her seat and walked to the front door. She cracked the front door and watched as Paul walked out into the street and looked up at the castle. From the distance, Michele could see him waving at someone. She looked up at the castle a saw her half-sister, Amarina, waving at him. She closed the door and thought: *Oh great. Now I'm chasing him off into the arms of another woman. I need to decide, sooner rather than later, whether or not I want a relationship with Paul or Jayden.*

The next couple of days, Michele and Leewan worked diligently in caring for Mayra while she went through withdraws – putting Michele's and Paul's relationship on hold. Paul, feeling left out, disappeared for hours each day. Michele was distraught; she had suspicions that Paul was meeting up with her half-sister but she didn't confront him since she was torn between her feelings for him and Jayden and didn't have any time to sort them out.

By the third day, Mayra's severe withdrawal symptoms had abated, leaving her in a stupor. A nurse stopped by that day to start Mayra on intravenous feedings. When Paul returned from his evening walk, he asked Michele if they could talk. When she blew him off again, he marched up to his room and punched a hole in the wall while thinking of Jayden. The wall instantly repaired itself. *What the hell?* he thought. He sat down on his bed and stared at the wall. *Maybe I should take the hint and just go back to the states.*

Chapter 64

The next morning, Prince Macalla returned from his tour. After he stopped by the castle to talk with his mom and dad, he went to the guest house to see Michele and to check up on Mayra – he brought Jayden with him. When Jayden walked in the front door, behind Macalla, Paul stared at him with anger pulsating through his veins.

Leewan greeted Macalla and Jayden with a hug then Michele followed suit.

Macalla was the first one to address Paul while he stood there with his blood boiling, "Some vacation, huh? How are you holding up?"

Paul swallowed hard, took a deep breath to calm his nerves, then replied, "Alright. I guess."

Macalla looked at Michele and said, "The two of you need to get out of the house. My mother said you sounded excited to come and explore the castle. Why don't the two of you come to visit me later this afternoon? I can show you the catacombs… if you want to see them?"

Michele glanced at Paul, then replied, "We might just do that."

"If you need a break too, Leewan, my mother said she could send a nurse over to relieve you."

"No. I'm fine. Tell your mom thanks though."

"Will do. So… where's Mayra? I heard she wasn't doing so well."

"She's in the backroom," Leewan replied. "Follow me."

When Macalla walked into the sitting-room, he stopped dead in his tracks at the sight of Mayra: gone was the spirited, young woman with a sparkle for life in her eyes, replaced by an unresponsive, older woman with lifeless, blue eyes. He walked up to the bed, took her hand, and called her name. When she didn't respond, he looked at Leewan with tears in his eyes and said, "So the rumors are true? Mayra has lost her mind?"

"The doctor doesn't know that for sure. Only time will tell."

*****

After Macalla and Jayden left, Michele asked Paul, "So, do you want to go explore the castle with me --later on today?"

"You can just go explore them with Jayden if you want. I might stay here and talk to Leewan -- make my arrangements to head back to America."

"What? Why?"

"You know why. You've barely said boo to me the last couple of days.... And I see how you look at Jayden."

"Paul." Michele reached out to touch him but he jerked away. "I told you I was just upset about my mother. I don't want you to go."

"If that's true. Then tell me you don't have any feelings for Jayden."

"I. I don't know. There's this strange pull but...."

"Oh! Fuck it. I'm going for a walk. You have fun on your tour." Paul stormed out the front door.

Michele stood in the front foyer debating what to do. *Am I supposed to go chase after him or give him some space?* She watched as Paul rounded the corner then closed the front door. With tears in her eyes, she ran up the stairs. She needed time alone-- to think. The glass cupola on top of the house sounded like the best place to be. When she got to the third floor, a flash out of the corner of her eyes stopped her from ascending the rooftop stairs. Slowly, she walked towards the end of the hall and noticed that the door to Martha's old room was wide open. Michele tried the light switch without any luck so she turned on her cellphone's flashlight. As she walked into the room the door slammed shut behind her. She jumped, turned around, and tried to open the door – but it was locked. She looked at the doorknob and began to panic: *This doorknob requires a key from both sides?* Michele started jimmying the doorknob while saying "Open, Open, Open." Then she screamed when she heard a loud thud behind her. "Who's there?" She looked in the direction of the noise and noticed a large book had fallen off a bookshelf. She glanced around the room and saw a wall full of shelves, a table with some chairs, a dresser, and an old, four-poster bed with a couple of bedside tables. Turning her attention back to the door, she tried to open it again. When the door wouldn't budge, she took her phone and tried to call her grandmother. *Oh, hell no. No phone signal in this room!* Michele started calling for help while pounding on the door. *Shit! Leewan will never hear me from up here.* She took a step back and tried to use her magic to push the door open. *Fuck! It won't budge.* Looking around the room she said, "Martha. If you are here. I could use a little help!" Michele heard a fluttering sound and looked back to the book that was lying on the ground. The pages were turning back and forth until they finally stopped on a specific page. Michele walked over to the book and picked it up. Using her fingers to save the page, she closed the book to read the cover: *The History of the Hidden Islands of Honiawae.*

Looking around the room, Michele said, "If I am supposed to read this book --it would be nice to have better lighting." Instantaneously, numerous candles that were situated on the opposite wall's shelves burst to life. Michele walked back across the room, set the open book down on the table, then looked at all the lit candles on the shelves. *I wonder what's in all those jars?* She walked over to the shelving system and started reading some of the labels: *bay root, sage, rosemary, lavender...* As she was exploring the shelves, a couple of candles floated over to the table. Michele followed the candles over and tried to read the first paragraph. "This lighting is still too dim. Can I take the book to the glass cupola if I promise to bring it back?"

All the candles in the room started to flicker, then extinguished out. Michele thought: *Oh shit! I think I pissed her off.* The bedroom door blew open. Michele looked around into the darkness and said "Thank you!"

Chapter 65

Michele took a seat in the glass cupola and proceeded to read the page the book had selected. It was about a boy born seven years before Michele named Jayden. *What the hell!*

Michele flipped a page back and started skimming the names.

Jayden's parents were William and Juliet Hoekstra of Gatherson's Island.

Juliet's parents were Sidney and Rochelle Winters of Gatherson's Island.

Rochelle's parents were Theodore Macbeth of Honiawae Island and Beatrix Deneen of Gatherson's Island.

Michele thought about this information for a minute. *Hmm... For some reason the book wanted me to see this. Looks like Rochelle was born out of wedlock. Her father, Theodore, was from this island. The same island my grandmother grew up on. I wonder if Leewan knows anyone with the last name of Macbeth?*

Michele's cellphone started to ring. She glanced at her caller ID then answered, "Hi dad."

"Hey. I have some free time now if you and Paul want to stop over for lunch. Then after lunch, we could explore the catacombs."

"I loved to. Let me find... I mean get around, then Paul and I will head over."

"Sounds good. See you soon."

"Wait! Dad."

"Yes."

"Do you know off hand what Leewan's last name was before she got married?"

"Macbeth. Why?"

After a silent pause, Michele continued, "Oh nothing. I just found a history book that includes a family tree."

"You should bring it. Then when I show you the tombs, you'll understand your family's history."

"I'm not sure if I can take this book out of this house.... If you know what I mean."

"Not really. But I have heard stranger things happening at that house."

Michele hung up the phone and thought: *I wonder if Leewan had an Uncle or brother named Theodore? Hmmm. I promised Martha I wouldn't take the book out of the house.... But I never promised I wouldn't take a couple of pictures of it with my cellphone.*

*****

Michele started walking down the stairs with the book and thought: *Maybe I'll drop the book off in my room to read later.* When she started descending the stairs off the third floor. The book flew out of her hands, down the hall, and into Martha's old bedroom. Michele jumped when she heard the door slam shut. *Oh shit. I think I pissed her off again!* Michele backtracked to the bedroom door, but it was locked. Holding her hand on the door, she whispered, "I didn't break my promise. I was planning on returning it. I just wanted to read it some more… Forgive me… And thank you!"

Michele walked down the stairs to her room and tried to call Paul. When he didn't answer, she walked downstairs to find Leewan. When she reached the foyer, she could hear Paul talking in the kitchen so she hid behind the kitchen wall to eavesdrop.

"I understand how you feel Paul. I just think you need to give Michele a little more time. She's been under a lot of stress."

"I just don't know how much more of this I can take. She's been acting so distant lately. And then this thing with Jayden."

"I agree. But if you do decide to go back to the states without her, we need to discuss your memories."

"Erase them all! I don't care anymore."

Michele took a deep breath and covered her mouth.

Leewan continued. "I'm going to tell you something I haven't even told Michele yet -- about the chosen one."

"The chosen one?"

"Yes. There's been a story, passed down from generation to generation, of a chosen one. This person will marry an outsider, have unlimited power, and change our way of living... That's why a lot of the people here on the islands are afraid of Michele. If she is the chosen one, she is supposed to change the status quo, and most people are afraid of change and what change can do to their peaceful way of living."

"So that's why some of the people here overreacted and thought Michele and I were going to expose the islands?"

"More than likely. But maybe the change is finding my daughter—if she ever wakes up and is not totally brain damaged from years of drug use."

"Do you think I'm the outsider that is supposed to be her husband."

"I thought so... but now I'm not sure. The problem is Jayden. I don't know where he is from. Michele told me her necklace started to glow when she was around him and that he has the whispers of a dream power – which is rare. I planned on looking into it. Sorry. I failed to do so.... With all that's been happening. Maybe all I have to do is to ask Jayden. Maybe he would tell me where he is from?"

Michele burst into the room. "I think I know where Jayden is from."

Paul and Leewan looked up in surprise. Leewan asked, "How much did you hear?"

"Enough."

Paul looked down at the table.

Leewan continued, "How do you know where Jayden is from? Did he tell you?"

"No. Martha did."

"Martha Black? My great, great, great grandmother?"

"Yes. I mean no. She didn't actually tell me. But she showed me a book on the history of the islands. The book opened to a family tree of sorts, about Jayden."

"Oh! And what did it say?"

"Do you know a Theodore Macbeth?"

"Yes. He was my mother's younger brother, my uncle? He died in the line of duty when he was in his thirties."

"Well. According to the book I read. Theodore Macbeth is Jayden's great-grandfather."

"That can't be true. My uncle never married; but since my mother died when I was born, I never really got to know him. My evil stepmother would tell me stories about him and how he was a no-good-for-nothing, just like my mom.   She said my mother was the town tramp and my uncle -- a lady's man. Supposedly my uncle liked his women almost as much as he liked his ale. According my stepmother, my uncle had a different barfly at every port, and he didn't die in the line of duty – he was killed for fooling around with someone else's wife."

"So, he could have had a child by a woman named Beatrix Deneen of Gatherson's Island?"

"I suppose so."

"So, that would make Jayden my distant cousin."

"Yes! You could be right."

Paul stood up and smiled, "Jayden is your relative. That's why you feel a connection."

"Must be. Sort of a brotherly love."

Paul gave Michele a big hug, kissed her on the check, then said, "I'm sorry Baby. Instead of being jealous and should have been more supportive of you."

"That's ok. I didn't understand it either." She looked at her watch. "My dad's expecting us for lunch. Will you be ok grandmother, if Paul and I leave you alone with Mayra?"

"Sure. Sure. Go have fun."

Chapter 66

When Michele and Paul showed up at the castle's formal dining room, Michele's half-sister, Amarina, said, "Great. They finally showed up. Can we eat now?"

Lalirra patted her daughter's arm and said, "Pretty soon, dear." Then she smiled at the king.

Chloe jumped from her seat to meet Michele. "Come on in dear. We've been waiting for you."

Michele looked at the royal party all dressed up in gowns and suits again; then she looked down at her own outfit and Paul's. "Are you sure it's okay if I just wear shorts and a t-shirt."

"Of course, dear. We…" Chloe swept her arm back to include the royal party, "… have to dress the part since the people of these islands come to us for advice and leadership. When your dad was your age. He wore jeans and a t-shirt while out riding the countryside. He liked blending in and socializing with everyone. Your dad and I always thought-- it's not the clothes that make the person, nor the family they were born into. It's what's in here…" Chloe pointed to her heart, "…that makes a person special."

Michele smiled and hugged her grandmother.

After everyone was seated, Lalirra spoke up. "I've heard congratulations are in order. You've found your mother."

"Yeah. But I heard that she's a vegetable," Amarina added, then shucked down in her seat, worried Michele might make her take a shower again.

Michele smiled when she saw her little sister give her some respect, then said, "No one knows for sure. She might wake up any day now."
****

After lunch, Macalla put his napkin on his plate then asked Michele and Paul, "Are you guys ready to go and explore?"

Michele looked at her grandmother and asked, "Are you coming too?"

"I would love too, but as the queen, duty calls first." She rang the bell to call attention to the servers.

As Macalla started to standup, servers started filing out of the kitchen and the door behind Chloe opened. Macalla looked at the front entrance and said, "Great. You're here. Just in time." Then he looked at Michele and said, "I hope you don't mind if Jayden tags along. He thinks his great-grandfather's tomb is down there."

Michele looked questioning at Paul. He replied. "I don't see any harm with Jayden tagging along."

*****

Macalla led the way through the castle to the ceiler's door. After the group descended the stairs, Macalla explained the layout to Michele. "This catacomb was developed by the first settlers in the early 1700s as an underground escape route. It runs the length of the city and has another entry/exit on the other side of the river, in the surrounding forest. The tunnel under the river is damp, but it's sound since it has been reinforced over the centuries with a little hard labor and some magic." As they started to walk into the catacombs, Macalla continued, "As we walk through this mausoleum, you'll notice that your family's concrete, burial vaults are on the right side while my family's vaults are on the left. Our deceased ancestors were buried in accordance to the year they died. Some of them have cement statues in honor of them and some don't."

The first tombs the group came to was Martha Black's on the right and Abraham and Elizabeth Williams's tomb on the left. Michele looked at the statue of Martha, then started tracing it with her finger and said, "Whomever carved this statue did a great job. She looks beautiful. Did she ever marry?"

"No. But rumor has it, that she was pregnant by her one true love when she fled the witch trials. She dated some suitors from the islands, but none of them could ever reach the high standards of her first love."

"She never told anyone who the father of her baby was or what happened to him?"

"If she told her best friend Elizabeth, the world will never know. Of course, there were rumors. Some say he was a common man who died trying to protect Martha's parents and others say he was some great sorcerer that was killed by a mob of people during the witch trials."

The group continued down the tunnel. As they did, Michele payed more attention to her family tree on the right side. On the right side, Martha's daughter's, Sasha's, grave came next, then her children along with their spouses, and so on. Some of the graves where stacked on top of each other, three high. While they continued to walk, Macalla asked Jayden, "What was your great-grandfathers name?"

"My mother told me he was from one of the founding witches' bloodline. Theodore Macbeth, or something like that."

Macalla stopped dead in his tracks and looked at Michele. Michele blushed and said, "Yeah. I just figured that out today... That's why Paul and I were late for lunch. Jayden and I am related through Theodore Macbeth. He was my grandmother's Leewan's uncle."

Jayden stared at Michele in shock. Paul just smiled.

Chapter 67

When Michele and Paul returned to the guest house, Mayra was sleeping peacefully in the hospital bed and Leewan was sitting quietly next to her, reading a book. When Leewan saw the couple, she signaled for them to follow her into the kitchen. Once in the kitchen, Leewan told them, "I put some lasagna in the oven, but it won't be done for a while yet; so, in the meanwhile Michele, can you tell me more about Martha's book. Where is it now?"

Michele explained how she found the book and how it returned itself to Martha's room. "I promised her I would return it, but I guess she didn't want it leaving the third floor. I wonder if there's another book, similar to it in the library."

"Perhaps. Did you guys have a nice day exploring the catacombs?"

Michele recapped the day's events with Leewan and told her how Jayden went on the tour with them.

Leewan smiled and said, "My family circle is getting bigger. I thought our family tree would end with me, but now I have my daughter back, my granddaughter, a son-in-law to be, and my uncle's descendants. I need to go to meet Jayden's parents someday."

Michele looked at Paul. Paul shrugged his shoulders and said, "I did tell your grandmother I planned on marrying you someday… But we both thought it was best if we finished high school first."

"Then maybe we should go out tomorrow and find that bubblegum ring… make it official." Michele laughed.

"Does that mean you still want to marry me, someday?"

"Yes, Paul." She grabbed his head and gave him an exaggerated kiss on the cheek. "Now help me explore the library before dinner."

*****

Paul started searching one side of the library while Michele tackled the other side. Michele started skimming the titles of some of the books, then said over her shoulder, "If you find any books written about the history of the islands, just stack them up on that table for us to review later."

Paul started grabbing some of the books and stacking them on the table. Most of the books Michele saw were documentaries on specific people or events. When she reached the end of one of the bookshelves, she noticed a candle wall-sconce that was hanging crooked on the wall. She reached for the sconce, to straighten it, and one of the bookshelves turned inward, opening up a passage.

Paul turned his head when he heard the shelf move. He looked at the opened passageway and said, "Wow! Why do you always get to find all the cool stuff."

Michele turned on her cellphone's flashlight and looked into the passage. "Looks like it leads to some stairs. Shall we?"

He nodded his head and followed her down the spiral, cement steps. At the bottom of the steps, they met a brick wall. Paul laughed, "Looks like it's a dead-end."

Michele put her hand on the wall and could feel cool air creeping through the cracks. "It must lead somewhere."

"Let me try." Paul shoved his shoulder into the wall but it would not budge.

"Let me try opening it with my magic." Michele put both hands up and pushed at the air. The wall cracked opened like a door on hinges. She pushed the air more until the door was opened wide enough to pass. The couple squeezed into the next room and found themselves in the catacombs -- behind Martha's statue. "Wow! Cool. It's a passage to escape the guest house, but the occupants needed magic to open it."

Leewan came down the steps behind them and almost gave the couple heart attacks when she said, "Dinner is done…. Sorry, didn't mean to scare you." She looked around at the catacombs. "It's been a long time since I've been down here. I always knew there was an escape route from the guest house, but I never found it! Glad you guys found it; now if we ever want to sneak into the castle or outside of the castle's walls -- we can."

Leewan turned and started back up the steps, "Are you guys coming?"

Paul started following Leewan and said, "Yes. I am. I'm starved."

Leewan shouted over her shoulder, "Don't forget to close the door behind you, Michele."

*****

Paul helped Leewan get Mayra into the wheelchair for dinner. During dinner, Mayra was more awake and able to feed herself with her hands -- so Michele tried talking to her. When she didn't respond, Michele tried holding her hand to see if any of her healing powers would help; however,

Mayra just jerked her hand back and continued to play with her food.

After dinner, Paul helped Michele get Mayra back into bed. Once in bed, Mayra looked at Paul and started screaming, "No. No. Please don't. Not again!"

When Paul tried to calm her down, Mayra started swinging at him.

Leewan shouted, "Hold her down Paul. I'll grab her Ativan injection."

He held her arms down while talking to her; "You're alright Mayra. No one here is going to hurt you!" Michele held her mother's legs down while Leewan gave her an injection in the thigh. After a few minutes, Mayra started to calm down. Michele and Paul released their hold and looked at Leewan. Michele asked her, "How often do you have to give her a shot?"

"I've been trying to ween her off all the seditions, guess I was doing it too fast."

"Will she be alright?"

"She should sleep tonight. The two of you can head on up to bed. I'll call you if I need any more help."

The couple said their goodnights to Leewan, then went upstairs. Outside of Michele's bedroom door, Paul gave Michele a kiss goodnight then apologized again for being so jealous. When he turned to go to his room, Michele grabbed his hand and pulled him into her room.

"Whoa! What about your grandmother?"

Michele grinned and said, "Like she doesn't already know."

Chapter 68

The next afternoon, while Michele and Paul were reviewing some of the books they found in the library, Michele said, "Let's take a break and explore the forest at the end of the catacombs."

"Sounds like a plan to me. I'm beginning to see double." Paul walked over to the sconce and turned it. The bookshelf hiding the passage turned inward. "After you, my dear."

Michele walked down the stairs and used her magic to push open the brick door.

Once inside the catacombs, the couple made their way towards the sound of the dripping water. Michele's dad never took them to the end of the tunnel, he just told them about it.

"I don't know," Paul said, "It doesn't look safe to me."

"Come on scaredy-cat. How bad can it be? My dad said it has been reinforced over the years."

"I think it could use some more repairs."

Paul started walking down the incline, into the cool, damp tunnel. He used his flashlight to look at the ceiling and said, "Look at all those cracks with water leaking in. This tunnel might be the last resort to escape, but I don't think we should explore it, just for the fun of it."

Michele looked at the cracks and said, "I wonder if my healing power can work on walls?" She placed her hands on the wall, as high as she could reach, then closed her eyes and whispered, "Make these walls strong."

Paul watched in amazement as the walls pulled themselves tightly together and the constant dripping stopped. "Nice job."

"Well thank you."

The couple continued walking at a downward angle for another thirty feet before the tunnel leveled out then started to slope back up. When they came to the end of the tunnel, they found another dead end. Unlike the brick door at the bottom of the stairs, this one looked like a solid, large rock. Michele held her hands up and pushed into the air. The rock didn't budge so she tried again without any success. "Well, that was fun. Guess we might as well head back."

"Let me try." Paul walked up to the rock wall.

Michele laughed. "If I can't push it open, you sure in the hell can't."

Paul pretended to be hurt by Michele's remark, then said, "It doesn't hurt for me to try. Besides, maybe there's a lever or something?" He inspected all the sides of the rock. When he didn't find any lever, he put his arms straight out to feel the surface of the rock -- and fell right through.

Michele let out a yelp when Paul disappeared through the rock; then she walked over to the rock with her hands straight out and walked right through it. On the other side of the mirage, she found Paul lying on the ground. "Are you ok?"

"Told you I could open it." He stood up and dusted off his jeans.

The couple looked back at the mirage, then walked around it to look at the river. On the other side of the river, Michele could see the castle wall and towers. "This spot is beautiful. And the mirage of the fake, white rock fits right into the surroundings."

Paul looked behind him and said, "Let's follow this deer trail to the top of the hill. I'm sure the view is even better from up there."

When the couple made it to the top of the hill, Michele could see a 360-degree view of the island: On one side she saw the ocean. Then following the horizon, she turned to where the ocean met the land. The land consisted of lush green valleys with farms houses and mountains in the distance. Turning all the way around, she looked back at the castle with the surrounding village. "This is so beautiful."

"What are you doing here?" said a voice from behind them.

Paul and Michele spun around to face an older lady with long-wavy, silver hair. She held her cane up in anger and said, "I asked you a question."

Michele spoke up, "We're sorry. We didn't realize we were trespassing."

"How did you get up here? There's only one road up here, right past my house."

Michele thought: *Do I dare tell her about the tunnel? Is she a friend or foe?*

Paul spoke up. "Sorry for the intrusion. We are here visiting family and just wanted to explore the island. We can make our leave if you can just point us in the right direction. It seems like we've lost our way."

The elderly woman thought about what Paul said for a minute then asked, "Are you, Michele and Paul?"

Paul started to reply, but Michele nudged his arm with her elbow and said, "No. We're…"

The old lady interrupted with a twinkle in her eye and said, "About time you came to visit me, Michele. I'm Agnes Bates, the keeper of Martha Black's history book. I almost 95 years old. I've waited a long time to meet you so I can pass the wand, so to speak."

"You knew about me?"

"Of course! Didn't you read the entry I made in the history book about you?"

"No. I didn't get time. I only read about Jayden, then Martha took the book back from me."

"Martha's funny that way. She doesn't let anyone take the book out of her room."

"She let me take it to the glass cupola."

"She did? Well! I guess the chosen one does get more privileges."

"Why does everyone keep calling me that? I'm not even sure if I want to live on the islands."

"That doesn't matter. You can live wherever you want to live, as long as you come back to visit every so often."

"What else can you tell me about the chosen one."

"I said too much already." Agnes started having a coughing fit.

Michele walked over to her and asked, "Are you ok? Do you want me to try to heal you?"

Agnes stepped away. "No. Don't waste your time dear. Your magic won't work on me. Besides, I lived almost a hundred years. I'm ready to pass the wand. Not sure how many more years I can hold on, so you better get busy."

"Busy? Busy doing what?"

Michele and Paul heard a rustling noise in the bushes behind them. They both turned to investigate the noise, but it was only a deer. When Michele turned back, Agnes was gone. She looked at Paul and asked, "Should we go and try to find her house?"

Paul pointed to the distant sun setting on the water. "I don't think we have time today. We better start heading back."

*****

When Paul and Michele returned to the guest house, Mayra was sleeping and Leewan was reading one of the books from the library. Leewan looked up at the couple when they walked in and said, "Your dinner is still warm in the oven. Chloe stopped over earlier with some of her staff. They brought us some prime rib, loaded potatoes, and dinner salads. She said she was sorry that she missed you but she wants you to call her. I guess she and the king are taking a ride out to some of the villages tomorrow; they want to take you and Paul so they can introduce you to some of the prominent leaders living on this island."

"That was nice of her to bring us dinner, I'll call her right after we eat. I'm sure Paul is starving – I heard his belly growling all the way home." Michele looked at Paul and laughed.

He nodded his head and said, "I am starving... And prime rib sounds delirious."

"Did the two of you have a nice time exploring?"

"Yes, we did! And that's something I need to talk to you about." Michele took a seat next to her grandmother and told her about them exploring the underground tunnel and how she added just a little bit of magic to help reinforce it.

"Nice job! I heard the tunnel was starting to leak again. It's just one of those things that need constant upkeep."

"And the rock mirage is a nice touch for covering the opening into the forest."

"I've heard about that rock, but never actually saw it."

"Do you know a witch named Agnes Bates?"

"No. But I've heard rumors about her. Supposedly she was a very powerful witch. She lived on Black Sands Island. She was a school teacher that specialized in teaching young witches how to use their powers -- for the better. One of her powers included the wisdom to foretell the future. She's the one that advocated a chosen one coming in the future... But I heard she disappeared a good twenty years ago -- after she retired from teaching. Why do you ask?"

"We met her. At the end of the tunnel. She said she is the keeper of Martha's history book."

"Oh. That's very interesting. What else did she have to say?"

"That she was glad to finally meet me since I'm supposed to relieve her of her duty and that I'm the chosen one."

Leewan smiled, "So I was right!"

"I guess so. But what if I don't want to be the chosen one. I'm only a teenager and don't know what I want to do with my life."

"Don't worry about it, darling. You have time."

"I don't know about that. Agnes told me I needed to get busy, then she disappeared."

"So, finding Mayra wasn't the big change. Hmmm."

*****

After dinner, Michele called Chloe to thank her for the dinner.

"I'm glad you enjoyed it. Did Leewan tell you that the king and I want to take you and Paul on a carriage ride tomorrow?"

"Yes. That sounds nice. But what should we wear?"

"That's up to you dear. You know I don't care; however, your grandfather does like to dress the part. So, if you and Paul decide you want to go clothes shopping in the morning, I would be happy to go with you."

"I think I would like that."

"Great. Can you meet me at the castle for breakfast, say eight o'clock sharp? That would give us plenty of time to pick out some outfits before the king is ready to leave."

"We'll be there."

"Oh. Before you go. Let Leewan know – if she wants to come to breakfast, I can always send someone with nursing experience to relieve her."

"Thanks. I'll let her know."

*****

Before retiring for the night, Michele popped downstairs to relay Chloe's message to Leewan.

"That's nice of Chloe, but I still don't feel comfortable leaving her with anyone else. If she ever wakes up, I want to be here."

Michele walked over to the hospital bed. She grabbed her mother's hand and said, "Mom, it's your baby Michele. Can you hear me?" Mayra just started uttering something incomprehensively, jerked her hand away, then started reaching for something in the air. With a tear in her eye, Michele turned toward Leewan and said, "Goodnight." When Michele reached the top of the stairs, she walked over to Paul's closed door and knocked.

"In a minute."

Michele thought: *What the hell is he doing behind a closed door?*

When he opened the door, he had a big smile on his face. In one swift move, he knelt in front of her and offered her a small box with a ribbon tied around it. Michele's hands flew to her face in surprise. Paul handed her the box and asked, "Will you marry me?"

Michele just stared at the box, through her fingers for a couple of seconds, before she replied, "Are you sure you want to marry me? Now that you know the real me. You had your whole life planned out with college, a career, then settling down with a normal person. I don't know what my future holds. Hell. I don't even know where I want to live. You have your family to think about back in the states."

Paul stood up, took her hands, and said, "We can take life one day at a time. See where the road leads us. All I know is, I want to spend the rest of my life with you. I love you, Michele."

She looked at him through teared-filled eyes and answered, "If you're sure."

Paul hugged her and whispered in her ear, "Yes I'm sure! But if you're not... we can call this a promise ring." He held the box up to her and asked, "Will you wear this ring and promise to include me in your plans – no matter what you decide to do with your life?"

"Yes. I promise!" She took the box, started untying the ribbon, then asked, "When did you get this? Did you find a bubblegum machine?"

Paul laughed, "Just open it. You'll see."

Michele opened the box and found a small, gold band with a small, red stone in the shape of a heart. "It's beautiful. Where'd you get this?"

"I got it from Leewan. When I asked her what she thought of me proposing to you -- she was more than ecstatic. Then I asked her if I could borrow some money to buy you a ring – I told her I could pay her back Queensland by withdrawing some of my college savings from an ATM. She told me she had a better plan, then showed me some of her mother's jewelry she's saved."

Michele tried the ring on. "So, this use to belong to my great grandmother... I love it!" She jumped into his arms, kissed him, then said, "Come stay in my room."

Chapter 69

Paul watched as Michele tossed and turned in her sleep. He wanted to wake her from her dream but after the last incident, he feared he would be interrupting something important.

Michele was standing in her Uncle Joe's and Aunt Gloria's kitchen. Gloria was talking on the phone. "I can't reach Michele either. I tied calling and calling and all my calls went straight to her voicemail. Her voicemail is full now and she hasn't returned any of my calls. I even tried calling her grandmother's, Leewan's phone."

Michele thought: *She must be talking to Paul's mom.*

After a brief pause, Gloria continued, "I don't know what else to do. I'm worried sick. My husband Joe even tried tracing the location of her phone, but it's like she fell off the face of the earth. Michele did say they had bad phone reception on the island but you would have thought one of them would've called us by now, it's been over a month. Maybe we should send someone to the Island of New Caledonia to search for them, make sure they are alright. Joe said he can't call the local police since we don't even have her grandmother's address. Joe and I did go over to visit Leewan last fall, it seemed like a nice place to live, but we never thought to write down her address. I even searched Michele's room but I can't find the original letter Leewan sent her – to find a return address."

Michele thought*: Oh shit! What if she does find that letter with the return address of the Island Dreams Dress Shop in Yeppoon, Australia.* She sat straight up in bed. Paul looked at her and asked, "Was it bad?"

"Our parents are worried about us. They're thinking about calling the local police to help find us. We need to go somewhere soon --where we can call them. That stupid boundary spell!"

*****

Michele and Paul showed up for breakfast at 8 o'clock sharp. Her grandmother Chloe greeted them at the castle's dining room entrance as usual. After hugging Michele and Paul, everyone took their seats. Michele smiled at her father while eavesdropping on Amarina's conversation with her step-mother, Lalirra. "At least she made it on time, but when is she going to learn how to dress?"

The king must have overheard her comment since he replied, "Amarina. One shouldn't judge people by the way they dress."

Amarina blushed and dropped her head. Michele thought: *Grandfather must have kept his word and talked to them about their rude comments.* She looked at her grandfather and asked, "Will Lalirra and Amarina be joining us on this trip?"

"No. I thought it would be better to just take you and Paul. So, the people of our community can meet the both of you without any distractions."

Chloe smiled at Michele and added, "The uprising was over the concern of you and Paul -- the outsiders bringing change. We think it's best for the people to meet you in person and come to their own conclusions – that you and Paul are just normal people, or a normal witch in your case, just

like them – and are no threat to their way of
living!"

*****

After breakfast, the guards escorted
Michele, Paul, and Chloe to a waiting carriage just
outside the castle's main entrance. As the couple
rode down the road with the queen, the citizens of
the village would wave, bow, and curtsy. Michele
felt like she was riding in a parade; she smiled and
waved back to all the passing people.

At the dress shop, the coachman helped the
passengers down then guards opened the shop's
door for them. When Michele walked into the
shop, she saw a line of sales associates displaying a
variety of dresses and gowns for her to choose
from. A man walked up to Paul, bowed, and said,
"This way Sir." He led Paul towards the back of
the shop. Paul glanced over his shoulder while
walking and said, "Show me what you pick out so I
know how formal you want to look."

Michele smiled and said, "Nothing too
formal, we're just going for a ride in the
countryside."

Michele walked down the procession,
shaking her head no to all the fancy ballgowns and
dresses. Looking at her grandmother, she asked,
"Do I have to wear something so flashy? I would
prefer a nice sundress with rhinestone sandals."

The queen clapped her hands twice. The
sales associates jumped into action: returning the
gowns to their appropriate displays, then rushing
around the store picking out different outfits for
Michele to choose from. After selecting five

outfits, Michele retired to a changing room to try them on while Chloe sat and waited. When it was all said and done, Michele settled on a flowered, royal blue and white sundress with some matching rhinestone sandals. As she spun around in front of Chloe, she asked, "Do you like this outfit?"

"The colors of our island. Very nice and sensible."

A sales associate knocked on the door, then peeked her head in. "Sorry to intrude my queen, but Paul's wondering if Michele has time to come out and look at his outfit?"

Michele ran to the door. When she stepped out of the changing room, she couldn't believe her eyes: Paul looked handsome in a Hawaiian floral, royal blue and white, shirt with blue dress pants. "Wow. We match." She grabbed his arm and poised for Chloe.

Chloe smiled and said, "Not quite what my husband might expect, but I love it!"

*****

When the carriage returned to the castle, a guard announced to King Levi and Prince Macalla that the caravan was ready to roll. When the king climbed up in the carriage to sit with his wife, he looked at Michele and Paul sitting in the seat across from him. After looking at their outfits for a minute or two, he nodded his head in approval and said, "Not at all what your half-sister would have selected, but I do appreciate your style and the colors you have selected."

During their ride through the countryside, Michele's dad rode his horse next to the wagon while guards in blue and white uniforms rode their steeds in the front and the back of the carriage. A couple of guards in the front of the carriage carried flags: one of the flags represented the Island of Honiawae and one of the flags had seven stipes representing all the Hidden Islands of Honiawae.

Michele enjoyed the scenery of the island while her grandfather pointed out his pineapple fields and discussed the plans for the day: "The pineapples we grow here are sold on the islands and in Queensland. And the first place we will be visiting is on the west shoreline. It's a small village called West Point. The leader of that village is a close friend of mine from my younger years when we attended school together. We should be able to see the outskirts of the village in about thirty minutes."

As the group rode along in silence, enjoying the warm weather, Michele bought up her dream. "Grandma, is there anyway Paul and I can call our families back in America. They're worried about us and plan on either contacting the local police on the Island of New Caledonia or sending someone over to search for us."

"Oh, dear. We can't have them doing that," Chloe replied then looked at Levi.

"No, we can't. Hmm. Looking at his son Macalla he asked, "What are you doing tomorrow?"

"Just planned on attending the morning meeting with the guards. What do you have in mind?"

"Maybe you could take my yacht out into the ocean to find a spot where Michele and Paul can use their cellphones to call their families?"

Macalla looked at Michele and said, "I would love to."

The queen looked at her husband and asked, "Maybe I could ride along too, or do you need my presents at court?"

"Let me look at the agenda when we get back. I don't think we have any pressing issues."

Michele stood up and gave the king a hug, "Thanks, grandpa. You're the best."

The king felt a little awkward with the show of affection but was able to pat her back, lightly, as she hugged him.

By the end of the day, the group had visited three different villages: West Point, Mountain Valley, and Riverview. All in all, it was a great trip. Michele and Paul really enjoyed having the chance to get out and view the island, and the people of the island seemed to really like them. All of the villages greeted the royal party with food, spirits, and song. During the introduction ceremonies, Michele dismissed most of the formalities and requested that the visitors and any children that wanted to meet her, to come forward so she could shake their hands personally. Paul stood by Michele's side as she greeted the people from the villages. Michele didn't forget about his presents since she introduced him to everyone she met as her best friend and confidant.

As the caravan was leaving the last village, Michele asked the queen, "Can we drive by Leewan's place on the way back? Or is that too far out of the way?"

"Not at all, dear. It is a little bit out of the way, but I think we have time?" She looked at the king for confirmation. The king nodded at his son,

Prince Macalla. The prince kicked his horse so he could catch up with the head of the caravan to relay the change of plans.

Chapter 70

At Leewan's house, Michele walked into Mayra's old bedroom and thought: *What should I take back to my mother to help her remember?* She walked around the room and started rummaging through the drawers and closet. Then she looked at the table with her mother's rock collection and the items displayed on top of the dresser. She walked over to the dresser and started looking at some of Mayra's old pictures -- while thinking: *Maybe this picture of her with my dad will jar her memory and this other picture might be her as a young girl -- with Leewan and her first horse?* After she picked up the pictures, she glanced at the rock collection again. *And maybe, I should give my mother the rock I took home to America, along with these pictures. That rock did help me locate her.*

When Michele returned to the carriage, Paul was in deep conversation with the king. Both of them abruptly quit talking when she approached and the king had a big smile on his face. Michele's dad helped her up into the carriage before mounting his horse. Michele looked at Paul, then her grandfather and said, "Do I dare ask what the two of you were discussing?"

Paul smiled and said, "Nothing much. Just my future plans and how I plan on marrying you."

"And my grandfather approved of those plans?"

The king smiled and nodded. The queen spoke up, "Yes Michele. We both approve. Your grandfather might wear an armor of steel, but he's a lover at heart." Chloe winked at her husband and squeezed his thigh.

"What about you, dad?"

Macalla smiled down from his horse and said, "I just want you to be happy. And if Paul brings you happiness, I approve."

*****

When the carriage arrived at the castle, Michele gave the king and queen a hug while Amarina and her mother, Lalirra, watched from their balcony, "Thanks for the tour. It was great!"

As Michele started to get down from the carriage, the queen looked at Paul and asked, "Aren't you going to give us a hug."

"Yes. Of course. I… just didn't know if it was proper."

"Who defines proper?" Chloe chuckled, "Besides, you're practically family. Now give me a hug."

Amarina looked at her mother and said, "I don't like it. I don't like it at all."

"I know dear. Don't worry. My mother is working on a plan to drive a wedge between them. Hopefully, the plan makes Michele want to go home and never return again."

*****

When Paul and Michele walked into the sitting room, Leewan was trying to brush Mayra's hair. "This stupid brush. It doesn't work well on your mother's hair and half of the bristles have broken off. Do you happen to have an extra brush, Michele?"

"No. But I know where one is." Michele put the pictures face down on the end table then ran up the stairs to grab the brush and her mother's rock. When she returned, she handed the brush to Leewan and said, "Here. I saw this brush in the third-floor bathroom the last time we came to visit. Do you know who it belonged to?"

Leewan looked at the rhinestone-handled brush and said, "No. But I guess it will work."

As Leewan brushed Mayra's hair, Michele placed the rock in her mother's bed then watched as it began to glow. Paul tapped Michele's arm then pointed at the brush. When she looked at the brush, she noticed the rhinestones on the handle -- were glowing too.

Mayra turned her head slowly, looked at Leewan, then asked, "Where am I?"

Leewan almost dropped the brush and looked up at Michele. "She's waking up!"

Michele rushed up to the bedside. Mayra looked at her and asked, "Who are you?"

"I'm your daughter."

"My daughter? I don't remember a daughter."

"And I'm your mother, Leewan."

"Leewan?"

"Yes, dear. You're safe now. You're back home."

"Home?"

"Yes. You're home. We are on the Island of Honiawae. We are staying at the castle's guest house."

"Island? Castle? Can I sit up? I have a pounding headache."

"Yes. Yes. I'll help you." Leewan helped Mayra sit on the edge of the bed. Mayra shrieked when she saw Paul. "Stay away."

Leewan reassured Mayra, "That's just Paul. Your daughter's boyfriend. He's not going to hurt you. Come. Do you want to sit on the couch?"

"Daughter's boyfriend?"

"Yes." Leewan helped Mayra to the couch then looked at Michele. "Can you call the doctor? His card should be on the end table."

*****

After evaluating Mayra, the doctor discussed her prognosis with Leewan, Michele, and Paul in the front foyer. "She has amnesia. At this point, I'm not sure if she will ever get her memory back or not. All we can do is reassure her that she is safe and wait. It might also help if you can share childhood stories with her, something might trigger her memory."

After the doctor left, Michele told Leewan of their plans to take King Levi's yacht out in the morning. "Paul and I need to call our families back in the states since I had a dream last night."

"Are they ok?"

"Yes. They are just worried about us and are thinking about contacting the Island of New Caledonia's police department since they haven't been able to contact us."

"Then by all means... the two of you should go! I'll be fine here with Mayra."

Chapter 71

The king's yacht, fully equipped with servers, crew members, and guards, pulled out of the channel into the wide, open sea. Chloe told Michele and Paul, "We should be out of the boundary spell by now -- if you two want to check your cellphones." They both tried their phones without any luck.

Chloe shook her head and said, "Not sure how far we'll have to travel to get signal, this might be an all-day cruise. Well... We might as well make the best of it. Anyone hungry for some breakfast?"

"I am," Paul replied.

Michele giggled, "You're always hungry."

During breakfast, Michele told Chloe and Macalla how Mayra woke up, with the help of a little magic.

"Did she ask about me?" Prince Macalla asked.

"No. Unfortunately, she has amnesia. She doesn't even recognize her own mom at this point, but the doctor is optimistic; he said she should get most of her memory back -- over time."

"That's great news," Chloe declared. "I bet that's a relief for Leewan."

"She was quite ecstatic when Mayra woke up."

After breakfast, with no phone signal available, the group started playing euchre – girls against the guys. After a couple of hours of playing, Michele and Paul were still unable to call home. When Michele set her phone back on the table, Chloe noticed the red, heart ring. "Where did you get that?"

"Oh. This used to belong to Leewan's mom. Leewan gave it to Paul so he could give it to me as a promise ring."

Macalla looked at the ring then at Paul, "A promise ring – you say?"

Paul shifted in his seat under Macalla's stare, "Umm. You said whatever makes Michele happy. Remember?"

Macalla let out a laugh and patted Paul on the back. "Yeah. You're right. So, you just remember that. You better make her happy... or I might have to hunt you down."

"Dad!" Michele replied.

"Only kidding. Congratulations!"

Chloe just shook her head.

"What's wrong?" Michele asked.

"It's just that ring. It's nice and all. And very special since it belonged to your great grandmother... But I think you deserve something... bigger."

"I'm happy with this. It comes from Paul's heart. I don't need something big and flashy. Besides, Paul can't afford anything like that."

"Oh, nonsense. We'll just consider it a loan. A girl as special as you deserves a big diamond. We are so close to the mainland now that we might as well stop at my dress shop in Yeppoon and look at their rings."

"We don't need to do that! Besides, Paul can't take out a loan. He might not even have a job when he returns to the states."

"Can't we just look? I can pay for it and Paul can just pay me back -- say in 20 years."

"Let me think about it." She looked out the window and saw land in the distance. Then she looked at her phone and said, "I have four bars now. Excuse me while I go somewhere to call my aunt."

Paul looked at his phone, then said, "Guess I'll go call my mom."

*****

By the time Michele and Paul were done talking to their families, the yacht was docked.

Chloe looked at Michele and asked, "How were your aunt and uncle?"

"They were good. Just worried. I told them that the phone signals are horrible here and that it might be easier for me to send them a letter --weekly. Does the island's fishing boat take mail to the mainland?

"Yes of course. Maybe you should write too, Paul. So, your parents don't worry."

"That does sound like a good plan."

"Well, now that that's done, are the two of you about ready to do some shopping?"

"I guess we can look. If you insist?" Michele replied.

"I do."

Macalla nodded his head in agreement.

*****

The staff at Island Dreams were surprised when the queen and prince walked in; some of them stood at attention and some of them ran to the back office to find the manager, Elanora. When Elanora walked out, she excused the rest of her staff, then asked, "What gives me the honor to have all three of you in the store at once?"

Queen Chloe said, "We had to come to the mainland for Paul and Michele to finish some business; then we thought since we are here, we should stop by so Michele and Paul could look at the rings you have on display."

"Oh! Congratulations! Follow me. We have plenty of rings for the two of you to choose from. Are you looking for a full-set, with the wedding bands included, or just an engagement ring?"

Michele looked down at her red, heart ring and said, "I'm quite happy with this promise ring, but I guess I can you look at your display."

Elanora looked at the ring and said, "It is a nice ring. But it looks a little snug. You could always wear that one on your pinkie finger and find a nice diamond to complement it. Follow me."

Michele grabbed Paul's hand for support and followed Elanora to the jewelry cases. Chloe pointed out some 3-carat diamonds, but Michele kept looking back at a smaller, princess cut diamond with paved diamonds surrounding it. "Try that one on!" Chloe pointed to the diamond Michele was looking at.

"I don't need that big of a diamond. It probably costs too much.?"

"Don't worry about the cost. Pick out something you like."

Paul smiled and said, "Go ahead. Try it on. I think it will go well with your great-grandmother's ring. Plus, it'll make me feel better. Your great-grandmother's ring is special, but this ring will be something we picked out together... and I have twenty years to pay it off."

Michele glanced at Elanora and nodded. When Michele tried it on, she whispered, "It's beautiful."

"We'll take it.... before she changes her mind," Chloe declared with a small chuckle.

*****

On the cruise back to the hidden islands, the group was served dinner -- with lobster as the main course. After dinner, Chloe insisted they ride on the top deck so they could watch the sunset. Sitting next to Paul on the top deck, Michele twisted her wrist back and forth, admiring how her new ring sparkled in the sunlight. When she looked up, she noticed Paul was watching too. She leaned over, kissed him on the cheek, then whispered, "Thank you! I love you!"

Chapter 72

By the time Michele and Paul returned to the guest house, Leewan was tucking Mayra in for the night. Michele walked up to the bed, kissed Mayra on the cheek, and said, "Good night mom."

"Good night... Michele. Right?"

"Michele smiled, "Yes."

"And that is Paul. Your boyfriend. Right?"

"Yes."

"Goodnight Paul."

"Goodnight Ms. Johnson."

"Who's Ms. Johnson?"

"You are. Since you're Leewan Johnson's daughter."

"Oh… So, I never married?"

"Not that we know of?"

"So, I guess I am Ms. Johnson then. I like the name Mayra better."

"Then Mayra it is," Paul smiled and kissed her on the forehead.

Michele started to walk towards Leewan and saw the pictures she bought back from her grandmother's house. She picked them up and carried them over to Mayra, "Oh! I forgot all about these. I took these pictures from your childhood bedroom at Leewan's house."

Michele sat on the edge of the bed, handed Mayra one of the pictures, then started running her fingers through her mother's hair. While Mayra looked at the picture, Michele could feel her fingers start to tingle. Michele laid her hand flat on the back of Mayra's head while Mayra started tracing the horse in the picture. Michele felt a current running through her hand while Mayra started tracing the lady in the picture. "Is that you, Leewan?"

Leewan smiled and said, "Yes. And that's you as a little girl. Do you remember that horse? I bought her for you on your 8th birthday. You named her Windfire."

"Vaguely."

Michele took the picture away and handed her the next picture.

Mayra traced the picture with her finger and asked, "Is that Macalla?"

"Yes!" Leewan said.

"I think I remember him. Didn't I ride horses with him?"

"Yes!"

"And I also went to the garden to meet him, to break up with him since he was betrothed to Lalirra when... Oh my God! I was kidnapped! And I was pregnant with his baby. Michele! Are you my baby?"

"Yes, mom. I'm your baby."

Michele learned over the bed, with tears in her eyes, and hugged her mother.

"Help me up. I'm not ready for bed. I need to tell you all what happened. I never meant to abandon you, Michele, I was drugged."

Michele and Leewan helped Mayra back to the couch.

"Do you want me to get you something to drink?" Leewan asked.

"No. I'm fine. Let me start from the beginning – what I can remember."

Michele and Leewan sat with Mayra on the couch while Paul took a seat in the recliner. Mayra dropped her head down into her hands. Leewan patted Mayra's knee and said, "Take your time dear. We don't have to talk about this tonight if you're too tired; we'll always have tomorrow."

Mayra lifted her head and said, "No. I'm fine. I want Michele to know the truth. As I was saying, I remember going to the gardens to meet Macalla."

Leewan replied, "Yes. That's the last time I saw you. You told me you were going there to break up with Macalla. Do you know what happened?"

"Not really. Someone came up behind me and put a cloth over my face. When I woke up, I was tied up on a ship."

"They must have used chloroform or something," Paul interjected.

Leewan nodded, "Did you see who tied you up?"

"Yes. It was two of the Taylors' men. When I asked them where I was, they started arguing about not letting me wake up, and then they gave me some sort of injection. After they gave me the injection, I asked them why they were doing this to me. They started laughing and said because I was a little tramp, knocked up by the prince, and the Taylors didn't take too kindly to tramps getting in the way of their daughter's happiness. That answer really surprised me since I never told anyone that I was pregnant."

Leewan nodded, "They must have been following you and Macalla all along. I'm just surprised your dreams didn't warn you. They must have had a witch or a warlock working for them -- that knew some sort of incantation that could block your whispers of a dream power."

Mayra nodded her head, then continued, "Then, before I passed out again, I asked them where they were taking me. They laughed and said I should be happy; they were taking me to a man involved in sex trafficking – so I should fit right in."

"Oh my!" Leewan said. The mole, that the Taylors executed for treason, told us he took you to a Russian agent, but I never thought the agent could have been involved in sex trafficking. We need to tell Macalla."

"What mole?" Mayra asked.

"I'm sorry dear. Continue your story. We can tell you our side of the story later."

"Well. The days get fuzzy after the boat ride. All I can remember is living in a dark and dungy cage with only a cot, a thin blanket, and a pail. Men would come to my cell frequently, injected me with drugs, then have their way with me. After a while, I was begging for the drugs. The men that were holding me captured told me they would give me the drugs and some food if I would cooperate and perform unheard of duties. At the end of my duties, if the customers were happy, I could get my fix. If a customer complained, they would beat me and throw me in my cell to suffer withdrawals. After a while, my capturers realized I was pregnant. Some of the customers like pregnant women but most of them preferred someone else. Sometimes I left in my cell for days, starving and withdrawing from heroin."

"Oh, my poor baby!" Leewan hugged her. "I'm so sorry! I never quit looking for you."

Michele interrupted, "When I first found you in my dreams, you were left for dead by some garbage dumpster. How did you escape? Or did they dump you there?"

"I did finally escape. As I said, they would leave me for days withdrawing, so when the hallucinations decreased, I would regain some of my bearings. One night, when I was beginning to regain some of my composure, I stared at the lock on my cell door and wished it would open... And to my surprise... it did! I was determined to escape so I dragged myself on my hands and knees until I could find a wall for support. I remember staggering down some alley, searching for someone to help me. I must have collapsed before I found any help since the next thing I remember -- is waking up in the hospital and seeing a large surgical dressing on my belly."

Paul looked at her with empathy and asked, "Why did the hospital send you to Brightside?"

"I guess I went a little crazy since I was still craving a fix and my baby was missing. The hospital staff found me in my room with the room torn up and me screaming. They probably thought I was some crazy, drug addict. All I know is Brightside must have done a good job keeping me sedated since I vaguely remember being there. How old are you Michele?"

"17."

"17! Wow. Was I there that long? The Taylors need to pay for taking my life from me."

Leewan spoke up, "And so they shall! I will call the queen now -- tell her you woke up and we need to schedule a meeting tomorrow. You should get some rest tonight. When the story is revealed, I'm sure there'll be hell to pay."

Chapter 73

The next morning, Michele helped her mother to the shower then started searching for something for her to wear. After searching through some of her things, she looked at Paul and said, "I can't give my mom any of my clothes since all I have is mainly shorts and tank tops. And she can't wear any of those clothes we bought back with her from Brightside – they're just plain ugly."

"What about Leewan's clothes?"

"Mayra needs something classy to wear when she is presented in front of the court to speak; and maybe something a little sexy for my dad."

Paul laughed, "Are you trying to be a matchmaker now."

"Well... Why not. Besides, my dad doesn't give one lick for that so-called wife he has now." Michele slammed her dresser drawer shut.

Paul smiled then said, "Let's go ask your grandmother. Maybe she does have something that will suit you!"

The couple raced down the stairs and found Leewan in the kitchen. Michele blurted out, "Do you have anything classy but sexy for Mayra to wear to the castle?"

"In a matter of fact, I do. I knew I brought it from my house for some reason. I wore it to a ball at the castle a couple of years ago. It's a simple, black dress, about knee length; it has a lowcut neckline and slit up the side."

"Sounds exactly what I'm looking for."

"I even brought the matching black onyx necklace surrounded by zirconium diamonds."

*****

Paul helped Leewan in the kitchen while Michele and Mayra primped up in her room. While Leewan was cooking and Paul setting the table, someone knocked at the door. Leewan looked at Paul and asked, "Can you see who that is?"

"Sure." When he opened the front door, the king, queen, and Prince Macalla were standing there. "Come on in."

Leewan looked at the royal party from the stove and said, "I thought the meeting was around 11 a.m. in the council room?"

"Change of plans, there's been another incident," replied Chloe.

"Another incident?" Leewan turned off the stove and walked over to the foyer.

Just then, Michele walked to the open balcony on the second floor. She looked down at the guest in the foyer, then called, "Mother. They came here."

Mayra walked out to the balcony, then started descending the stairs. Macalla gasped and his heart almost skipped a beat as he watched her descend the stairs. She looked beautiful... with her natural, blonde hair styled to frame her face. She had that sparkle of light back in her blue eyes – the sparkle he had fallen in love with all those years ago. And the dress. Boy did she look sexy in that dress. The dress showed off her full-figure with just a tease of cleavage.

Queen Chloe stepped up when Mayra reached the bottom step. She gave Mayra a big hug and said, "Welcome back child." After she hugged her, she stepped back and said, "Let me have a look at you." Mayra curtsy and smiled. Chloe said, "Beautiful as ever."

When Mayra looked at Macalla, she smiled. Chloe glanced at her son just staring at her and thought: *He still infatuated as ever over her.*

She nudged her husband to get his attention, then tilted her head towards their son so he could observe Macalla's reaction to seeing Mayra.

King Levi cleared his throat, breaking the moment between Mayra and Macalla, and asked, "Well. Do I get a hug too?"

"Of course," Mayra said as she walked over to the king, hugged him, then kissed him on the cheek.

The king blushed, then looked at Leewan and said, "We came to you instead since there's been another rumor started. Is there someplace we can all sit?"

"Another rumor?" she replied. We can all have a seat in the back sitting-room..... Follow me."

The group started making their way to the back room. Macalla waited for Mayra, then put his hand on the small of her back as she walked down the hall under the balcony. In a husky voice, he asked, "Where's my hug?" Mayra stopped, looked at the prince, then fell into his arms. When she finally stepped back, she had tears in her eyes.

"What's wrong love?"

"I have so much to tell you." She wiped a tear from her cheek, then continued, "But we should listen to your news first. My story might take half of the day."

*****

Michele and Paul sat on the hospital bed so the king and the queen could have the recliners while Macalla, Mayra, and Leewan took a seat on the couch. After everyone was seated, Chloe asked, "Do you still need the hospital bed?"

Leewan spoke up, "No. We moved Mayra's belongings to the fourth bedroom on the second floor."

"Great! I'll send someone over later to get that bed out of your way."

"Thank you!" Leewan replied, then looked at the king. "So, what's the new rumor all about?"

The king cleared his throat then nodded at Macalla. Macalla reached into his pocket and pulled out a folded sheet of paper. He passed the paper to Leewan while saying, "My guards found this poster nailed to trees throughout the countryside. We have also had calls from the neighboring islands, demanding information in regards to these posters."

Leewan looked at a picture of Michele then read the caption below it out loud, "Warning. Impersonator. New evidence shows this outsider, who calls herself Michele, is really a descendent of the evil sorcerer, Mukai, from Scorpion Island. She used her magic to alter the paternity test." After she read the poster, she handed it over to Michele and Paul.

"Who is Mukai?" Michele asked.

Queen Chloe interjected, "Mukai was just like the poster states... pure evil. He was a powerful sorcerer who wanted to be the king of the Hidden Islands of Honiawae. He and his followers would kill or persecute anyone that refused to follow him. He had big plans for his followers. He wanted them all to return to their homelands to seek revenge from the descendants of the people that held the witch trials -- for what they did to their ancestors. He didn't think it was right for his people to have to hide and he wanted them to take back the lands that were rightfully theirs."

"He wanted to kill incident people that didn't have anything to do with the witch trials?"

"Yes. And if people didn't agree with his plans, he would order raids on their villages."

"So, how did they stop him?"

"The king's army, along with the help of a lot of good witches, trapped him in a gold lamp."

"Sort of like the stories I heard about finding a Genie in the Lamp?"

Chloe chuckled, "Yes. I suppose you are right. But hopefully, no-one ever finds his lamp. They threw it into the mouth of a dormant volcano on Scorpion Island."

"Why are they saying I am a descendent of his?"

"During the war, a lot of his close followers escaped the islands along with his lover. Who knows where they went? I suppose his lover could have been pregnant with his offspring."

Leewan spoke up, "That's all nonsense!"

The king nodded his head and said, "We agree! It's all nonsense. But you know how some people are – they'll believe anything."

"Well, I think the Taylors are behind this rumor too!" Michele replied. "After you hear my mother's story, I think you'll agree."

Everyone was quiet while Mayra retold her story. At the end of her story, Macalla grabbed her hands, looked into her eyes, and said, "I'm so sorry."

"It's not your fault."

Macalla looked at his mother and said, "The Taylors need to pay for these crimes they committed against the kingdom and all the turmoil they have produced with these outrageous rumors."

Chloe nodded then looked at her husband.

King Levi cleared his throat, looked at Mayra, and said, "I'll send guards over to bring Moki and Merrin Taylor in for questioning."

Macalla cleared his throat, "And don't forget. I think the Taylors might have tried to poison me during my last visit. If we can't find any witnesses for the crimes committed against Michele or Mayra, maybe we can find a witness that the Taylors ordered someone to poison my drink?"

Chapter 74

Early the next morning, the king's army accompanied by Macalla and Leewan, showed up at the castle on Keelonie Island. The Taylor's guards saw the ships approaching and immediately complied: they raised their white flags, assisted with the docking of the boats, and welcomed the prince. After the guards disembarked, a lot of them started to surround the castle while Macalla and Leewan led a dozen or more guards to the main entrance. When the Taylors' guards, stationed near the castle's entrance, saw the prince coming, they rushed into the castle to wake up the warden and his wife.

After hearing the pounding on her bedchamber's door, Merrin open it and asked, "What's the meaning of this?"

"The prince is here, my Lady."

Merrin looked at her husband in shock, then told the guards, "We'll meet him in the formal dining room. Inform the servants that we are having a guest for breakfast."

When Moki and Merrin walked into the formal dining room with their guards, they were surprised by the number of guards, all dressed in blue, standing at attention. Looking over towards the table, Merrin saw Leewan sitting next to the prince. She grabbed her husband's arm and whispered, "This can't be good."

Moki shook off his wife's handhold, walked up to the prince, and bowed. "What gives me the honor of your presents this fine morning -- Prince Macalla."

The prince nodded at his guards. Four of his guards detained the Taylors while the rest of them pointed their rifles at the Taylors' guards.

The prince looked at the Taylors and said, "We are here to take the both of you in for questioning for crimes committed against the kingdom."

"What? Unhand me!" Merrin exclaimed. "I've done nothing wrong."

Moki looked at his wife then said to the prince, "We will follow you peacefully. I have only done what is expected of me for maintaining peace on this island. I have not done anything against the king's orders. Please don't let the people from this island see us being dragged away."

The prince nodded his head. The guards released the warden and his wife. "Very well. As long as you both walk peacefully to the awaiting ships, no force shall be used."

Moki bowed, then said, "Thank you, my Lord."

*****

Moki and Merrin were immediately taken to the throne room to stand before the king and queen. Their daughter, Princess Lalirra, sat in her thrown to the far right. She looked down at her parents, worriedly. After Prince Macalla took his throne next to his wife, the king cleared his throat and said, "Moki and Merrin. You are brought here today for questioning on the conspiracy of the kidnapping of Mayra. How do you plead."

Moki Taylor spoke up, "What? We have done no such thing. This is an absurd accusation."

"So, you deny the charges?"

"Yes. We deny the charges."

"How do you plead to the charges of trying to poison my son?"

"What?" Moke looked at his wife then back to the king. "We deny any accusations of ever trying to poison Prince Macalla."

Merrin nodded her head in agreement.

"Very well. Guards. Lock them up in the high bedchamber. They are not allowed any visitors or contact with any outside people until a thorough investigation can be conducted."

The guards started pulling the couple away.

Lalirra looked at the king with pleading eyes and said, "Wait! You can't do that! They're my parents. Aren't they innocent until proven guilty?"

The king looked at Lalirra and replied, "And Macalla is your husband. My son! If your parents tried to kill my son they will be executed for treason."

Lalirra watched in horror as the guards dragged her parents away.

*****

The investigation started the very next day on the island of Keelonie. Jayden, Dwayne, and Charles were in charge of rounding up all the servers that were working the night of Macalla's visit. They put all the servers in one room so they could send them in, one by one, to be interrogated by the prince, Leewan, and Diane. By the end of the day, it was beginning to look like the Taylors would have to be excused of all the charges.

"Maybe I did just have an allergic reaction to something I ate?" The prince looked at Leewan with sad eyes.

"Nonsense. I know the Taylors must have had something to do with all of this mess."

Jayden opened the door and said, "Here's the last server that was working that night, Kaena." He brought in a young girl who was shaking from head to toe. "She told me that the night in question was her first day on the job."

Leewan smiled, "It's okay. Have a seat dear." After Kaena took a seat and Jayden closed the door, Leewan continued, "You can just relax. We're all friends here. You're not in trouble. We just need to know if you know anything about the possible poisoning of the prince."

Kaena nodded her head.

"Did Jayden tell you already who we are?"

She nodded again.

Leewan smiled then told her, "I need you to hold Diane's hand. As you have been told, Diane here can read minds, so she will know if you are lying."

Kaena joined hands with Diane. Diane thought: *Great! This girl is already sweating and shaking. She might be hard to read.*

Leewan continued, "Now think back to your first night on the job. Was there anything unusual?"

Kaena started shaking her head and said, "No. Like I said. It was my first day on the job so I'm not really sure what would be considered unusual. I was just there to severe the ale."

Diane nodded at Leewan.

"Wait! I did think it was odd when the Lady of the house called me aside. She told me I was doing a great job -- then she noticed that my pitcher was about empty. She handed me a cup of ale and asked me to do her a favor. She said the prince had requested a special brew and would I be kind enough to deliver that cup to the prince -- on my way back to the kitchen."

"Do you know if the castle makes its own special brew?"

"Not that I know of. I think the lady made her own special brew by adding a couple of drops of some dark, red liquid to the mug before I took it."

"Do you remember what she added?"

"I'm not sure. She got the liquid from a vial she had in her purse. After she put several drops in the mug, she winked at me and told me to deliver it to the prince straight away."

Leewan looked at Diane, Diane nodded.

"That will do. Thank you."

"Am I in trouble?"

Leewan patted her hand. "Not at all. But we will need your statement at Merrin Taylor's trial. Do you feel safe enough to go home or should we put you in a witness protection program?"

"Can I go back with you? If Merrin did poison the prince, who knows what might happen to me?"

"Yes. You can come back with us. We can give you one of the rooms at the king's castle... and your own security guards. For now, you can just hang out with me until we leave."

"Great. Can I call my mother?"

"I think you should wait until we have you safely tucked away at the castle."

"Ok."

Leewan turned her head to address Macalla. "Did you get all of that recorded?"

Macalla nodded then went to the door to talk to Jayden. "We need to send a search party up to Merrin's bedchamber to look for a vial of dark, red liquid; Kaena saw it in her purse."

Chapter 75

Macalla sat in his bedchambers contemplating what his life might have been like if he had married Mayra. His thoughts were interrupted when he heard a soft knocking at his door. When he opened the door, he found his wife, Lalirra standing at the threshold, "What are you doing here?"

"Can we talk?"

Macalla sighed, left the door open, and walked away. Lalirra entered the room, closed the door softly behind her, then followed him into the room. Macalla pointed at a table and said, "Have a seat." After the couple was seated, he asked, "What do you want now?"

Lalirra tried to pour on her charm and batted her eyelashes. "Are you going to release my parents now? I'm sure this was all just some misunderstanding."

"Ha!" Macalla jumped out of his seat. "No Lalirra. This isn't just some misunderstanding. Your mother tried to poison me. We have proof. We found a vial of liquid in her room. It is being tested now. If it is poison, she will be hung for treason."

"You found a vial in her room?"

"Yes! In her purse! And we have a witness."

Lalirra started sobbing. Then she stood up, went over to Macalla, and started begging. "You can't kill my mother! Please... I'll do anything. Think about me. Think about our daughter! My mother was just trying to protect me... and our future together."

Macalla jerked away from her. "What future together. A loveless one!"

"If I testify against her. Can you change her sentencing? Maybe just put her in prison... for the rest of her life?"

"We don't need you to testify. As I said, we have proof!"

"But do you have the proof of what she did to Mayra... of what she did to your illegitimate daughter, Michele?"

"What do you know about that?"

"I swear, I didn't know anything at the time. But my mother told me after the fact. I could testify insanity... How the love of a mother trying to protect her only child was driven to insanity -- causing the mother to think irrationally and do foolish things.... Please Macalla. If not for me, do it for your daughter, Amarina. None of this is her fault."

Macalla walked over to the window and mumbled, "Tell me what you know."

*****

After Lalirra finished her story -- all Macalla could see was red.

"Well... do we have a deal?"

"Your mother should hang for all her wicked deeds."

"How can you say that. My mother acted out of love...... for me. A lot of people are blind when it comes to love and do foolish things."

"Foolish! You call what your mother did to Mayra... to me... just foolish. I call it downright evil. Besides, I don't need you as a witness. You just confessed everything to me."

"I'll deny it all. I'll say you must have been dreaming... my mother did no such thing. It'll be your word against mine. And everyone knows how you can't stand me already."

"I never said that!"

"You don't have to say it. It shows."

"Does our daughter know?"

"Yes. She knows there is no love lost between us."

"Does she know I love her?"

"She does. But it wouldn't hurt for you to tell her more."

Macalla nodded his head.

"So…. if you won't spare my mother's life for me…. you should spare it for our daughter. Prove to her you love her."

After a moment of silence, Macalla said, "I'll think about it. Now leave."

"Will you talk to your parents about it?"

"Yes. But I don't think they are going to like it any more than I do."

"Just try…. Please…." Lalirra quietly left the room.

*****

When Leewan came home from the investigation on Keelonie Island she found Michele, Paul, and Mayra talking in the back sitting-room. Leewan walked into the room and announced, "Good news. It looks like we found a witness and the poison Merrin used on Prince Macalla. It would have been nice to find a witness to verify the story of Taylors ordering the kidnapping of Mayra, but I think they made sure that trail was covered -- when they executed their spy that was tracking you, Michele, back in Michigan."

Michele jumped up and handed Leewan a sheet of paper. Leewan looked at the picture and asked, "Who's this?"

"I don't know. I thought maybe you could tell me! I was doodling on a pad of paper while we were sharing stories about our past endeavors. The man in the picture is the same man I saw popping up in my dreams last night. I think this man knows something about our case since my dreams kept showing me images of that man's face, the alley with Mayra lying by the dumpster, and an orphanage."

"It's worth looking into. What stories did Mayra tell you?"

"We were just comparing stories like – homeschooling compared to public schooling and how Paul and I met compared to how my mother and Macalla met."

"Oh! Well hold that thought… I'll have one of our guards out front deliver this drawing to Jayden… see if he can find this man. When I come back, I want to hear some of these comparisons -- see if I did a good job at homeschooling Mayra or not." Leewan chuckled, then ran down the hall.

Chapter 76

The next day, the occupants of the guest house were summoned to the castle's council room for a meeting. Macalla stood up when he saw Mayra walk in and pulled a chair next to him out for her to sit. After everyone was seated, Michele noticed that her step-mother and half-sister weren't present.

King Levi was the first to speak. "The test results came back this morning. The dark, red liquid found in the vial inside of Merrin Taylor's purse was positive for Mezereon, a poisonous, red berry." He slammed his fist down on the table. "That bitch tried to kill my son!"

The queen looked at her husband and cringed. "Remember your blood pressure, dear. She will get her just punishment."

"But why do we need to have a trial. I say she's guilty. Take her out to the firing squad now."

"This is the warden's wife, the mother of our daughter-in-law. We need to give her a fair trial, open to the public. Besides… your son did not die -- thanks to Michele."

"Let's do the trial tonight then."

Chloe laughed. "Now you're being unreasonable. We don't even have a jury! And we need to notify all the wardens of the other islands, the noblemen, the news channel, and the general public."

"They already know they are imprisoned in the castle --pending charges for poisoning my son!"

Macalla cleared his throat.

Chloe replied, "I'm sorry dear. I completely forgot. You're the one that requested this meeting. Go ahead… You have my complete attention." Chloe smiled and nodded her head at her husband.

"Yes, son. Go right ahead."

Macalla told the group everything his wife had told him. After he was done talking, the room was so quiet, you could have heard a pin drop.

Leewan was the first to speak up. "Does your wife know that her testimony could put both her mother and father in prison for life?"

"I'm not sure if she thought about that. She just wanted to save her mother's life, on the plea of insanity." Macalla reached for Mayra's hand and squeezed it. Then he looked at his dad and said, "What do you think? Do we give Lalirra a chance to testify? If she indicts both of her parents for the kidnapping of Mayra and the persecution of Michele, will you lessen the sentencing to life in prison?"

"We need to take a vote. I, for one, want them both sentenced to death! I would think you would want the same thing?"

"I did. But I do have my daughter, Amarina, to think about. She might hate me for life if I voted to sentence her grandparents to die by execution. And what about my wife Lalirra. She didn't know about the kidnapping or the poisoning until after the fact… but she did know about the rumors her mother started. When this all comes out in the open, I hope you don't expect me to stay married to her."

The king stared at Macalla, then looked at his wife.

"Why are you looking at me? I always told you I didn't agree with arranged marriages."

The king looked back at Macalla, "So, what do you propose we do?"

"First we should vote. See if we all agree to lessen the sentencing for Amarina's sake."

"Very well," the king replied.

Chloe looked at Paul and asked, "Paul, will you be so kind and grab that pad of paper and some of those pens off the side wall table behind you?"

"Will do." Paul got up from his seat and grabbed a handful of pens and the pad of paper. After everyone had a piece of paper, the king announced. "Write either life or death on your paper, then fold it up and pass them to me."

After the king reviewed everyone's votes, he announced, "The sentencing has been reduced to life in prison. You can tell your wife, that I shall abide by this vote if... she abides by her word to confess all their crimes."

"And what becomes of Lalirra?" Macalla asked.

"She should be punished for obstruction of justice," the king demanded.

"But she is the mother of my youngest daughter."

"Then what do you suggest?"

"I was hoping you would let me divorce her. In the divorce settlement, we would give her the castle on Keelonie Island and make her the Lady of the house. After Lalirra accepts her new title, I want to have a long talk with Amarina. Let her know how much I love her and let her decide on where she wants to live: with me, her mother, or both."

"That sounds fair to me," Chloe interjected. "How about you, dear?"

The king looked around the table, scratched his chin, then said, "I think that sounds fair as long as there are no objections."

Michele squeezed Paul's hand, then said, "Amarina is my half-sister. I think we need to do right by her. What do you think, mom?"

Mayra nodded, smiled, then thought: *She's just like me at that age -- thinking of the welfare of others first.*

*****

The trial was scheduled a couple of days out so the appropriate people could be notified. During the waiting period, Michele hung out at the house with her mother, grandmother, and Paul. They all shared stories of days gone past, and Mayra and Michele practiced a little of their telekinesis. Michele enjoyed the time getting to know her mother and grandmother better but she still wanted some time to be alone with Paul. A couple of times, during the waiting period, Michele encouraged Paul to sneak away with her. On the first day, the couple just stole away to the glass cupula to people watch. The next day they snuck down the library entrance to the tunnel under the city. They explored the graves in the catacombs then walked, hand in hand, through the long tunnel under the river. The rock mirage at the end of the tunnel didn't stop the couple this time -- as they approached it, they just continued to walk right through it -- to the open forest on the other side. While in the forest, Michele and Paul searched for Agnes Bates's house to no avail.

Chapter 77

On the day of the trial, Michele stared out the kitchen window and asked, "How are we ever going to make it to the castle, unnoticed, with all those people?"

Leewan looked at her and asked, "Why do you need to be unnoticed?"

"Some of those people out there are from other islands… and they might still think I'm an impersonator."

Leewan thought about what Michele said for a moment, then said, "Come with me. There's a bunch of old clothes up in the third-floor storage room. We can pick out outfits for all of us so we can disguise ourselves as locals."

When Michele got to the second floor, she rounded up Paul and Mayra to follow them to the third floor. Mayra laughed when she picked out a long, flowery dress with a matching bonnet. "How old did you say these clothes are?"

Paul picked out a white, ruffling shirt and a tailed tuxedo. "I could go as an aristocrat!"

Michele laughed and said, "From which century? Maybe if you dig a little deeper, you can find a matching white wig."

Leewan called out from the back of the room, "I found some outfits that are a little more up to date back here."

Paul and Mayra put their outfits back into their respectful boxes then followed Michele back to where Leewan was standing. Paul looked at the clothes rack and said, "Someone took a lot of time preserving these outfits. Do we dare break their plastic wraps?"

"You don't have to silly." Michele took one off the rack and said, "Look. The plastic has an opening on the bottom."

Paul blushed slightly then grabbed a guard's outfit off the rack. "I could go as a guard."

Leewan shook her head, then laughed, "I guess you could if you wanted to stand around keeping the peace -- instead of sitting down with us."

"I'll pass."

After the group found something to wear, to help them blend in, they returned to their rooms to get dressed.

*****

Leewan notified the guards at the door that they didn't need an escort to the castle -- they just needed them to make a distraction while they snuck out to blend into the crowd. The guards nodded and went to the front gate. They left the gate cracked open while they made a huddle with four other guards in front of the gate—forcing the crowd to bottleneck around them.

Once the distraction was in place, Leewan told the group, "Michele, you sneak out first with Mayra. Follow the crowd into the castle, but when the crowd turns right, the two of you go left. Paul and I will meet you down that hall."

When the group met up in the hall, Leewan said, "Follow me." She then proceeded to lead them to the back entrance of the throne room. The guard at the back entranced didn't recognize them at first and asked, "What are you doing here?" Michele pulled off her bonnet and let her hair fall down. The guard immediately bowed and said, "Sorry. I didn't recognize you." Then he immediately opened the door for the group to enter.

Leewan took the lead and led the group across the room, behind the thrones. Macalla looked over his shoulder when he noticed someone walking behind him. Michele smiled and gave a half-wave to him; Macalla replied with a wink.

The group followed Leewan under the side balcony to their reserved seats. Michele looked around the throne room that had seating for over 500 people. It was filling up fast. She looked at Leewan and asked, "Who are all these people?"

"Nobles and citizens from all the seven islands."

A hush fell over the crowd when some guards entered with Moki and Merrin Taylor in handcuffs. After the king nodded his head, the guards escorted the couple down the long aisle, between the pews, to stand before the royal court. A group of seven jurors, consisting of one representative from each of the islands, sat to the left of the thrones under a balcony.

After the clock charmed eight times, the king stood up to address the audience. "Welcome my good people of the Hidden Islands of Honiawae. We are here today to ensure a fair trial for the Warden of Keelonie Island, Moki Taylor, and his wife, Merrin. The king nodded to the herald. The herald walked out to the middle of the throne alter and announced, "The first charges to be addressed against Moki and Merrin Taylor are the charges of kidnapping Mayra Johnson, the persecution of Michele Armstrong, and two counts of slander and libel against Michele Armstrong." As the herald read the charges, Merrin let out a gasp of surprise and the audience started murmuring. The herald continued in a loud voice, "Moki and Merrin Taylor, please tell the court how you plead to these charges."

Moki spoke up. "We're not on trial for any of that. This is preposterous. There is no evidence to tie us to any of those charges."

King Levi spoke up, "Does that mean you deny the charges?"

"Hell yes! I deny those charges."

The king looked at Merrin and asked, "And how do you plead to those charges?"

Merrin looked at her daughter, Lalirra. Lalirra just looked down and started twirling her thumbs.

"Speak up Merrin! How do you plead?"

"Not guilty your majesty."

"Very well. The court calls their first witness."

Everyone started looking around the room for the witness. Lalirra just sat in her chair staring at her folded hands. The king spoke up, "Lalirra, did you have something to say?"

Michele whispered to Leewan, "She's changing her mind."

Leewan grabbed Michele's arm as Lalirra started to rise. Merrin nearly fainted as she watched her daughter walk slowly to the podium with one hand on her chest.

When Lalirra reached the platform, the herald swore her in then nodded to the king.

"Lalirra, please tell the court how you know the defendants"

"They are my parents."

"What can you tell us about your parents' involvement in the kidnapping of Mayra."

Lalirra spoke softly into the microphone, "First off, I want Mayra to know I didn't know anything about any of this until my mother told me. My mother, Merrin Taylor, told me about the kidnapping after one of her spies confessed to Leewan that he was following the Taylors' order to kidnap Mayra. After that spy confessed to Leewan, my mother covered up his confession by having him executed for treason, then creating a story of her own. My mother's story detailed how that spy acted on his own accord. According to her story, that spy confessed to her, that he and his partner raped Mayra in the gardens when they both were impaired on liquor; after the rape, they realized who she was and decided they had to get rid of her – so they took her to the mainland to deliver her to a man that they knew was involved in sex trafficking. My mother lied and killed that spy to cover up the truth!"

The crowd went wild and Merrin started screaming, "Liar, Liar. I never told you that! Why would you make up such a story? Did Michele use her magic on you to make you lie?"

The king screamed, "Quiet!" The noise in the room died down. Then the king looked at Lalirra and asked, "Did your mother tell you why she sent those spies to America, to find Michele."

"Yes. She wanted Michele eliminated since she was a loose thread. If she ever discovered her true roots, she might try to find her mother and possibly expose the kidnapping... and she was also a threat to my daughter's inheritance."

"Did your father, Moki, have anything to do with this crime?"

"It was my father who spared Maya's life. My mother wanted her eliminated since she and my betrothal, Prince Macalla, were lovers and she was carrying his baby. My father is the one who convinced my mother to get Mayra out of the picture by selling her to a man he knew from Russia -- who was involved in sex trafficking."

The crowd started rumbling again.

Lalirra continued, louder, "But I want everyone to know. My mother only did what she did because she loves me. She wanted me to marry the prince. She wanted me to be the future queen of the hidden islands. I guess her love for me was overpowering. It caused her to make irrational decisions. She didn't want some peasant girl or some child born out of wedlock -- to stand in my way of true happiness."

Moki stood by his wife and said, "That's all hearsay. It's her word against ours. And I stand by my wife. Someone is forcing Lalirra to tell these lies."

The crowd went wild. Prince Macalla walked up to the podium and held up his hands, "Quiet! Please! I know this testimony might come as a shock to some of you, but we need to keep quiet so the jury can hear everything the witness has to say."

The crowd quieted down some. After obtaining some sort of order, the prince looked at his wife and asked, "Is there anything you can tell us about the false rumors about Michele?"

"I'm not sure if my parents started the first rumor about Michele planning on exposing the hidden islands, but I do know that my mother was planning something to make people distrust her. She said she had a plan that would drive a wedge between Michele and the island people, and make Michele want to go back where she came from."

"These are all lies," Merrin proclaimed. "Do we get a chance to testify and tell the truth about all these lies?"

The prince looked at his dad – the king nodded his head and said, "You both will have a chance to speak after Lalirra. Lalirra, is there anything else you wanted to say?"

"No. I said everything that I know."

The king nodded his head, then said, "Thank you. You may be excused. Guards! Please bring Moki Taylor to the stand."

*****

After Moki and Merrin Taylor testified, sticking to their stories that they had nothing to do with the outrageous things their traitor spies did or the vicious rumors about Michele, it didn't look good. Michele looked over at Leewan and whispered, "They're going to get off scot-free. No jury, in their right minds, would ever convict them on the hearsay from one witness."

The king stood at the podium and announced, "Before we move on, are there any other witnesses in this room that would like to make a statement?"

The audience looked around and started murmuring, but no one stepped forward.

The king continued, "So if there is no-one else, we will…."

The king was cut off by Jayden barging in through the back door with another man. "I found another witness to the crimes made against Michele and Mayra."

Michele nudged Leewan and said, "That's the man I drew."

Leewan nodded her head.

Jayden walked up to the front of the room and discussed something with the king. When the king looked up, he announced. "I would like to call Robert McCool to the stand." Merrin's eyes got big when she saw Robert. The king walked back to his seat and let Jayden asked Robert the questions.

"How do you know Moki and Merrin Taylor?"

"I'm a private detective on the Island of Keelonie. A couple of years back I was summoned to the Keelonie Castle to meet with Merrin Taylor. When I got there, she wanted to know if I wanted to earn some extra cash. Business was slow, so I agreed to hear what she had to offer."

"And what was the job she had to offer?"

"To see if I could track the whereabouts of Mayra and her fifteen-year-old daughter. Merrin told me that she had heard rumors that Mayra Johnson was living in Moscow. She didn't want to get Leewan's hopes up, so she wanted me to investigate, see if it was really her or not. I did think it was odd when Merrin told me a couple of times to make sure Mayra or her daughter didn't know I was searching for them. She said she heard rumors that Mayra actually ran away from the islands with some guy – and might run if she knew someone found her. Merrin insisted she just wanted to make sure they were safe before she told Leewan about them."

"Lies. Lies," Merrin shouted. "You have no proof."

"That's where you are wrong. As a private detective, I always keep receipts and records of my work. You might have insisted on paying me in cash, but I had your keeper of the coin write me a receipt. I also kept a duplicate copy of the file I gave you."

"So, what does that prove. It doesn't prove I sent any spies to America to eliminate Michele and it doesn't prove I had anything to do with the disappearance of Mayra in the first place."

Jayden held up a file he had in his hands. "Then tell me, Merrin. What did you do with the information Robert gave you? Did you tell Leewan?"

"No, I didn't. Because it was a dead-end road. He couldn't find Mayra."

"No. But he told you where Michele was. He even told you the names of her adoptive parents from America. What did you do with that information?"

"Nothing!"

"Then how did your two spies get that information from you?"

"They must have stolen it."

"And why would they care about Michele?"

"Because one of them could have been her father. I don't know why people do what they do. You know one of them confessed to me and my husband --that he raped Mayra."

"Mayra stood up enraged, causing Amarina's empty throne to fly off the alter and stop - mere inches away from hitting Merrin. "Liar! I was not raped by any of your spies. You and your husband sold me to a guy involved in sex trafficking. Your spies told me the whole story on the boat ride to Queensland! And how can Michele be the daughter of one of your spies and the daughter of the evil sorcerer, Mukai? Maybe I should just hang you now, for taking my life away from me!" Mayra lifted one of her hands and telepathically lifting the thrown chair by Merrin a couple of feet off the floor. "Let me take her to the witch council. They'll get the truth from her!"

Merrin and Moki looked at the chair shaking in front of them, then back at Mayra. Merrin was in shock that Mayra got her memory back. She turned and looked at the king. Trembling, she begged, "Don't let her hurt me. I'll confess to all of it if the court will take mercy on me. As my daughter said, she had nothing to do with any of it and I just wanted what was best for her."

The king cleared his throat and asked, "So, how do you plead to all of these charges."

"Guilty."

The crowd went crazy.

The king stood up, raised his arm, and yelled, "Order. Order,"

The crowd quieted down some.

The king continued, "And how do you plead to the next charge of poisoning my son."

Merrin softly replied, "Guilty."

Moki looked at his wife in shock.

*****

After the Taylors were sentenced to life in prison on Rocky Trail Island, Prince Macalla followed his sobbing wife from the room. When they reached the inner hallway, Macalla grabbed her by the arm and said, "We need to talk."

Lalirra wiped her eyes and asked, "Why. You heard my mother. I had nothing to do with any of it."

"I want a divorce."

"But you can't. It's against the laws of the kingdom."

"And my father is the king, so he can change the laws."

"I think I can fight that decision. Doesn't changing a law require a vote or something?"

"Do you really want to drag this out? Throw all our dirty laundry out for the world to see. I'm prepared to offer you your parents' castle. You would be the Lady of the House."

"Lady of the House, you say."

Macalla could see the wheels spinning in Lalirra's brain. After a minute or so, Lalirra replied, "What about our daughter? She goes with me!"

"I thought we should give her the option."

"Like hell. She's going with me."

"Lalirra. You know I love our daughter. Don't you think we should make this as peaceful as possible for her?"

"Ughh. I'm her mother. I know what's best for her!"

"What do you think about us going to talk to her? Tell her we are splitting up. She can choose to stay here with me, go with you, or make arrangements to spend time with both of us."

"No!"

"Lalirra. You're being unreasonable."

"My mother and father just got sent away for life, and you're calling me unreasonable!"

"At least your mother wasn't sentenced to death. You can always go visit her."

"I know," Lalirra said through tear-filled eyes. "I'm just afraid Amarina will choose to stay with you... Can't we just offer her time to stay with both of us?"

Macalla stepped back, surprised by her suggestion. "I thought you told me she felt distant from me?"

"I did. But I said that out of spite -- to hurt you. She talks about you all the time. She even does silly little things -- trying to get your approval. The other day she asked me if she could take riding lessons, so maybe you would take her out to the countryside for a ride."

"She said that?"

"Yes."

Macalla stared at the floor, angry at Lalirra for keeping things from him. When he finally looked up, he said, "Shall we go talk to our daughter. I'm sure she's waiting to hear the verdict of the case... Then later, we can discuss a shared living arrangement with her."

Chapter 78

The next day after the trial, Leewan cooked an assortment of foods for breakfast. When Paul, Michele, and Mayra came downstairs, they were surprised by all the food on the table.

"Wow," Paul said. You must have been up all-night cooking."

Leewan laughed, "Not all night. But I did get up pretty early. We need to celebrate."

Mayra picked up a biscuit and asked, "Is this from your famous homemade receipt?"

"Yes. I'm glad you remember. Now eat up everyone.... since I want everyone to pack up after breakfast. Paul and Michele only have a couple more weeks to visit, so I thought it would be nice if we could spend that time together, at my cabin."

Michele looked at Leewan and asked, "How do you know I haven't decided to stay here?"

"Cause I'm your grandmother. And I know things."

Michele laughed as she grabbed a couple of slices of French Toast.

*****

King Levi, Queen Chloe, and Prince Macalla all stopped by the guest house before everyone left. While standing in the foyer, Chloe hugged Michele and said, "I'm going to miss you."

"We're just going to Leewan's house for the next couple of weeks."

"Well then... you make sure you call me if you need anything. And stop by and visit me before you leave for home... unless you changed your mind and are planning to stay?"

"I will stop by... And no, I want to finish my high school year in America. But I do plan on coming back next summer, and maybe Christmas Break."

Chloe smiled and said with a chuckle, "You better."

Chloe went on to hug the rest of the group while Macalla walked up to his daughter and said, "Are you sure I can't send a dozen or more guards with you guys? To keep you safe."

Michele laughed, "Dad! Are you forgetting there are three capable witches here? I doubt anyone would dare to cross all three of us."

"You never know. Just make sure you call me if you need anything. And I was thinking, maybe I'll come to visit you at Leewan's house. I could bring some horses with me... so we could all go riding."

She glanced at Mayra talking with Chloe, then said, "That would be great, dad."

Macalla hugged her, then whispered, "I love you, and I'm proud of you."

"Thanks, dad. I love you too."

Macalla stepped aside to talk with Paul. The king stood back by the door. Michele walked up to her grandfather and gave him a hug. "I love you too, grandpa!"

The king blushed slightly and patted his hand on her back. When she stepped back, she looked at her grandfather, kissed him on the cheek, then said, "Thanks for everything. And I'll come back to see you before Paul and I leave."

"I would like that."

When she turned around to see if everyone was ready, she noticed dad talking to her mother and thought: *They sure do make an attractive couple. I hope they start riding together when I'm gone.*

*****

When the group walked out of the house, Michele glanced back and swore she saw a shadow of a ghost standing by one of the windows in the glass cupula. She thought: *Goodbye Martha. I'll be back!*

Michele hugged her dad one more time before climbing in the back of Leewan's traveling wagon. "You should come to visit us soon at my grandmother's house."

"I'll check my schedule and let you know."

"Thanks, dad." She kissed him on the cheek then climbed up in the seat next to Paul and gave him a wink. Paul laughed softly, grabbed her hand, and said, "Matchmaking again I see."

She smirked, then said, "A girl can dream, can't she?"

The horse, Windfire, whinnied at the site of Mayra walking out to the wagon. Mayra walked up to her old horse and started petting her. "It's been a long-time, my old friend. I hope my mother took good care of you?" The horse snorted. Mayra laughed and patted her on the neck.

Leewan called from the driver's seat, "Come up here and ride with me. You can drive us all home."

Macalla helped Mayra up to the box seat. Leewan handed her the reins.

"Take care Mayra," the prince said as he looked up into her bright eyes.

"I will. And don't be a stranger."

As the wagon traveling down the village streets, towards the castle's main gate, Paul and Michele waved out the windows to the passing villagers. A lot of the locals, that either heard or saw the results of the trial, bowed to Michele as she traveled passed.

The ride through the countryside was peaceful: with the sun shining, wildflowers blooming, and the birds singing. When the group arrived at Leewan's small, white cabin, Paul volunteer to take care of Windfire and unload all the luggage. While Michele helped him with Windfire, Leewan took her daughter into the house. Mayra walked around the cabin, touching everything while reminiscing her childhood memories. Leewan watched her from the distance, then said, "You get to stay in your old bedroom. I left everything the way you had it."

"Is Michele going to sleep in there with me or is she sleeping in your room?"

"She can stay with Paul in the living room, on the pull-out couch."

"What! You're going to let them stay out in the living room... together!"

Leewan smiled, "You were younger than Michele when you were sneaking off with the prince. I just pretended I didn't know. At least Michele is on birth control."

"And how do you know that?"

"I saw it in her room at the guest house when I went to get the dirty clothes out of the laundry hamper."

Mayra shrugged her shoulders and said, "I guess... your house – your rules."

Paul walked in carrying some of the suitcases. Mayra thanked him, grabbed her suitcase, and dragged it into her old bedroom. After she put it on her bed, she looked around and thought: *Just like I remembered.* When she opened the suitcase, she saw the rock Michele had borrowed. She picked it up and put it back in its rightful place with the rest of the rocks she had collected over the years. The rock glowed for an instance, then faded back to its normal form. Turning her attention back to her suitcase, she grabbed the picture of her and Macalla. With a tear in her eye, she put the picture back on her dresser. Michele walked into the room and saw her mother staring at the picture. Hugging her mom, she said, "I'm sorry for the way things turned out, but I'm so glad I finally found you!"

Mayra hugged her daughter back and said, "Me too, baby. Me too."

*****

The next day, Leewan dragged out her book of spells and dropped it on the kitchen table. "I figured you'll need some lessons before you go back to the states."

Michele put her hand on the purple velvet cover and thought: *Is there a spell to make someone love you?* The book didn't open. Michele smiled.

"What are you thinking?" Leewan asked.

"Oh, nothing really. What do you think I should try first?"

"How about a mind-erasing spell? Maybe you can do that too? You might need it back in the states."

Michele thought about a mind-erasing spell, the book opened to the page. Michele read the incantation then asked, "Can I take this book back to Michigan with me?"

"Sorry. Mayra and I might need it, but you could take some pictures of specific spells that you might want to try or might need. If you need more, you could always come to visit me in your dreams."

"True. But I do wish I could just call. Maybe someday I can figure out how to break that old boundary spell."

"I don't think you should mess with it. You might accidentally expose the islands to the world."

"Don't worry. I would never do that."

Chapter 79

"They're here!" Michele ran into the house to alert Leewan and Paul. The group ran out of the house and saw Macalla and his daughter, Amarina, riding their horses up the road with three extra horses in tow. Mayra mounted Windfire as Amarina delivered a horse to Michele.

"Thank you!" Michele said as she took the reins of the horse her half-sister was ponying.

"You're welcome," Amarina replied softly.

"I like your riding jeans."

Amarina looked down at her riding outfit and replied, "They are more comfortable than the dresses my mother used to make me wear."

Macalla looked at Michele and said, "This is Amarina's first long ride. She just started taking riding lessons last week."

Michele looked at Amarina and said, "She looks like a pro to me."

*****

The group rode down the road two by two. Macalla and Mayra led the way. Michele road next to Amarina and Leewan next to Paul. The ride through the countryside was peaceful with all the green foliage and flowering shrubs. After a while, Michele broke the silence by saying, "I'm sorry about your grandparents."

"It's not your fault." Amarina shook her head then continued, "I'm sorry for all the things they put you and your mom through. And I'm sorry for being so mean to you when I first met you."

"That's all under the bridge now. I was hoping we could start over on a clean slate."

Amarina nodded her head.

Michele reached her hand out and said, "Hi. I'm Michele. You're long lost sister that you never knew you had."

Amarina laughed, then shook her hand. "Hi, I'm your younger sister. Welcome to the Hidden Islands of Honiawae."

"So…. I know it's none of my business. But I know it must be hard on you with our dad and your mom splitting up. Have you decided where you want to live?"

"I plan on staying with our dad during the summer, then my mom during the school year – visiting dad every other weekend or so."

"That's nice."

"I suppose."

After a while of silence, Amarina asked Michele, "How do you know Jayden?"

"He's my distant cousin. Why do you ask?"

Amarina turned red, then softly said, "Oh. Nothing. I just think he's cute."

Michele laughed, "He's way too old for you!"

"I know a lot of people that end up marrying a man a good ten years older than them. Besides, I'll be turning 16 soon."

Michele looked down at her horse, then back to Amarina. "If you want me to introduce you, I can the next time I come to visit. Maybe Christmas Break."

"You would? That would be great!"

"We're here!" Macalla called from the front of the possession.

Michele looked around and saw a large rock by a river, surrounded by trees. She smiled as she thought: *This is the same secluded spot my dad showed me during my last visit; the same spot he used to ride to with my mom when they were teenagers. I bet he brought Mayra here on purpose!*

Macalla jumped off his horse, then helped Mayra down from hers. After setting her on the ground, he turned to the others and said, "Amarina and I bought a packed lunch from the castle."

*****

After tying up their horses, Michele and Amarina carried their saddlebags over to the spot Macalla picked out – under some palm trees. Leewan grabbed a couple of blankets she found in her saddlebag and laid them out on the ground. After the picnic area was arranged, she stood up to look around. "This is a great spot for a rendezvous: right next to a river with a great view of the mountains in the distance. Plus, it's secluded. People riding down the road would never notice anyone was back here."

Michele walked over to the large rock that blocked most of the view from the road. On the backside of the rock, she noticed the initials: *MW + MJ.* She squatted down next to the rock, traced the engraving with her finger, then smiled as she pictured her young parents sitting here, engraving their initials into the rock, all those years ago.

Paul walked up behind Michele and startled her. She pointed to the engraving. Paul shook his head, kissed her on the forehead, then said, "Your matchmaking skills might work. Take a look at your mom and dad."

Michele turned and noticed her parents walking hand and hand down by the river. Looking back at Paul she said, "I'm happy you made this trip with me. I like making memories too."

*****

After the group enjoyed a meal of fried chicken, potato salad, macaroni salad, and baked beans, Amarina pulled out a box of chocolate chip cookies. "Does anyone want to try one of my homemade cookies? I'm taking cooking lessons from one of our cooks, so I thought I would try making something for our trip."

"I would love one," Michele said with a smile.

Amarina passed the box around. Paul gobbled down two of them, then said, "These are delicious! Maybe Michele should take some lessons too."

Michele punched him in the arm. Paul laughed, then tackled her on the blanket. Once he had her pin to the ground, he said with a laugh, "I love you the way you are… I'm just saying a little cooking class wouldn't hurt."

Michele started to struggle. Leewan laughed and said, "I think you're right, Paul. Maybe I've been too easy on her. I should make her help with the cooking more often."

Paul let her up. She slugged him in the arm again and said, "This isn't fair. Two against one."

Everyone laughed.

Macalla looked at his watch and said, "We better get going."

Paul stood up and offered Michele his hand. She ignored his hand and pushed herself up off the blanket. Paul followed her to her horse. "Don't be mad. You know we love you. Can I help you get up onto your horse?"

Michele turned and looked at him with his sandy, brown hair blowing in the wind and dreamy, brown eyes with long lashes: *How can I stay mad at him?* "Sure." Michele lifted her foot so Paul could give her a boost. Once seated on the steed, she looked at him and said, "We can race down the road. Whoever loses has to help Leewan with dinner."

"That's not fair. You have more experience."

"So. Your horse might be faster. Is it a deal?"

"Deal."

Michele told the others the plan while Paul mounted. Leewan and Mayra rode down the road so they could indicate the finish line, while Macalla and Amarina stayed back with the racers—to ensure a fair start. When Leewan waved from a good distance away, Macalla said, "On your mark. Get set. Go!"

Paul's steed took off with a leap. He gripped the saddle tight, hanging on for dear life, while the horses raced head to head. When he looked over at Michele, he noticed how she was encouraging her horse to run faster. Following Michele's lead, he kicked his horse, snapped his reins on both sides of the horse's neck, and screamed, "Yaa!" The horse responded to the command and started running faster, leaving Michele's horse in the dust. Paul's body tensed as the horse flew down the road. He held a death grip on to the saddle while thinking: *Oh shit! How am I supposed to stop this horse?* Paul's horse flew past the finished line. He tried to pull up on the reins and screamed, "Whoa," but the horse kept running.

Michele passed the finish line and kept riding in pursuit of Paul's horse. Leewan flipped her wrist and moved a downed tree into the path of the runaway horse, but the horse just jumped it. Michele's horse was dead on the trail of Paul's, but too far back to help. Michele screamed, "Stop," and everything froze except for Leewan's, Mayra's, Michele's, and Amarina's movements. Paul's and Michele's horses were in mid-stride. Michele looked back at Leewan and Mayra and said, "A little help, please."

Leewan, Mayra, and Michele all dismounted their frozen horses. After getting off her horse, Mayra looked at Michele and said, "Wow. Did you do that?"

She nodded and replied, "Yep. But we need to hurry. Not sure how long this hold might last."

Amarina looked at her father and the frozen horses in amazement. When she looked up the road, she saw the other three witches moving, so she dismounted and started walking up the road to join them.

Leewan and Mayra followed Michele down the road to Paul's horse. Michele looked at her grandmother and said, "Can you put Paul on the back of your horse?"

Leewan flipped her wrist and moved Paul to the back of her horse.

"Now. I think we should move all our horses to the front of the line so we can try to stop the runaway horse."

"Let me try one," Mayra asked.

"Be my guest," Michele replied.

Mayra moved her horse while Leewan and Michele moved theirs, Macalla's, and Amarina's horses. Amarina watched the movement of the horses in wonder. When she finally reached the group of witches, she said, "Wow! Who did that?"

Leewan replied, "We all used our power of telekinesis to move the horses. Your sister did the freezing."

Amarina looked at Michele and asked, "How come you didn't freeze me?"

Michele shrugged her shoulders, then looked at Leewan. She replied, "Must be your starting to come into your powers. You do turn 16 in a couple of months."

"You mean... I might be able to do something like this?" Amarina waved her arm out to encompass the situation.

"Not sure what your powers might be. Only time will tell."

"Cool."

Michele smiled at her and said, "It is kind of cool. If you need any help, you can always call Leewan or Mayra while I'm gone. But for now, we all need to get into position." The witches mounted their horses. Michele looked at the others and asked, "Are we ready?"

"Ready for what?" Amarina asked.

"When I unfreeze the horses, get into a line so we can try to capture Paul's runaway horse."

"Sound good. I'm ready!"

Michele screamed, "Go!"

Paul's runaway steed continued running, straight towards the group of horses. Paul woke up with a start and grabbed ahold of Leewan. Macalla woke up disoriented but was able to manage his horse and moved into the line next to Amarina. As the charging horse saw the other horses, it began to slow to a trot. By the time the horse met the line, Macalla was able to reach out and grab one of the horse's reins. He pulled on the rein and yelled, "Whoa boy!" The horse reared slightly, then settled down next to Macalla's horse.

Michele looked over at Paul. Paul asked, "How did I get here?"

Michele smiled, "A little magic. Are you okay?"

He looked down at his arms, then replied, "I think so. Thanks!"

"No problem... but I think you should have to help Leewan with the cooking since I saved your life."

"But I won the race!"

Michele smirked, "Then I guess we're even. So, we both get to help make dinner."

"Deal."

"Are you ready to get back onto your horse?" Michele asked.

"I would prefer to ride double, in back of you!"

"No problem."

Leewan kicked her horse so it would line up with Michele's horse. Once they were even, side by side, she said, "Slide on over."

"I can't do that!"

Leewan laughed and said, "Here. Let me help you." With a twist of her wrist, Leewan transferred Paul over onto the back of Michele's horse.

Grabbing ahold of Michele's waist, Paul remarked, "Hey. That was freaky."

"You're welcome," Leewan replied with a laugh.

*****

By the time the group returned to Leewan's place, there were guards positioned all over the place. Macalla rode up to one of the guards and asked, "What's going on?"

"Queen Chloe sent us to follow you...in case there was any trouble."

Michele heard the end of the conversation and asked, "Why would there be any trouble?"

The guard looked at Macalla, Macalla told Michele, "I guess some of the citizens of the islands are still concerned since they heard of your plans of returning to the states. They are worried about you and Paul exposing the islands."

Michele looked at Paul. Paul shrugged his shoulders.

Chapter 80

After everyone left, Mayra took Windfire into the shed to brush her down while Paul and Michele went inside to clean up and help Leewan start dinner.

Leewan grabbed the cookbook and said, "I'm going to teach the two of you how to make a chicken pot pie."

"Shouldn't we start with something easy – like hamburgers?" Michele replied.

Leewan laughed and said, "Hamburgers are too easy. The two of you need to learn how to follow a recipe."

While Michele was rolling out the crust and Paul making the cream sauce, Michele asked Leewan, "Why do you think some of the islanders are still worried about me and Paul exposing the islands?"

Leewan glanced at Paul, then replied, "Probably since they heard that you are not planning on erasing Paul's memories. Some islanders might be worried that Paul will tell outsiders, especially if the two of you ever break up."

Michele looked at Paul. Paul interjected, "I don't want someone messing with my memories -- ever again!"

"I know Paul. And I wouldn't blame you. I wouldn't want someone messing with my memories either."

Leewan shrugged, "So, now that you know the reason. What should we do about it?"

Michele shrugged her shoulders and looked at Paul. "Any ideas?"

"Nope."

*****

Mayra took a bite of the chicken pot pie and said, "This is really good. The two of you should open a restaurant."

"I wouldn't say that," Michele laughed.

After dinner, Mayra volunteered to clean up while the rest of the group retired to the sitting room. Leewan grabbed the TV remote then looked at Paul and Michele and asked, "The two of you want to watch a movie on the DVD player or the news from the one local channel available on the hidden islands?"

"That's it!" exclaimed Paul.

Leewan scrunched up her face and looked at Paul with confusion. "Yes, that's it. You already knew we only have one local TV channel here due to the old boundary spell. The DVD's we have -- are purchased in Yeppoon then brought back here by the ship to be sold in stores."

"No. Not that. But the local news could help Michele. She could give a public speech at the castle, from the front balcony. She could reassure the people that the rumor about us exposing the islands isn't true... And the news channel could record the message so all the islands would get the message."

"That might work?" Michele looked at Leewan for support.

Leewan shrugged her shoulders and said, "Guess it couldn't hurt."

"I'll give Chloe a call," Michele replied.

*****

Three days before the couple was supposed to leave for home, the group packed up their bags in Leewan's wagon and headed into town to stay at the castle's guest house. The king and queen had made all the arrangements for Michele's public speech, and Prince Macalla made all the arrangements for taking the couple back to the airport in Brisbane, Queensland.

After the group dropped their luggage off at the guest house, they all decided to go with Leewan to the livery stable to drop off Windfire and the wagon.

"You guys don't have to help me. I'm used to it," Leewan replied.

Mayra insisted, "But you shouldn't have to do all the work yourself. Besides, Windfire is my responsibility too."

Michele interjected, "Plus, it's a great day to be outside in the sunshine. It'll be fun for all of us to walk back together." She looked at Paul, and he replied, "I'm game. Leewan shouldn't have to do all the work. She can even stay here if she would prefer to rest."

"Heavens, no! Let's all go then."

After the wagon pulled up to the livery stable, Paul helped the stable boy unhitch and put the wagon in storage while Mayra took care of Windfire. When the work was done, the group started walking down the street towards the guest house.

The walk from the stables to the house wasn't that far, but Paul didn't think they'd ever get there with Leewan stopping to talk to everyone on the street. They barely made it another ten steps before she stopped again for the umpteenth time. Paul smiled and pretended to be happy while Leewan introduced him to a couple. After the introductions, he tapped his foot impatiently and listened to his stomach rumble. Michele elbowed him in the ribs, then laughed, "Is my man getting hangry?"

Paul gritted his teeth and whispered back, "Yes. I'm going to waste away to nothing if I don't get something to eat – soon!"

Michele chuckled, then taped Leewan on the shoulder and asked, "Do you mind if Paul and I run over to that shop and grab some munchies?"

The woman Leewan was talking to look at Michele and said, "Oh dear. Are we keeping you from a luncheon engagement?"

"No. Not at all. It's just my boyfriend. He hasn't eaten anything since breakfast."

The man looked at Paul and said, "Come with me, son. We own that pasty store right over there. Anything you want is on the house."

Paul winked at Michele, then walked away with the man.

"I'm coming too," she shouted and started following them.

Leewan looked at the lady, and said, "Maybe we should all go and check out your store?"

"It'd be my pleasure. Follow me."

*****

When the group finally made it to the guest house, the front door flew open, and Chloe stepped out. Gesturing for the group to come in, she said, "There you are. Come on in. The lunch I had the castle send over is getting cold."

Michele walked into the kitchen and looked at all the food on the table. Her stomach protested: *No more food!* But Michele knew she better eat something or Chloe would be upset. Putting her arm around Paul's shoulders, she said, "Are you hungry?"

"Guess I could try a half sandwich and some of that homemade soup."

While the group picked at the food, Chloe told Michele and Paul, "I brought some outfits over for the two of you to try on for your public appearance tomorrow."

"Oh!" Paul replied with his mouth half full.

"Yes. Since the two of you will be on display on the castle's balcony, you'll need appropriate outfits that represent the positions you hold -- a princess and her right-hand man."

"Do I have to dress that way all the time now?" Michele asked with a big frown on her face.

"No. No. Don't worry Michele. You only need to dress the part for public appearances. The news crew will be filming you and Paul live. We want all the citizens of these islands to know that the two of you are part of the royal court."

"Where are these dresses?"

"I have two racks of clothes in the sitting room. One for you and one for Paul."

Michele wiped her mouth with a napkin, then looked at Paul and asked, "Are you ready?"

*****

After trying on multiple gowns and dresses, Michele settled on a long, formfitting, royal blue dress with a V-neck and waist-line, crystal pin. For shoes, she picked some white sandals with blue and white crystals. When she walked out into the sitting room to show everyone her selection, Chloe started clapping her hands in approval.

Leewan let out a long whistle when Paul walked into the room wearing a royal-blue and silver uniform. Looking at Mayra, Leewan asked, "What do you think mom? Do they make an attractive couple or what?"

"Yes. They sure do. I couldn't be prouder."

Chapter 81

Michele stood nervously on the balcony while looking down at all the people in the street. She reached for Paul's hand and squeezed it tight. "I don't think I can do this. Will you read my speech for me?"

Michele turned towards the castle, she needed to get something to drink, some air, or something. When she turned, trying to escape, Paul refused to let go of her hand. Looking towards the castle, she saw her dad, Prince Macalla, and her half-sister, Princess Amarina, standing in the doorway. Macalla winked at her and loudly whispered, "You got this girl!" Amarina smiled and gave her a thumbs up.

Macalla, seeing her apprehension, walked out onto the balcony. He raised his hands; a silence fell over the crowd. He looked at his daughter, with a death grip on the microphone, and asked, "May I?"

Michele gave her dad a little, nervous smile and handed him the microphone.

"Welcome. Welcome. All my good people for the Hidden Islands of Honiawae. For those you, who have never had the chance to meet my oldest daughter, this is Michele." Macalla covered the microphone and whispered, "Wave."

Michele waved to the crowd. The crowd cheered.

"And this is Paul Hudson, Michele's fiancé."

Paul flinched, looked at the prince, then waved to the cheering crowd.

My daughter planned this event so everyone would have a chance to meet her before she returns to America to finish her senior year. Michele also planned this event since she knows some of you still fear her. We all have heard the stories, passed down from one generation to the next, of a chosen one coming – and changing our world. At this point, I don't even know for sure if

Michele is the chosen one…. Especially since I always thought I was."

"The crowd laughed."

Macalla held his heart and continued, "What? I'm heartbroken. You don't believe I'm the chosen one?"

More laughter came from the crowd below.

"Needless to say. I think I better give the mic to Michele now. I think she has some words she wants to say."

Macalla started to hand the mic to Michele, but she shook her head. He wrapped one of his arms around her and pulled her to his side while speaking into the mic, "Unlike me, I think my daughter is a little shy." Then he looked at Michele and whispered, "Just pretend you are talking with me." He looked back at the crowd and said in a loud voice, "So, Michele, do you think you are the chosen one?"

"Yes."

The crowd all started grumbling. Someone screamed, "Blasphemy! Don't let them leave without erasing their memories! She and her boy toy will be the death of us all!"

The prince held up a hand to quiet everyone down without any effect. Another person screamed, "She is the daughter of the evil sorcerer, Mukai!"

The king and queen walked out onto the balcony. The king held one of his hands up then grabbed the mic with the other. "My granddaughter is not on trial here! She came on her own accord so she could reassure everyone that she has no plans on destroying our way of life. Please let her speak! If you do not want to listen to her speak, leave now -- or you'll be forced to leave by my guards."

The guards surrounding the crowd stood at attention.

The king looked at Michele and said, "The floor is all yours, my dear. Please tell the people why you think you're the chosen one, then tell them what you came here to say."

Michele smiled slightly, grabbed the mic, and started mumbling, "I met this lady…"

"Quit mumbling!" called a heckler from the crowd. He looked at some guards walking towards him, then said, "Guess I'm out of here. I doubt she has anything important to say anyways."

Michele looked at the man with anger in her eyes, then spoke louder. "I met Agnes Bates and she told me I was the chosen one!"

The crowd all started mumbling at the mention of Agnes Bates. Then someone from the crowd shouted, "Agnes Bates died years ago!"

"No, she didn't. She's the keeper of Martha Black's history book. She lives at the end of the tunnel, on the other side of the river. She told me I was the chosen one and that I was supposed to relieve her – as the keeper of Martha's book."

"So, what are you planning to change?" shouted another person from the crowd.

"I don't have any plans to change anything, and I would never jeopardize the homes or the lives of my family. I like it here! And I plan to come back and visit my family and update Martha's book as needed, but the only thing I want to do now -- is to finish my last year of high school in America. I don't know what I want to do after high school, but I do know that I want to spend the rest of my life with Paul." She looked at him; he squeezed her hand, then kissed her on the forehead.

A little girl, seating on her father's shoulders, shouted, "Marry her Paul."

Michele looked down at the little girl and recognized her. "I think we both better finish high school first, Zoe."

Zoe giggled and told her dad, "That's the nice girl that gave me my first horseback ride. I like her."

"The father held up his fist and said, "Hail to Princess Michele! Hail to Princess Michele!"

Zoe's grandparents from Keelonie Island joined in, then a few more people, until half of the crowd was hailing her name.

Michele waved and smiled until one woman screamed, "How are we guaranteed that your boyfriend won't tell anyone about the hidden islands?"

Michele glanced at Paul then looked back at the crowd. "I guess you'll have to trust him as I do. I love Paul, I love my family, and I love these islands. There's nothing I wouldn't do to help protect the privacy of these islands if I thought they were in jeopardy of being exposed."

Paul grabbed the microphone from Michele. "I love this girl and I want to spend the rest of my life with her. If she does choose to live here on the islands after we graduate, I would hope that everyone here would accept me as one of their own. These islands are like a paradise. I would never jeopardize this kingdom."

Someone screamed from the crowd, "What if the two of you don't make it ... or decide to go your separate ways?"

"I hope that doesn't happen, but to help this community feel safer, I will let Diane erase my memories... or at least bury them -- until I come back to visit again."

Michele looked at Paul in shock and said, "You what? You don't have to do that!"

He nodded his head and said, "It's the right thing to do."

*****

After the event was over, Chloe ran up to Michele and hugged her. "That went well. Now it's time for your going away party."

"My what?"

"I couldn't send you back to America without a party... now could I?" Chloe locked her arm with Michele's and said, "Come on Paul. The party is for you too!"

Michele looked at Chloe as they walked down the hall. "We didn't need a party."

"Oh yes, you do! Don't worry. It's just a small party. Some of the nobles from the other islands, some of my friends from here, and of course, your family."

Michele looked at Paul, shook her head, and thought: *Doesn't sound like a small party to me!*

Chloe led the couple down the hall to a private, plush powder room. "Both of you wait in here while I go check to make sure everything is set."

Michele looked around the powder room. It was divided into two sections. The first section had fancy love seats, chairs, end tables, and mirrors. The second section had private, restroom stalls, a long counter full of sinks, and more mirrors. Michele walked down the section to use one of the restroom stalls then stopped, dead in her tracks, when she opened one of the stall doors. "Paul. Come look at this. These stalls have bidets, end tables, and TV monitors on the doors."

"Now that's a true throne," Paul laughed.

Chloe reappeared at the entrance door. "Are the two of you ready?"

"Just give me one second, please," Michele replied.

*****

Chloe led the couple down the hall to a large, double door. At the threshold, she turned around and started straightening Michele's dress. After she was satisfied with the appearance of the dress, she took a once over at Paul, then said, "The two of you need to walk in as a couple. Michele, please take Paul's arm."

Michele laughed, then took Paul's arm. Chloe nodded, then pushed the automatic, door button on the wall. When the doors opened, the herald announced, "Princess Michele Armstrong, escorted by Paul Hudson."

The crowd inside the ballroom started clapping. Michele blushed. Paul escorted her down the stairs. While walking through the procession line, Michele met and shook the hands of so many people that her head was starting to spin. At the end of the line, she found her family... waiting patiently. Leewan looked at her and said, "Follow us, dear. I'll show you to our table."

*****

Michele and Paul sat in the middle of a long table with her family. She looked around the ballroom; it was decorated with blue and silver tapestries and white, Christmas lights. Round tables were placed sporadically in front of the long table. Michele watched as the guest started to take their seats and servers started bringing out salads.

Paul looked at Michele and said, "Your grandmother sure does know how to throw a party."

Michele laughed and said, "I feel like we're getting married or something."

Paul laughed, "Well maybe we should. It's not like I'll remember."

She hit his leg with her knee and said, "Not funny."

After dinner was finished, an orchestra started playing music from the corner of the room. Paul looked at Michele and asked, "May I have this dance."

Michele walked out to the crowded dance floor with Paul. While resting her head on his shoulder, she looked at all the other couples dancing next to her and thought: *Who are all these people?* Then she noticed her dad dancing with Mayra and thought: *Chloe did do a great job planning this party!*

*****

It was close to 11 p.m. by the time the group made it back to the guest house. Michele and Paul ran up to their rooms to change while Mayra and Leewan went out to the sitting room to watch the evening news. When the newsman started talking about Michele's speech, Leewan looked at Mayra and said, "I better go get them." She walked to the bottom of the stairs and called, "You're on TV now. You better get down here if you want to watch it."

Michele rushed down the stairs tying her housecoat with Paul dead on her heels. When they walked into the room and looked at the TV, it showed a news reporter, sitting at his desk, with a big picture of Michele and Paul behind him. The news reporter was saying:

Princess Michele, or should I say the chosen one? Will surely be missed when she goes back to America. During her visit here, she has bought back harmony to the islands. I still find it hard to believe, all the horrible things the Warden of Keelonie Island and his wife did to her and her mother. Life in prison isn't punishment enough. So glad Mayra made it back alive.

Michele looked at her mother and smiled.

Chapter 82

That night, Michele heard a voice calling her name: *Michele… you need to update the book!* She peeled Paul's arm off her body, slipped out of bed, and proceeded to the third floor. As she walked down the hall, she noticed a light coming from Martha's old bedroom. When she walked into the room, she saw a lamp on the table next to Martha's history book. The book was opened to a blank page with a pen and a folded-up piece of paper lying next to it. She took a seat and unfolded the piece of paper. It was a note from Agnes Bates:

> *Dear Michele,*
>
> *It was nice meeting you the other day. You are more than I could have ever expected. I hope you like the lamp better than Martha's candles. Not sure how much time I have left. I need you to take over updating the book. Please add a section about you found your family and your summer vacation.*
>
> *Sincerely,*
> *Agnes Bates*

Michele folded up the letter, slipped it into her pocket, then thought: *Shit! I'll be up all night.* She rested the tip of the pen on the paper and thought: *Where do I begin?* Then she remembered her conversation with Agnes: *She said she made an entry about me?* Flipping through some of the pages, she thought: *I'll never find what she added. Maybe if I close the book, it will work like Leewan's magic book?*

Michele closed the book then thought about what she wanted. *It worked!* She looked at the page and noticed it was the family tree... and there it was -- her name and birthday under Mayra's and Macalla's names. It said: *Michele, the "Chosen One." Adopted from Baby House #42, Moscow, Russia, by a couple from America: Jerry and Daria Armstrong.* She thought: *Wow. I wonder when Agnes added that?*

Michele closed the book again and thought: *Take me to the page where I need to start writing.*

*****

Paul woke up to an empty bed. He grabbed his housecoat, ran out into the hall, and called, "Michele!"

Michele was just coming down the stairs from the third floor. Paul ran over to her and said, "You're up early. We don't have to be ready to leave for a couple more hours."

Michele yawned, handed him the note she had in her pocket, and said, "I know. But I had to update the book last night. Not sure how great of company I'll be on our way back."

He read the note then looked at her and said, "Go pick your clothes out for today. I'll finish packing your belongings and let you sleep -- until we are ready to go."

She yawned again, then said, "You're an angel."

*****

Paul answered the door and found Jayden standing there.

"Are you and Michele ready to go?"

"I thought Macalla was taking us?"

"He's coming too. Is there a problem?"

Paul shook his head, "No problem. Wait here, I'll wakeup Michele."

Leewan and Mayra met Michele in the foyer. Mayra hugged Michele and said, "Have a good time in America. I'm going to miss you!

Make sure you call me frequently… in your dreams."

"I will mom. I'm glad Leewan and I was able to find you."

Mayra stepped back and turned her attention to Paul while Leewan stepped up to hug Michele. "Don't be a stranger. If you need anything, you can always meet me in your dreams… You do plan on coming back?"

"Next summer for sure. Not sure if I can afford to come during Christmas break."

"Oh, nonsense. Your father can afford it -- if you and Paul want to come."

Michele smiled. "Then it's a date. I love you."

"Love you too!"

Michele and Paul followed Jayden to the carriage. The king, queen, and Amarina were standing there so they could say their goodbyes too.

*****

The yacht ride to the mainland was rough. "I think I'm going to be sick." Michele ran from the dining room table to the bathroom -- leaving Paul alone with Jayden, Macalla, and Diane. Paul looked around the room, feeling a bit awkward. When he returned his attention to the occupants sitting around the table, they were all staring at him. To break the tension, Paul looked at his empty plate and said, "Thanks for serving us such I great lunch."

Macalla replied, "We couldn't send you off without a good meal. I know how awful the food can be on those planes."

Paul nodded his head then looked towards the bathroom door.

Jayden spoke up, "I hope there are no hard feelings left between us. I know you didn't like me too well when we first met."

"Nope. We're good."

"I'm glad she found that history book. It totally explains why I felt an overwhelming need to protect her... since we basically family."

Paul continued to nod his head.

Prince Macalla looked at Paul with a straight face and said, "You better take good care of my daughter back in the states or I might have to come over looking for you."

Paul swallowed a large lump in his throat and said, "I'll try."

Macalla laughed and slapped his hand down on Paul's back. "I know you will. I'm only kidding."

Diane looked at Paul and said, "It was very considerate of you to let me erase your memories of the islands; are there anything specific memories you want to remember?"

Paul glanced at Macalla and blushed.

Macalla glared back and said, "Don't tell me you've been sleeping with my daughter!"

Paul squirmed in his seat, then said, "Then I won't."

Diane cleared her throat, then continued, "Any other request?"

"I want to remember all of Michele's family. I know I can't keep the memories of her grandparents being the queen and king, or that her father is a prince, but can you make other important jobs for them – so I can remember them by name?"

"Sure. I can make them owners of a big business, and Macalla is one of the big bosses. I'll even replace Mayra's memory – may be to something like she ran away to get married in Moscow all those years ago; to a man Leewan despised. She gave Michele up for adoption since she was being abused. She finally came home to live with her mom on the Island of New Caledonia since she was homeless in Moscow… How's that?"

"That should work… When I come back to visit, can you return my memories?"

"Of course. Just like I did this time."

Paul nodded. Michele came out of the bathroom and asked, "How much longer before we are in Queensland?"

Jayden looked at his watch, then replied, "About an hour."

Diane looked at Michele and asked, "Anything you want to say to Paul before I erase his memories?"

Michele looked at Paul and said, "You don't have to do this. It's not too late to change your mind. Nobody but us will know."

He shook his head, "I told the people I would. I can't go back on my word."

Michele smiled and said, "I love you!"

*****

Michele listened while Diane hypnotized Paul and replaced his memories; she wanted to hear all the details so she could try to keep the story straight when they got home. When Paul woke up, he thought he had just fallen asleep on the boat ride to Queensland from the Island of New Caledonia.

Michele sat on the edge of the couch and said, "Well good morning, sleeping beauty. We're almost to Queensland. We should both call home, let our families know we are on our way."

Continue to Book 3-- In the Whispers of a Dream Series: To Live Happily Ever After or Die Trying.

Sign up to email link to be notified when the next new book is published at:
https://books2read.com/author/evelyn-green/subscribe/1/220835/

Made in the USA
Monee, IL
28 November 2020

49808243R00233